Spirit Dad

by

Anne Talmage Cooksey

This book is a work of fiction. Names, characters, places, and incidents are either the product of the author's imagination or are used fictionally. Any resemblance to actual persons, living or dead, or to actual events or locations is entirely coincidental.

This book may not be re-sold or given away to other people. If you would like to share this book with another person, please purchase an additional copy for each person you share it with.

Copyright © 2016 by Anne T. Cooksey. All rights reserved. Including the right to reproduce this book or portions thereof, in any form. No part of the text may be reproduced in any form or by any means, electronic or mechanical, including photocopying, recording, or by any information storage and retrieval system, without the written permission of the author.

Version 2016.09.25

In memory of my father

USCG LCDR, Stuart Talmage Scharfenstein

Prologue

1.

"You're right. He *does* have more money than God. But the company's soul isn't for sale. Yes, it *is* my decision. And it's final."

Forbes Harding hung up. The long, grueling day, fielding phone call after angry phone call, was over. Done. No going back now. Not that he'd want to. He felt around in his jacket pocket for a piece of candy. Nothing.

He glanced at his watch. It was four-thirty. Perfect timing. Forbes had developed a habit of stopping by the pharmacy before heading home. He strode out of his office, catching the elevator door just before it closed. He could use a walk right about now.

Outside the office building, Forbes looked up. This morning's dismal weather, heavy with rain, had given way to the weak February sun, breaking through the clouds and lifting Forbes' spirit. He knew he had made the right decision. He felt better than he had in weeks. He'd call Melissa...take her and the girls out to celebrate.

He inhaled a deep breath of the crisp air and grinned.
"What a great day!"

2.

"Target is leaving the building and heading for destination. Are you in place?" the electronically altered voice demanded.

"Yes. The security system is offline. The city bus just pulled up. My men are entering now. There are eleven people inside, not counting mine," the man responded calmly, a veteran of many successful hits.

"Excellent. The more confusion, the better. At my signal, fire. Remember, no kill shots. Lots of blood, lots of noise...but no casualties. Thirty seconds to create complete chaos and disappear. He's mine. Anyone other than the target dies, my money will not reach your account."

"You're the boss. Target is approximately six feet from the entrance."

"Five feet."

"Four feet."

Three.

Two.

One.

3.

Forbes moved toward the candy aisle. He saw several of his colleagues. One waited in line for prescriptions while another loaded up on decongestants and cough drops. February had been a brutal month for flu. He bumped into a woman and her daughter arguing. He apologized and went around them.

As Forbes reached for the familiar pink and white box, he heard shots ring out. Pop! Pop! Pop! Bang! Bang! He froze. The sounds came from all directions at once. Rapid fire spits tore the silence. People screamed. People ran. Merchandise displays exploded and fell.

Forbes tackled the disoriented women beside him, sending them crashing to the floor.

"Stay down!" he commanded.

Keeping his head low, Forbes crept to the end of the aisle and peered cautiously around the corner. And ran smack into the chest of another man.

The man said something. Forbes shook his head, indicating he couldn't hear. He felt the muzzle of a gun push into his chest, dead center. Shocked, Forbes looked up into the man's face in disbelief. Click.

"Nooooooooooo!" Forbes roared. The bullet shattered his breast bone, rupturing his heart. His lifeless body fell backwards, spraying the terror-stricken mother with blood.

The gunman melted silently into the background. Gone.

****

Back in his car, the gunman wrapped the weapon in his handkerchief and tucked it in his interior jacket pocket. He placed his realistic silicone mask (affectionately nicknamed "The Senior") and matching arm sleeves into the black gym bag on the seat next to him. It had been worth the fifteen hundred dollars for the set--even the extra thirty for the nose and ear hair. He laughed, thinking about the bank robber who hadn't had the foresight to use a fake name, address, and credit card, ending up in jail when the police traced his purchase back to him.

"Amateurs…, he scoffed.

He lit an unfiltered Marlboro and took a deep drag as he watched bloody, panic-stricken people stumble out to the sidewalk, crying and moaning for help. Police sirens wailed. Ambulances screeched. He smiled.

"They're mine now, Forbes. They'll do whatever I want, when I want. And you can't do a thing to stop me."

Chapter One

Samantha Harding stepped back. She closed her eyes and tried to count to ten. At three, she thought, "screw it. Pigzilla is going down…" She launched herself full force at Anime Bloom, a bottle-blonde bombshell in pajama jeans who had trash-talked Sam's mother one too many times. If Sam had her way, neither of them would live past the next five minutes.

One busted lip, one black eye, one nasty gash on the forehead, and one bloody scalp later, four teachers pulled the girls apart and yelled at them to break it up. Sam found herself sitting back outside the principal's office for the third time that week. And it was only Tuesday.

"Sam, whatcha doin' outside Davies' office again? Who you been throwing shade on this time?" asked Michael.

"Shut it, Michael. Save it for someone who cares! Mrs. Belcher sent me…again. Said I started the fight with that fat panda. She said rearranging Anime's face was the last straw," Sam answered.

"Anime? She's like twice your size. You don't want to take that on." He sniffed in her direction. "You hungover? You drinking again last night? I knew I should have followed you home…you are gonna ruin your life. Have you no respect for me? I called and called you! You didn't answer or text me back. I am getting grey *hairs* from you, girlfriend." Michael pushed his face close to hers, willing Sam to look at him.

"I cannot take you seriously with those neon green glasses, you freak." Sam rubbed her eyes and gingerly felt her lip under the ice pack. She sighed and leaned back against the faded wood paneling in the hallway.

"Samantha? Come in my office, please." Mr. Davies stood in his doorway.

"Hey, Mr. Davies...be easy on my girl, Sam, here. She's a mess and all, but I've got her back." Michael looked concerned.

"Thank you, Michael. I'll take your input into account. We have a meeting this afternoon regarding your eligibility to be elected to the National Student Achievement Society. Michael, I'm very impressed. You seem to have the whole package: extra curricular activities, 4.0 grade point average, advanced placement courses. You might be the first sophomore to gain entrance," said Mr. Davies.

"Thank you, sir. My mom and dad are pretty jazzed about it. Got their hopes up pretty high. I think they see a doctor in their future. Um,...but what about Sam, sir?"

"Go on back to class, Michael. I'll make sure she gets the help she needs. I'll send her along when we're done."

"Yes, sir." Michael shifted back and forth on his feet. He leaned toward Sam and said in a low voice, "be cool, Sam. Mr. Davies is one of the good guys."

Sam lifted her chin and glared at Michael. Life was so easy for him. He just seemed to float along, making friends and rising to the top of this crummy high school.

Sam grabbed her backpack and pushed by Mr. Davies. She paused and chose the left seat in front of his desk. The last time she sat in that chair, Mr. Davies had to take a phone call. When he faced away from her to look out the window during that conversation, Sam drew a picture of Woodstock from the Peanuts cartoons underneath the desk's front overhang. It comforted her to see it still there.

Mr. Davies shut the door. He went around his desk and sat down. He didn't say anything at first, just shuffled the papers on his desk and cleared his throat a few times.

Sam refused to say a word. Not one word.

"I am not going to give him a single opening," she thought. "And I'm not going to cry. I am sick of crying. I don't care if he is nice. I don't care what he thinks. He has no idea. No idea at all. I just want to be left alone. Maybe I can spend the rest of the afternoon in the nurse's office. Mrs. Henley is cool. She never asks stupid questions or tries to make lame attempts at conversation. She just leaves me alone."

Mr. Davies cleared his throat. "Alright...Mrs. Belcher says you attacked Anime. The three other teachers agree. Now, one did say she saw Anime and her friends approach you first and say something. Said it looked like the fur was going to fly right before it did. However, you did attack Anime first and attempt to strangle her with both hands. Strangle her?" He looked over the top of his glasses and raised his eyebrows. "Really, Samantha? This is high school. Not an episode of the Kardashians. You've been in detention numerous times this semester, been put on probation, suspended for two days, and now spend more time in my office than in class. You seem determined to get in trouble. Your talks with your guidance counselor are going nowhere...you just sit there. Now you're getting into fist fights. Sixteen-year-olds need to behave with more responsibility."

Mr. Davies paused. "It's October. Your father died in February, Samantha. I've made allowances and special arrangements. But you don't appear to be making any noticeable progress. Your mother agrees with my recommendation that you see a family therapist whose specialty is dealing with the loss of a parent. I've made it mandatory for you to meet with her twice a week on campus for an hour each time in order for you to continue here as a student. I know this is difficult for you. Do you have anything to say?"

Mr. Davies looked at Sam. Sam looked back at him. Her

face ached, her jacket was ripped, and her scalp burned where a section of hair was missing. She sat there, miserable and angry. And silent.

He nodded. "Your first session is tomorrow after school at three o'clock with Miss Jenkins, the family therapist. You'll meet in Room B in the Learning Center. I truly hope this helps you, Samantha. Let's see how the next few weeks go until the end of the semester."

Mr. Davies picked up a folder on his desk and pushed back his chair. "You have a good friend in Michael, you know. Try to live up to what he sees in you, okay? From what I know of him, he's one of the good guys."

Sam's eyes widened at hearing Mr. Davies use the same phrase Michael had used.

"You may stay here in my office until your mother arrives. I've already called her to come and pick you up."

Sam sat bolt upright. Her voice shook. "Why did you call my mother? I don't want to see her! You told Michael I'd be back in class! I don't want to go home right now! Can't I just stay in the nurse's office until school's over? *Please* don't make me go home."

"Sorry, Samantha, your mother is already on her way."

"You can't do this! I can't go home right now. I can't see her right now!" Sam yelled. Her hands balled up into fists, pounding on Mr. Davies' desk.

"That's enough, Samantha! This is exactly why I can't have you stay here. You need to go home and let your mother take care of you." Mr. Davies poked his head into the adjoining office. "Moira? Come sit here with Samantha until Mrs. Harding gets here, please."

Sam stopped. She stared at him and shook her head.

"What's the point?" she thought wearily. "You don't live in my world, do you? And neither does Michael. You're both completely blind to what's right in front of you. Whatever."

Mr. Davies looked at Sam, his eyebrows drawn together in

concern. For a moment he appeared conflicted about sending her home.

"Samantha…," he began. He glanced at his desk calendar.

His packed schedule overflowed with meetings and appointments scribbled in various colored inks. Plus, Samantha couldn't stay at school after instigating a fight. Appearances were important, especially now with the local attention the school enjoyed with educational grants and the possibility of the Achievement Club being inducted into the National Chapter.

Moira, Mr. Davies' administrative assistant, walked in. She put her hand under his elbow to propel him toward the door. "It's time to go, Mr. Davies. Your one o'clock appointment with the school superintendent has been moved to the South Wing Conference Center. Samantha will be fine. I'll stay with her until Mrs. Harding gets here."

Mr. Davies popped opened his briefcase and slipped the folder inside. He took a last look at Sam sitting there, small and quiet once more, her fingers tracing a pattern on the front of his desk. He started toward her, but Moira shook her head. She gave him a gentle push out the door.

As he headed down the hall, Mr. Davies caught sight of Melissa Harding coming in the front door, accompanied by a well-dressed man in dark glasses. Mrs. Harding looked expensive and elegant in an ensemble that hugged her curves and displayed her generous assets along with a fair amount of skin.

The man held the door for Mrs. Harding. Inside the foyer, he stopped. He pulled her to him and ran his hands up the front of her body. He kissed her neck, then her lips. Breaking the kiss, she straightened the front of her blouse and whispered something in his ear. The man removed his sunglasses, nodded, and rewarded her with a tight smile.

Mr. Davies looked at his watch. He kept walking.

Chapter Two

Mrs. Harding's perfume reached the principal's office moments before the woman appeared in the doorway.

"Samantha, dear...let me see...oh, honey, your lip! And your hair, sweetheart, your pretty hair. What were you thinking...why on earth would you try to choke a girl? This Anime...she needed stitches?" asked Melissa Harding in a low, cultured voice.

Samantha didn't move. She endured her mother's soft murmurs and pets without objection. She looked down at the desk, her finger tracing and retracing the little Woodstock.

Moira looked at Mrs. Harding. Samantha's mother was no longer the heartbroken widow whose beloved husband had been killed. That Mrs. Harding had been grief-stricken and lost, with conservative clothing and a soft beauty. This Mrs. Harding was intimidating with collagen-plump lips and a two hundred dollar haircut.

Moira put out her hand. "Mrs. Harding, I don't know if you remember me. I attended your late husband's funeral."

"No, I don't remember you." Mrs. Harding dismissed her coolly. "Kameron, gather up Samantha's things and walk her outside to the car while I meet with....I'm sorry, what's your name again...Norma? I shouldn't be more than a few minutes. Samantha, dear, go with Kam."

Sam looked at Moira. Then she looked at Kameron. A shudder rippled through Sam's body, so slight Moira couldn't be sure it happened at all.

Sam stood. She removed the ice pack. Her swollen lip had dried blood crusted at the corner. She looked old and sad.

Kameron touched Moira's shoulder. "Thanks for watching out for Samantha. She won't be causing trouble again soon. Melissa will set her straight." His smile didn't reach his eyes.

Moira stepped back, putting distance between herself and Kameron. She wasn't usually ill at ease with people. Moira shivered, goosebumps covering her forearms.

Kameron picked up Sam's knapsack. "We'll be in the car, Melissa. Don't rush. I didn't plan on going back to the office today."

Mrs. Harding glanced at Kameron. "Ten minutes. I'll be out in ten minutes." Kameron put his arm around Sam's shoulder, steering her in the direction of the front door where the town car waited.

Moira watched them go. Mrs. Harding looked down at her cell phone and tapped her french-manicured nails on the screen with precise irritation. Moira reached for Samantha's file and began going over the details.

At the front door of the school, Kameron separated from Sam. He walked out first, toward the car parked at the bottom of the steps in the middle of the school's circular driveway. The black car's windows were shaded with a dark tint. Sam followed, the icepack pressed to her swollen lip again.

Kameron looked down at his phone and sent a quick text. "Just letting Robert, my driver, know we won't be leaving right away. He's across the street picking up lunch. I'll let him know when your mother is ready." He opened up the back door. "Get comfortable, Samantha. Pour yourself a drink. You'll find soda in there...or something stronger if you'd like. I'll take a look at that lip of yours and check on the actual damage..." His eyes glittered dangerously.

The door closed behind him.

"Definitely not one of the good guys," Sam thought wearily, hoping the next few minutes would pass quickly.

Chapter Three

Samantha ran up to her bedroom, locked her door, and refused to come out. Her mother knocked, wanting to talk. Sam didn't know why her mother even bothered.

There was no way she was having some fantasy heart-to-heart with capital M mother while Kameron lurked in the background. He and the rest of the boy toys grew six extra hands every time Melissa's back was turned. So far they were satisfied with a few minutes of heavy breathing and rough embraces that left Sam's tender skin red and scraped. For now, that is. Her mother seemed intent on working her way up to the big leagues. Sam felt sick about the implications.

Mrs. Harding gave up and left a tray of covered food outside Sam's door. Around nine o'clock, Sam watched Kameron walk outside to his car, parked in the driveway under her window. She held her breath and stayed well in the shadows. His driver opened the back door.

Kameron paused and turned. He gazed up at Sam's window for a few minutes before disappearing inside. The headlights beamed and the engine purred to life. The sound of gravel crunching under the tires faded away in the darkness.

Sam sagged against her turquoise Paris Sketch wallpaper in relief. She crossed her bedroom, padding across the thick carpet in her bare feet, and unlocked her door. She ran across the hall to Sarah's bedroom. Sam tried the door, happy to find it locked. She called Sarah on her cell and let it ring three times before hanging up and trying again.

"Sam?" Sarah answered the second time.

"Yeah, baby, it's me. Open up. I'm right outside."

Sarah unlocked her door. Her bedroom was a Pottery Barn explosion in pink, green, and white. Primrose wallpaper covered the walls. Her princess canopy bed overflowed with stuffed animals. The table in the center of the room was piled with tempera paints, brushes, colored pencils, charcoal, chalks, drawing pencils, and art paper. Taylor Swift's song, *Shake it Off*, was playing on Sarah's iPod speaker dock system.

"What happened to your mouth, Sam? Your lip is all puffy, like Mom's...except just on the bottom." Sarah reached out to touch Sam's lower lip with her finger, but Sam stopped her hand in mid-air.

"I got into a fight with Anime at school. She opened her stupid mouth again. She looks worse than me, though. She had to get stitches because she tripped over her own fat feet trying to push me and hit her head on the water fountain," said Sam.

"Whoa. Does it hurt? Your hair looks funny. There's a piece missing off the top. I can see your scalp. It's all bare and scabby-looking. Did she do that, too?"

"Yeah, she did that, too. And yes, it hurts. A little. This is a case of don't do what I do, do what I say. Don't get into fights at school, alright? They're more trouble than they're worth. I just lost my temper, big time. Along with my hair. Remember when I tell you to always count to ten and the bad feelings will lose their power? I didn't make it to ten. Not even four. The bad feelings won and I got a fat lip. And a bald spot."

Sam walked over to the art table. She picked up Sarah's latest drawing, a decent sketch of their dad. Sarah drew it from a photograph of Forbes opening a Christmas present last December. It really looked like him. It wasn't a surprise, though, considering Sarah spent all her free time working on her art. Sam, on the other hand, struggled to keep her head above water.

"Time for bed, Picasso. I'm impressed. I actually recognized Dad in this one. If I get a frame, can I have it?" asked Sam.

Sarah nodded. "I had trouble with the tree. But it was easy to draw Dad this time. It was weird, Sam, y'know? I could almost feel him in the room with me while I was sketching. Not spooky weird like he was a ghost or something. But friendly weird, like he was watching over my shoulder. At one point I thought I even smelled the cologne we used to buy him for Father's Day. Hugo Boss No. 6, remember? We thought it was so funny when he'd say to Mom, 'you're not the boss of me--I'm the boss' in his fake British accent and she'd pretend to order him around. Then she'd crack up. Mom never could keep a straight face around him." Her voice trembled. "I smelled him, Sam. I did."

Sam reached out her arms and folded Sarah into a hug. "I get it, short stuff. I do. I feel him, too. But it's time for bed. I wanted to let you know my door's unlocked. It's just me and Mom at home. Get undressed and brush your teeth. It's already nine-thirty! Mush!!"

If Sam could get only one thing right, it would be to keep her baby sister far away from whatever drove her mother into the arms of all these men with their big bank accounts and lavish gifts. So far, as long as Sam was willing, the creeps didn't try to get near Sarah, her eleven-year-old sister.

Sarah had no idea why Sam had a special ring pattern or why Sarah had to keep her cell phone in her pocket at all times. Sam didn't explain why Sarah had to stay in her bedroom and keep the door locked if there was anyone in the house besides Sam and her mom. Sarah idolized her big sister. Sarah trusted her and did what she asked without question.

Sam said good-night to Sarah and snuggled her down with the Ten Chosen Ones...Sarah had her stuffed animals on their own rotating sleep schedule. Back in her room, Sam shoved her giant collection of stuffed Snoopys and Woodstocks onto the floor. She sat on her bed with the lights off, headphones in, music on. Life had become so crazy complicated since their dad died.

Her mother went off the deep end in the middle of last summer. The first few months after her dad died were horrible, but her mom functioned. They were still a family...sort of.

"We ate dinner together at least, if you count take-out and pizza delivery," Sam remarked out loud to the empty room. "We sat on the couch and watched Netflix forever until we fell asleep." She punched her pillow. "Then Mom had to go to New York for a weekend at the end of July and come back all different...a plastic replica who barely notices us anymore." For the millionth time that week, Sam wished she could talk to her dad.

Her phone buzzed. Another text from Michael. Fifteen so far tonight. "Tomorrow," she thought. "I'm not in the mood to answer any questions."

Sam swallowed mouthfuls of scotch from a bottle hidden in a boot in her closet, trying to blot out all the painful, ugly parts of the day. She fell fast asleep, fully dressed, on top of her covers.

Chapter Four

At five minutes after three the following afternoon, Sam went to the Learning Center and knocked on the door of Room B. Her heart rocketed around the inside of her chest like a panicked bird caught in a grocery store. Her mouth felt dry. Sam drained the rest of her Dr. Pepper, wishing she had another.

"Please come in, Samantha," a voice called from inside.

Miss Jenkins sat in a comfortable, overstuffed, yellow and blue flowered chair. She relaxed back in her seat, her high-heeled boots propped on a matching footstool. She wore a soft navy-blue corduroy jumper over a white turtleneck. Over this, Miss Jenkins wore a bulky, hand-knit, pink and white cardigan sweater.

"Shut the door behind you and come sit down." Miss Jenkins gestured to a matching yellow and blue chair with a throw pillow embroidered with the words, *WHAT YOU SAY IN HERE, STAYS IN HERE*.

Sam looked at the pillow and raised an eyebrow at Miss Jenkins. "Do you really expect me to believe that? Because it's written on a pillow? It's not even a good meme. It's a loser meme."

Miss Jenkins laughed. "Thanks. First time I've been called a loser in the first five minutes. By the way, you're late. I like to start on time."

Sam rolled her eyes. "This is dumb. I'll sit here for an hour, but this a waste of time. I'm not talking. You already know everything about me from my file," she said. "This is pointless."

"Silence is power, Samantha. When someone demands our silence, they control us. When someone refuses to speak, it's often the *only* thing they feel any control over."

Sam stared at Miss Jenkins. This woman talked too much. She looked down at her cell phone. Ten minutes after three. Only five minutes had passed.

"Oh.My.God. This is torture." Sam grimaced silently. Michael said he would wait for her at her locker before they caught the late bus together. He was mad at her for not answering his texts last night.

"He'll get over it," she thought.

"One other thing, Samantha. No cell phones. Turn it off and place it on the table next to you. Mine's already off. See?" Miss Jenkins held up her cell phone. She placed it on the little end table next to Sam. "Your turn."

"No. No way." Sam couldn't believe her ears. She wasn't turning off her connection to Sarah for anybody. "I can't. It stays on. You can hold it. Here. I won't look at it. But it *has* to stay on."

Sam held out her phone to Miss Jenkins. Her voice sounded thin and small. Sam really needed water. Her throat was closing up. She was gonna choke and die in the therapist's office. "Do you have any water?"

"Over in the corner. See the little fridge? Water and soda. Take your pick." Miss Jenkins took Sam's cell phone and gazed at the screen saver. It showed a picture of a little girl who looked like Sam flying a kite on a beach with a tall, bearded man.

Sam hurried over and opened the compact refrigerator's door. Grabbing out a water bottle, she unscrewed the cap and gulped the water down as fast as she could. She snagged a Dr. Pepper as well. After she drained the water, Sam tossed the bottle into the blue recycling bin and headed back to her chair.

Miss Jenkins gestured to the phone in her lap. "Who are the

people in the photo, Samantha?"

"My dad and my little sister, Sarah," Sam said in a rush. "Would you please turn the screen off? I don't want to wear down the battery. I need it to last."

Sam hated having the phone out of her reach. It was never, ever out of her possession. She sat on her hands to keep them from shaking.

"If we turn it off, your battery will keep full charge. Tell me what's making you fearful about turning it off, Samantha? We only have thirty minutes left," said Miss Jenkins gently.

To her horror, Sam felt tears prickle in her eyes.

"No, no, no, no, no!" thought Sam.

Her breathing quickened. She opened her mouth, then closed it again, not trusting herself to speak. She bit her injured lip so hard she tasted blood in her mouth. Despite her best efforts, her large, green eyes filled with tears which spilled down her cheeks.

"It's okay, Samantha. We don't need to shut it off. Look, I'm turning off the screen to save the battery. Breathe in...and out...slowly. Again." Miss Jenkins reached for the tissue box on the floor next to her footstool and handed it to Sam.

She waited for Sam to wipe her eyes and blow her nose. Minutes ticked by. Miss Jenkins sat quietly.

"Sarah can't reach me if you turn it off," Sam muttered.

"What about your mother?" Miss Jenkins offered.

"She's...not as available. She has a lot of appointments and stuff."

"I see. Was she always this busy? I mean, before your dad's death?"

"No. I mean, yes, but not like this. Whatever...I just know my dad would want me to make sure Sarah can always reach me. I have to keep the phone on."

"Connections are important." Miss Jenkins looked up at the clock on the wall behind Sam.

"Our time's almost up, Samantha. Before you go, I have an

assignment for you to do before our next meeting on Friday. I would like you to take some time each evening and write a letter to your father. You can write in a notebook or a journal. You can write a letter on the computer, print it out, and put it in a drawer. Whatever way makes you the most comfortable. It doesn't matter what you say. No one is going to read it but you. Will you do this for me, please?" Miss Jenkins watched Sam's face.

Samantha hesitated, then nodded.

"Good. Friday at three o'clock?" asked Miss Jenkins.

"Yeah, sure. I guess. It's not like I have a choice." Sam reached for her phone and stuck it in her pocket.

She picked up her backpack and slung it over her shoulder. She refused to make eye contact with Miss Jenkins. Instead, she headed for the door to go meet Michael.

She let out her breath in an exasperated puff when she realized she forgot to snag her Dr. Pepper off the table. Sam wheeled around to scoop it up when she noted with annoyance Miss Jenkins stood right behind her, holding it out.

"Thanks," Sam grunted as she grabbed her soda, reluctantly meeting Miss Jenkins' eyes.

"You're welcome. And, Sam?"

"Yeah?"

"Be on time."

Chapter Five

Michael leaned against Sam's locker, whistling the latest Beyonce hit. He seriously crushed on that woman. What did Jay Z have that he, Michael Coolcat Bateman, didn't have? Okay, money...and more money. But beyond that? He was the man! Today he slayed the ladies, stylin' a flowered bowling shirt, jeans, and turquoise sneakers with glasses to match. Who could resist?

"C'mon, Sammie-girl," said Michael. "What's taking so long? Where are you anyway? Nobody ignores my texts--I am an Instagram maniac with a super-sized flock of obsessed followers who totally live for my *Living Like a Celebrity* posts and Vine videos!" He laughed to himself at the social media hype.

"What would these follower people think if they saw me burning the midnight oil and studying until I fell asleep with my face in my physics book?" Michael wondered.

It had taken all his charm to convince Mrs. Belcher to let him take her senior AP physics class. It didn't hurt that he was a straight A student or that he'd hopscotched through Chemistry, Trigonometry, and Advanced Algebra in ninth grade and was working on killing the Calculus book in less than a semester.

"One way or another, I'm getting a full ride to Cornell on scholarships," he mused.

"Let's go," Sam snapped. She blew by him, heading for the bus.

"You okay? You look like Rudolph's ugly sister." Michael saw traces of tears on Sam's cheeks as he ran to catch up. "C'mon. Don't look at me like that. I'm kidding. You look like Rudolph's fat sister."

Sam cracked a faint smile. She bumped her shoulder into his and pushed open the exit door. He hurried after her.

"Wait up! I want to know what happened last night. You cut me, Sam. You cut me deep, you cold piece of lunch meat. I cried myself to sleep." Michael caught up and danced ahead of her.

"Nothing happened. Shut up until we get on." Sam stopped in front of the bus door and waited for the driver to open it. Michael stood behind her singing along to his iPod with one earbud in.

"Negative traits make negative space, blah, blah, blah that's the human race? What the hell are you listening to? Beyonce doesn't write that crap." Sam threw her backpack on the floor and sat next to the window.

Michael eased his six-foot, two-inch frame down on the seat next to her. He did a flippy hand dance and head weave in time to the song. She yanked the headphones from his iPod.

"Stop, just stop. Point of no return. Respect my ears, dude." Sam looked out the window, then back at Michael.

"Tell me. Why didn't you come back to class? I looked for you, but you vanished. Is there some secret school torture chamber for pig attackers?" Michael kept it light, but Sam looked awful.

Her mother was tripping these days and Sam was getting so thin it looked like she was disappearing. He had known her since they were seven years old. They had been best friends ever since that first day of school in the second grade when she had befriended him on the playground at Stanwich Country Day School. No one else would talk to him or play with him.

She had taken him by the hand and pulled him into the game she and her friends were playing. After that, he was golden. They were best friends for life.

"Davies called my mother. She and Kameron came to the school. And brought me home. That's it. Mommie Dearest kept trying to talk to me. That wasn't going to fly, not with bae in the house. They make me sick. She makes me sick. So I just checked on Sarah and went to sleep," Sam continued.

"What about today? You looked like somebody ran over your best friend--by the way, that's me so I'm taking it personally--when you got out of that appointment. Who did you see? Why in the learning center? What was it for? Do you have a parole officer now or something?" He peppered her with questions, anxious for the answers. She really did look rougher than usual.

"Davies is making me go to a therapist. Sigmund Freudette. Because I am a head case. Because my father died. Because I'm violent. It's mandatory. If her little magic therapy wand doesn't make all my bad feelings go away, then he'll kick me out of high school land." Sam sighed bitterly.

"Damn! How did it go--she all textbook and what do you see in this ink splat-like?? What's your first memory in your crib? Do you have a poop fetish? Does the name Anime make you turn green and grow humongo muscles and throw cars? And when you gave her the silent treatment, was she thera-pissed? Ha! Get it? Thera-pissed, therapist?" Michael crossed his eyes and spoke primly in a fake German accent.

"No, you idiot! For a genius, you say the dumbest things!" Sam opened her Dr. Pepper and took a long drink, then burped loudly in his direction for punishment. "Worse...she asked for my phone and wanted to turn it off."

"No way."

"Way."

"What happened?"

"I got all sweaty and started crying. Zero cool. She didn't

make me, didn't say anything. Just gave me tissues and waited until I dried up."

"Did you tell her? About Sarah, I mean?" asked Michael.

"Yeah. I told her Mom is sort of on her own planet these days. Not let's get a social worker involved unavailable, but just busy with appointments and work stuff. I said Dad would want me to be there for Sarah, like 24/7. She didn't say anything. That was the whole appointment. Oh, wait, she said I was a control freak or something." Sam leaned her head on Michael's shoulder. "I have to go back on Friday at three."

"That was unremarkable, boring even. She was cool about the phone and you just had to sit there? Maybe she can help, Sam. You need to talk to somebody," said Michael.

"I talk to you."

"It doesn't get better, though. Your mom is still an alien and you're a toothpick. I'm worried you're gonna disappear and blow away. And you can't disappear 'cause Grayson asked where you were yesterday. I think the boy likes him some Sammie-girl. Especially since you went all WWE on Anime. Impressive, you were."

"Gray?" Sam's head snapped up. "He spoke? He asked about me? That's a first."

"I know. Looks like your man-crush finally noticed you...happy?" Michael was glad to see Sam's face brighten.

"Wow. I don't know what to do about it, but wow. I'm getting off at the next stop. Sarah's at Magda's this afternoon. I said I'd walk her home." Sam finished her soda and tucked the empty can in the side pocket of her knapsack. "Don't study all night, geek. You're gonna end up starting college in two months like Doogie Howser and I'll never see you again. Fail a course or something for me, will you? I need you...even though you think it doesn't help." Sam stood up as the brakes screeched and the bus came to a stop. "Say hi to Mom and Pop for me. Tell them I'll come over this weekend. They can feed me and Sarah till we're stuffed. Later, tater…"

Michael stood up to let her out. "Answer my texts, Sam. I mean it. I need to know you're okay just as much as you need to know Sarah is. Freak."

"K. Pinky swear." She hooked her pinky around his and held it there for a second.

He stepped back, reassured for the moment. He watched her walk to the front of the bus and step down onto the sidewalk. For a brief moment he thought he smelled men's cologne. He looked around at the remaining bodies on the bus, intent on their various screens, and shook his head. It was gone. Funny. He put his headphones back in and hit PLAY.

Chapter Six

"Sam! Oh, Sam! Samanthaaaaaaa!" Sarah burst out the front door, leaped down the flagstone steps, and bolted across the manicured lawn. She waved a yellow paper in her left hand. Sarah barreled into Sam on the sidewalk, talking a mile a minute.

"Look, Sam, look! I won! I won! The Halloween art contest! All the kids in the fourth, fifth, and sixth grade were in it. I won the mixed media category! I made a Hansel and Gretel house out of recycled plastic bottles with a huge paper mache spider stretching across the roof and a spider web made out of mesh bags. I painted it with glow-in-the-dark paint and used a blacklight flashlight...the one Daddy used with my Halloween costume last year. Look, Sam! Look at my ribbon!"

Sarah didn't stop to pause as the words tumbled out of her mouth. Her face lit up with a huge smile. She pushed the ribbon into Sam's hand, trying to catch her breath.

"This is the entry form for the Community Center Halloween contest. There's only two more days left to enter. Help me fill it out, Sam? Please?!" Sarah flapped the yellow sheet of paper in Sam's face.

"Wow, chica! Nice going! Mixed media, huh? Pretty big potatoes for a small fry like you! Congratulations! Sure, I'll help you fill it out. Gotta support our resident artist! How come I didn't see you working on this at the house?" Sam held Sarah's hand as they cut across the lawn.

"It was a school project. I found stuff I could use in our recycling bin. And in a couple of the neighbors' ones, too. I washed them all out and brought them to school in my backpack. Magda gave me the mesh bags. She said they'd look cool with paint on them. Something about texture," Sarah shrugged.

Sarah let go of Sam's hand and opened the screen door. Together, they entered the cheerful foyer. Sam dropped her backpack on the front bench.

"Hi, honey! How was your day? What did you think of Sarah's win? I am tickled pink her talent is getting the recognition it deserves..." Magda's words died away when she got a good look at Sam's lip.

"Samantha Elizabeth Harding...why is your bottom lip all puffy and bruised? Did someone hit you at school?" Magda demanded.

"Sam started it! She lost her temper at Anime. She couldn't help it. The counting to ten thing didn't work and Sam tried to choke her to death!" Sarah looked proud of her older sister.

"Both of you come into the kitchen. I'm baking an apple kuchen. There's some cinnamon spice cake cooling on the counter. I'll put the kettle on and you can tell me all about it. It's almost five o'clock, Sam. You're usually here on the early bus. Why the schedule change today?" asked Magda.

She bustled the girls through the spacious family room with its comfortable, sectional seating and sat them down at the generous kitchen table. The roomy captain's chairs were perfect for curling up and relaxing.

"I have to see a counselor twice a week because of the fight. I had my first session today," said Sam.

She took a bite of the cinnamon spice cake. It tasted good, but it hurt her lip to eat. Sam put down her fork. She'd just wait for the tea.

Magda worked busily at the center island cutting up chunks of butter and liberally sprinkling brown sugar and cinnamon onto the apples in the pie crust. Her hands flashed like lightning as they moved between the various crocks that held her ingredients.

"Whoops, not that one. One of these days I'm going to add a sprinkle of Fred and then where will we be?!" Magda glanced upward and chuckled.

Sam smiled to herself. Magda's husband, Fred, had died of cancer a few years back. Magda kept the urn of Fred's ashes with her in the kitchen where she spent most of her time cooking. She was almost *always* adding in a little bit of Fred.

Magda talked to Fred all the time. Other people might find it creepy that her husband's cremated remains were in a beige ceramic urn on her counter next to her stove, but not if you knew Magda. Fred belonged there.

Fred's urn blended with all the other mismatched ceramic canisters she used for her flour, sugar, coffee, popcorn, rice, and dried beans. Every morning she poured coffee for herself and an extra cup for Fred, then settled in for a nice one-sided chat. Magda often said the only difference between Fred and her was a single heartbeat...why stop the conversation?

"Okay, missy...spill. Why the cat-fight at school? Who is Anime?" Magda opened the oven, slipped the apple kuchen inside, and shut the oven door.

"She's...she's popular, gorgeous, and mean. Really evil. She and her nasty friends say bad things about Mom. I've sucked it up for weeks, but she follows me around with her minions until I can't take it any more. I tried to keep my temper, but my head fuzzed out and I hit F5 hurricane status in like four seconds. Next thing I knew my hands were around her guppy neck...I think it saved her. I couldn't get a good grip, so I punched her in the face and gave her a black eye." Sam looked at Magda who didn't say anything, just listened with a thoughtful expression.

"Mr. Davies, the principal, called Mom. He said I have to go to special grief counseling with this lady, Miss Jenkins. If I don't improve, I'll probably get kicked out of school."

"How did it go?" Magda asked.

"It was okay. She isn't a jerk or anything. She gave me this homework thing to do."

"What kind of homework thing?"

"She wants me to write letters to Dad. Like in a journal or something. I have to write one a night."

"That sounds like a good idea, Sam. I kept Fred's Facebook page open and sent him messages after he died. I knew he couldn't respond, but it made me happy to think that somewhere in the universe he was getting them. When our loved ones pass on, that doesn't mean that they aren't with us spiritually, surrounding us with their love and protection. Death only refers to the physical body, Sam. After our bodies die, our souls live on. Your dad is with you during all your highs and lows, your ups and downs. He knows when you are hurting or scared or angry. Maybe if you could talk stuff over with him on your end, you might feel less like lashing out at stupid bullies. He can hear you, sweetie. And I know he's doing his best to watch over you and keep you safe."

"Mag? How do you know when Fred is around?" asked Sam. Sarah cocked her head and looked at Magda with intense eyes as she cradled her mug in both hands.

Magda gazed at the girls. She'd been waiting for this question. Every time she was with them, she could smell a faint whiff of Forbes' cologne near them. He loved them to the moon and back...still did. But it seemed to be getting stronger as the months went by.

Magda had asked Fred about it this morning while pouring his coffee out on the patio. No response: no slight breeze on the back of her neck, no whiff of cigar smoke, nothing. It was like a television with rabbit ears. Some days it was hard to get reception.

"Well, honey, sometimes Tigger stares at Fred's recliner and meows his head off. Animals can sense spirits easier than we can. That's a sure sign Fred is hanging out. Other times I might catch the faintest odor of cigar smoke or a burning candle in the laundry room or in the bedroom hallway. Sometimes I'll feel a cool breeze but there isn't a fan on or a window open. It takes a lot of concentrated energy for him to make the smallest sign he's around. I've heard stories of lights or televisions going on and off. Fred's never done that, but he probably could if he felt it was important to send me a message."

"Did it scare you the first time you felt him near you?" asked Sam.

"Not really. It's the same old Fred keeping me an eye on me and listening to me talk a blue streak over coffee." Magda got up and checked the timer. She opened the oven door and peeked in. The apples bubbled away under the streusel topping.

"Your mother called and asked if you could stay for dinner. She's meeting Peter Ambroglia at the club to go over some of your dad's estate papers. It seems there's been another delay in your father's life insurance settlement. Your mother sounded frustrated." Magda pulled out the ingredients for grilled cheese. "But don't you worry, Peter will get it straightened out. Your dad knew what he was doing when he made Peter the executor of his will. He wasn't your father's Executive Vice President of IT at NatureLight for nothing--he's a genius at all that paperwork."

Magda pulled out a large pot and clunked it down on top of the stove. Soon organic chicken broth, chopped chicken breasts, peas, carrots, egg noodles, and spices were simmering away. The delicious aroma of the soup mingled with the scent of warm apple kuchen fresh out of the oven.

Sam and Sarah went to get their homework out of their backpacks. They ate dinner two or three times a week with Magda while their mother was out. Usually, after they finished their work and cleared the dishes away, they played Clue or

Parcheesi until Sam walked them home.

Sam lingered in the foyer. Sarah left to start her math pages at the big kitchen table. Sam wandered into the living room. The grand piano sat in the corner covered with framed photographs. Her family, especially her dad, figured prominently in many of them. They had spent many happy years in the company of Magda and Fred.

Sam's eyes welled up with tears as she looked at the pictures. Magda walked into the room and turned on a corner lamp. Without saying a word, she stood next to Sam and put her arm around her shoulder. Sam leaned against her.

"So many nights I sit in the bottom of my closet, wrapped in one of his old shirts. It smells like him. It does, Mag. It still smells just like him. It makes me feel like he's hugging me or something. It's so lame." Sam swiped her hand hastily at the tears on her cheeks. "I felt so safe when he was alive. Like he stood between me and everything. Nobody makes me feel that way anymore. Sometimes I even climb out of my window and sit on the roof at night. It's as though the closer I am to the stars, the closer I am to him. No wonder they think I need a shrink," Sam confided.

"He's right here with you, Sam. I promise you, your dad is watching over you. And none of that is stupid or lame. I've done it all...it's comforting." Magda squeezed her tight and went back to the kitchen to check on the grilled cheese.

Sam went to the foyer and unzipped her backpack. She reached in and pulled out her English assignment. Out of nowhere, a breeze sprang up and caressed her face. She felt the air around her grow cool. The scent of Hugo Boss surrounded her.

"Daddy?" she breathed.

Outside in the quiet neighborhood, a black Lincoln town car drove slowly up the street, past Magda's house, on its way to the Harding mansion.

Chapter Seven

Melissa Harding sipped her drink. She contemplated the man across the table. Peter Ambroglia looked distinguished in his impeccable, tailored suit. "Is this necessary, Peter?"

"Yes. It is. What's wrong, Melissa? Don't want to stop screwing around long enough to attempt to settle your dead husband's estate? Forbes would be disgusted to see you like this. Frankly, I'm disgusted," said Peter dispassionately.

He glanced around the bar. The Happy Hour crowd had left, leaving only a few diners passing time as they waited for their tables in the club's restaurant. He opened his briefcase and drew out some papers.

"Cut to the chase, Peter. You're boring me. Give me some good news regarding the estate, the insurance, or something. Throw me a bone." She crossed her long, graceful legs and sank back in her red leather armchair.

"The estate is still in probate. It will take at least a year. You know that already. It's the life insurance policy that's complicated. Because the death is still an open file with the police department, the insurance company won't release the funds. The police aren't convinced it was an open and shut case of being in the wrong place at the wrong time. The witnesses at the shooting think Forbes was singled out. No one else died, even though there was clear opportunity. It's a gray area. Even though you have been technically cleared as a possible suspect, you're the one to benefit the most from his death. So the wheels grind very slowly. Every "t" needs to be crossed and every "i" dotted before they will sign off and hand you a check." Peter looked over at Melissa.

"So no money...yet," said Melissa calmly. But as she sipped her drink, her hand trembled, betraying her agitation.

"No. You and Forbes kept the money from your father's estate separate in your name, correct? So you have plenty to continue supporting you and the girls until this is hammered out, yes? As I recall, your inheritance was formidable. Charles Crafton was a god in the investment banking world. He gave me my start, always willing to hear my ideas about automating the systems and updating the bank's technology. Add him to the list of people who would be dismayed by your present behavior." Peter handed two forms and a ballpoint pen to Melissa.

"Sign at the red sticky arrow here...and here...and here. These are to release the autopsy results from the hospital and the witness testimonies from the police department to the insurance company."

Melissa signed her name on all three spaces with a flourish. After she handed the papers back to Peter, she reached into her handbag, drew out her compact, and re-applied her lipstick.

"Well, I guess that's that. Unless you have more good news for me?" she challenged.

"Actually, Melissa, I'd like to know how the girls are doing. I haven't seen them since last June when you brought them by the office to see Bailey, Forbes' assistant. We were all very happy to see them. Forbes used to bring them by quite often." Peter tucked the signed papers into their folder and slipped the file back into his briefcase.

"I guess they're fine, Peter. What else can they be? Their father was killed. How would you be? Samantha is a typical, preoccupied teen and Sarah has her nose buried in her art projects. Oh, and Samantha has been in some trouble this semester. She got into a fight with one of the girls at school.

The principal is handling it with some mandatory grief counseling. That nonsense should be in the rear view mirror in a few weeks...end of story." Melissa seemed more irritated than concerned.

"I know you think they're handling it, Melissa. However, as Forbes' friend, I think he would feel better, and I know I would, too, if I called you every now and then to check on them...especially Samantha with her grief counseling."

"Whatever, Peter. Call me. If you want to be in the loop, I'll keep you in the loop. But please see if you can exert some influence to get the insurance money moving. I'd prefer it in my hands in trust for the girls instead of the insurance company's hands."

"I'm sure you would." Peter rose from his chair. "I'll be in touch, Melissa." He picked up his briefcase and walked out of the bar.

Her phone buzzed. She looked at the text from Kameron.
???

Melissa tapped out a reply.
Sorry. Still in meeting. Running late. Wait at the house.

She dropped the phone in her bag without bothering to check for his response. Melissa shuddered, unable to push down the fear that threatened to paralyze her. She thought back to the phone call she had received earlier that day--the same phone call she received like clockwork, every week, since July. The same disguised voice threatening her. Threatening to harm her daughters in terrible, detailed, horrifying ways if she didn't follow his instructions precisely. She lifted her glass, but it was empty.

Melissa beckoned to the waiter, an attractive, muscular man in his early thirties. He hurried over.

"Yes, Mrs. Harding?" He stood next to her.

"Bring me another, please, Matthew. Make it a double." She stroked his forearm with her fingertips. "I'll need a ride home. What time are you through?"

Chapter Eight

At nine o'clock, Magda kissed the girls goodbye. She watched them walk down her driveway together.

She called from the front door, "Let me know if you need anything! I'll be up for a while!"

The girls turned and waved. They headed down the sidewalk toward their house at the end of Hawkins Lane. It was only nine houses away, but the property lines grew farther apart as the mansions grew larger, culminating in the castle-like grandeur of the Hardings, with its beautiful English gardens and gated grounds.

"Do you think Daddy is watching us right now, Sam?" asked Sarah. She held Sam's hand tightly as they walked along the side of the road.

"I guess. It's not like he has anything better to do, right?" Sam wished the city had put in more street lights. It was so dark at this end of Hawkins. She could see their house all lit up at the end.

"Mom must be home," she thought. "That's weird. She told us last week to turn lights off to save money on the electric bill. Which is also weird...times ten. Why is the driveway blazing like the yellow brick road in Oz? That's not very energy efficient."

"Come on, Sam! Let's run! I'll race you!" Sarah dropped Sam's hand and flew down the remaining length of pavement to the front gates.

Sam took off after Sarah. Something wasn't right. A brisk wind blew up, swirling leaves and sticks in little tornados around the landscape lighting. Suddenly, the lower half of the driveway plunged into darkness. Sam put on a burst of speed and caught up to Sarah before she ran out of the protection of the shadows. She grabbed Sarah's arm and pulled her behind a large group of rosebushes.

"Sam? Wha…"

"Shh. Hang on a minute." Sam poked her head out and saw Kameron's town car parked in front of the garage. His driver leaned against the door texting on his cell phone. She blocked Sarah's view with her body. She knelt down next to Sarah in the dark, reached for her own cell phone, and called her mother.

"Hello? Samantha?" said Melissa.

"Mom, are you home from your meeting?"

"Not yet. I should be there in an hour or two. Put Sarah to bed. I'll check on you both when I come in." Mrs. Harding sounded distracted, laughing at something someone said in the background.

"You don't have to. I was just calling to tell you we're staying at Magda's for the night." Sarah stared at her big sister, silently shaking her head in disagreement.

"That's good, dear. Tell Magda I appreciate it. I'll call her tomorrow." Her mother hung up before Sam could say another word.

Sam peeked out from behind the bushes again. She could see the vague outline of someone, probably Kameron, rolling down the car's rear window.

"Sam, what is going on? We're home. Why did you pull my arm and push me down behind this bush? Why did you tell Mom we're still at Magda's? And why did the lights go out?" Sarah knew by the look of grim determination on Sam's face to keep her outraged comments to a whisper.

"Because we're not staying, short stack. Mom's not coming home until later. I'd rather be back at Mag's. I don't know what happened to the lights. Maybe it's some new energy saver timer. You know Mom and all her messed-up ideas on saving money these days. Just c'mon. Let's go." She reached for Sarah's hand. Together they retraced their steps, heading for the warmth and safety of Magda's.

Ten minutes later they were back in Magda's big, warm kitchen. Magda had a guest room upstairs with two twin beds that the girls had stayed in many times over the years. After their father died, Magda took it upon herself to outfit it with several changes of clothes for the girls to use on the nights they stayed over.

Tonight Magda didn't ask any questions, except to make sure their mother knew they were staying over. She took one look at Sam's face and bundled Sarah upstairs to take a warm bath and get ready for bed. She knew Sam would tell her what happened when she was ready.

Sam took out her computer from her knapsack and connected to Magda's WiFi.

"The password is so typical," she thought. "ILoveFred#999." She was still so unglued by what happened. "I wonder if Mom knew Kameron was waiting at our house?? I would've had to fend off Super Creep for hours, plus Sarah would have been there, too. Cheezits, what was Mom thinking?" Sam shook her head. "This is Level Psycho."

Sam breathed deeply. She ran over the bizarre events of the evening in her head. Daddy's cologne on the breeze earlier. The lights blazing in the driveway illuminating the car. The wind blowing debris around. The lights going out.

"No freaking way. It couldn't be...," Sam said to herself. "I wish...but Michael would think I'm a head case for sure if I told him I thought my dead father saved our butts. I am so losing it!"

Sam tried logic. "Mom's been coming home late. She wants to leave the lights on for us so she must have put some on a timer system to save electricity. No big mystery. And Dad's dead. End of story. Just dumb luck we missed Kameron. My life isn't a sci-fi TV show and Daddy isn't flying in from the spirit world to save us. So I might as well write the stupid homework letter and get it over with."

She opened up her browser and went to her Facebook page. She hadn't been on in ages. She used Instagram or Kik these days when she even felt like being near social media. She clicked on her photos and looked at the pictures of her Dad and Mom.

"Yeah...ancient history," Sam muttered. She went to her father's Facebook page and clicked Message.

Hi Dad:

I'm supposed to write to you because I punched a girl in the face at school. I have a shrink for grief counseling to help me with my anger issues. You probably already know this. Magda says you're watching over me and Sarah. I don't know what I believe. I wish you weren't dead. Nothing is the same anymore. Mom is crazy. She's not Mom anymore. Something happened last July. She changed into this person I don't even recognize. She brings home these guys who buy her all these presents. They're all over her and she lets them. Worse, they..."

"Sam? Hello?" Magda had been in the kitchen for a few minutes. She had waited for Sam to take a break, but the girl had been so intent on her writing she didn't have a clue Magda was even there.

"What? Oh! Sorry...writing the message to my dad on Facebook..."

"Go ahead and finish, honey. I'll be over here on the sofa reading."

Sam looked at her message. She deleted the last two words.

"I'm taking good care of Sarah, Dad. I won't let anything happen to her. No matter what. I promise. I miss you so much, Daddy. I hope you get this somehow.

love, Sam"

She added a Woodstock emoticon and hit Enter. Finally, Sam shut down her computer and yawned.

Magda stuck a piece of mail in her book to save her place. She put it down on the seat next to her. She yawned as well.

"Was it hard? To write to your dad?" asked Magda gently.

"Not really. Doing it on Facebook and sending the message made me feel as if I was really sending it to him. Like he's out there somewhere off planet and can actually read it." Sam paused. "Thank you for letting us come back and sleep here. Mom wasn't home yet. I called her, but she didn't seem in a big hurry. She said she'd give you a call tomorrow."

Sam sat down next to Magda. She struggled to find the right words to say. "I just didn't want to stay in that big empty house all by myself with Sarah. It felt better coming back here."

"You're welcome here day or night, Samantha. Your mom and dad kept me together during Fred's cancer. There is nothing I wouldn't do for you and your family. But I can tell by the look on your face, sweetie, that something rattled you. I won't push it. When you're ready to talk, I'm here. I know your mother has been through huge amounts of stress after your dad's death, but it's not okay for you to be put in difficult or uncomfortable situations that are beyond your coping skills." Magda looked as though she wanted to say more, but stopped and rose from the couch. "Alright, time for bed."

Later, after her shower, Sam sat on her bed and sent a text to Michael.

Staying overnight at Mag's. Mom had late meeting. See u at school.

"No way I'm gonna tell him about walking home and seeing Kameron's car," she mused. "Michael would flip out."

Sam glanced at Sarah sleeping in the bed next to hers, cuddled up with Magda's cat, Tigger. She got into bed, snuggled into her pillow, and stared at the ceiling.

"I guess I'm on my own," she thought sleepily. "I wish I could tell somebody. I'm afraid it's only gonna get worse. Somebody must know what happened to Mom last summer...."

Chapter Nine

Magda stared out the window over her kitchen sink. The rain fell in sheets, making everything look bleak.

"Brrrr…," she shivered, buttoning up her sweater. "I'm glad I drove the girls to school before the storm started."

She reached up and took two ceramic mugs from the cupboard. Fred took his coffee black while she enjoyed a good amount of half and half in hers. He had always joked she liked a little coffee with her cream.

"Alright, Fred." She brought the two cups over to the kitchen table and sat down. "Here's the thing. I'm calling Melissa right now. I want you to listen in on the conversation so we can discuss it when I'm through." She dialed Melissa Harding.

"Hello?" Melissa answered briskly.

"Hi, Melissa. It's Magda. How did your meeting go last night with Peter?"

"Same old, same old. No news. More paperwork to sign which means more hold-ups on the insurance money. The estate can't be settled until a year from Forbes' death which means my hands are tied in that as well. Unbelievably frustrating!"

"I'm so sorry, Melissa. I just wanted to let you know that Samantha and Sarah are both off at school. No bumps there except I'm a little concerned about Samantha's fight at school.

She told me she was seeing a grief counselor in order to keep from getting expelled."

"Yes. I know, Magda. What is she thinking? Aren't things bad enough right now without her getting into fights at school? I have too much on my plate every day without having to run to the high school every time she gets sent to the principal's office. I'm glad she's going to grief counseling. Maybe that Miss Jenkins can get through to her. I certainly can't," Melissa snapped.

"I think grief counseling is a good idea. It might help. She told me she's supposed to write a letter to Forbes each evening to get out her feelings. She wrote one last night in the kitchen. Messaged it to him on his old Facebook page. Writing down my feelings after Fred died was so beneficial. Hopefully, these notes to Forbes will give her some comfort. Did she tell you why she got into the fight?" Magda spoke carefully.

"No. She locked herself in her room and wouldn't even talk to me. That isn't surprising seeing as she barely speaks to me at all these days or spends any time at home lately unless Sarah is there. And Sarah is usually at your house so I never see Sam at all unless I pass her in the evening as I'm going out."

"She said she was defending you, Melissa. Some girls at school have been trash-talking you for weeks as Samantha put it. She couldn't take it any longer."

"That's news to me. It's also ridiculous. Why would *I* be a topic of conversation for high school girls?"

"Well..you have been attracting a lot of attention around town lately. And their mothers talk. And Sam goes to the same high school as their daughters," said Magda, shocked by Melissa's cluelessness.

"Explain *attention*, please," said Melissa stiffly.

"Oh, come on, Melissa. You've been entertaining different men in revolving door style since last summer. That isn't like you. I lost my husband, too. I understand fixing yourself up and treating yourself to nice things after months of intense grieving. Granted, it's paralyzing...but the men? Forbes hasn't been dead a year and your name has been linked with several eligible men in Beaconsfield since last summer, including some that aren't so eligible...as in married." Magda sounded as dismayed as she felt. "Are you in some sort of difficulty, Melissa? These are very wealthy, powerful men who have few scruples...not like Forbes, at all. In fact a few of them had bad blood with Forbes, especially when he blocked NatureLight from doing business with them. I remember several conversations with him about that. It upset him greatly. He called it dirty money."

"Funny you should mention NatureLight. I'm in Forbes' office right now taking care of some board issues. Thank you for taking care of the girls...you're the best. I couldn't do this without you. I'll pick up Sarah at six o'clock." Melissa disconnected the call without another word.

Magda stared at the cell phone in her hand.

"I'm speechless, Fred. That's a first. Don't we make a fine pair..."

Chapter Ten

Melissa locked the door of Forbes Harding's office in the NatureLight Building. She sat down at his desk and gazed at the pictures of her family that still hung on the walls and lined the shelves. She reminisced about happier times on their boat in the Bahamas, skiing in Aspen, hiking in Oregon, posing in Disney World, and enjoying other family vacations through the years.

"Oh, Forbes...," she whispered. "Help me."

With shaking hands, Melissa drew a piece of paper out of her leather Gucci handbag.

All household bills have been paid for the month as well as school tuition. You have a date with Marvin Buehler at 6:00 pm. His limo will pick you up at 5:30 pm. He has $4000 cash for you. Next time make it home to meet your date. Kameron was disappointed. Disappointment is not tolerated. Your daughters are lovely, aren't they? Kameron thinks so, too.

Melissa brought her fist up to her mouth and moaned soundlessly. She reached for her cell phone and tapped out a quick text to Magda:

Something came up. Won't make it home tonight. Please keep girls overnight? I know they're safe with you.

As she hit Send, someone knocked on the office door. She crumpled the note into a tiny ball and shoved it deep into her purse.

"Melissa? Are you in there?" asked Peter.

She took a moment to compose herself, then walked over and opened the door.

"Yes, Peter?"

"Private meeting? I don't remember Forbes ever locking the door."

"If he ever did lock the door, it was because I was in here and you weren't invited. Do you need something?" Melissa knew she had to get to the salon. Four thousand dollars meant absolute perfection.

"Claws in, darling. I saw you come in earlier. I wanted to see how Samantha was doing."

"Fine. Her therapist is having her write letters to Forbes to get out her feelings. She decided to use social media and message him her thoughts on Facebook. I guess writing a letter was too low-tech for a teen these days. So, that's a start." Melissa walked around the desk to gather up her coat and purse.

"You kept his old Facebook page? Lots of photos and memories there." Peter held Melissa's coat for her. Resignedly, she allowed him to help her.

"Yes. I didn't know how to get rid of it. Forbes never really used it except to post pictures and send messages to the girls while he traveled. So he and his memories live on in the Cloud. How nice. I'll let Samantha know you were concerned. I'm off to an appointment," she said, walking down the hall toward the elevators.

"Are you alright, Melissa? You seem a million miles away." Peter followed her and pressed the elevator button.

"You know me, Peter. I'm a survivor. Always have been. Just concentrating on keeping all the balls in the air." The elevator doors opened and she stepped in.

"If you ever want…," Peter began.

"No. Just no." The sound of her brittle laughter floated out as the elevator doors closed.

Chapter Eleven

Samantha ran down the hall. She burst into class right as the bell rang. Anime's foot poked into the aisle. Sam tripped over the ginormous day-glo pink sneaker and faceplanted in the second row of desks.

Anime and her friends snickered as Sam struggled out from under her backpack and hauled herself up the side of her desk. She managed to crawl into her seat *and* keep her mouth shut. Sam's inner ninja wanted to jump across the desks and land a spinning kick right in Anime's gut.

"That's a good way to get sent directly to Davies' office, do not pass go, do not collect two hundred dollars. And by the way, you're expelled. Awkward. I wish Michael the Boy Genius could witness my extreme temper control," Sam thought, glaring at Anime.

"Pass your homework up to the front of your row. Open your books to Chapter Four: How to Measure Angles in Radians. Read the explanation on the first two pages of the chapter and do the first five problems at the top of the third page." Mrs. Belcher collected the homework pages from the front row desks. "Anime, get your things and report to Mr. Davies' office. You will complete all fifteen problems on the third page of chapter four in Detention this afternoon at three o'clock. Are we clear?" Mrs. Belcher stared at Anime pointedly for a long moment, then at Sam, then back to Anime.

Anime looked at Mrs. Belcher and turned an ugly purple-red color, a disturbing sight with her zombie forehead stitches and bleached blond hair. She turned and gave Sam the stink eye and mouthed something nasty. Sam reconsidered the ninja move. Anime slung her backpack over her shoulder and stamped out of the room.

Sam breathed a sigh of relief and turned her attention to her math book. For once she wouldn't be the one sitting in detention this afternoon.

"I have way more important things to do, starting with going through Mom's stuff with Michael. There's gotta be something that'll shed some light on this whole crazy, upside-down reality," she promised herself. "I'm gonna find it or die trying! If trig doesn't kill me first..."

****

"Chica, chica, chica...slow down! Wait!" Michael leaped off the bus, trying to keep up with Sam who zoomed down the sidewalk like an F-16 fighter jet, intent on her mission. "Honey, pay attention! I am breaking a sweat here!"

"Hey, butthead...Jay Z called. He wants his attitude back. Hurry up! Sarah's at Magda's and Mom's out for the rest of the night. We have plenty of time to search," Sam called over her shoulder.

"Search for what? You never told me what we're looking for!"

"Anything, Michael! Anything that will explain why my mother is from Planet X these days! I'm tired of this...I want some answers!"

"Girl, your karma's gonna get you."

"It already did. And I'm not waiting for it to circle back and get me again."

Sam punched in the key code and opened the front door. She threw her backpack down in the foyer and pulled off her jacket.

"Whoa! Nothing says welcome home like a mansion made of money. I still can't get over how you live. And you like my mom's crowded kitchen better? Let me take your temperature…" Michael looked around and whistled. "Damn! I could see the Arrow or Batman living here. With some hot chick sister who needs to take me into her confidence…that's the "t" on that…ooh, we could turn it on up…" He stared at himself lovingly in the mirror, striking poses and flexing his muscles.

"Earth to Michael?! Are you done? You can't flex what you don't have, dude. Come on…my Mom's been using Dad's old office on the second floor. Stop staring at everything like you've never seen it before…I can tell you're running superhero scenarios through your head. Focus, Teen Titan." Sam ran up the carpeted stairs, through the gallery, and down the hall. She stood in front of the closed office door and turned the handle, but the door wouldn't open.

"Locked?! Since when? Sarah and I always played in this office. It hasn't been locked since…," Sam's voice trailed off. "Since Dad died. I can't believe I haven't been in here since then."

"You okay? I mean, I can go get tissues or something if you gonna cry it out right here and now. I can handle it. You go ahead." Michael started backing away toward the bathroom on the second floor.

"What?! No, no. I'm okay…it…I just didn't realize how much time had passed. Don't pass out on me. See? No tears."

"Yeah, well, you're really good at preparing for crises after they happen, y'know? We don't know what we're gonna find behind that door. I'm gonna go get the Kleenex just in case." Michael returned in a flash with a handful of tissues stuffed in his pocket.

"Thanks, bro. You're such a Boy Scout." Sam smiled, but then her smile disappeared and was replaced by a look of frustration. "I never saw a key. Dad never locked it. I guess I could try picking it. It can't be that hard. Thieves pick locks all the time. Maybe I could google it."

"You gonna google how to pick a lock? Haven't you ever gotten locked out before? Or gotten locked in the bathroom when you were little? We used to have to spring my cousin all the time. All you need is a screwdriver. Did your Dad have a toolkit in the garage?" Michael headed down the hall, talking over his shoulder.

"Yeah, just go through the kitchen. It's on the workbench. Just get the screwdriver, not the whole toolbox. Those tools haven't been moved since Dad died."

"Obviously!"

"I don't want Mom to get suspicious or anything!" Sam waited anxiously, relieved he decided to snoop with her.

No matter what they found, Michael had her back.

Chapter Twelve

Michael returned, brandishing the flat head screwdriver like a lightsaber. "Kssssshhhhhing! Ksssssshhhhhhing! Kssssssshhhhhhing! Move out of the way--the Force is with me!"

Sam laughed. "If only it *was* a light saber! I could do some real damage with that thing!"

Eight seconds later, they were in her dad's office. Papers were piled everywhere: on the floor, the desk, and the filing cabinet.

"Um....what are we looking for again?" said Michael.

"Anything dated the last weekend of July...receipts, notes, letters. I'll look through the stuff on the desk. You look on top of the filing cabinet. Then look through the drawers." Sam started going through the papers on the desk, one by one.

They worked for thirty minutes, flipping through the piles of papers without speaking. Finally Michael broke the silence.

"Everything on top of the file cabinet has to do with your dad's will. It's a lot of paper all saying the same stuff...your dad was worth a pile of money. Which is good because if he wasn't, then your whole lifestyle was probably supported by drugs. Which it wasn't. Just sayin'. That's a good thing. Okay, I'll stop talking now."

"Everything on the desk is bill, bills, and more bills. The house, the car, phones, school...and a huge amount of clothes, shoes, jewelry, hair, nails, spa treatments--really high-end, premium designer stuff." Sam picked up one of the bills and examined it. "I mean, Mom took care of herself when Dad was alive, but this stuff is really expensive. My parents were more into traveling, charities, and setting up foundations. Dad didn't like to live lavishly while others around him struggled and worked to make ends meet, especially after the economy slowed down. He was old school. Very down to earth. God, I miss him! He would get really mad if he saw these…" She replaced a pile of bills exactly how they had been on the desk and wiped at the tears rolling down her cheeks.

Michael handed her some tissues with an "I told you so" look, complete with eye roll. Sam laughed, sniffed, and blew her nose. Michael shuddered.

"I am never having children," he said. "Too much mucus and fluid. Gross."

"What about inside the drawers?" asked Sam.

"All your Dad's files. Stuff about NatureLight, insurance, mortgage paperwork, life insurance. Oh, and in the back is a file stuffed with all the newspaper articles about the…your dad's…death and stuff. Did you look inside the desk, yet?"

"Yeah…except this one drawer that's locked. You wouldn't know how…?"

"Nope. You're gonna need the key for that one. Maybe in your Mom's room in a bureau drawer or something? What about the other drawers?"

"Files of bank statements for different accounts. That's not strange because when my grandfather died, my mom's dad, he left her a fortune. He was an investment banker who made a lot of money during the eighties, using a bunch of brand-new information technologies. Dad told me he and Mom kept that inheritance separately in her name. For tax reasons, I think."

"Maybe she's using her inheritance to pay for all this bling and upkeep?"

"Maybe…" Samantha found the files pertaining to her

mother's inheritance account and began to leaf through them. "That's weird."

"What?"

"The statements end in July. There isn't an August or a September or anything after July."

"Maybe they're in a pile of mail somewhere."

"No...this is all mail on the desk. And it's all been opened. Nothing from that bank for that account. Look at these files...same bank, different accounts. All the statements are there. But not her inheritance account. The last statement is dated July fifteenth." Sam looked confused.

"Maybe they're in the locked drawer, Sam. Maybe your mom didn't want anyone to see how fast she was going through her money. All the bills are paid, right?"

"Yeah...wait. There's something on the bottom of the drawer." She felt around with her hand and pulled up a slip of white paper. "Michael! It's a deposit slip for twelve thousand dollars. Cash. Deposited into her regular checking account. Where would she have gotten twelve thousand dollars?"

"eBay? She selling jewelry and stuff?"

"eBay doesn't do cash. It's cashless. It uses credit cards or Paypal. Remember when your Dad was selling that vintage action figure on eBay and I helped him set up his Paypal account? If you use Paypal, the money is directly deposited or taken out of your Paypal account. Then you can transfer it over to the bank account that's attached to your Paypal account." Sam stared at the deposit slip, then placed it back in the drawer where she found it. "What's that you're looking at?"

Michael held up the book he had pulled from a corner bookshelf. "It's your Mom's high school yearbook from her junior year. Look at her, Sam! A cheerleader and everything! National Honor Society, Homecoming Princess...and hot! I mean, um...very nice-looking in my best friend's mother sort of way. And I'm not the only one who thought that. Listen to this:

Lissy Baby, I know we've been through alot this year, but you mean everything to me! Always remember Close Encounters of the Third Kind double feature at the drive-in! You rocked my world! I will always be here to take care of you and make you smile! I'd sacrifice anything for you! You are mine, baby. Together, forever. I would die for you! One more year and we graduate! Love, Tucker

"Uh-huh. You know what that means. Your mother did it in the back seat of a car in high school. Cheerleader Barbie and PreMarital Sex Ken. I did not need to know that about your mother. I need instant amnesia or something. Oops, sorry!" An envelope that had been stuck in the back pages slipped out and fell on the floor.

Sam walked over and picked up the envelope. It wasn't sealed. Inside she found a yellowed newspaper article, dated March 4, 1978. The headline read, *Star Athlete Murdered, Town Mourns Mysterious Death of Beloved Teen, Tucker Callahan.*

"What's it say? Read it!" demanded Michael.

"This star football player, Tucker Callahan, was found dead in his car, shot in the head after taking my mom, Melissa Crafton, home from a party at the home of her best friend, Kate Lambert. My mother was brought in for questioning, along with a bunch of other kids who attended. There were a bunch of kegs at the party, no parents were home. I guess she was the last one to see him alive. Oh, my God, Michael. That's awful and horrifying. She never, ever told us about this. How horrible for her."

"Somebody wanted him dead, Sam. It's not self-defense or an accident if somebody shoots you in the head. Fast forward to this year and somebody wanted your father dead, too." Michael stuck the yearbook back on the shelf and looked around the office. "Are we done here? 'Cause I'm starting to feel like somebody's looking over my shoulder. I think we better go. We got some clues...they don't make any sense, but it's a start. We can head to the library and see if we can dig up more articles about Callahan's death."

"What about the locked drawer?" Sam felt close to

something important. She didn't know what...but something.

"Samantha? Michael? Are you two upstairs?" Melissa Harding's voice floated up to the second story balcony. Sam froze.

Michael shook his head and mouthed, "be cool, Sam. Answer her."

He double-checked the positioning of all the papers and gently pushed her out of the office. He re-locked the door quietly.

Sam, realizing she still held the envelope with the newspaper article, shoved it in her sweatshirt pocket.

"Yes, we're up here on my computer googling funny cat videos," Sam called out.

Michael looked at her with disbelief. He stalked down the hall to Sam's room, muttering "I will get you for that!"

Sam ran down the stairs. She collided with her mother who juggled garment bags and shopping bags.

"What are you doing home, Samantha? I texted I would be out most of the night and you were to go to Magda's house. I don't think it's appropriate for you to be entertaining Michael in your bedroom without an adult in the house for supervision," said Melissa.

"You have got to be kidding! Who's on your agenda for the evening...and breakfast?" Sam glared at her mother, conscious of the newspaper article in her pocket.

"Samantha, I...," her mother's voice faltered. Despite the professionally applied makeup and elegant hair swept up off her neck, her mother's eyes were bright with tears and she seemed unusually fragile. "I can't even begin to have this conversation. I am late. Please, all I ask, and I know your father would ask the same, is do as I say and go to Magda's. Your one job is to keep an eye on Sarah and keep her safe."

"Don't you dare bring Daddy into this! He would never understand what you are doing to us, to me! You are everything those girls said you were! What is wrong with you?

Everything I do is to keep Sarah safe because you are doing nothing except spending money and bringing those awful men home. I would trade you for Daddy in a heartbeat! I hate you! I wish you were dead!" Sam ran back upstairs and slammed her bedroom door.

Melissa Harding drew in a painful breath and headed to her own bedroom.

"Me, too," she thought. "Me, too."

Chapter Thirteen

Later that evening, after Sarah fell asleep, Sam dropped into a chair at Magda's kitchen table. She dragged out her computer and stared at it. Magda munched on popcorn while watching an old *Murder She Wrote* in the family room. Sam sighed and opened up her Facebook account.

Dear Dad:

It's me again. Nothing much happened today. Pigzilla tripped me in class and got in trouble. That's good. But she'll be out for blood tomorrow. I'd fake being sick, but I have stupid Miss Jenkins after school. Mom's out again. Michael and I snooped through her stuff today. Don't be mad. I have to figure this out. There's some bank account stuff missing and we found out somebody killed her high school boyfriend before graduation. Did you know? And she had sex with him. Miss "Don't Have Sex Before You're Married." Nothing makes sense anymore. You're dead and Mom has this weird secret life. I'm afraid, Daddy. I wish you could do something. Like make Mom be a mom again. I hate these guys she goes out with. The way they look at Sarah and me makes me feel sick. Mom doesn't know, but they try stuff with me when she's not in the room. I have to keep them away from Sarah. If you weren't dead, this wouldn't be happening. Whatever. This is useless. Having a crappy time on Earth. Wish you were here.

love, Sam

****

The next morning, Michael and Sam got off the bus at Stanwich Academy and stood on the front steps. Sam swallowed the last of her Dr. Pepper too quickly and it went down the wrong pipe. She coughed, cleared her throat, and hacked, trying desperately to breathe.

"Oh, Sam-a-lam-a. Keep it corked. That's disgusting. Like a hairball or something," Michael gagged.

"Dying here, you jerk...," Sam wheezed.

"Better clean it up quick. Strong, silent, and cute coming straight at you."

"Noooooo....," she protested.

Sam heard Grayson say, "are you alright?"

"Y-y-y-ess," she stammered, praying her burning cheeks and watery eyes weren't too noticeable. "Just, um, allergies?"

Michael grinned and shot up the stairs into the school. Grayson stood next to her, waiting for Sam to catch her breath. She looked up at him, not sure why he was still there.

"I was wondering...I mean...I wanted to ask if you wanted to, um, hang out some time," said Gray in his deep, rumbly voice as he stared at the ground.

"What do you mean?"

"Like go to a movie or hang out at the mall or something." This time he looked directly at her with a hopeful look on his face.

"I didn't see the new Marvel movie yet," said Sam.

"Me neither. We could go tomorrow. I'll pick you up at your house around seven o'clock and we can go to the seven-thirty showing."

"Okay." Sam smiled. Inside, she high-fived herself and turned handsprings. On the outside, she kept cool. She had been crushing on him forever. She didn't want to spook him.

"Okay." He nodded and gestured for her to go up the stairs before him. "Bell's gonna ring."

They walked up the stairs, down the hallway, and into

homeroom, slipping into their seats just seconds before the bell rang. Sam's eyes widened when she realized she hadn't given him her cell phone number. She tore a piece of paper out of her notebook, scribbled her number on it, and handed it to him. Their eyes met briefly and he nodded. Neither one noticed Anime watching them.

Chapter Fourteen

"How did the letter writing go, Samantha?"

Sam looked at Miss Jenkins, sitting across from her, comfortable in her casual Friday jeans and oversized, pink cashmere boyfriend sweater. Sam didn't want to talk about letters or her dad or anything at all. She had been asked out by Grayson Gates. Grayson Gates! Their desks had been near each other ever since grade school. He was really smart, never spoke unless necessary, and was a star middleweight on the high school wrestling team.

"Alright, I guess. I mean, I wrote them." Sam glanced out the window, wondering to herself if Gray would take the late bus home or if he had driven to school that day.

"What emotions did you feel while you were writing?"

"I don't know. Mad, sad, stupid? I mean it's just nutso writing to somebody who died, isn't it? It goes nowhere, y'know? It's pointless. It's not like he can do anything about anything. He's dead!" Sam didn't want to do this right now. All her happy, fizzy feelings about Gray were slipping away.

"Did you tell him what you were feeling? Did you tell him why?" Miss Jenkins asked, pushing Sam a little harder.

"Oh my God! Yes! I did! Okay? I told him everything! I wrote it all down. But it doesn't do any good, does it? He's not going to come back and fix it, ever! He died and he left us and no amount of stupid letters is going to bring him back!" Sam snarled, pounding her fists into her thighs as hard as she could. She leaned back, squeezing her eyes shut in frustration.

"You're right. No letter is going to bring him back. But the letters help you, Sam. The very act of writing to your father brings up all the feelings you try so hard to bury. The only way to get rid of all those messy, scary feelings is to bring them out into the open. Hidden away, they become powerful, out of control, even dangerous. When you bring them up and out, I can help you work through them. But it *is* work--hard work." Miss Jenkins watched Sam's face.

"You have no freaking clue, do you?" Sam thought, silently staring at a point on the wall above Miss Jenkins' head. "I've already done this so-called *work*. I've cried, screamed, yelled, even thrown stuff when the pain got bad. I have scars on my wrist to prove it after I punched out my bedroom window. But at least Mom was present. Completely. With both of her arms wrapped around me and Sarah until we fell asleep. And until I know what sent Mom off the deep end, all the dumb letters to Dad are useless."

Another minute or two ticked by. Sam still hadn't said a word.

"Okay. Let's try something else. Let's talk about your relationship with your dad. Tell me something about him, a favorite memory or gift he gave you," said Miss Jenkins.

Sam looked at the clock. Fifteen more minutes left. She looked at her cell phone sitting on the table and remembered she had to drop off Sarah's art contest form at the Community Center before five o'clock.

"I can take the late bus to Lockwood Avenue, drop it off, then walk home from there," Sam planned.

"Samantha?"

Sam shrugged. Again she refused to say anything.

"This is going nowhere, fast," she thought bitterly. "Let's focus on the dead guy in the room and some airy, fairy happy memories. That'll fix everything and solve all my problems.

Oh, and bring world peace while we're at it."

"Samantha, you've spent a lot of time in the school nurse's office this fall. She noticed your weight has dropped significantly in a short period of time. Do you feel it has? What's going on with that?" Miss Jenkins didn't seem bothered by Sam's lack of response. She waited, allowing the silence to grow.

"I'm not hungry," Sam muttered finally, her eyes downcast. "And....Woodstock."

"What do you mean, Woodstock?"

"The memory. Woodstock. The little yellow bird on Peanuts. My Dad loved Woodstock--said he reminded him of me. Dad said I was little and feisty like Woodstock. I have a whole collection he gave me." Sam cleared her throat and grew quiet again.

"Thank you."

"For what?"

"For sharing that with me. It wasn't easy to do." Miss Jenkins looked at the clock. "Okay, we're finished for today. Would you please humor me and continue writing the letters to your Dad?"

Sam stood, reached for her cell phone, and jammed it in her pocket. "I'll think about it."

"Okay," Miss Jenkins agreed. "See you next Wednesday."

Sam slung her backpack over her shoulder, took her Dr. Pepper, and left the room without saying goodbye. She hurried toward Michael's locker to meet him, hoping Gray would be waiting with the other kids for the late bus. As soon as Sam turned the corner, she ran smack into Anime.

Chapter Fifteen

"What's your rush, crazy? Did your shrink keep you overtime?" Anime smirked. "I want a word with you. In here." She shoved open the door to the girls bathroom with one hand and held it there, waiting for Sam.

Sam hesitated. "If I go in there," she thought quickly, "I'm dead meat. Anime's groupies are probably waiting inside."

She moved toward the door slowly, her half-finished Dr. Pepper still in her hand. In one swift motion, Sam threw the soda in Anime's face and ran in the opposite direction. Anime reached out and grabbed the strap of Sam's backpack. Sam slipped out of it and kept running. She blew past Michael's locker, yelling "pig attack!" and headed straight through the doors to the late bus.

Michael slammed his locker shut. He headed in the opposite direction, back toward Anime. He looked at the tall blonde dripping with soda and snickered. He snagged Sam's backpack from the floor.

"What's the matter, girl? Miss your mouth?" Michael asked.

"I'm gonna kill her--this is so not over. She is so dead." Anime mopped her face with her sleeve. Her friends hovered around her, mingling their own threats with Anime's.

Michael rolled his eyes.

"Really? Dial it back, Anime. Too much hot air is leakin' out of your balloon, girl." Michael laughed and walked away, hurrying to catch up to Sam.

"Yeah? You tell her to stay away from Gray or she'll really be sorry!" Anime yelled at Michael's retreating back.

"Whatever! Get a life, Anime!" Michael answered without turning around. He flipped his finger up in a familiar salute and kept walking.

****

Michael and Sam boarded the late bus. He handed over her backpack as soon as they were settled in their seats.

"Thanks. You didn't have to...I didn't have anything important in it," Sam explained.

"I figured. I just wanted to see if you did any damage."

"Hah! Waste of a good Dr. Pepper, right?" Sam laughed out loud. It felt good.

"Yeah...she was mad!"

Sam looked out the window. She didn't see Gray. She guessed he'd driven to school today.

"Oh, man...I just remembered! It's a good thing you did get my backpack. Sarah's art contest form is in there. She would have been so disappointed if I didn't get it in on time. Thanks...I owe you!" Sam realized.

"No problem. What happened with Gray this morning?"

"He asked me out."

"No way. He doesn't talk. What did he do...use sign language?"

"No, silly. He actually spoke. It was kinda cool."

"So...?"

"So...he asked me to a movie tomorrow night. He's driving. I was so moony I almost didn't give him my cell number."

"Be careful, Sam."

"Why? Gray's not the type to try anything."

"No kidding. I mean watch out for Anime. I think she likes him. You've been pretty lucky so far. You've always been able to outrun her or outmaneuver her. But you hanging with Gray might make her go psych ward. Be careful."

"That's creepy. Okay, I will. Thanks," said Sam. "What are the odds of ending up in the same universe as Anime and liking the same boy? Why can't anything in my life be uncomplicated?"

"I don't know. But, you know what's nice, Sam-a-lam-a-ding-dong?" Michael puppydogged his head onto her shoulder.

"What? You haven't called me that in forever. Please don't ask me to sing *Summer Lovin'* with you--it's so seventh grade."

"Yeah...well, you *were* good as Sandy. Your Mom and Dad went to every performance, remember? I used to watch your Dad from behind the curtain--he had the biggest smile every night. No, I just wanted to say it's nice you haven't smelled like a drunk skunk for the past few days. Maybe the therapy stuff is helping?" Michael sat up straight as the bus rolled to a stop.

"Maybe. I don't know," said Sam vaguely, not wanting to talk about it. She gathered her things and moved to the front of the bus. "Tell your parents I'll be over for dinner around five-thirty with Sarah."

Sam jumped off the bus and waved at Michael. She waited for the bus to take off again before crossing the street to the Community Center. The wind picked up and whirled a burst of leaves in her wake as she dashed up the front walkway to the building. Sam pushed the front door open, pausing when she caught a whiff of her dad's cologne.

She looked around, then up at the sky and said, "Plenty of time, Dad. I've got Sarah's entry form right here. She'll be in the contest. Don't worry."

Sam stopped and looked over her shoulder. "Great. Now I'm talking out loud to my dead father. Thanks, Miss Jenkins. How to be a social reject before my time...hope nobody heard me."

Sam headed inside to drop off the form.

Chapter Sixteen

Dear Dad,

Okay. How was your day? Do you even have days? What's considered a day to a dead person? Is it all one big never-ending day? Never mind. I'll start. My day was decent. This boy, Gray, asked me out. I never told you about him because I never thought I ever had a chance with him. I've liked him since fourth grade. I know, stupid. So today I found out he likes me back. That was cool.

I told Miss Jenkins these letters were dumb. I lied. I just don't like her digging around in my head. I like writing to you. It makes me feel like you're around. Like you can still hear me even if I can't hear you. I wish I could hear you. I wish you were just on some long vacation and you were really getting these messages. I wish you would show up with a giant stuffed Woodstock. I wish this was just a horrible dream. But I know it's not. I miss you so much.

I love you.

Sam

Sam pushed her computer aside and relaxed back on her bed. It had been a nice evening.

She had picked up Sarah from Magda's. Together, they walked over to Michael's house for dinner. Michael's parents were warm and welcoming. Mrs. Bateman clucked and fussed over her and Sarah until Michael said he was starting to get jealous. She made sure to eat enough dinner to satisfy Mrs. Bateman's eagle eye even though she wasn't hungry. She escaped with Michael to the family room before dessert while Mrs. Bateman asked Sarah about the Community Center art contest.

"I found something out about your Mom this afternoon on the internet." Michael beckoned Sam over to his laptop he had out on the big center table.

"That doesn't sound good. What did you find?"

"You know that boyfriend of hers that got killed before graduation?"

"Yeah."

"The police brought your mom in for questioning. As a suspect."

"My mother? My mother can't step on ants. She carries spiders out of the house in paper cups so she doesn't damage their legs. No way could she be involved in his death. He was her boyfriend. She loved him. They did it and everything." Sam's voice rose in agitation.

"Shhh...keep your voice down, chica. It just said her fingerprints were all over the car and she was the last one who saw him alive. So they brought her in."

"But they didn't put her in jail or anything, right? Her friends must have seen him drop her off at their house. She was with them when he died."

"Yeah. But one of the articles stated one of her friends said she'd been crying and acting weird."

"Maybe she had her period. Crying and acting weird doesn't make you a murderer."

"There were witnesses who said your mom was with them at the time of death. So, yeah, she was cleared, but your grandfather had to hire a lawyer and everything to make it go away. Like being an accessory and stuff. Did you find the key to that locked drawer yet?" Michael asked.

"No. Not yet. Maybe I'll look tonight after Sarah's asleep," said Sam.

****

Comfortable against her pillows, Sam looked at the clock. It was only ten. Her mother, if she came home at all, wouldn't be in until after midnight.

"No time like the present," she decided.

Grabbing her cell phone, she put it on vibrate and stuck it in her pocket. Once inside her mother's room, Sam started poking around. The chaise lounge hid beneath dozens of elegant dresses. The dresser peeked out under heaps of scarves, jewelry, and lingerie in complete disarray. Dozens of pairs of shoes littered one whole corner of the room. Her walk-in closet overflowed.

"Where are you getting all the money for this, Mom?" Sam wondered.

She rifled through her mother's jewelry boxes and bureau drawers. Nothing. She attempted to put stuff back the way she'd found it, but gave up, figuring it was already so messy her mother wouldn't notice. No key on the night tables or in their drawers. The bathroom search turned up nothing. Sam wandered inside the walk-in closet. She moved aside hangers and looked behind clothes. Her toe stubbed something hard.

"Ouch! What the…?" She bent down.

Sam uncovered an old wooden art supply box. She tried to lift it out, but it was too heavy. She knelt down and inched it out, little by little, to where she could open the lid. She ran her fingers over the top where her mother's name, Melissa Crafton, was engraved on a metal plate. Inside were charcoals, pencils, pastels, tubes of watercolors, erasers, and brushes all jumbled together. It hadn't been touched for years.

"What, now you're an artist? Why is this a secret? We know Sarah had to have gotten it from somewhere. Why is this hidden in your closet? Sarah would love to see this…." Sam was mad enough to just take it and give it to Sarah, but then her mother would know she'd been snooping.

Frustrated, she slammed down the lid and pushed it back into place. Her hand felt a tiny pull-out drawer in the front. Inside, she found a key. Before she could go try it, her cell phone buzzed.

"Hello?"

"Samantha? It's Mom. Is Sarah asleep?"

"Yeah. It's past eleven. Where are you?"

"Business meeting ran late." Her mother sshed someone in the background. Sam rolled her eyes. Her mother couldn't lie her way out of a paper bag. "I need you at the house to watch Sarah tomorrow night."

"Can't. I'm going out."

"Some of your father's business associates are coming over for cocktails at five o'clock. Magda can come get Sarah at seven. As soon as she's picked up, you may go."

Sam could hear a man's voice calling for her mother to get off the phone.

"Sam," her mother's voice was barely audible. "I need you. Sarah can't be in the house alone tomorrow evening. Please." Her voice shook.

"Alright, I'll be there. Why? What's going on? Are you okay?" said Sam, mad and confused.

"Yes, darling." Melissa resumed her normal volume. "I have to run. I won't be home until very late. See you in the morning." She ended the call before Sam could say anything.

Sam took the key and headed for her father's office.

Chapter Seventeen

The next morning Sam checked her phone. Six texts from Michael waited for her.

What do you mean your mother's money is gone???
What was in the drawer?
Is this on vibrate?
Not going to stop texting until you get out of bed.
Not going away.
Texting every emoji one at a time until I get a phone call!

Sam leaned over to snag her phone, tangled her legs in the comforter, and fell out of bed in a heap of covers. She reached up for her pillow and settled herself in a makeshift nest on the floor. Michael answered her call on the first ring.

"Finally!" Michael grumbled.

"The missing bank statement was in the drawer. The account had been cleaned out. The balance was zero. ZERO, Michael. Every bit of her inheritance from my grandfather VANISHED. That was an investment account, Michael. It was huge. I checked the statement against the last one in July. The money disappeared in less than twenty-four hours."

"When?"

"That same Friday in July when she went into New York for the weekend. There was also one hundred thousand dollars in cash in the drawer. CASH, Michael. That explains the cash deposit slips, but not where it's coming from. And a

Valentine's Day card with the same date that said "Mine, Forever."

"From your Dad?"

"How could it be from my Dad? He's dead. And, no. I didn't recognize the handwriting."

"A Valentine's Day card in July? That's random. And so not normal."

"None of this is normal, Michael. It's bizarre. Why would my mom empty that account? And if she didn't, who did?"

"Maybe she got spooked by all the legal stuff and took out the money. Hid it in a mattress somewhere. A big mattress." Michael whistled in appreciation.

"She's not senile. That's something crazy, old people would do. Dad was serious about investing and growing money. They never touched principal funds. That account was different, too. It was like a special signatory account. It couldn't be accessed without certain protocols."

"Protocols?"

"These protection devices they put on accounts, I think, so somebody couldn't kidnap my mom and make her empty it. Something like that. I used to hear them talking about it at night after dinner."

"The icky part is the Valentine. That's like stalker stuff. Why would she keep it?"

"I don't know. I don't know about any of this. I can't ask her 'cause then she'd know I snooped. I put the key back exactly where I found it in this big wooden art case with all these old art supplies. I'd never seen it before. I know Sarah's never seen it."

"Okay. This is alternate reality stuff. Just take a break for now. We'll start putting the pieces together tomorrow. Big date tonight, sister soul."

"I know, right?"

Sam heard pounding on her bedroom door.

"Gotta go. Call you later." She hung up.

Sarah was yelling her name. Sam threw open the door. Sarah tackled her, grabbing her by both arms.

"Sam!"

"What?!"

"A package came to the front door for you. I heard the doorbell ring, but when I got there all I saw was this box. Open it!" Sarah pointed to the large box next to her on the floor.

Sam picked up the brown shipping box and brought it into her bedroom. She took a pair of scissors and sliced open the top. Inside was a large, beautifully wrapped box with a giant bow. Her name, *Samantha*, was written on a tag attached to the ribbon.

She untied the bow and tore off the wrapping. When Sam removed the lid, she froze. Inside was a large, plush Woodstock.

Chapter Eighteen

Sam's eyes widened when she saw the stuffed animal. She fell to her knees and covered her mouth with her hands, unable to speak. Frightened, Sarah ran to get Melissa.

"What on earth...? Samantha? You look like you've seen a ghost!" said her mother.

Sam pointed to the hapless Woodstock, still in the tissue paper.

"What is wrong with you? I don't understand. You love Woodstock. Peter called yesterday. He asked if he could send you and Sarah some presents. He's been worried about you two...said he rarely gets to see you anymore at the office. I told him you and your father had this thing about Woodstock and you hadn't had a new one since he died. Peter sent this for you and a huge box of art supplies for Sarah. Stop being dramatic and enjoy it. Honestly! Let's go, Sarah. You can help place the flower arrangements."

Her mother turned and walked away saying something about the caterers arriving, but Sam didn't pay attention. She pulled the Woodstock out of the box and placed it gently on her bed with all the others.

"Oh, Daddy...," she whispered to herself.

****

Cars began pulling up to the Harding mansion at five

o'clock. Sam watched the women, wearing heels and little black dresses, sparkle like diamonds on the arms of the men in designer suits. She sniffed the different perfumes as the scents drifted up into her bedroom window.

Sam recognized many of the guests from her father's office. A familiar black Lincoln town car pulled up the drive. When the driver opened the passenger door, Kameron got out.

"Of course he would be here," Sam thought. "How could I be so stupid?"

Kameron glanced upward. He saw her stricken expression, smiled, and headed inside. Sam planned to keep as far away from him as possible until Gray came to get her.

One of the company limousines arrived last. Sam watched Peter Ambroglio step out, then offer his hand to the woman inside. She liked Peter. He had always been kind to her whenever she visited her father's office, asking about school and stuff. It had been really nice of him to send her a gift. She studied the woman on his arm.

"Tall, pretty, blond...very classy, Peter," said Sam, impressed. "Maybe she's the one who'll finally get you to the altar. Too bad for all the other high-heeled hopefuls lining up at your door." Sam remembered how her father had often encouraged Peter to marry and settle down.

Sam kicked herself for thinking somehow the Woodstock had come from her dad.

"Yeah, like he's magically alive somewhere, trying to send me a message. Even if Magda is right and Dad is watching over me, there's no way he can buy stuff on Amazon and have it delivered. Dream on," she thought.

Sam's phone buzzed.

"Hello?"

"You ready?" asked Michael.

"Yeah."

"Finally choose the outfit?"

"Yup. Leggings, mini blue jean skirt, cropped T-shirt,

hoodie, boots. Okay, Versace?"

"Who? Yeah...it's all good. It's a movie, not a promposal."

"I wish. Text you when I'm home. Bye."

"Bye."

Sam called Sarah with their special ring, then knocked on her door. The lock turned and Sarah poked her head out.

"I'm going downstairs, Boo. Mom said I had to mingle and say hi to the people who worked with Dad. Stay up here. I'll come get you when Magda's here to pick you up," said Sam firmly.

"You look nice, Sam. You put stuff on your eyes. It makes you look really pretty."

"Yeah? Thanks, squirt. Lock it up--I'll be back."

Sam headed down the hallway past her Dad's office. She found the door wide open and a folder left out on the desk. Mom must have been in a hurry. Usually she straightened everything away and closed the door to discourage stray guests who wandered upstairs.

Sam went inside to put away the folder. When she picked it up, a sheet of paper fell out. It was this evening's guest list, written out in the same handwriting as the valentine in the locked drawer. A star highlighted a name she didn't recognize. A note at the bottom said:

Enjoy the party. I know I will.

Sam slipped the list back into the folder with trembling hands.

"What are you involved in, Mom?" Sam wondered uneasily.

Chapter Nineteen

Waitresses with trays of canapes and glasses of champagne circled the rooms on the main floor with professional ease. A guy in his thirties manned a full-size bar in the massive living room. Sam recognized him from the club. He caught her eye and waved.

She walked over to the bar and nodded hello.

"Hey. Sorry, I don't remember your name," said Sam.

"Matthew. From the club? I used to wait on your family in the restaurant when Mr. Harding was alive. I'm...um...sorry about your loss. Your Dad was a really nice man. One of the good guys, y'know?"

"Yeah, Matthew. I know. Thanks. Have you seen my Mom?"

"Yes. She just walked through here with Mr. Goss."

Sam's ears pricked up. That was the name with the star next to it on the guest list.

Matthew looked around. "Lots of money walking around in here tonight. Lots of heavy hitters, if you know what I mean. And Leopold Goss? He's got more money than God." He hesitated before continuing. "None of my business, but I don't trust him. Something about his eyes, y'know? Cold. Now your Dad? Lots of money, but true blue." Matthew took a long pull on a beer he was nursing under the bar. "Your mom is special...she deserves better."

"Okaaaay...awkward. I'm just gonna go find my mother. Nice seeing you." Sam made her way out of the living room.

"Jeez...does the whole world have a thing for my mom?" Sam complained under her breath. She glanced into the library packed with inebriated guests having a loud, lively conversation about local politics. No mother.

In the dining room she caught sight of Peter Ambroglio and his date. Knowing her father would have wanted her to be polite, she waited for a break in their conversation and thanked him for the gift.

"I'm glad you liked it, Samantha. I've missed seeing you. This is my friend, Janet. I'd forgotten what lovely parties your mother throws," Peter remarked.

"Yes, she does. Thank you again, Mr. Ambroglio."

"You're old enough to call me Peter now. Times change."

"Alright. Thank you, Peter. It was nice meeting you, Janet."

Sam left the dining room, but not before she overheard Janet remark about her mother's exquisite taste and unique sense of style.

She heard Peter reply, "Yes. Melissa's an artist. She used to paint. She had amazing potential. Unfortunately, she never pursued it."

Sam wandered toward the kitchen. She couldn't believe what Peter had just said.

"Does everybody know you better than me, Mom?" Sam muttered.

"Hello, Samantha. Talking to yourself?" Kameron towered over her.

Distracted by Peter's comment about her mother, she had wandered too far into the dim, back hallway near the kitchen. Sam spun around to go back the way she came, but Kameron blocked her.

Sam heard people moving in the kitchen. Dishes and glasses clinked. A utensil clattered to the floor. Someone swore loudly, then laughed.

Kameron stepped closer, backing her up against the wall. Her heart pounded. The party noises faded into the background as she frantically tried to figure out an escape route.

"Mmmm. You look...so good." He pushed his heavy, muscled body next to hers and ran both hands up the outside of her slender, goose-fleshed arms, whispering what he'd like to do to her. His breath reeked of alcohol and cigarettes. Kameron's hands dropped to her waist, sliding up and under her cropped t-shirt. He breathed heavily onto her neck, running his tongue up and over her jawline.

When Kameron closed his eyes and bent down to cover her mouth with his, Sam angled her hips closer. His murmur of pleasure became a groan of pain as she stomped her sturdy-heeled boot squarely on his instep. She jammed her knee up between his legs with as much force as she could, grabbed the coat stand, and pulled it over on top of him. Kameron dropped to the floor, clutching himself, covered in a heap of raincoats, hoodies, and windbreakers.

Sam whirled to make her getaway. His hand snaked out and grabbed her ankle. She gasped, lost her balance, and fell on top of him. He twisted her long hair in his hand and pulled her face close.

"Not so fast," he growled. He flipped her around until she was underneath him. His leg pushed hers apart, one hand still twisted in her hair, the other rubbing his thumb over her bottom lip. She looked up into his determined eyes and knew she was in trouble.

"We can head out to the garage this way." Sam heard her mother's voice coming down the passage.

Kameron released her, his eyes warning her to be quiet. Sam stood quickly, stepping over the coats to put as much space as possible between her and Kameron.

"Samantha? What are you doing? Oh my goodness, Kameron, why on earth are you on the floor with all those coats?" Her mother, Peter, Janet, and three other guests all crowded in the hallway, staring.

"My fault," said Kameron. "You mentioned you were going to show some of your guests Forbes' classic 1955 Mercedes 300SL Gullwing. I saw Samantha at the party. She nicely offered to let me have a sneak peek. But the coat stand and I came to blows."

"Looks like the coat stand won," said Peter. He looked at Samantha, her hair messy and tangled.

She shifted from one foot to the other, not saying a word. Peter offered Kameron his hand, but Kameron waved him off.

"Oh, dear," said Melissa quickly. "Kam, come with us. I'm so sorry you fell. The lighting is terrible back here." She hooked her free arm through Kameron's and took a sip of the drink in her other hand.

"Samantha, you need to get going. It's almost seven. Oh, and comb your hair, dear, you look like you've been through a windstorm. Other than that, you look very cute. Have fun tonight!" She blew Sam a kiss. "Come, everyone. Watch your step."

Melissa headed, arm in arm with Kameron, out the back door toward the carriage house across the lawn. Sam stood there for a second. Mingled waves of anger, fear, and relief washed over her.

"Are you coming, Peter?" Janet asked.

"Yes. Are you sure you're alright, Samantha? You're very quiet." Peter didn't have a high opinion of Kameron at the company. And he was pretty sure Kameron wasn't the type to lose his balance due to a bunch of coats.

"Yeah. Fine," Sam mumbled. She stood the coat stand up and picked up the jackets. She reached in her pocket and checked the time on her cell. "I've gotta go."

Sam headed back through the house toward the family room. On her way she snagged two glasses of champagne from a waiter's tray and downed them both, one after the other, handing the glasses back to the startled waiter. When she reached her destination, she smiled at Matthew, bent down behind the bar, and pulled out an unopened bottle of scotch whiskey.

"Samantha...," Matthew began.

"It's okay, Matthew. Mom asked me to bring it out to the carriage house. She's having a private showing of one of my father's automobiles. I guess she's looking for the highest bidder and needs something to loosen up the purse strings."

"Your mother's a smart woman, Samantha. Do you need me to carry out some glasses?"

"No, I've got it. Thanks." Sam turned and walked out, this time heading straight for her bedroom.

Chapter Twenty

Sam looked in her bathroom mirror. She'd switched to a long sleeve tee that didn't show the bruises on her arms from struggling with Kameron. She massaged her neck muscles, rolling her head from side to side. The champagne and two shots of scotch had calmed her down and pushed the memory of Kameron's hands and lips to the back of her mind. Magda had just called and said she was on her way. Sam gargled with mouthwash.

"I can't believe I let that jerk corner me!" Sam checked her hair and makeup in the mirror with shaky fingers. "Thank God, Sarah is safely tucked in her room. If he ever tries to touch her, I will kill him. Complete and utter death delivered to that pond scum by my own two hands!"

She gathered up her hoodie and her wallet. Sarah sat waiting for her in her room. Together they rushed, hand in hand, down the staircase toward the front door.

"Hurry, Sarah! Magda's waiting," Sam urged. "Gray's probably out there, too." Sam had told him to wait outside. It was too crazy to try to introduce him to Mom with all these people here. Not that Mom would notice or care.

At the bottom of the stairs stood a small cluster of guests. No one paid any attention to the girls descending the staircase except one older man. He broke away from the group and stopped the girls before they could get halfway across the foyer to the front door.

"You young ladies are in a hurry. You must be Melissa's daughters." The man positioned himself between them and the door. "I'm a good friend of your mother's, Leo Goss."

"Nice to meet you, Mr. Goss. I don't mean to be rude, but we're late." Sam felt trapped under the weight of Leo's calculating gaze.

"This must be how a mouse feels right before the cat pounces," she thought.

"You're Samantha." Leo wasn't impressed. "And this...this must be Sarah. Don't be shy, Sarah. I don't bite. What a pretty little girl you are. Your mother is a terrible one for never having any pictures of you. You have such beautiful long blonde hair."

Leo reached out to stroke her head with his hand, but Sam stopped him. She knocked his hand out of the way with a swift, protective instinct.

"Don't touch her!" she hissed, thrusting Sarah behind her. Leo's smug, greedy expression vanished. Something ugly flared in his eyes. He moved toward her.

At that moment, Magda sailed through the front door and called out, "Hello? Sam? Sarah?"

Melissa Harding strode with purpose through the foyer toward Leo. And Gray, looking like a young, buff superhero, stepped out from behind Magda.

"Gotta go!" Sam said quickly.

Chapter Twenty-One

The IMAX Cineplex overflowed with people out on a Friday night. Harried parents hanging on to two or more excited children carrying buckets of popcorn, sullen teenagers more interested in their iPhones than the person standing next to them, and senior citizens out for a relaxing evening...all stood in line. Sam and Gray, loaded up with Milk Duds, Twizzlers, popcorn, and Cokes, headed to Theater 5 for the latest Captain America movie.

Sam didn't say much on the drive over. She appreciated the fact Gray wasn't talkative. Other than saying hello to Magda and Sarah and telling Sam she looked nice when he opened the truck's door for her, he remained quiet. Sam, on the other hand, felt stressed and slightly wasted. She just wanted to sink down in the darkened theater next to Gray and lose herself in the movie.

Her mother had swooped down on Leo Goss, gushing about some guest he just had to meet. She draped herself against him, tucked his arm firmly around her, and insinuated her body between himself and her children. Melissa drew his face to hers possessively, kissing him on the lips.

Leo Goss had studied Sam's defiant face over her mother's head before he allowed himself to be pulled away. Magda hastily shooed a big-eyed Sarah out the door. Sam and Gray followed. Sam cringed at the memory of Gray's face at the moment he realized that was her mother locking lips with the toad king in front of everybody.

"These seats okay?" Gray nodded toward the row on his left.

"Yeah, fine." Sam stood there until she realized Gray was waiting for her to go into the row first. "Oh, thanks."

She sat down in the middle. Gray sat next to her.

"Big party at your house, huh? Those were some pretty sweet cars parked outside. The valet dude looked a little nervous about my truck." Gray's father ran a landscaping service company. Gray worked for him on the weekends.

"Sorry you had to come inside. I meant to be out sooner," Sam explained.

"No problem. I'm glad I got to meet your little sister and...Magda? They're nice," Gray assured her.

The theater grew dark and previews of upcoming movies began to play. Sam relaxed, finally beginning to enjoy herself. She peeked sideways at Gray, who munched on his popcorn while laughing at a comedy bit up on the screen. She couldn't believe she was on an actual date with him. Sam smiled and looked up at the screen. The main feature started.

Halfway through the movie, she needed to go to the bathroom.

"I'll be right back," Sam whispered.

Stepping over knees and feet, Sam made it to the end of the row and hurried to the ladies room. On the way back, she spied Anime and one of the guys who worked at the movie theater talking in a corner. Hoping she had gone unnoticed, Sam slipped through the door to Theater 5 and went to take her seat. Grateful she had avoided another confrontation, Sam sat down in her seat next to Gray and settled in to enjoy the rest of the movie.

Leaning down to pick up the pack of Twizzlers that had fallen out of her jacket pocket, she was confused to hear jeers and catcalls echo through the room. Laughter and "whoo-hoo's!" were mingled with angry shouts.

"Get that off the screen! Go back to the movie! C'mon!"

voices called.

"Get what off the screen? What's going on?" Sam turned her head toward Gray, her body still bent down while her fingers searched the floor for the missing candy. She turned her face toward the screen.

And thought she was going to throw up.

Chapter Twenty-Two

Sam saw her mother up on the screen, in living color and larger than life, for the whole world to see. Melissa Harding, half-naked, exchanged steamy, passionate kisses in some hotel room with Leo Goss whose hands roamed all over her. The six seconds of video repeated itself again and again.

"Oh, no!" Sam cried.

She hurled herself past Gray, dumping her Coke and tripping over knees and feet in her haste. The lights came up. Sam ran up the aisle and out the door, searching wildly for Anime.

"ANIME!" Sam howled in frustration, the events of the entire day crashing down around her.

Sam heard laughing. She whirled around to see Anime exiting the theater, staring at her phone screen. Anime looked up at Sam, shaking and wild-eyed in the hallway.

"Well, that was educational," Anime snickered. "Maybe your mom could take over the sex ed classes at school. Oh, wait...there's no porno class." She held up her phone, waving it tauntingly at Sam. "It's on Vine, Instagram, and Facebook, too."

Gray ran out of the theater in time to see Sam approach Anime with murder in her eyes. He caught up to her and spoke in a quiet voice.

"Sam...," Gray cautioned. "This isn't school. They'll call the cops. And you already have alcohol on your breath."

Sam stared at him in disbelief.

"Sorry, but it's true. I'm not judging or anything." Gray held her gaze, his honest eyes filled with worry.

"What's the matter, Sam? Can't handle Gray seeing your mom at the movies?" Anime took a step closer.

"Shut up, Anime," said Gray, standing close to Sam.

"I will kill you for this, Anime. I will kill you for doing this!" Sam's voice ended in a shriek. Her eyes blazed. Her hands itched to wrap around Anime's throat and squeeze as hard as she could.

"What are you saying, crazy girl? Kill me for doing what?" Anime looked at her. "You think I did this?" She shook her head. "Nope. Nice try, looney bird. I wish. Pretty impressive tech hack, though, whoever did it. It's your mother's own fault for letting her candyman make selfie sex vids on his cell."

"I saw you! I saw you with that game hacker right before it happened. You followed my mom somehow and got him to hack the footage of her off some server...then you got him to upload it...everywhere!" Sam yelled. A crowd formed around them in the lobby.

"Prove it. You have nothing. Except a slut for a mother." Anime smiled maliciously at Gray. "Like mother, like daughter?"

Sam gasped and tears filled her eyes. "I hate you, Anime. You're gonna pay for this. I will hurt you so bad. You will wish you never messed with my family," she choked out.

"Come on, she's not worth it, Sam. Let's get out of here." Gray took Sam's hand. He led her through the lobby and out to the parking lot.

Sam's phone buzzed.

"Hello?"

"Samantha! Thank goodness you answered. Have Gray drive you to Memorial Hospital. Your mother was attacked!"

Chapter Twenty-Three

Dear Dad:

My life is ruined. I can't go back to school. I can't live in this town. Really awful things are happening. Mom got mugged outside a hotel tonight and landed in the hospital. I don't know if she's doing drugs or if she's doing crazy stuff because she needs money. I don't know what she thought she was proving with Leo Goss but now everyone has seen her disgusting video. I mean, doesn't she care about me and Sarah? I can't face Gray. He must think I am such a total loser. I can't even look at him without seeing that horrible, sleazy vine video playing over and over again. I just want to die, Daddy. I want to lay down, close my eyes, and die. I can't take this. I wish...

Sam stopped typing and looked over at the next bed where Sarah curled under the covers, sound asleep. She took another swallow from the scotch bottle she had stuck in her backpack when Magda had run her home to get her laptop. The strong liquor burned her throat. She took a final drink and hid it away again.

...you were here with me. I wish you could tell me what to do. I don't want to be here anymore, Daddy. I feel so alone. Sarah could go live with Magda. I'm tired of all this. I don't know if I can figure out what's going on with Mom, and after tonight, I don't know if I care.

I don't even know if I can keep Sarah safe anymore. I need you, Daddy. I just want to be with you. I can't see a way out of this anymore. I wish...I wish with all my heart that you weren't dead. I don't know how to do this without you.

love, Sam

Sam looked at the time. It was already one o'clock in the morning. She hit enter and stared at the screen. A mental image of her mom, bruised and bloody, floated in front of her eyes. The doctors had decided to keep Melissa overnight in the hospital for observation.

****

Melissa's driver took her to the downtown Hilton after the party. Before Melissa walked two steps toward the hotel entrance, a dark blue Nissan with tinted windows roared into the driveway entrance of the hotel.

A stocky man in a black ski mask jumped out of the rear of the car. He attacked her on the sidewalk. He grabbed her by the neck, punched her hard in the ribs, and threw her to the ground. Within seconds he was back in the car. It raced away before panicked onlookers could react or call for help. No one got the license plate number and no one was able to identify the driver. It happened too fast. Melissa was taken to the hospital in an ambulance with a couple of bruised ribs, some nasty contusions, and a mild concussion.

At the hospital, Gray handed Sam over to Magda. He started to say something about the evening, but Sam cut him off.

"Thanks for driving me. I have to go now." She walked inside the hospital without a backward glance.

She texted Michael from the hospital. He texted back. He'd already seen the video. Everybody was talking about the big screen version on Kik.

How's your mom?

She'll live. Cops think it was a random mugging, except they didn't take her jewelry or purse or anything. Weird.

Want me to come over to the hospital?

Yes. Wait, no. Don't bother. We're leaving soon.

Heard you threatened Anime. True?

True. My life is totaled. And I know Anime did it. Not to mention made the entire world want to wash their eyeballs.

It wasn't that bad. At least the dude had clothes on. I don't think I could have recovered from that.

Yeah. You and me both.

We still on for tomorrow? The detective thing?

I don't know. I'm not feeling very motivated. I think I'd rather drown myself.

I'm coming over.

NO. Don't worry. I won't do anything stupid. At least not until I kill Anime. gtg, Magda is leaving. Text you tomorrow.

K. I've got your back, Queen.

Thanks.

****

Sam sighed. She didn't feel like getting undressed. The events of the evening seemed far away. She felt drowsy, secure in the safety of this room, in this house. Away from all the wackos on the planet who made her life miserable. She shoved her computer off her lap and leaned back on the pillows. Within minutes, Sam fell asleep.

In the middle of her dream about a giant Captain America ringing her doorbell and holding up his iPhone, complaining "your mother has more followers than I do!", she woke up and realized the dinging sound was coming from her computer. She couldn't have been asleep for more than an hour or two. The street lights were still shining. Sam rubbed her eyes a couple times and squinted at her open laptop.

She sat up straight and reached for it, almost knocking it clear off the bed in an effort to bring it close to her face.

"What the hell?!" whispered Sam.

On the screen was a response sent from her father's Facebook page.

samantha
help
me
stop
them

Chapter Twenty-Four

"This isn't happening," Sam thought. She looked at the cryptic message on the screen.

Sam glanced around the room, then at Sarah. Nothing had changed. Tigger, Magda's big tomcat, lay next to Sarah, burrowed in the blankets. He opened one sleepy eye at her with a reproachful look, then stretched out to his full length and went back to sleep.

Sam stood up and went across the room to peek out the open window. The curtains remained unruffled in the breezeless night. Nothing stirred on the quiet street.

She picked up the laptop and put it on the antique desk in the corner. Taking a quilt off the bed, she wrapped herself up and settled into the sturdy desk chair. She eyed the computer as if it were a bomb about to go off.

Sam took a deep breath and typed:

Who is this?

She hit enter before she could change her mind. After a minute there was an answering ding.

dad

The screen showed whoever was on the other end was still

typing. Sam watched in shock, unable to tear her eyes away. The rest of the message appeared.

danger
mom
sarah
you

Then nothing. Nothing at all. Sam sat there with tears running down her face, hugging herself as hard as she could. Deep down inside, she wanted to believe her father was somewhere out there in the universe and had figured out a way to reach her, but her mind just couldn't believe it. She rejected the possibility immediately.

"This is some sick joke...some twisted person's way of tormenting me. Why not? Guess I'm fair game," Sam thought.

The ding came again. This time a photograph appeared of her father holding her and Sarah on the beach at Gulf Shores at sunset when they were younger. They had just finished building a huge sandcastle with turrets and shell decorations.

Sam remembered her father saying to her mother, "Tide's coming in. Quick, get a picture! These girls put a lot of sweat equity into this castle!"

Sam hesitated. That had been a big saying of her dad's. He had always wanted them to do their best--to put 110 percent into their hard work and efforts so they would feel real pride and ownership in life, not just have stuff handed to them.

Sam turned off the message notification sound on her computer. She didn't want Sarah to wake up. She typed:

What did you say to Mom before she took this picture?

The response came quickly.

sweat equity

hard work
need you
stop killer
not easy

Sam began to type questions as fast as she could. "If this is you, prove it," she muttered.

Where did you propose to my mom?
What was Magda's husband's name?
What did you always bring me as a present?
What was the last gift I gave you?

In a few moments, she was looking at all the correct answers to the first three questions.

portofino
fred
woodstock

She waited. No one, not even Sarah, knew she had slipped a box of her father's favorite candy into his jacket pocket before he left for work on the day he had been killed. In a few minutes, a picture of a box of Good & Plenty candy appeared in the message feed.

"Oh, dear God, Daddy," Sam breathed. "It *is* you."

Sam fought to remain calm. If what he said was true...she began to type as fast as she could.

Your murderer is after us? Why? What do I do? Where do I start? Mom got beaten up tonight, Dad. She's in the hospital. How do I stop this? Help me, Daddy!

Another message appeared.

terrible danger
do whatever
it takes
count on you?

Sam's fingers flew over the keyboard.

Yes, Daddy, yes! Whatever you need me to do, I will do it! Help me protect Mom and Sarah! Help me find who killed you, Daddy!

More words appeared in response.

murdered
find them
make them pay

"Yes, Daddy," Sam whispered.

Suddenly an electrical spark shot out of the wall outlet where the computer cord was plugged in. The computer screen went blank. The laptop shut off. A strong breeze whipped in the open window and blew the curtains out straight. Tigger woke up, growling. He stood stiffly on all four paws and stared at Sam, his hackles raised, as the smell of Hugo Boss drifted through the room.

Chapter Twenty-Five

Sam examined her laptop in frustration. It sat on her desk, useless. Every time she tried to power it up, nothing happened. She climbed on to her bed and sat back on the pillows, upsetting a pile of stuffed Woodstocks. She pushed them to the floor. Sam shook her head, remembering the messages from the night before.

"Nobody would believe me...just nobody. Forget a shrink...they'd just lock me up and throw away the key," she decided. She tapped the Facebook app on her phone and clicked on her father's last message.

"This is actually better," she thought. "Now that I know he's for real and not some stupid assignment, I can talk to him anywhere." She sent him a message.

I'm ready, Dad.

Magda had gone to pick up her mother from the hospital. Sarah had gone to spend the afternoon at a friend's house. Sam tried again.

Daddy, are you there?

Her phone dinged. It was Michael, texting her about this afternoon's sleuthing.

Sam-a-lam-a!
What?
You okay?
I'm good.
For real?? What happened to "my life is over" status? Death by booty call vine?
I'll make Anime pay. Don't worry. I've got this. Can I call you later?
When? I have Youth Group tonight at seven. We're looking up criminal records online this afternoon, remember?
My laptop is dead.
How?
It's fried. We have to use yours.
OK. What time?
Four.
Get your Mom's id numbers--driver's license and social. And a credit card in case we have to pay for records search.
Yeah. Maybe I'll do some online shopping, too. She owes me.
Mmmm...pat your weave and wind it back, girl.
What??!!

Sam's phone chirped. A Facebook message had come in. She texted Michael quickly:

K gtg c u later.

Sam scanned the new message from her dad.

office
get
gun

"Gun?" said Sam. She was shocked. "I never heard Mom or Dad mention anything about guns. Ever. Mom would have freaked if Dad had a gun in the house."

Your office at home? Or your office at NatureLight?

naturelight

Where is it? Is it locked up? Do I need a key?

mirror
safe
43
54
27

Sam shoved her shoes on while typing her response.

What mirror? In your office?

go now

Wait! How am I supposed to get in? Is there a key or some card I can use or something? Hello? Dad?

Nothing. The conversation ended as abruptly as it had started.

"Okay," Sam mused. "I'm not going to let you down. If you want me to go now, I'll go. Guess I'll figure it out."

She checked her wallet to make sure she had bus fare downtown. Sam dumped her backpack out on the floor, then stuffed a couple t-shirts inside to wrap around the gun.

"Good thing there are no metal detectors on the city transportation system, otherwise I'd be walking home."

She changed her clothes, grabbed a jacket, and ran down the stairs. Sam was about to leave when she remembered Magda had put all her mother's personal effects from the hospital into a large plastic bag. That plastic bag was hanging on the newel post, waiting for someone to carry it upstairs.

"And that somebody would be me," she murmured. Reaching inside the bag, Sam pulled out her mother's purse.

Inside was her wallet. Sam opened it up and ticked through all the credit cards, looking for her mother's NatureLight passkey.

"Got it!" she exulted.

She paused, then grabbed a MasterCard as well. She shoved both into her pocket. Next, Sam plucked out her mother's driver's license and social security card. She laid them next to each other on the carpeted stairs and took a picture with her phone before returning them to her mother's wallet. Finally, she gathered up her mother's things, crammed them back into the plastic bag, and raced upstairs to throw the whole mess on her mother's bed before running out the front door.

"Nice job," Sam congratulated herself. She flew down the street, eager to carry out her father's wishes.

Chapter Twenty-Six

NatureLight's corporate headquarters took up a full city block in the business district. The corporation prided itself on flexible hours for its employees. It wasn't unusual for many of the offices on all fifteen floors to be in use on the weekend. Operations managers, scientists, and different members of their teams could be found working on any number of projects any day of the week. The international green technology company developed systems to ensure safe, clean, and affordable water resourcing and to protect a sustainable supply.

Sam got off the bus two stops before the big CVS pharmacy on the corner where her father had died. She hated that place. Sam preferred walking a couple of extra blocks and going in the west entrance of the parking garage instead of taking the shortcut where it butted up against the back of CVS Pharmacy.

When Sam arrived in the parking garage, she swiped her mom's passkey and took the elevator up to the fourteenth floor to her father's office. She had dressed like one of the teen interns who earned school credit in exchange for long, tedious hours collating environmental data, taking inventory in the science labs, and entering geographic statistics into the computer.

"I hope I look nerdy enough," she thought.

The elevator opened. She walked out of the elevator, down the hall, and into her father's office. She looked around for a mirror, but there wasn't one in sight. She sat down on the big leather couch and took a deep breath.

"Where's the mirror, Dad?" Sam asked nervously.

Sam glanced around the spacious office, with its connected conference room. Her gaze fell on two ordinary doors across from the couch. She remembered Dad had his own private bathroom. She walked over, opened one of the doors, and found a closet. A baseball bat leaned against the back wall next to an old pair of her dad's sneakers. A light blue button-up sweater hung on a hanger.

"Rockin' the Mister Rogers look, Dad."

Sam's phone chirped. She drew it out of her pocket and looked at a text from Magda.

Have your mom. Taking her to the pharmacy, then to the office. She'll be home later.

"Great! That makes no sense...most people go home and put their feet up after spending the night in the hospital. Whatever. She cannot find me here! I would be seriously screwed! We gotta hurry, Dad!"

She put her phone on mute and stuck it back in her pocket.

Sam opened the other door and found the bathroom. She flicked on the light and saw a mirror above the sink. She pulled it open. No safe. Just a medicine cabinet filled with mouthwash, some shaving cream, and a razor. Disappointed, she looked around. She saw some vintage wall art on the opposite wall with twelve mirrored squares in a distinct pattern.

"It's gotta be behind one of those squares. If not, I have no clue...," Sam grumbled.

Not knowing which square, if any, the safe was behind, Sam started at the top and worked her way downward. On the tenth square, she hit the jackpot. The mirrored square swung away from the wall on two hidden hinges. Using the combination of numbers from her phone, she opened the safe.

"Whoa..." Sam turned on her flashlight app and took a

good look.

"Handgun. Okay. This better not be loaded, Dad," Sam said. "I'm gonna have to look up on the internet how to tell if a gun is loaded. It's not exactly a normal conversation starter. A box of ammunition. Great. I'll have to look up how to load it as well. And, a knife. Two knives? I get the Swiss Army knife, but why a utility knife?"

She picked it up and pushed the button on the side forward. A short blade extended. She felt it with the end of her finger and drew blood.

"Ouch! That's not your everyday box cutter." She retracted the blade. Next Sam picked up several pairs of latex gloves. "Man, this is serious stuff, Dad. Were you a spy in your secret life? What is it with you and Mom?"

Sam wrapped the gun in a t-shirt and put it, plus the box of ammunition, the knives, and the gloves, in her backpack. She closed the safe, returned the mirrored square to its position, and turned off the light switch.

"Done!" She checked her cell phone. "Not bad, only seven minutes. Time to rock and roll."

She prepared to leave when she heard noises down the hall. Anxiously, she peered around the edge of the door. Horrified, she saw her mother and Don Thompson, a tall, red-haired man who had been at her mom's party the night before, coming right toward her. Don had a firm grip on her mother's arm, propelling her along. Neither one looked happy.

Sam pulled her head back inside the office and looked around for a place to hide, her heart pounding in her chest. She ducked into the closet and clicked the door shut seconds before they entered.

"As long as you're here, pour me a drink," Melissa demanded. "What is so important you couldn't have called or texted me?" Sam could hear the man laugh, then the sound of ice rattling in glasses. "How did you know I would be here, Don?"

"I didn't. I had work to do. I saw you get dropped off. Lucky for me, I like looking out the window. You stood me up last night."

"Newsflash! I spent the night in the hospital because I got mugged outside the Hilton last night. I didn't stand you up! I was the victim of a crime!"

"You look fine to me, Melissa. You also looked more than fine on my Facebook feed last night. The way I see it, I'm the victim. To the tune of about twenty-five hundred dollars. Cash. I waited for you at the Hilton. You told me to go ahead and you would meet me at the room. So I'm giving you the opportunity to make good. Right now."

"Take it easy, Don. I'm not going anywhere. I had a rough night. I promise I'll make it up to you if you give me a few days." Melissa turned on the charm, her voice low and suggestive.

"Gross!" Sam thought, more than a little worried. "This guy is serious." She pulled out her phone and sent a message to her dad.

Dad! This guy, Don, has Mom cornered in your office. I think he's going to hurt her! What do I do??? If I have to shoot him, is this gun loaded???

She watched the screen, praying he would answer.

not loaded
don
one of them
blue porsche
use gloves
knife tires
take bat
use stairs

Are you serious? You want me to go down the stairs to the parking garage and vandalize his Porsche? How's that going to help Mom?

key alarm
go off
mom escape
tires first
then windows

Sam could hear her mom struggling in Don's arms.
"Please, Don! That hurts. At least let me....ouch! Let go! You're hurting me!" Melissa whimpered in pain.
"You said you needed something in here. You know what I think? I think you're stalling, sweetheart, hoping you could talk your way out of this. Not happening. I paid a pretty price for the privilege of your companionship. I made a deal. I intend to get my money's worth." Melissa's protests were muffled, then abruptly cut off.

Sam dropped to her hands and knees, peering under the closet door. Don had her mother up against the bar, kissing and pawing her. Melissa's legs gave way beneath her. Don didn't hesitate. He scooped her up against his chest and half carried, half dragged her out the door and down the hall toward his office at the far end.

Sam looked at the phone in her hand. A new message appeared.

GO!

Chapter Twenty-Seven

Sam snapped on a pair of gloves from the backpack and slipped the utility knife in her pocket. She grabbed the baseball bat from the closet, ran out of the office, and headed toward the stairwell, her backpack bouncing on her back. In the parking garage, she stopped to catch her breath.

"I'm never gonna get to his car in time to make his damn key alarm go off!" she fumed.

She started running through the garage, looking for the car, when a fire alarm on the wall caught her eye. She pulled. Immediately deafening alarms sounded. She spotted his Porsche and looked up. The security camera over the car was broken, hanging by a few wires.

"Dumb place to park, ape-man," she noted. Sam had two minutes to wreck his precious car before the fire trucks arrived. "Perfect."

She freed the knife from her pocket and stuck it into the sidewall of the first tire, jimmying it back and forth to make a two-inch slash. She heard a steady whoosh of air emit from the tire. Sam yanked it out and repeated the action on the other three tires. Out of the blue, the car's headlights and tail lights started blinking. The radio turned on and began to switch stations, as though an unseen finger were punching the buttons.

"I'm hurrying, Dad!" Sam grunted. She took the baseball

bat in both hands. Picturing Don's repulsive face, she smashed both headlights and side view mirrors. Panting and exhilarated, Sam busted out the driver's side window, then the passenger's side for good measure. In the distance, she heard sirens.

"This is awesome!" she thought, energized by the rush of power zinging up and down her spine. "I wish Kameron's car was here...I'd smash it, too!"

Fire engines screamed by the parking garage and arrived in front of the building. Slipping through the rows of parked cars, she strolled out the east pedestrian walkway and into the empty back parking lot of CVS. She tossed the baseball bat into the dumpster. She tore off the gloves and tucked them in her backpack.

Sam cut around the side of the drugstore. She crossed the street and headed into the park opposite the front entrance to NatureLight. Camouflaged by trees, Sam turned to watch the chaos. She could see people standing outside by the fire trucks, including her mother. Melissa was talking on her phone. A man ran toward the parking garage. With a thrill, Sam recognized Don.

"Surprise!" she murmured, grinning.

Sam took out her phone and sent a quick message to her dad.

Mom's safe.

Chapter Twenty-Eight

Sam rang Michael's doorbell. When he opened up the door, she blew past him and raced ahead into the family room. "Come on! Let's get started!"

"Hello, Michael? How are you doing? How is your day? What is with you, Sammie girl? Where have you been? You're bouncing around like a rabbit on crack! Did you take something?!" Michael crossed his arms over his chest and waited.

Sam's cheeks glowed bright red. Her eyes sparkled. She crackled with energy.

"Everything's different, Michael! I feel different...better! Like I'm alive again!"

Michael put his hand on her forehead and shook his head.

"Nope, no fever. What happened in the last couple of hours?"

"Stop it, you moron! I'm fine. Better than fine. I feel ten feet tall." Sam danced around the room, laughing. "I mean it! Let's go! I want to get some real information on my mom."

"Did you bring her info? And a credit card?"

"Got it."

"Okay, then. Let's dig."

An hour later, their eyes burned from going through all the numerous documents and police records on the different websites.

"Wow. I didn't know we could get this much information

on the internet." Michael leaned back and yawned.

"Yeah, but it didn't really tell us anything we didn't already know. The police brought her in as a main suspect in Tucker's death, but released her when witnesses came forward testifying she was at the party the whole time after he dropped her off."

"That's just it. I still don't get it. Why was she a suspect at all? Sounded like she and Tucker were gonna get married and everything."

"The anonymous caller. He insisted Mom had something to do with it. Described her, the gun, the argument they had at the party...," Sam squinted at the screen in front of her.

"Hey, slow down. What argument? Where did you read that?"

"In the police dispatcher files. Here..." Sam pulled the document up onto the screen.

Michael read it over her shoulder. "But that means the anonymous caller must have been at the party."

"Yup. They questioned everybody on the guest list. But remember, this was a huge party. There could have been any number of people who crashed." Sam leaned back.

"I guess people were partying, figured everybody there was legit, and somebody slipped through the cracks. Ten bets this anonymous caller who id'd your mom was the perp."

"The what?" Sam wrinkled her nose at him.

"Perp. Perpetrator. The killer. Don't you watch CSI, NCIS, or any of the other thousands of crime shows on the boob tube?" Michael rolled his eyes.

"Don't say boob tube. That's so eighties. Perp is bad enough."

"No murderer, no murder weapon, no motive, and no way to trace the anonymous caller thanks to the dinosaur era our parents came from." Michael's fingers drummed on the table in frustration.

"So...whoever killed Tucker tried to frame my mother. Sort

of like what they're trying to do now by keeping my father's case open and not releasing any of the insurance money because she benefits most from my dad's murder. Oh my God, Michael! Do you think these cases are related?"

"Nah. If we can buy this stuff on the internet, the cops can look at it for free. It would be all over the news if there was any chance these cases were related."

"I guess so. My brain hurts. Want me to use Mom's credit card and buy you some new sneakers? Nikes?" Sam looked at Michael.

"Not on my server, you juvenile delinquent. I'm not getting traced to a stolen credit card. I would be screw-be-doo-be-doo'd to the fullest extent of the law. I'm the one whose dad is a police officer, remember?" Michael spoke into the air. "Did you hear that, NSA goons? I'm the honest one!"

"More like the paranoid one. I've gotta go. See you on the bus tomorrow?"

"Yeah, unless some teenage crook I know orders me a Porsche 911 and has it delivered before seven o'clock in the morning."

Michael thought that was hilarious until he looked at Sam. Her face turned pale. She looked sick.

"Kidding! What's wrong, Sam?"

Michael reached out to touch her arm, but Sam jerked away. She picked up her jacket and headed straight for the front door.

"Sam, don't forget your backpack." He bent to pick it up, but she ran back in a flash.

"Give me that!" she cried.

He put his hands up and backed away. "Are you alright?"

"Yes. I just don't feel so good all of a sudden. Sorry. See you tomorrow. Text me later if you put together any more clues."

She backed out of the front door, clutching her backpack tightly. Once outside, she turned and bolted down the steps toward home.

Chapter Twenty-Nine

Monday, then Tuesday, came and went. Sam felt stuck in a bad dream. Every night she wrote to her father with no response except for *"good"* and *"wait."*

"It's like my own Magic Eight Ball," she thought. *"Reply Hazy, Try Again…"*

Anime antagonized her every chance she could by sharing Melissa Harding's six-second vine video with every account she could on Instagram and Facebook. The loop count was in the thousands.

"All I need now is for it to go viral and Mom to appear on *Ellen*. Last nail in the coffin of *my* social life," Sam figured. She avoided Gray as much as possible.

Sam spent hours pacing, wishing for some way to dispel her nervous energy. Even Magda and Sarah wondered what had gotten into her. Sam couldn't tell them she ached for the adrenaline rush she'd gotten while puncturing the tires and bashing in the car. For a few moments she felt on top of the world and in control...able to stop people who hurt others.

A picture of the smashed Porsche had been in the local newspaper with the headline, "Vandals Destroy Private Property at NatureLight."

"That's Don Thompson's car," Melissa gasped. Sam didn't say a word, just smiled to herself.

The contents of the safe lived in a hatbox in the back of her closet. Her laptop worked again. In the evening, Google taught her how to how to empty bullets out of the gun safely and how to load it again if necessary. Sam learned bullets were called rounds and how to chamber one. She wiped her history clean every night in case someone stole her computer.

"Look who's paranoid now," Sam murmured.

****

"Samantha? Samantha!" Miss Jenkins caught up to her in the hall on Wednesday morning between classes.

"What? Oh, sorry. Did you need something?" She didn't realize Miss Jenkins had called her name.

"Yes. I want to make sure you remember to come by my office after school for our meeting. It's been several days since we've talked. Lots can happen. Three o'clock. See you then?" Miss Jenkins smiled at Sam.

"Yes. Sure. I'll be there." Sam didn't have the heart to tell her she had totally forgotten her mandatory or else therapy session. She'd rather go kick someone's butt.

****

The final bell rang. While pushing through the crowds of students, Sam's phone vibrated. Keeping an eye on the bodies in front of her so she didn't cause a wreck, she looked at the screen. Her heart raced. Her pulse quickened. Excitement washed over her slight frame as her throat tightened in anticipation.

tonight
9:30

Sam skidded into the therapy office. She opened the little refrigerator and grabbed a Dr. Pepper. She threw her cell phone onto the table between herself and Miss Jenkins, popped open her soda, and drank half the can without stopping.

"Wow," said Miss Jenkins, her eyebrows raised. "Your energy's awfully high. Good day at school?"

"Nope, school sucks. Don't play dumb. That vine video made the rounds everywhere, even the teachers' accounts, thanks to Anime."

"That was unfortunate," Miss Jenkins agreed. "A lapse of judgment on your mother's part, but she *was* the victim of pirated footage. I'm sure the police will be able to find out who targeted your mother and punish them appropriately."

Sam threw her head back and laughed, long and loud. It took a minute to get herself under control.

"What world do you live in, Miss Jenkins? The police aren't looking for anybody...they're sharing it themselves. Hackers are like magic: they take what they want, do what they please, and disappear without a trace. Information technology is the biggest security risk in every organization in every country on the planet. I can find out everything about you, all your most private information, with enough money and the right hacker."

"This isn't about me, Samantha."

"Actually it is. It's about everybody. I'm vulnerable. My mother's vulnerable. You're vulnerable. We all are. But I'm not afraid anymore. I know Anime did this. And I will make her pay."

"Samantha, I know you're angry. A great deal has happened to you. But revenge and making someone pay only keep you stuck in a very dark place. How are the letters to your father going?" Miss Jenkins wrote some notes down on her legal pad.

Sam gazed at Miss Jenkins. She looked around the comfortable therapy room, then back at Miss Jenkins' concerned, caring face.

"She's clueless," thought Sam, "Nice, but completely clueless. She actually believes a few letters to my dead father and a couple hours of therapy per week are gonna make everything peachy keen. Not in this lifetime."

"You know? They are going really well," Sam lied. "I keep a big folder of them. Each night I write out my feelings on this pretty stationary that my dad gave me. I'm writing down as many memories as I can. It helps me remember. I've stopped feeling so angry and out of control since I started."

Sam kept talking, making it up as she went along. Miss Jenkins nodded at appropriate moments and took several pages of notes.

"This is easy," realized Sam silently. In no time at all, the session ended.

"Alright. Time's up, Samantha. I'm very pleased at the progress you've made. Your teachers, as well as your principal, Mr. Davies, have been worried about you. They didn't want you to feel you needed to face these challenges alone."

"Thanks, Miss Jenkins."

"See you Friday at three, Samantha."

Sam walked out and shut the door behind her. She leaned against the wall in the hallway.

"Oh, Miss Jenkins," Sam thought. "I don't feel alone anymore. I have my dad back. And we have a job to do."

Chapter Thirty

Sam took the late bus home alone, wondering what had happened to Michael. Sarah sat on the steps of Magda's house reading a book. She looked up when she saw Sam.

"Hey, Sissy!" Sarah grinned. "I got a book at the library. It's a new Goosebumps about a haunted hotel."

"Well, don't get all freaky about ghosts now." Sam tugged Sarah's blonde braid.

"I won't. The ones I know are cool. Fred and Daddy are good ghosts. Magda was talking to Fred before when I was inside. She told him to calm down. He kept knocking things over so I came out here to read. Funny, huh?"

"Yeah, funny. I'll be out in a bit." Sam took the steps two at a time and pushed open the door.

Magda sat at the kitchen table, a big mug of coffee between her hands, talking to someone Sam couldn't see.

"Must be Fred," thought Sam.

"I don't know what's gotten into you today, Fred. You've got Tigger thoroughly spooked. He won't come out from under our bed at all," Magda fretted.

"What's going on?" asked Sam.

"Nothing to worry about, dear. I just think Fred is trying to tell me something. He's frustrated I can't understand. He's quiet for now." Magda took a sip of her coffee. "He hasn't been this active in a long time. I can't imagine what is so important he had to knock down my antique rosebud vase. He knows I love that! And every single picture of you girls and your father were face down on the piano this morning. Why would he have done that?" She looked at Sam in exasperation.

Sam kept her face blank as she put a reassuring hand on Magda's shoulder. "No clue. Maybe Tigger jumped up on the piano while chasing a moth. You know how excited he gets about moths."

"Maybe," Magda mused. "But why weren't all the pictures knocked down? Oh! The brownies! I almost forgot!"

She bustled over to the oven and pulled out a large pan of butterscotch brownies. The fragrance made Sam's mouth water.

"I know you're not very hungry these days, Samantha, but do you think you might like a few of these to take home with you tonight?" Magda didn't look very hopeful.

"I'd love some. Do you mind if I have two now and a glass of milk before dinner?" Sam sat down at the table.

"You bet! Not at all! You won't spoil your appetite?"

Sam smiled. "I don't think so. For the first time in forever, I'm actually hungry."

After Magda served Sam her brownies and poured her a glass of milk, Sam started on her homework. By the time she finished her third trigonometry problem, Michael texted.

News, Queen!
Why weren't you on the bus, dweeb?
Went to the library, then the police station.
What news?
Facetime me.

"Magda, I'm gonna go sit outside and call Michael. I need a break from trig. Plus, I want to find out why he wasn't on the bus today."

"Sure, honey. Send your sister in, please. She needs to start her homework."

After Sarah went inside, Sam walked down the steps. She

sat cross-legged on the lawn by the sidewalk, enjoying the last of the October sunshine. She opened her phone and called Michael. His face appeared on her phone screen.

"Spill!" Sam ordered.

"Are you eating a brownie? I want one!" said Michael jealously.

"Suffer!" She stuffed the rest of the brownie in her mouth and motioned him to continue.

"It was the same gun, Sam. The same gun was used to kill your mom's boyfriend in high school AND your dad last spring."

"What? The police didn't find either murder weapon. How can you possibly think it was the same gun?"

"Ballistic fingerprinting." Michael looked smug.

"Speak English?!"

"One of the librarians helped me find articles on it, including ones he wrote himself. Turns out he's like an expert or something. Would not shut up--I mean, I talk a lot, but he put me out of *business*! My ears hurt! He knew his stuff, though. I went to the station and read both police reports. The marks on the bullet used to kill Tucker are an identical match to the marks on the bullet used to kill your dad. Same gun! It's still out there!"

"That's impossible."

"It's in the reports. I took pics with my phone to show you. Want me to send them? Or do you want to meet tomorrow after school?"

"Both. Oh, wait! I start volunteering at the Community Recycling Center tomorrow after school. I got the schedule yesterday. Every Thursday afternoon, three-thirty to five-thirty."

"Since when do you volunteer? Those places are dangerous. Remember the guy who got crushed to death in the cardboard compactor?" Michael made a face.

"Since my future college resume is empty. We all can't be

related to Einstein, geek. And I doubt they let the volunteers near the compactor. We're more like customer service. Hi, I'm Sam. May I help you carry your cardboard crap?"

"Don't quit your day job. I'll meet you there when you're done. We can compare notes on the bus ride home."

"Okay. Hey, Michael. Thanks. You're really a good friend for doing all this."

"Back atcha', Queen." Michael hung up.

Sam stood up and stretched. Both men her mother had been involved with...dead. A high school football star named Tucker and her beloved father. And the killer was still out there somewhere. She looked down at the pictures of the ballistic reports Michael had sent.

She shivered in the cool, October air. The sun sank behind the trees. The temperature dropped. She felt really, really cold all of a sudden. Her teeth started to chatter. Chills ran up and down her spine. Two young boys shot down the sidewalk on their bicycles in front of her. Unnerved, she jumped back with a gasp.

One boy said rudely, "Whatsa matter, scaredy cat? Someone walk over your grave?"

The boys pedaled away, laughing and high-fiving each other. She watched until they disappeared around the corner.

Sam glanced over her shoulder. "Not if I can help it," she said to herself.

Chapter Thirty-One

It began to rain after dinner. Lightning lit up the sky. Thunder crashed. Magda insisted on driving the girls home. She tucked Ziploc bags of butterscotch brownies into each backpack. She bundled the girls into the car, admonishing them to run between the raindrops and keep their feet dry. A few minutes later, they pulled up to the front door of the Harding's mansion.

"Your mother's home early. That's nice," noted Magda. "Looks like she has company. Do you recognize that car, Samantha?"

Sam knew right away it belonged to Kameron. His driver sat at the wheel, out of the rain. Probably scrolling through his Facebook feed while he waited for his boss.

"No. Probably someone from the company. They stop by a lot since Dad died. Always needing something signed. Mom said Dad left a lot of unfinished negotiations for some pretty big projects. I'm sure whoever it is will be gone soon. Thanks for dinner and the ride! I'll make sure Sarah's ready early. Thanks for driving her to school tomorrow morning. Her latest art assignment's too big to carry on the bus. Come *on*, Sarah." Sam talked fast, anxious in her haste to send Magda on her way.

"I've got to get inside," thought Sam. "I need to message Dad."

Before Magda could reply, Sam hustled Sarah out of the

car. She pushed her through the rain and into the house. Sam turned and waved goodbye before shutting the front door.

The doors to the downstairs library were open. Sam could see her mother and Kameron deep in conversation, sitting across from each other, papers scattered on the coffee table between them. Kameron sat with his back to the doors. Melissa looked up and saw Sam. She gave an imperceptible nod, not pausing in her conversation. Sam grimaced and went upstairs to settle Sarah in for the night.

****

"Good night, munchkin. Did you brush your teeth and floss after all those brownies?" Sam smiled at her sister surrounded by tonight's Ten Chosen Ones.

"Yes. They were so good. I saved one for my lunch tomorrow at school."

"Shouldn't have told me!" Sam pretended to dive for Sarah's backpack. "I ate all mine!"

"Sam! Don't!" Sarah sat upright, indignant in her pink and white lace nightgown, knocking her carefully arranged stuffed animals all over the bed. "Now look what you made me do!"

"Just teasing! Here...lay back down!" Sam picked up the plush toys, one by one. She fired them gently at Sarah who laughed and arranged them back where they belonged.

After Sarah said her prayers, Sam kissed her on the forehead.

"Sleepy?"

"Yes." Sarah yawned. "Love you."

"Love you, too. See you in the morning."

"Check on me?"

"Always. Every night, sweet pea."

****

As soon as Sam was inside her bedroom, she messaged her dad.

It's nine-thirty. Kameron, the product defect, is downstairs with Mom. What's the plan?

*kameron's house
break in
get file in desk*

I don't know where he lives. How am I supposed to break in and get some folder? I hate Kameron. He knows I hate him. He makes my skin crawl. He won't give me his address. How am I supposed to get it? How do I break in?

*sorry
too hard
too much*

No, Daddy. I'm sorry. I can do this. I'll think of something. I'll figure it out. How do I know what folder?

no

Wait. You said yourself we're all in danger. I have to keep Sarah safe, Daddy. Please?

too risky

Sam got mad and stamped her foot. She paced back and forth on her carpet. What she could say that would convince him to let her at least try?

If I'm old enough to be in danger from these killers, I'm old enough to try to stop them, Daddy. I have to do this! I love you so much. I can't sit here and be afraid anymore. They murdered you! I can do it! Please!

middle drawer
new guinea
irrigation
so
grownup
be
careful
love y...

The message cut off at that point. Sam tried again, but he didn't respond. By now, Sam knew exactly what she had to do to get into Kameron's apartment.

"I hope you're as big a slime as I think you are," she said. She put on a little lip gloss, brushed her hair until it shone, and changed into a cropped t-shirt.

Sam headed downstairs in her bare feet. She could barely stand the sight of Kameron. The thought of being near him made her sick. But she needed that folder.

"You can do this," Sam encouraged herself. "Just let him think *he's* getting what *he* wants..."

Chapter Thirty-Two

Sam knocked on the library doors. She waited until her mother acknowledged her presence before entering. Kameron followed her with his eyes. Sam tried not to flinch.

"Samantha, what is it? What do you need?" Her mother didn't look pleased to see Sam at all. "Shouldn't you be asleep by now?"

"I couldn't sleep. Would you make me a vanilla steamer, Mom, the way you used to? Please? I think it would help. I'll keep Kameron company. You don't mind if she makes me one, do you, Kameron?"

Sam settled herself in the chair opposite him and watched his expression. He shrugged casually, but his eyes flickered with interest.

"I'll only be a few minutes. I want you to get to bed as soon as possible, Samantha." Her mother hurried out of the room.

Kameron patted the sofa cushion next to him. "I'd like to get you to bed as soon as possible, too, Samantha. Change your mind? Didn't think I'd have the pleasure again so soon."

Gathering her hatred for him around her like a protective shield, Sam moved across the room. Before he could react, she climbed onto his lap and kissed him deeply, wrapping her arms around his neck.

Breaking the kiss, she looked into his shocked eyes and whispered in his ear, "Tomorrow. After school. I get out at three. I could be at your place by three-thirty. What's the address?"

Kameron tangled his fingers in her hair, pulled her head

back, and kissed her neck roughly. His breathing quickened. "The Gables at Fox Haven. 412 Stevens, Unit B." His other hand brought her close against his chest.

"Do you have a key in case I'm early?" Sam murmured.

She unhooked his hand from her hair and pressed her lips to the center of his palm, shuddering at his sweaty, lotion-scented touch. Grabbing his other hand in hers, she leaned in and nuzzled her cheek against his face.

Kameron, mistaking her shivers of disgust for quivers of ecstasy, slobbered wet kisses on her ear. He whispered hoarsely, "Key code. 3559."

He reached for her again, but Sam was too quick. She shifted her weight, wriggled off his lap, and sat back in the chair across from him in a heartbeat, pulling out her phone.

Kameron began to protest, but stopped when he heard sounds of her mother approaching--the teaspoons rattling on the tray.

Sam spoke into her phone rapidly. "Gables at Fox Haven, 412 Stevens, Unit B. 3559?

She looked at him when she finished, a question in her eyes. He nodded, letting her know the address and code were correct.

"Tomorrow, three-thirty?" asked Sam. She licked her lips, staring at him.

Kameron nodded again and straightened his clothing. He didn't look happy about having to wait until tomorrow. Sam stood up when her mother came into the room and set the tray on the bar.

She brushed close to Kameron while Melissa's back was turned, pouring Sam's steamer. Sam lingered against him for a brief moment. His hand caressed her midriff, drifting upward. She felt him struggle to maintain control.

Then she took her mug of warm, steamed milk, said her good-nights, and escaped.

Chapter Thirty-Three

Sam's adrenaline cranked into top gear the next morning. She hadn't slept well. Too keyed up after her nauseating performance with Kameron, she couldn't get to sleep right away. A long, hot shower helped rid herself of the memory of his rubbery lips and fleshy hands.

"I should burn these," she thought, picking up the clothes she had worn last night, sniffing them, and dropping them into the laundry hamper after spraying them thoroughly with Febreze. "Troll doesn't come out."

After Magda picked up Sarah and took her to school, Sam went around to the rear of the house and sneaked back inside. Melissa exercised on the treadmill in her bedroom, making a phone appointment for another fitting or tightening or whatever she did. Sam had checked her mother's schedule the night before. Melissa planned to be at the office for some meeting at ten o'clock.

"Hurry up, Mom! You are taking forever!" Sam hissed under her breath.

She was edgy and fidgety. She needed her mother out of the way for the next part of her plan. Throwing herself on her bed in agitation, Sam covered her face with her hands and tried to calm her nerves.

Ten minutes later, Sam poked her head out into the hallway for the millionth time. At last! She heard the sound of the shower being turned on in her mother's bathroom. When the bathroom door finally clicked shut, Sam cruised into her mother's room and grabbed her mom's cell phone. Quickly she scrolled through her mother's recent calls until she found Kameron's number. First she sent the contact to her own phone, then she called Kameron from her mother's phone.

"Hello? Melissa?" said Kameron. "I'm about to step into a progress meeting. Please don't tell me you won't be here for the board meeting at ten. I told you last night how important it was for you to be present to represent Forbes' interests. Melissa? Melissa?! Are you there?" Frustrated, he disconnected the call, muttering about wasting his time with pocket dials.

In less than an hour, she heard a car pull into the driveway. She watched Melissa leave the house and merge onto the backseat. Happy to see the car and her mother disappear in the distance, Sam turned her attention to her new career choice-- breaking and entering.

She tied her long hair back in a ponytail and skillfully applied makeup, adding several years of maturity to her youthful face. She put on an outfit she had pilfered from her mother's closet. The tan, Italian cashmere, v-neck dress with a tailored, sophisticated, soft black leather jacket, along with a black leather Kate Spade backpack looked really good on her. She surveyed herself in the mirror from all angles, satisfied with the outcome.

"If I pair this with Mom's Kate Spade heels, some of her daytime jewelry, and some Jennifer Lawrence attitude, my 'twenty-something business casual assistant helping out the big boss' look will be Oscar worthy. Netflix, you are my true love," Sam murmured.

She placed a pair of jeans, a long-sleeved white t-shirt, socks, sneakers, and a plain blue sweat jacket into the roomy Kate Spade bag. She hesitated, then added a pair of her dad's vinyl gloves and the Swiss Army knife. She sent a quick text to Michael.

Have a bad sore throat and headache. Sleeping. I'll let you know if I make it to recycling.

Then a message to her dad.

On my way.

Chapter Thirty-Four

It took eight minutes for the downtown bus to arrive at the stop near Kameron's. The condo's lush complex was conveniently located within walking distance of the Promenade at Beaconsfield, an open-air shopping center with a nostalgic Main Street flair, beautiful landscaping, and the popular IMAX Cineplex. It catered to the west end neighborhoods of Beaconsfield with its upscale national and local stores and five-star restaurants. All the teens in Beaconsfield headed there on the weekends.

"And where my date happened to be ruined last Saturday night, thank you very much, Anime, you life wrecker," Sam remembered, cringing.

"Focus!" she said, irritably. "Not the time."

Shoving thoughts of publicly humiliating Anime in many different and painful ways out of her head, Sam marched down the sidewalks connecting the winding streets from the bus stop to the front entrance of The Gables at Fox Haven, determined to complete her mission.

She stumbled once in her high heels, flapping her arms like a startled chicken in her efforts not to land on her butt, and caught herself just in time. A young mother dressed in yoga pants, a Fabletics sports bra, and trendy Christian Louboutin trainers pushing her child in a giant jogging stroller gave her a sympathetic glance.

"Yeah. I don't want to be me either, right now," Sam thought. Feigning a self-assurance she did not feel, she strode down the front walkway.

As she passed the small security station, she flashed a smile at the middle-aged guard. He barely looked up from the iPhone that was resting on his formidable beer gut encased in a stained company uniform. Relieved, Sam continued walking.

412 Stevens, Unit B was the second unit on the right. Sam tapped in the four numbers of the key code and let herself in. Once inside, she took a look around, astonished by the sheer, over-the-top grandeur. The condo had an open floor plan with soaring living room ceilings. Every square inch had been filled with priceless carpets, huge pieces of Chinese lacquered furniture, works of art depicting Samurai warriors on the walls, and large Asian art pieces.

"It's like a freaking retirement home for ninjas." Sam's mouth dropped open.

She searched all over the first floor looking for an office area or a desk of some sort, but found nothing that normal. Sam looked at her phone. It was eleven-thirty. She needed to hurry. She wanted to be long gone way before three o'clock. She climbed the thickly carpeted stairs to the second floor.

Every door in the long hallway was shut. Sam turned the handle of the first door on the left, pushed it open, and flicked on the light. She stifled a shriek, then realized she wasn't about to be eaten by gaping jaws. The room was filled with Chinese masks hanging on the walls, dragon kites suspended from the ceiling, and a vast collection of ceremonial swords, weapons, and contraptions that looked suspiciously like torture equipment. She closed the door, not wanting to get too up close and personal with any of it.

"Really disturbing," Sam observed. "I hope that isn't his idea of a fun first date. No one should be allowed naked near those machines. No one." She shuddered at the thought.

"I hope there isn't a body in the next room or worse…"

Sam's imagination began to get the better of her.

Her heart pounding, she checked the rest of the upstairs. Nothing else out of the ordinary: master bedroom, guest bedroom, two full bathrooms, and a home gym.

"Not that you ever use it," she muttered.

Sam went back downstairs to the main level and took the carpeted stairs to the huge finished basement. It had been divided into a home office, a state-of-the-art twelve-seat man-cave movie theater, and a full bar with a small dance floor complete with disco ball. The man-cave even had a real life-size movie theater popcorn machine.

"Guess you can find anything on eBay for the right price," Sam commented.

She opened the door to the office and turned on the lights. The room was filled heavy mahogany furniture, black leather armchairs, and a massive antique desk. The whole place looked more for show than anything else....like someone threw up a whole bunch of money and left. Sam sank into the high-backed leather desk chair and pulled open the middle drawer. She peered at the mishmash of papers and files. Grabbing with two hands, she pulled it all out and placed it on top of the desk.

She glanced through the loose papers. Nothing interesting. Turning to the stack of files, she flipped through them one by one. Finally, toward the bottom of the pile, she was rewarded by a file labeled "New Guinea Irrigation." She tucked it in her backpack and shoved the remaining heap back in the drawer. One lone piece of paper escaped. It fluttered to the floor. It was a receipt for one Commercial Movie Theater Popcorn Machine purchased from eBay for eleven thousand, five hundred dollars.

"I knew it!" She stuffed it back in with the rest of the jumbled mess, shut the drawer with a triumphant bang, and raced upstairs, intent on vacating Kameron's as quickly as possible.

****

Back on the bus heading downtown, Sam checked her phone. It was two-thirty.

"Time to send sleazeball Kameron a Dear John text," she thought with satisfaction.

Can't make it. Forgot I have to volunteer at Community Recycling Center this afternoon.

Sam pressed Send.

"Kameron's gonna be mad. Too bad. So sad. Guess who won't be waiting for you in Torture Land? In your dreams, sucker!" Sam smiled in relief at her successful heist.

And stopped smiling when she read his return text.

I'll meet you there and bring you back to my place. Canceling isn't an option. I have big plans for you, little girl. Gonna take all night long.

Chapter Thirty-Five

Melissa Harding entered her deceased husband's office. She shut and locked the door behind her. She sagged against it, her legs threatening to buckle. She went to the bar and poured herself a generous drink. She drained it with a shaking hand, then threw the glass at the wall. The heavy crystal shattered and fell to the floor, streaks of liquor staining the wallpaper.

"They were all there! Every one of them sat at the board meeting, Forbes! Every last one. Watching me, knowing I had no choice, enjoying every minute. Every single man I've had to...," Melissa said brokenly.

Tears streamed down her face. She crumpled on the long leather sofa, then gasped as pain blinded her. Her bruises were fading, but her aching ribs would take a while to heal completely.

"If you can hear me, if you still exist somehow...help us, Forbes. Magda believes Fred can hear her...I need you! I am afraid for the girls, Forbes." Melissa struggled up, rummaged frantically in her purse, and pulled out a piece of paper. "Look at this! Look at this, Forbes! I sat at that board meeting this morning and cast the deciding vote for the *Samantha Project*. I agreed to go against everything you ever stood for...every humanitarian ideal you believed in when you started this company!"

Melissa stood up. She paced back and forth. She stared out

the floor length windows that afforded a panoramic view of one of the most affluent towns on the East Coast.

"I signed my name to a document that will allow the most despicable man in town, Leopold Goss, to launder all his drug and human trafficking money through the New Guinea Irrigation Project, now called the *Samantha Project*. Named after our very own daughter. Isn't that ironic, Forbes?" she cried.

Melissa sat down at the desk and whispered, "It gets worse, Forbes. Leopold Goss is going to ask me to marry him and I have to accept. I have to accept him, Forbes. I have to allow that monster in our lives." She tore the paper up and threw the pieces in her handbag. "There's no one I can go to for help, Forbes. No one…"

Melissa broke down, sobbing. "Whoever murdered you has made it very clear. They own me, Forbes. I have to do everything they say--everything! Or they will kill the girls!"

Suddenly the lights in the spacious office flashed on and off, then on again. One by one, they exploded with electric blue flashes. The glasses stored on the shelves in the bar began to rattle, then burst, one right after the other, glass shards flying. The temperature dropped. A wind whipped around her and sent everything on the desk crashing to the floor.

Melissa started screaming.

Chapter Thirty-Six

The Community Recycling Center seemed empty when Sam arrived at three-fifteen. The educational facility, *The Trash Gallery*, operated tours with hands-on exhibits in a building adjacent to the actual recycling plant. During the day it teemed with school groups and tourists. By three o'clock, *The Trash Gallery* closed for the day before the volunteers arrived. The Program Director organized the volunteers into groups which assisted the many cars coming in to drop off their glass, plastic, paper, and cardboard recyclables.

Sam used the fifteen-minute window to duck into the bathroom to change. She shucked off the dress, jacket, and shoes as fast as she could. It felt good to put on her familiar, comfortable clothes. She jammed her sneakers back on her feet. Her hands shook.

She had sent an immediate message to her father.

Daddy. I got the folder. But I pissed off Kameron. He's coming after me at the recycling center. What do I do?

Nothing. Sam tried again, her fingers cold and numb as she tapped out another plea for help.

Daddy? Please, Daddy? Please answer me. I need you. I'm scared.

*go to
center
safe in
crowd
use what's
there
hide
don't let him
hurt you
stop him*

How Daddy? How??????

*whatever
it takes, baby
he's one
of them
you can
do it*

"Whatever it takes, huh, Dad? Okay. No one is going to touch me. Not today. No way. I am not some piece of fruit, ripe for the picking. I'm ready for you, Kameron." Sam squared her shoulders.

She left the educational facility and crossed the parking lot to the small building where the volunteers gathered. She signed in and placed her backpack in a locker. Sam tucked the Swiss Army knife and latex gloves into the front pocket of her jeans. She placed the locker key band around her wrist and tightened it so it wouldn't slip off.

In the main room she positioned herself near a window to listen to the volunteer welcome and instruction speech so she could keep an eye out for Kameron's black Trans Am. Sam doubted he'd come with the Lincoln and his driver. He wouldn't want any witnesses.

"If I get in his car today, I won't be returning any time soon. And, if he is involved in Daddy's murder, maybe never," she thought. She tapped her foot nervously.

"I am not a victim," said Sam silently to herself, repeating the key phrase from the self-defense for women course her father made her take at the police station the summer before he died. She took a deep breath, willing herself to be brave. Somehow she would strike first.

"Samantha Harding?" The coordinator had to say her name twice before Sam, embarrassed, raised her hand to let him know she was present. He tossed her a pair of work gloves. "You're in Group One. Today is sorting day. Group One will sort the aluminum and tin cans. Group Two will sort glass and plastic bottles. Group Three will sort other clean, plastic containers. And, finally, Group Four will sort cardboard, newspaper, and mixed paper. Each item will be brought to its designated area. All garbage and non-recyclable items will be tossed over the side of the garbage pit into one of the five large dumpsters. Doesn't matter which one, but please aim. You don't want to be climbing down there because you missed. Any questions? No? Okay, let's go."

Sam followed the other volunteers out the door and across the pavement. She didn't see anybody she knew which was good. Anonymous was good. She scanned the parking lot, but no Trans Am yet. About fifty feet in front of the garbage pit, someone had parked an orange forklift. She had seen some like it at Home Depot, lifting building supplies around the store. As she walked over to her station, she glanced inside the forklift and saw the key dangling in the ignition.

"Why?" she wondered. A minute later, she found out.

A worker in a yellow hard hat climbed inside, sat down, and started it up. It began to move forward. He drove it about twelve feet and stopped. A group of volunteers loaded a huge stack of flattened cardboard onto the fork. The forklift rose into the air. The worker drove over to the compactor, which was several hundred feet away from the volunteers, and deposited the load with the rest of the cardboard waiting to be crushed. Then he drove it back to its parking space to wait for another large load prepared by the volunteers.

Sam checked her phone. It was three-fifty.

"Kameron should be pulling in any time now," she thought.

She pulled up her sweat jacket hood and tucked her hair inside. When cars pulled in full of recycling, she immediately started pulling out boxes and bins to be sorted. She didn't want to call attention to herself by standing around doing nothing.

Suddenly a black Trans Am roared across the pavement into the parking lot. Sam froze, hoping some plan would fall from the sky into her panic-stricken brain and save her. Kameron didn't pull into line behind the other cars. He cut in front of everyone, squealed his tires, and came to a smooth stop in front of the fork lift.

He stepped out of his car and looked around. He gestured at the group of volunteers, expecting one of them to come over to him. They all just spread their hands and shrugged, unable to hear him over the mayhem of machines and car engines. He looked annoyed. If it hadn't been so awful, it might have been funny to see him fuming in the middle of Prius-driving hipsters getting their recycle on.

Kameron's eyebrows drew together in thunderous rage. Sam knew that look. She didn't have much time. She had to move fast before he sniffed her out like a pack of dogs at a barbeque.

All at once Sam's brain cells lit up like a pinball game.

"If I could just get over to the forklift without him seeing me," she thought, "I could use the forklift as a diversion. Get it started, throw it into forward, and bye-bye Trans Am. Straight into the garbage pit."

That would keep him busy for hours, even days. She could

grab her bag and take off. Even stay at Michael's or Magda's for a few days until she and her dad flushed out the killer.

"Come on, Kameron. Go ask the nice people where I am. Stay distracted," Sam breathed. She leaned over to the person next to her and said loudly, "I'll be right back. I have to use the bathroom."

Sam headed toward the bathroom, then veered to the right. She circled back around the line of cars until she hid behind the forklift. From where she crouched, she could see Kameron looking for her, asking people questions.

"Yeah. Probably lying through your Hollywood whites about how my mother sent you to pick up poor little fatherless me. Well, I'm not in this alone anymore, you lying piece of roach poop...," Sam gritted her teeth. "It's now or never."

She ducked down on the driver's side of the forklift and poked her head into the cab. She stretched her hand toward the "Start" button when she realized the forklift had an acceleration pedal. Somehow, she had to get it to stick down or the forklift wouldn't move.

"The gloves!" She reached into her front pocket for the latex gloves. She tied the index fingers of both gloves together, then pushed the accelerator pedal down halfway. Wrapping one end around the pedal to hold it in place, she secured it tightly to the base of the brake.

She looked up and peeked out the side window. She saw Kameron talking to one of the women. Sam could see her pointing toward the bathroom. Kameron nodded and headed in that direction.

"Move!" Sam pushed the "Start" button. Nothing happened. "C'mon!"

Staying low, she turned the key, then hit the start button again, and reached up with her right hand to the gear shift on the steering column. She pushed it into drive. The forklift began to move steadily forward.

"Yes!" Sam turned to flee, but stopped in her tracks when

she realized the wristband of her locker key had looped over the gear shift. She tried to pull up, but only succeeded in tightening the band more firmly around the base.

She couldn't move!

Chapter Thirty-Seven

The heavy forklift inched forward. It hadn't caught anyone's attention...yet. Sam clawed at the wristband, desperate to figure out a way to cut herself loose before she landed in a whole mess of trouble.

Still crouched on her knees, Sam leaned against the driver's seat. She felt the outline of the Swiss Army knife in her front pocket. Reaching in, she pulled it out with her free hand and opened it with the hand trapped on the steering column. She stuck the blade under the strap. With one firm cut, she sliced it in two and stumbled clear of the forklift.

"Ow, ow, ow...," Sam hobbled in pain, still bent in a u-shape. She couldn't feel one of her feet and her hand throbbed.

She couldn't go retrieve her stuff from the lockers. Kameron lurked somewhere by the restrooms. One of the larger recycling trucks sat by the *Trash Gallery* entrance. Sam crisscrossed between the cars in the parking lot until she stood in back of the big truck.

"Come on, creepazoid. Hurry up!" Sam waited for the moment Kameron would emerge and see his car. "I need to blow this popsicle stand...and fast!"

Meanwhile, the orange forklift closed in on the sleek, black car. Kameron walked out of the volunteer building, his head moving back and forth as his eyes scanned the Center's grounds. When he saw his Trans Am, they widened. He began to run.

"Nnnnoooooooooooooo!" Kameron bellowed.

The crunch of metal against metal reached Sam's ears. She watched with satisfaction as Kameron ran. He flung open the door, got in, and started his car. The engine roared to life, but it didn't matter. The entire fork carriage wedged flush against the Trans Am, with both forks underneath it. The car couldn't go forward or backward. Kameron's face turned an angry, mottled red as he yelled and cursed.

"Turn off that damn machine! Someone stop this thing!" He threw the gear shift into reverse, then into drive, but his car didn't move. The acrid smell of burnt rubber filled the air as he spun his tires in a frantic attempt to save his beautiful Trans Am. It crawled closer and closer to the edge of the garbage pit.

"Get out of the car, you idiot," Sam muttered.

But Kameron waited too long. The front and back tires on the passenger side teetered on the crumbling rim of earth. There was no room to step out and get around the car to safety.

"Help me!" Kameron screamed.

"Dude! Climb on the roof and jump clear!" shouted one of the volunteers.

Sam stared in horror. She needed to run, to get far away from here, but she couldn't stop watching.

Kameron climbed out the open window and pulled himself, red-faced and panting, onto the roof of his car.

"Jump off, man! Jump to the side!" Everyone watched breathlessly as Kameron slid his way to the hood of his car and prepared to step off.

The car began to tip. The gravitational pull of the vehicle sped up the momentum of the forklift. In less than thirty seconds, the car and forklift had disappeared over the edge.

And so had Kameron.

Chapter Thirty-Eight

"Melissa? Melissa! Open up! Melissa!" Peter Ambroglio pounded his fist against the solid door. Men and women crowded in the hallway behind him. Heads poked out of offices. Melissa's screaming could be heard throughout the entire floor. "Dear God, Melissa!"

"Stand back!" Peter backed up, then launched forward driving his shoulder like a battering ram against the heavy wood. It splintered, but didn't give way. He tried again. This time the door swung open and he rushed inside.

Melissa sat at the desk. Her hair-raising screams gave way to muffled sobs as she buried her face in her hands. Peter looked around the room in horror, taking in the wreckage. Lamps lay shattered on the floor, blackened electrical outlets still smoked, and light fixtures hung by their wires from the ceiling. The crystal glassware and decanters had exploded: jagged pieces of glass covered the bar and puddles of liquor stained the rug. Framed pictures and papers peeked out from under the debris on the floor.

"Melissa! What happened! Are you alright? It looks like a bomb went off in here!" Peter put his arms around the weeping woman and pulled her close. "Shh. It'll be okay. You're not hurt. You're not, are you?" He held her at arm's length and examined her closely. "Thank God, you're not cut. All that glass!"

Melissa looked at him. Mascara ran down her cheeks, her eyes loomed large and frightened in her pale face. She sat there in shock, unable to speak.

"Andrew!" Peter called.

"Yes, sir?" Peter's tall, dark-haired assistant appeared at his side.

"Get the janitorial staff in here. Clean up this mess. Call an electrician. I want all the wiring and outlets in this office tested to determine the problem and fixed. Next, replace everything that was broken. Put this office back to it's original condition. Pronto."

"Yes, sir. I'll take care of it right away, sir." Andrew left to alert the cleaning staff and make some calls.

Peter stood up and shooed the wide-eyed office employees back to their own areas. "Melissa? Take my arm." He spoke gently to her as though she were a child. "We're going to my office."

Placing one arm around her waist to steady her, Peter brought her down the hall to his own executive suite. The unexplained wreckage in Forbes' office dismayed and disturbed him.

Peter helped Melissa to a chair. He shut his office door firmly on the last of the office gawkers hovering in the distance.

"Drink?" He watched her face. Color slowly returned to her cheeks.

"Please. A double." She checked her face in her compact and flinched. "I look like a complete disaster. I...I apologize for that awful scene."

"Melissa. I don't know exactly what happened in there, but you don't owe me any apologies. If it weren't completely ridiculous, I would say you look like you'd seen a ghost! For a minute there, I wasn't sure if I'd be able to get through to you." Peter leaned back in his chair, looking at the widow of his closest friend. She was falling to pieces before his eyes, slipping further and further away from the woman he knew.

"You seemed agitated during the board meeting. Did someone say something to upset you?" Peter questioned.

"No. No one said anything. I just...found it difficult to be there. Overwhelming, actually, to sit in Forbes' seat and know I cast the deciding vote on the *Samantha Project*. This is not what Forbes had envisioned for the company." Melissa took a sip of her drink with an unsteady hand.

"As a matter of fact, Melissa, I'm surprised you signed. Leopold Goss has been trying to get his hooks in this company for years. When the other board members put pressure on Forbes to take Goss on as the primary investor, Forbes tabled the project. I agreed with him. After his death, the pressure began again." Peter paused, taking a sip of his own drink. "To me, money is money. I've heard the rumors regarding Goss but, so far, they are unsubstantiated. Your refusal to sign would have been a roadblock to give us more time, but now...so be it." He steepled his fingers, shaking his head.

"Time to move on, Peter. Forbes always took the moral high road. That's a luxury I can't afford." Melissa checked her phone. "Thank you for being so kind to me. It's been a rough couple of hours. I need to get ready for a dinner engagement."

"In light of the circumstances, perhaps you should cancel...?" Peter's words died away at the look on her face.

"Not an option, Peter. I'm having dinner with Leo. It would be rude to cancel. Besides, I'm looking forward to a night out on the town after today." Melissa spoke lightly, but her eyes warned him off.

"Please. Be careful, Melissa. I said the rumors were unsubstantiated, but that doesn't mean I trust him." Peter cleared his throat. "I do have another matter to discuss with you. The life insurance company finally returned my calls. Forbes' life insurance money has been frozen. The detectives handling Forbes' murder have decided to reopen Tucker Callahan's case," he informed her somberly.

Melissa's eyes closed. A look of grief crossed her face. She opened her eyes and stood. Her hard gaze met Peter's.

"And when were you going to tell me this?" Melissa demanded.

"I only got the call today, Melissa. They want you to come in for questioning tomorrow morning. I've already called your attorney's office. You were cleared, Melissa. It won't stick. We can fight this."

"We, Peter? I'm having dinner with one of the most powerful men in Beaconsfield. Maybe the *most* powerful after today. Tell the detectives I'll be there with my attorney." Melissa finished her drink, then moved to the door. She turned and looked back at him.

"I'll give Leo your regards. Who knows? Maybe you'll have a chance to dance with...what's her name? Janet? Maybe you'll have a chance to dance with Janet at our wedding." She opened the door and left, slamming it behind her.

Chapter Thirty-Nine

"Call 911!" someone shouted.

Sam didn't stick around. She bolted toward the volunteer building. People ran in every direction. The staff moved cars in the drop-off lane toward the exit in an orderly flow to make room for the emergency vehicles.

Sam opened her locker and grabbed her bag. Volunteers poured into the building.

"Did you see that?"

"Oh my God! Do you think he's dead?"

"My mother is never gonna let me volunteer here again!"

Sam heard sirens wailing in the distance. She pushed her way through the frightened, milling people and headed to the main street. She ran in the direction of the bus stop.

"Sam! Yo! Sam!" called Michael. He sat on the bench waiting for her.

"What are you doing here?" Sam cried.

"Meeting you, remember? You were supposed to text me when you woke up and let me know if you were gonna make it to your recycling gig. I didn't hear anything, so I went to the library and hung out until now. I figured you'd either be on the bus or you wouldn't. What the heck is going on in recycle land? I thought it was a pretty chill place--y'know, saving the earth for future generations?"

An ambulance sped by, then two police cars and a fire truck in close pursuit. He looked at her with big eyes.

"Not the compactor again!" Michael cringed. "That thing

should be outlawed. That last guy came out all flattened into a rectangle--like a human Lego. Ugh! The news coverage gave me nightmares for weeks!"

"I don't know! I had to go to the bathroom. When I got out, I heard everyone yelling and freaking. I didn't think I could do anything, so I left. The volunteers start to leave around now, anyway. I figure we'll hear about it on the news, y'know?" Sam watched the bus pull up. Her legs felt like rubber. She really needed to sit down. She didn't want to think about the scene she just left at the recycling center.

"Come on. I've got something to show you. I found a folder in a box of Dad's stuff today." Sam pulled Michael's sleeve. Together, they climbed up the stairs and settled themselves in two empty seats toward the middle of the bus.

"Nice backpack. Bit much of a fashion statement though, right? Oooooh...that leather is soft as a baby's butt, girl!" Michael patted her backpack like a puppy.

"Stop fondling my backpack, weirdo! Get a girlfriend!" Sam grumbled.

"I have a girlfriend. Her name is Netflix. I see her every night. Don't be a shater!"

"A what?"

"A shater. A hater throwin' shade on the ones he loves. Just sayin'." Michael reached out to touch the backpack again, but stopped when Sam glared at him.

Before Sam could reply, the bus pulled up to the next stop. An older couple got on. They sat down in a couple of seats a few rows in front of Michael and Sam. The man listened to the police scanner on his cell phone.

"Didja hear that?" the man said in a loud voice. "A forklift went haywire at the recycling plant and pushed a car into the garbage pit. The car's owner tried to save it, but he fell in, too."

"How'd he lose his shoe?" said the woman.

"Fix your hearing aid, woman! He didn't lose his shoe! He fell in, too!" the man said loudly.

"Is he dead?"

"Nah. Police said he'd already cleared the car before it fell in, but he lost his balance and rolled into the pit. He missed the dumpsters. Just bounced down the slope all the way to the bottom. Sounds like he's got some broken bones, though. Lucky to be alive if you ask me!"

"Ask you what?"

"Oh for heaven's sake! Never mind!"

The woman patted him on the knee. She turned to look out the window. The man shook his head and went back to listening to the live reports.

Sam felt all the tension drain out of her body. She hadn't killed him. But she did hurt him badly enough to stop him from coming after her. For now.

"I did it! I did what you said, Dad, and it worked!" Sam thought. She settled back in her seat next to Michael and smiled. She grabbed her phone and sent a quick message.

I took care of Kameron. What's next, Dad?

Chapter Forty

"Magda, could Michael stay for dinner? We have to finish a project." Sam neatly scooped four cookies off the plate on the counter and tossed two to Michael.

"What about me?" Sarah asked, looking at the cookies.

Sam dropped the other two on Sarah's math book before snagging two more for herself.

"Of course, dear. Michael, you know you're always welcome." Magda stuffed herbs under the skin of a whole chicken before sliding it into the oven to roast. "You two can take over the table in the library. That should give you enough room. Close the door if you need more quiet."

Magda put her new CD of the Broadway show *Cats* into the Bose system on the kitchen counter. She sang along as she prepared dinner. Sam looked at Michael and giggled.

"Thanks, Mrs. Muensterhaus." Michael stuffed another cookie in his mouth.

"Magda, dear."

Sam and Michael gathered up their things. Magda's version of *Memory* followed them. Sam made sure she closed the library door. Michael pulled out a notebook and a pen.

"Let's make a list of the info we have so far." He opened the notebook and wrote the heading, INFORMATION, with a list numbering one through ten.

"Okay." Sam grabbed a chair and sat down.

"Starting with your Dad's murder."

"Why?"

"He was the target. No one else got hurt. And he was shot dead, not wounded. Sorry, Sam, but you have to admit it wasn't random," said Michael.

"I know," she muttered. "Okay, what else?"

"Your mother changes into Robotica in July and becomes the hottest ticket in Beaconsfield."

"The same weekend her inheritance disappears...," realized Sam.

"And she gets the stalker valentine..."

Sam clapped her hand to her forehead. "Michael, I forgot to tell you. I found the guest list of the people she invited to last Saturday's cocktail party in my dad's home office. It was written in the same handwriting as the stalker valentine."

"The stalker is a party planner? That makes no sense."

"Ha-ha. Not funny. Everyone on the list is also on the executive Board of Directors at NatureSense, except Mr. Goss."

"Leo Goss? Richer than God Goss? He's really bad news, Sam. He's organized crime--doesn't tell where the bodies are buried--bad news. You saw him at your mom's party?"

"Yeah. Mom hung all over him. He creeped me out really bad." Sam remembered how Leo had looked at Sarah with greedy, hungry eyes. She shivered.

"Seriously, Sam. Goss is involved in big-time shady stuff. He keeps his hands clean, but Dad has nothing good to say about him. Dad's buddies at the precinct keep tabs on Leo. They all hope he slips up big time so they can pin something on him. His money is as dirty as it comes," said Michael.

"What about the bullets? You said something about Mom's high school boyfriend?"

"Oh, yeah. That's ballistic fingerprinting. Every gun that fires leaves a mark on the bullet. It's the gun's fingerprint, specific to that gun. If you find the bullet, you can trace back to the particular gun that fired it. I looked up the ballistic fingerprint on the bullet that killed your mom's boyfriend. It had the exact same fingerprint as the bullet that killed your dad. Which means both bullets came from the same gun."

"Okay, so now you're a boy genius super sleuth as well." Sam rolled her eyes.

"Hey, it's just my dad rubbing off on me. But listen to this, Sam. What if the killer is the same person? Find the gun and solve two murders. Huh? Am I right or am I right? I'm right!" Michael pumped his fist in the air and did a mock stadium run.

"Down boy--seems like a long shot. No pun intended," Sam winced. "But couldn't there be two guns out there with the same print, like from the same manufacturer? Or maybe it could be altered. I mean, it's not like a person's fingerprint or DNA."

"Maybe. I don't know. Sounded good, though," Michael shrugged. "When did you find this file you want to show me?

"Last night. In my mom's office. I went to take another look. I saw a corner of it sticking out behind the file cabinet. I guess it had fallen behind it or something." She handed him the file.

Sam felt bad about lying to Michael but she figured it was better to lie to her best friend then get him involved in her new secret life. The city's best detective was none other than Mr. Bateman, Michael's dad. There was no way she could tell him what she'd been doing.

"New Guinea Irrigation? Sounds like another one of your dad's water sustainability projects. Hey, Sam, look! It's called the *Samantha Project*. That's pretty cool. You have a conservation project named after you!" Michael sounded impressed.

"Give me that! What the….? He never said anything about naming it after me," Sam mused.

"It? You mean you knew about the New Guinea Irrigation part?" Michael asked, confused.

"No, I mean, um, I never knew they named any projects after me or Sarah. Seems odd," Sam stammered.

She kicked herself mentally for the slip. She had to be careful not to let on she knew more than Michael thought she did.

"There's an awful lot of papers in here. Looks like all the board members were pretty eager to fund this. This sheet is headed, *Aggressive Marketing Synopsis*. This one is all about rate of return on investment. This one is...oh no! Michael, this one is a proposal to bring Leopold Goss in as the primary investor at over forty-two million dollars." Sam couldn't believe her eyes.

"Forty-two million dollars? Let me see that. I want to see a number that big in print. Damn, girl! That is a lot of green! And if it's coming from Goss, that puts your daddy in bed with the Mob!"

"He wouldn't! Oh, Michael! He never would have done that! Dad always said any deal was only as good as the quality of the investors! He said his demand for transparency guaranteed only the best and the most honest!" Sam picked up the file and threw it across the table. It fell onto the floor, spilling all the papers out on the rug.

"Sam? What's that envelope?" Michael pointed at the scattered papers on the floor.

"What envelope?"

"This one marked *Private and Confidential*." Michael reached down, picked it up, and handed it to Sam. "Here. You do the honors."

Sam ripped open the envelope and unfolded the piece of paper.

"It's a private memo to the board members from my father. It says as owner of the corporation and Chairman of the Board, he cannot, in good faith, approve of or be involved in taking money from Leopold Goss and regrets that he is defunding and tabling the New Guinea Irrigation Project until alternative funding can be obtained at a future date." She looked over the top of the paper at Michael. "Michael, he doesn't call it the *Samantha Project*. Where did you see that name?"

Michael pawed through the papers on the floor.

"This one. See? It says the *Samantha Project* right here at the top in big letters below the date." He took a closer look. "Sam, all the board members are listed on here. It says all names listed herewith are legally bound co-investors of the *Samantha Project*. Goss is on here for forty-two million. All the others have big money amounts next to their names as well. Not as much as Goss, but each one is over a million. It goes on to say at the bottom that each investor will receive additional added benefits according to the terms of the agreement to be listed in individual letters to each investor." Michael paused. "Added benefits? What sort of added benefits? What letters? And who's writing the letters?"

"When's it dated, Michael?" Sam asked, feeling apprehensive.

"July 1st. Why?"

"My father's memo is dated February 27th. The day before he was murdered."

Chapter Forty-One

"Yeah? What is it?" Leo Goss grunted into his cell phone.

He checked his watch. The man on the other end of the phone yammered on and on. Leo kept one ear focused on the conversation while his mind wandered.

"I don't like to be kept waiting," he thought impatiently, "especially by some dame. Even one as beautiful as Melissa Harding. But...I can make an exception. After all, she did give me complete protection and credibility today--albeit under duress. I am now the biggest investor in the largest green sustainability corporation on the East Coast. All my money is flowing through the *Samantha Project*, coming out squeaky clean on the other side. No one can trace it back to me. I guess that deserves a big, fat diamond on her pretty little manicured finger."

He smiled and answered the man's question.

"Yeah, I saw it. Everybody saw it. Nice angles...your man did good work. Not every day I get to see myself in a compromising position with a beautiful, half-naked woman. If I hadn't been so well paid, I might have to sue."

He listened to the response on the other end and barked out a coarse laugh.

"I know. Victor's kid did just as she was told. Melissa's daughter will be ready to push over the brink soon. Then my new bride and I will send her away. Good riddance."

Leo paused. "Tonight's the night. You did tell her to make sure she accepts? Good. Getting roughed up by Jasper outside the Hilton helped her see the light, too, huh? Hah! My forty-two million goes away if she says no. I don't care what piece of paper I signed. I get it all, got it? Security, protection, and Melissa." He brushed an invisible piece of lint off his sleeve. "Y'know, if you ever want to stop all this cloak and dagger crap and join my organization, I'd make it worth your while. No? Alright, alright. I'll stick with your original plan as long as the money keeps coming. And if not, I'll figure out who you are, find you, and hang parts of you all over this stuck-up little town." He ended the call abruptly.

"Leo. I'm sorry I've kept you waiting." Melissa slipped into the seat across from him. The ambiance of the white tablecloths, exquisite cutlery, and delicate bone china soothed her senses and relaxed her frayed nerves. A string quartet played in a private room, the soft melodies drifting out to the main dining area.

"You look lovely." He scrutinized her appearance possessively.

He approved of her flowing white chiffon backless gown with icy crystal clear jewels adorning the semi-sheer mesh bodice. Her warm, blond hair curled softly around her shoulders, providing a stunning backdrop for her cluster drop diamond earrings from Tiffany's.

"Thank you, Leo. The earrings arrived this afternoon. They took my breath away. How did you know to choose ones that would compliment my gown so well?" Melissa could feel all the eyes in the restaurant watching the couple with covert malice. She straightened her shoulders and sat with the impeccable posture that came from years of classical ballet.

"For twenty-seven thousand dollars, sweetie, I knew they would go with anything...or nothing." He leered at her across the table. "I've taken the responsibility of ordering all your favorites this evening. I want this night to be memorable."

He gestured to her glass of wine. Melissa picked up the fragile stemware and drained her glass. He poured her another, a calculating smile on his face. She smiled back, suppressing the fear that bubbled up inside her each time she gazed into his flat, ruthless eyes.

Leo finished every crumb of his food, smacking his lips and washing it down with glass after glass of wine. Satisfied, he belched and leaned back. Melissa, on the other hand, barely touched her meal. She pushed it from one side of her plate to the other. After the waiter cleared the table and the two were sharing a bottle of champagne, Leo reached across the table and took one of Melissa's hands in his.

"You impress me, Melissa. You did something today your own husband couldn't do, despite all the time and money spent to prove bringing me in as the main investor in your company was the best decision. You trusted me. That means a lot. You're quite a woman, Melissa. You're beautiful, sexy to the point of distraction, and very intelligent. You knew the right thing to do...the only thing to do. For all concerned." Leo paused and looked around the room. "You're the only woman I want. Someone who'll be loyal to me to the end. For that, I intend to make you very, very happy. And all mine."

Leo stood up and walked over to Melissa's chair. He pulled her up out of her seat and clasped her in his powerful arms. He took one finger, tipped her head back, and focused his cool eyes on hers with laser-like intensity. He raised his voice. He knew every person in the dining room was waiting to hear his next words.

"Melissa, would you do me the honor of becoming my wife?"

Chapter Forty-Two

"This is evidence, Sam! You can't hold on to this. It might help the police find the murderer! What if it's Goss?" Michael spluttered. "I can't believe we have a copy of the memo your father wrote the day before he died!"

"Evidence every board member has, Michael. It doesn't prove anything, least of all who did it. It's just a clue. I don't want to do anything yet. I need to think about it." Sam wanted to wait until she had a chance to ask her dad.

"Why?"

"If it is Goss, I don't want him thinking we know anything at all. To him I'm just a dumb kid with an attitude. I'm not sticking my neck out for him to chop my head off without some real, hardcore piece of evidence to tie him to the murder. Otherwise, we may as well just hang a target on our backs. And if it's not him, then we've wasted everybody's time and earned a rotten enemy."

"Yeah, I guess you're right," Michael sighed, deflated.

"Ya think?! Ooh! You even admitted it! Two points for me, brainiac." Sam punched him on the arm. She gestured toward the papers. "Come on, let's get these cleaned up and go eat. I can't think about this stuff anymore. I'm on overload.

****

When Michael left after dinner, Magda called Sam into the

family room. Melissa planned on being late tonight, so Sam and Sarah were staying over. Sarah took the stairs two at a time on her way up to take a bath. Sam watched her go.

"Samantha, you were at the recycling center this afternoon, weren't you?" Magda asked.

Sam's roast chicken and mashed potatoes churned ominously in her stomach as she turned to look at Magda. She had been so wrapped up in the details of the memo and the bullets and stuff, she had forgotten about Kameron. She composed herself, wrapping her arms around her queasy belly, and looked innocently at Magda.

"Yeah, I admit it. I exercised my right to recycle today. I volunteered to help my fellow humans release their cardboard, cans, and bottles into these trustworthy hands." Sam waggled her fingers.

"Sam, I'm talking about the accident."

"Oh. Yeah, that. When I left for the bus stop, I overheard people freaking out about some guy who had fallen in the garbage pit. I guess somebody called 911. They cleared us out of there pretty quick. Why?" Sam asked lightly.

"I saw it on the news. It wasn't just some guy. It happened to be one of the board members of NatureLight. Kameron Richards."

"Tell me something I don't know," thought Sam to herself. She paused before responding.

"No way! Kameron? Why would he be at the recycling center?" Sam asked, hoping Kameron had kept his mouth shut and didn't say anything incriminating. It wouldn't look too good for him and would only make it worse for her.

"I don't have the slightest idea. Neither did the people at the recycling center or the police. His car somehow got caught on the forklift which malfunctioned and threw his car over the side. Kameron tried to save it, but only succeeded in falling in himself. Lucky for him he wasn't killed!" Magda clucked.

"Yup. That would have been bad," said Sam quietly.

"The reporter on the news said he sustained two broken legs, a broken arm, and a broken collarbone. He'll be in the hospital for quite a while," Magda sighed. "I don't mean to be glad about someone's misfortune, but I didn't like the amount of time he spent at your house. He gave me the willies. I had a bad feeling about him. I expressed it to your mother several times, but she just laughed it off."

"Does Mom know yet?" Sam wondered out loud.

"I don't know. She texted me to ask if you girls could stay over because she had a dinner engagement with Leo Goss. I'm sure she would have said something if she knew."

"Yeah, she had a board meeting this morning. Kameron would have been there. Magda, did my dad ever mention a water project in New Guinea to you before he died?" Sam asked curiously, changing the subject.

"No, honey. You know, he had such a positive, energetic attitude toward his sustainability projects. He made it his mission to search out and provide clean water for people in poorer countries. But you could cut the tension with a knife during the months before his death. He didn't talk much about it, but I knew something weighed heavily on his mind, like a dark cloud he couldn't get out from under. Too bad we'll never know what troubled him." Magda picked up her knitting. Sam had no clue what it could be. It had no recognizable shape.

"I'm gonna go up and shower. Good night, Mag." Sam leaned over and kissed Magda on the cheek.

"Good-night, sweetie. Glad you weren't involved in that accident. So many strange things happening these days, like that other car being vandalized at NatureLight. Makes you wonder…"

Magda picked up the remote. Angela Lansbury appeared on the screen in the midst of another mystery, this time involving a man and his dog.

"Wonderful," Magda murmured as she settled back to enjoy her favorite television series.

Chapter Forty-Three

Kameron's in the hospital. I didn't mean to hurt him. I really didn't. I just didn't know what else to do. And a part of me doesn't care. I hate him so much, Dad. I actually felt glad when he fell. I thought maybe if he died, I wouldn't ever have to worry about him coming near me again. Does that make me a horrible person, Daddy?

no
dangerous men
stop at nothing
i'm dead
you're not
proud of you
sleep
talk tomorrow

If you're okay with it, Dad, then I am, too. Together we'll stop them. All of them. No matter what it takes. I'll do whatever you need me to do. I love you, Daddy.

****

Melissa huddled in the back of Leo's limousine. She surveyed the fourteen-carat pear-shaped yellow diamond solitaire in its platinum setting. It sat like a plump manacle on her finger.

"If only I'd shouted a refusal at the top of my lungs, hurled the champagne bottle to the floor, and run as far away from

Leo as I could," she thought bitterly. "I wanted to. But I didn't dare."

The hypocritical congratulations of the patrons in the dining room were almost too much to bear. But she did. She suffered their air kisses, their hearty handshakes, and their sniveling prostrations of good will. As the fiance and bride-to-be of the richest, most underhanded, treacherous, power broker in town, they could no longer snub her at will. Melissa sighed.

"What is it, beautiful? Too small?" He laughed, noting the way she stared at the ring.

"What? Oh, no! It's perfect, simply perfect, Leo. You have exquisite taste."

"Yeah. I chose you, right? Classy ring for a classy broad." Leo fondled her, running his hands over the chiffon dress.

"Leo, the driver is watching." Melissa struggled to sit up.

"Yeah, well it's not like he's never seen you before, baby...your vine went viral." He pulled her into his lap and kissed her.

Leo's driver headed for the Hilton Arms where Leo owned the penthouse suite.

"Now that we're official, your dance card is full. You are out of circulation for good. Signed, sealed, delivered...you're mine."

Melissa didn't say a word. She felt as hopeless and ruined as the torn skirt of her chiffon gown.

"Tell your daughters we're going out for dinner tomorrow night as a family. I want to show them off. Have them dress to impress." He undid the clasp in the middle of her back.

"I'm not sure of their plans this weekend, Leo. I thought we could spend a quiet weekend ourselves. This is all very new and sudden. I'd like to break it to the girls gently." She struggled against his iron grip.

"Break it however you want to break it, but do it before dinner tomorrow night. That wasn't a request, Melissa. They'll be there. Time to get with the program. Oh, and the older one, Samantha? I have boarding school lined up for her. She leaves November first in time for the beginning of the second semester. That will give me an opportunity to spend quality time with our younger daughter...Sarah," he drawled.

"But Leo...," said Melissa.

She prayed she wouldn't vomit. Icy fingers of dread crawled up her spine. Suddenly her cell phone shrilled a loud, high-pitched sound. It blared non-stop. She pulled it from her bag, hitting the volume button and tapping the screen, but nothing happened. It wouldn't stop its ear-piercing sound.

"Give me that!" Leo grabbed the phone from her hand. He tried to turn it off. It wailed away despite his every effort to stop it. Finally, he lowered the power window, tossed her phone out on the road, and raised the window again. "There! That'll stop that racket! Jeez! What is that smell?" He rapped his knuckles hard against the glass partition. "Joey!"

"Yeah, boss?" Joey's voice came over the intercom.

"Too heavy with the cologne there, Joe. It reeks! I can't breathe back here. You know I got asthma! Save it for when we're out of the car!" Leo complained.

"Not me, boss. I know the rules. You told me no cologne when I'm working 'cause you got the asthma," Joey blustered.

"Ugh! What is that?" Leo lowered the window again. He stuck his head out into the night, taking great gulps of fresh air.

Melissa looked sad. She said, "It's a men's fragrance. Hugo Boss. Odd..."

"What's odd?" Leo reached into his pocket and pulled out a rescue inhaler. He took two puffs.

"Nothing. It's just....nothing." She realized her phone was gone. "Leo, my phone."

"I'll get you another one tomorrow. Don't worry about it."

"But Leo...," Melissa protested.

"No buts about it, Melissa. I got everything all figured out.

Just lay back and relax, baby."

This time, when Melissa submitted to his insistent hands, she thought she heard the faint sound of a man weeping. But when she tried to focus her attention, it disappeared. Only the wind could be heard, moaning softly through the open window.

Chapter Forty-Four

"Don't look now, but he who shall be nameless...Gray," Michael coughed the name into his hand, "is heading this way."

"What do I do?" Sam hissed. She wished the ground would open up and swallow her whole. She couldn't turn around and face him. He had seen way more of her mother than anyone alive should have been allowed to see.

"You could just turn around and talk to me," said Gray from somewhere above her left shoulder. "Um...and don't get mad at Michael. I asked him to leave. You've been avoiding me all week. You never returned my texts. I just wanted to see how you're doing after...y'know."

Sam turned around and saw Michael wiggle his fingers at her from the top of the school steps before he disappeared from view.

"Hi," she said, not quite sure what to say.

"Hi," Gray said. "That wasn't so bad, was it? Look, do you want to go out with me tonight? And not to a movie or anything with a screen?"

"I guess...yeah. This isn't a pity date or anything, right? We don't have to go out again because you feel sorry for me." Sam glared at him.

"Nope. I don't feel sorry for you one bit. If anything, I feel sorry for anyone who tangles with you. You're pretty fierce when you're riled up." He bumped her slender shoulder amiably with his broad one. "Pick you up at six? We can get something to eat and then go play laser tag. You ever play before?"

"No. What do you do?"

"Fire your laser gun at your opponent's kill zones and hit him before he hits you. Oh, and it's best to wear all black. You don't want to wear anything with white lettering or light colored because the blacklights will make you glow and stand out. I'll teach you...it's easy. You'll do great. It's really fun. We'll kill 'em!" said Gray enthusiastically. "It'll be a blast!"

The first bell rang. He smiled down at her. Sam smiled back.

"Come on, killer. We don't want to be late." Gray took her hand, not noticing the stricken look that crossed her face. "Did you study for the quiz?"

"What quiz?" Sam's head started to buzz with a loud, droning sound. Her vision browned-out around the edges. She missed a step and stumbled. She breathed rapidly.

"Hey, Sam! Sam!" said Gray, alarmed at the look on her face. "Sam, can you hear me?"

She sat down on the school steps and put her head down on her knees.

"Stay here, I'm getting the nurse!" Gray bounded inside. A few minutes later he returned with Mrs. Henley, the school nurse. She hurried to Sam's side.

"Samantha? Samantha?" Mrs. Henley sat down beside Sam and took her pulse. "I need you to breathe slowly, sweetie. In through your nose and out through your mouth. Come on, Sam. You can do this. In through your nose and out through your mouth. You're okay. You're having an anxiety attack."

The nurse turned to Gray. "She'll be fine, Gray. You did the right thing to come get me. You can go to class now. I'll have her stay with me for a bit, then she can return to class as well."

Gray sat down on the other side of Sam. Her breathing

calmed down. Her color returned to normal. She looked at him sheepishly.

"Sorry. I didn't mean to freak out on you," she said.

"I know, right? It's only a quiz. Now you probably won't even have to take it," Gray chuckled.

"Yeah, just a quiz. No major stress there," said Sam. "Pretty lame, huh?"

"Go rest. I'll see you at six." Gray tugged on her ponytail playfully and left.

"Okay. I'll be ready." Sam turned and watched him run up the school steps and into the building as she continued her slow, deep breathing at the nurse's encouragement.

She turned back in time to see a black limousine pull up in front of the school. Dismayed, Sam sat there as Leo Goss emerged first, followed by her mother. Then she caught the flash of the enormous diamond solitaire on her mother's left hand.

Without any warning, Sam passed out.

Chapter Forty-Five

Sam slammed into Miss Jenkins' office. She banged the door shut as hard as she could and threw her backpack on the chair.

"I'm done! Do you know who should be sitting in your office right now? Not me. Oh, no! Definitely not me. My schizo, flipped-out mother should be sitting in here! Get *her* in here! Make *her* look at your cheesy, worthless sayings and write letters to her dead husband! Dead as in murdered husband! Only been dead for eight months dead! Did I say murdered?! Maybe he'd tell her to get her act together and not act so stupid crazy! Get out your *feelings*, Sam! Don't be so *angry*, Sam!" Sam slapped both hands down on the low coffee table and fell to her knees. She howled in frustration. "Aaaghhhhh!"

Miss Jenkins rushed over. "Easy, Samantha! Breathe! What happened? It's eleven o'clock. Aren't you supposed to be in class?"

"I'm not going back to class, ever! And stop telling me to breathe! Everybody's telling me to breathe! There's no point in breathing! The lunatic and her fiance have decided, together….yeah, together…that I am being shipped off to boarding school in ten days. BOARDING SCHOOL! Because it would be best for me to be in an environment more suited to my behavioral issues! *He's* doing it! *He's* sending me away! He's not my freaking father. He's an awful, vile excuse of a human being!" Sam pushed the coffee table over and looked up at the psychologist, her face running with tears.

Miss Jenkins knelt next to Sam on the floor. "Who is sending you away? Take a minute and start at the beginning." She reached up and got the tissue box. She pulled out a couple and handed them to Sam.

"My mother and Leo Goss," Sam fumed, "are engaged to be married. As my new father and correctional officer, he gets to decide whatever he wants. And the humongous ring on my mother's finger has made her constitutionally unable to have a single independent thought of her own. So I am officially screwed. My father is dead and my mother is brain dead. Got any peppy pillow slogans for that?"

"Samantha, your mother's engagement is not the end of the world. The nurse called and told me you had an anxiety attack this morning on the school steps. That's serious. Perhaps this marriage will be a stabilizing force in all your lives. Take some of the burden off your shoulders. Let you be a teen again. Go on a date, have some fun, take life a little less seriously." Miss Jenkins rocked back on her heels and straightened up off the floor. She brushed off the knees of her jeans and pulled the table upright. "I'll talk to your mother about the boarding school. Perhaps I can get her to reconsider. You're making good progress here."

"Really?" Sam raged. She stood up and looked at Miss Jenkins.

"That's all you have to say? Sit back and enjoy the ride? My mother just welcomed a complete beast into our lives. I was told to cancel any dates because my schedule is now the sole property of Leo Goss." Sam felt so angry--hot lava bubbled in her veins.

"Samantha, granted, it's been a rough morning. I'm sure you think your life is over. It's not. It's natural for you to have these feelings. I'd be surprised if you didn't. But feelings and thoughts are not facts. Why don't you sit down? Let's talk about what you can to do to feel more comfortable during these tough times." Miss Jenkins spoke in a calm, sugar-sweet voice.

"No, thanks. I'm good. You're right. It's been a hard couple of hours, y'know? I think I'm going to take the nurse up on her offer. She already wrote me a note to go home. I'll go back to her office and call for a ride." Sam let out her breath slowly, realizing Miss Jenkins didn't want to hear what she really thought. "I have been stressing out lately."

"I think that's wise. Take some time for yourself." Miss Jenkins noticed the change in Sam's voice. She seemed more subdued and thoughtful. Miss Jenkins made a mental note to give Samantha's mother a call after the weekend to check on the teen. "Put it in perspective. Things have a way of working out just fine."

"Maybe. I don't know. It's a lot to take in, I guess." On her way out, she thought to herself, "I think I'll just go send a message to Dad."

Almost immediately the air around Sam's body grew cold. Her teeth chattered and her forearms pimpled in goosebumps. She felt the curious sensation of something brush by her and lightly touch her cheek as it passed. She whirled around, feeling an unmistakable presence directly behind her. Then, nothing.

"Is anything wrong, Samantha? Make sure whoever comes and picks you up stays with you. I don't think you should be alone." Miss Jenkins sat in the same spot, watching her.

Sam smiled to herself. "I won't be alone."

Chapter Forty-Six

An hour later, Sam curled up on Magda's flowered sofa. She wrapped a colorful afghan around her shoulders and sipped a cup of herbal tea. The tea tasted delicious. The mixture of chamomile, hops, and valerian root calmed her. She sent a text to Gray telling him she had to cancel laser tag. She suggested Saturday night instead, but hadn't heard back.

"I'm not sick, Mag," said Sam. "I just had an anxiety attack."

"Yes, you did. Then you passed out completely."

"You would have, too. She might as well be wearing a diamond ball and chain. I can't believe she told me at school. What parent tells their kid they just got engaged to the biggest schmuck in town at school! All the other guys were bad enough, but she was smart enough not to marry them. What's wrong with her!!" Sam threw herself back on the couch among the pillows.

"I haven't a clue. Your mother and I don't see eye to eye on much anymore, I'm afraid. Do I think this is a good decision? Nope! But I've kept my own counsel because I cannot do anything to jeopardize my relationship with you and Sarah. I love you two girls as if you were my own. Scoot over." Magda snuggled her close. "I have to be neutral. I will not put my two cents in and give Leo Goss any reason to cut me out of the picture."

"He wants to send me away, Mag. In less than two weeks. To a boarding school in Switzerland. I can't come home for Thanksgiving or Christmas. That's beyond crazy. I can't leave, Mag. I can't leave Sarah." The enormity of the situation overwhelmed her. She buried her face in her hands.

"We'll think of something, sweetie. I didn't get this far in life without some tricks up my sleeve. Maybe Fred can drop a few good ideas into my head. He's been pretty agitated. Tigger's hoarse from watching Fred's chair and meowing his head off. And my radio and tv go on and off at all hours of the day and night. He loved you girls to pieces. It's as if he's fired up about the whole mess as well."

"Maybe Fred and my dad could get together and start a fire or something. Let Leo Goss die from smoke inhalation, then burn to a crisp so he'd be out of our lives for good!"

"Samantha Harding! What a terrible thing to say!" Magda said, appalled. "Where did you ever get the idea that our dearly departed spirits would do such dreadful things?"

"I didn't say they would. I said they could, right?" Sam started to feel sleepy.

"Oh, honey. That's a Pandora's box of evil I wouldn't ever want to open. We'll figure it out. And let's just ask Fred and your dad to keep loving and protecting us, okay?" Magda got up and walked into the kitchen. She returned with a box and handed it to Sam.

"What's this, Mag?"

"Oh, I saw this on Amazon a couple days ago. Thought you might like it. It arrived this morning. You were your daddy's little Woodstock, Sam,...small, blonde, and full of moxie. His face would just light up when he would tell stories about your latest scrapes and adventures." Magda smiled at the memory.

"Thank you, Mag." Sam opened up the box. Inside was a plush Snoopy hugging a bright yellow Woodstock. "Oh, Mag...I love it!" She scooped it out and cuddled it in her arms.

"Well, I'm glad. I know you have a huge collection from

your dad. But this one reminded me of your dad holding you close, keeping you safe." Magda smiled, pleased Sam liked it.

"I don't have any of Snoopy holding Woodstock. This is the best!" Sam threw her arms around Magda and hugged her.

"Why don't you rest for a couple hours? Sarah won't be here until three o'clock. Your mother is sending a car to pick you up to get your hair and makeup done, plus a fitting for this evening's dinner." Magda kept her tone light, not wanting to upset Sam.

But Sam, her arms wrapped tightly around her gift, snored lightly. She was already sound asleep, burrowed beneath the afghan.

Chapter Forty-Seven

Sam shivered. Snow blew wildly, making it difficult to see. White flakes coated her hair and lashes. The afghan from Magda's couch flapped around her body. She drew it up over her head and leaned into the strong winds. Placing one foot in front of the other, she moved forward, desperate to find shelter.

Up ahead she heard keening and wailing. Fear tightened her throat. The snow lessened. Big, fat flakes drifted past her face. She wiped her eyes with a corner of the throw. She could see crowds of people. People she knew. Kids from high school. Michael's family. Sam squinted. Her mother stood next to Leo Goss, her arm held tightly in his strong grip. Sarah stood there as well, looking old and beaten. Magda held Sarah's hand in hers.

Michael stepped away from the crowd. He walked up to her. Took her ice-cold hands in his.

"Best friends. Remember? Together, forever, amen. I'll always have your back, Queen..."

"Michael? What's going on?"

Her father appeared and put his hand on Michael's shoulder.

"Daddy?!"

"Be careful, sweetheart."

The two turned, faded back into the crowd, and vanished.

"Wait! Wait! Daddy! Michael!"

She ran forward, slipping in the wet snow. The mourners drew back. Sam pushed her way through their bodies. She arrived, breathless, at the site of a new grave. Her heart skipped a beat. She turned around and tried to run, but her legs wouldn't move. The ground underneath her began to shift and soften. She sank down into the earth, a few inches at a time.

"No!" Sam screamed. "Help me! Someone help me, please!"

The crowd turned and left, leaving Sam alone. The cool, dark earth dragged her body downward. Her heart hammered against her ribs. She struggled in the dirt crumbling against her waist, then her chest. It reached her neck and made its way toward her lips.

"Daddy…help me..." she pleaded.

Chapter Forty-Eight

Magda returned from a quick run to the grocery store to find Sam writhing and mumbling on the couch. The afghan covered her face, winding around her shoulders in a strangle grip.

"Samantha! Shh! Honey, wake up! You're dreaming, sweetie! You're having a nightmare!"

Magda sat down next to the frantic, panting girl who woke up and looked at her with wide, frightened eyes. "It's me. Mag. You're okay. You're safe. It's just a bad dream. Hold on, I'll get you some Rescue Remedy. It's a Bach Flower Remedy. Good for shock." She dashed into the kitchen and snatched it off the counter. "Goodness, child, what a day you are having."

Sam shuddered at the memory of the cold, damp earth surrounding her body. Magda dropped down on the couch and smoothed back Sam's hair.

"If you aren't soaked with sweat...I never...here. Open up."

Sam tilted her head back obediently and opened her mouth like a baby bird. Magda squeezed four drops onto Sam's tongue.

"I'll give you another dose before you go." She gazed at Sam, worry drawing her eyebrows together. "Would it help to talk about it?"

"Not really. I don't want to think about it. I'd rather watch America's Funniest Home Video blooper reels or cat videos on my phone. Something really stupid and normal." Sam looked down at her phone. "Oh, look. A cat playing drums. That's about all I'm good for right now."

"Sounds like a plan. I'll leave you be. But I am right here in the kitchen if you need anything, you hear me?" Magda began unpacking the ingredients for chocolate peanut butter surprise cookies.

Instead of watching any more videos, Sam texted Michael. She needed to touch base with him right away.

Hey

"Come on, come on," she thought. Instead of a text, her phone rang.

"It's Michael, Mag. I'm gonna go sit outside on the porch and talk."

"Okay. Take a jacket. It's chilly." Magda sifted flour with a practiced hand.

"Hey, Queen! Whassup? Gray said you had a panic attack. Really? That's a new one. He said you were hanging out in the nurse's office but when I went to find you, you had flown," said Michael.

As soon as Sam heard Michael's deep voice riffing about panic attacks being non-existent in aliens, she closed her eyes and relaxed. She sat back on the porch swing, relishing the warmth of the sunshine on her face and the familiar sound of his voice cracking them both up. The terrifying details of her dream faded into the background.

"So how come you didn't come back to class, wimp?" asked Michael.

"You'll never believe me. I'll tell you, but you still won't believe me." Sam shook her head.

"Try me."

"I fainted for real."

"That's it?"

"Nope."

"You're killing me, Smalls. Give it up," said Michael

impatiently.

"I fainted because Leo Goss and my looney bin mother are engaged to be married and they are sending me off to a small country in Europe to be imprisoned for the rest of my natural school life."

"Shut your beak! I so don't believe you. What really happened?"

Silence.

"Damn," he said.

"I know, right?"

"This isn't the Dark Ages, Sam-a-lam-a. He has no legal say...he's not your father. He's just your mother's newest bad choice in a whole string of bad choices."

"She agreed, Michael. Signed the papers and everything. I leave in two weeks. Just in time for the second semester to begin. It's in Switzerland."

"Switzerland? Really? Swiss Miss instant cocoa land? They speak German, French, and I think, Italian. You don't speak any of those—plus, you failed Spanish."

"This is the detail you find interesting? They speak English at this school, dweeb. So they'll understand when I tell them where they can stick their courses."

"They can't do this, Sam."

"This is Leopold Goss, Michael. He can do anything he wants with my family, including killing my father! Period, end of tragic Lifetime movie!" Sam managed to say while holding back tears.

"Sam! You don't have proof yet. My father has been working for years at the department to pin something on Goss, but he's Teflon--nothing sticks!"

"What about the signatures? What about the private memo? What about the fact that my father ended up dead less than twenty-four hours after he shut down the project?" Sam cried out.

"Circumstantial, Sam. We don't know who pulled the

trigger. Nobody does!"

"I know he's involved, Michael! Leo may not have pulled the trigger, but he's in just as deep. I can feel it. I'll get the proof--or maybe I'll just kill him myself and put him out of his misery!"

"Whoa! Dial it back, girl. Prison orange is not a good look, alright? Don't do anything stupid, Sam. I mean it. You're kinda unstable right now. Jumpy-hyper, angry, sad, now this anxiety stuff...you're all over the place. I'll keep working on what we have. Hey, do you want to come over for dinner? Mom will pull out all the stops, spoil you a little. Get you back on a more positive vibe while I figure out some plan." Michael worried about Sam's new, vengeful attitude.

"Can't. Have to be at a command performance dinner with my new Daddy. Oh, yeah, after Sarah and I go to a fitting-slash-hair appointment with Malibu Mommy so we can all look like a remake of Charlie's Angels and make Leo proud. We can perform tricks for treats. Oh, wait. That's my mother. Me? I just get sent away," Sam fumed. "I have to go. Mom just texted. She'll be here in five. Talk to you later."

She hung up and ran inside to get her stuff. She stuffed Snoopy and Woodstock into her backpack.

"Gotta go, Magda. Mom's on her way with Sarah."

"I know. She just texted. Your mother wants you to stay here tonight after dinner. She and Leo are staying at his townhouse in the city for the evening to discuss wedding plans," said Magda. Her face betrayed her strong emotions.

Something crashed in the front room. Sam and Magda rushed through the door in time to see Tigger leap from the top of the baby grand piano by the window. He streaked through the house howling, his tail bushed out like a bottle brush.

"What the...?" The two stopped dead in their tracks.

Framed photographs and broken glass covered the floor. Both of them stared at the piano, softly playing Chopin's

Funeral March, unable to tear their eyes away from the sight of the keys being pressed down by invisible hands.

"Wedding, Fred! NOT funeral! Melissa is planning her wedding! What a mess--I swear, you frightened Tigger out of another life!" The piano playing stopped abruptly. Magda narrowed her eyes, hands on her hips. She shook her head at the mess and shivered. "It's freezing in here, too! Sam, go grab me the broom and dustpan, please? Then you have to skedaddle. I don't want to keep your mother waiting. And don't tell her about this, please? All I need is Leo Goss using paranormal activity as a reason to keep you children away from me...especially now!"

Sam dashed to get the cleaning supplies. When she returned, she bent down and pocketed a picture of herself and her dad taken two summers ago. In it they were laughing while making homemade pizzas in Magda's kitchen. Her heart broke into a million little pieces all over again as she stared at his familiar, beloved face. He never would have sent her away. Ever.

"Can I keep this, Mag?" asked Sam.

"Yes, honey. I'm going to have to get indestructible frames." Magda gazed around the room in despair. "What has gotten into you, Fred?"

"Here, Mag." Sam handed her the broom. "Um. Wow. That blew my mind...like something out of a horror movie. You sure you're okay here by yourself? Fred hasn't gone over to the dark side, has he? The walls aren't going to start dripping blood or anything, right?"

"I'll be fine. I never told you, but he has played the piano before. Usually something comforting or uplifting. Not helpful, Fred!" Magda spoke to a point somewhere above the piano. "I don't claim to be psychic but I believe Fred's just very upset right now. He doesn't like seeing your family fall apart and Leo Goss picking up the pieces. Now go! I'll see you later tonight." Magda urged Sam toward the door.

Sam didn't look convinced, but she picked up her things and headed outside. Magda watched as Sam ran down the front steps toward the limo.

"I don't like it any better than you do, Fred," she huffed. "Keep an eye on her, please!"

Chapter Forty-Nine

The limo headed to the Avalon Spa in New York City. The forty-five minute drive ended too soon. Sarah basked in her mother's presence, chattering away like a little squirrel--excited to be with her mother and sister. Sam gave her mother a disgusted look. She stared out the window until they arrived, lost in the ear-numbing sounds of her iPod's playlist.

Sarah's jaw dropped as she entered the spa. It welcomed them with soft lighting and soothing background music. A woman named Bianca with beautiful long black hair and a pleasant foreign accent greeted Melissa Harding with pleasure.

"Hello, Mrs. Harding. Everything is set for you and your girls. Mr. Goss called. The gowns sent over from Valentino's are with Jessalyn, your personal alterations specialist. After your fitting, Ayesha will come get you for your Brandied Cherry and Brown Sugar Glaze Manicure and Pedicure. Servio will apply your makeup. Harold will do your special occasion hair styling. Mr. Goss plans to be here promptly at six-thirty. Reservations are at Mancini's at seven." Bianca smiled. "May I get each of you a glass of chilled, fresh, raspberry-flavored water?"

Sarah's eyes grew bigger and bigger as Bianca described each step of the afternoon's treatments.

"Sam, we're gonna be beautiful!" Sarah breathed. Sam rolled her eyes and grimaced.

"I think you're beautiful just the way you are, short stuff. Daddy thought so, too. You don't have to dress up to please anybody," Sam whispered in Sarah's ear.

"Come on, girls." Melissa finished going over the details with Bianca. She motioned for her daughters to go up the red carpeted stairs to the second floor.

An expansive fairyland with floor-to-ceiling mirrors, lush upholstered sofas, and beaded, glittering dresses in rich fabrics met their eyes. Jessalyn stood waiting for them.

"Oh, Bianca. Before you leave us, would you please make sure everybody knows everything must be done with pure, organic materials with absolutely no added perfumes or scents. Mr. Goss is severely asthmatic," Melissa confided. Sam's ears perked up.

"Yes, certainly. Mr. Goss informed us of this as well. And may I say congratulations to you, Mrs. Harding?" Bianca noticed the breathtaking diamond on Melissa's left hand.

"Oh, thank you. He is very generous." Melissa smiled faintly.

"Yeah, like Bluebeard and his wives...," Sam muttered.

Bianca excused herself tactfully. Melissa turned and fixed Sam with a relentless gaze.

"Nothing is ever as it seems, Samantha."

"Really? I'm beginning to figure that out for myself." Sam switched topics. "What's this about Leo's asthma? How bad is it? You can't die from asthma."

"Actually, you can. He's allergic to certain things, like perfume, cigarette smoke, pollen, dogs and cats, especially cats. He is so sensitive no one who works for him can be around these things. His drivers even have to shower before driving him anywhere: no cologne, lotions, scents of any kind. I've stopped wearing perfume at all."

Sam didn't say anything. In fact she didn't talk at all for the rest of the afternoon. She put her earbuds back in, but didn't turn on her iPod. Her mind worked furiously. Leo had a weakness.

"And, somehow, I'm gonna use it," Sam vowed.

Chapter Fifty

Leo sat waiting in his limousine in front of the spa at exactly six-thirty. Melissa had watched the clock like a hawk, unwilling to be even a few seconds late. All three of them looked amazing in their Valentino evening gowns in deep autumn colors, their hair curled in riotous, feminine waves.

"Now...that's more like it," Leo said.

He sat in the rear of the car, facing forward. He looked approvingly at Sarah and patted the seat next to him. She cautiously made her way into the vehicle, not wanting to wrinkle her skirts.

In the jewelry Leo had sent over from Cartier and the sophisticated makeup, Sarah's natural beauty sparkled. She looked like a young, dazzling ingenue, her long blond hair tumbling down her back in Juliet curls with a circlet of flowers crowning her head.

"Hey, thanks, Leo." Sam pushed by Sarah. She plopped down next to him onto the seat he indicated. "An eye-opening experience, to say the least. Never saw so many women spending so much money on themselves at one time. I didn't know breaking a nail deserved emergency status. So many first world problems, so little time." She tugged at the side of her dress. "Mom, I think they sewed my dress shut."

Leo looked furious, his lips set in a thin line. Before he lost his temper, Melissa extended her hand as she settled into her seat across from him. "Such a lovely time, Leo. Let's have a glass of champagne to relax on the way to the restaurant. I feel like celebrating, don't you?"

Sarah sat down next to her mother, closest to the door, furthest from Leo. Sam smiled to herself.

Leo still looked irritated as hell. His eyes began to water. He fumbled in his jacket pocket for his handkerchief. Wiping his eyes, he started to sneeze. Sam watched with interest.

"Shut the door! Damn it! Shut the door, now!" His chauffeur slammed the door shut. He walked around to the driver's door and got in.

"What is it, Leo?" Melissa looked nervous. "Girls? You made sure you didn't touch any of the scented lotions or soaps, right?"

Sam and Sarah shook their heads. Bianca had followed them around like white on rice. Even if she'd wanted to, Sam couldn't have touched anything that might have set off Leo's allergies.

"Cigarette! Idiotic smoker! Loser!" He wheezed, taking out his inhaler. "Drive, Lennie!"

The limo pulled away from the curb in one smooth motion and headed to the restaurant. After a few moments, Leo looked like he felt better. He leaned forward and reached down into a small cabinet next to the wet bar. He pulled out a fresh handkerchief and tucked it into his interior lapel pocket.

When he looked up, he saw all three of them staring at him.

"What?" Leo griped. "Didn't you see the guy smoking a cigarette on the sidewalk? All that smoke coming right in through the door? What a jerk! I couldn't breathe." He coughed. It went on for a minute or two with an awful wheezing sound as he tried to catch his breath. He exhaled and took another puff on his inhaler, sucking the medicine deep into his lungs. "Don't worry, ladies. I'm not going to die any time soon. I've got plans for all of you...big plans."

Leo laughed and looked at Melissa. She busied herself

pouring drinks. His eyes slid over to Sarah and lingered for a long time. Sam watched him out of the corner of her eye. She felt a slow, murderous rage build up inside her chest. She glanced down at the cabinet that housed Leo's supply of fresh, unused handkerchiefs.

Her plan began to take shape.

Chapter Fifty-One

"Mr. Goss! Delighted to see you this evening surrounded by such beautiful flowers, no? Come, follow me. Your table is ready," said Adrian Manzanelli, the handsome, famous maitre d' at Mancini's. With a seemingly insignificant change of seating, he could make or break someone's career.

Mancini's...the place to see and be seen. Crowded with A-listers and politicians alike, it commanded the reputation of being *the* popular spot to seal a deal or make a new one. Only the very rich or the well-connected got reservations. If you didn't know anyone who knew anyone, you found yourself turned away quietly back out onto the sidewalk with the rest of the unworthy.

Leo grasped Adrian's hand. Sam saw several hundred-dollar bills pass between the two men. Leo pointed to a section of the restaurant. Adrian raised one eyebrow, thought a moment, then nodded. He called over the head waiter and whispered something in his ear. The head waiter rushed away.

Leo made the rounds through the restaurant with Melissa on his arm. He stopped to chat with several people Sam had only seen in magazines. Sarah looked completely starstruck.

"This is just wrong!" thought Sam, her eyes flashing. "What are we doing here? Leo Goss is a freaking criminal--he's got us dressed up like little petted poodles...parading us around like his personal show dogs...what the hell?" She scowled in mute protest.

The maitre d' came and stood by Leo's side.

"We made the change you requested, Mr. Goss. If you would, please, follow me?"

Leo, her mother, and Sarah went with Adrian. Sam hung back as her anxiety built. Leo circled back and came up behind her. He put his smooth, manicured hand on her bare skin. She flinched.

He drew back his lips with an easy smile. But his eyes told her a different story. He put his arm around her shoulder, bent his head, and spoke close to her ear. Only Sam could hear the whispered venom escape his clenched teeth.

"Do we have a problem, Samantha? Put a smile on your face. This is not the time or the place to make a scene. Do what I say or you'll find yourself on a red-eye flight out of town this evening. I promised your mother two more weeks. I don't keep promises." He turned her around. She stood facing him, staring up into his eyes.

Leo put his hands on either side of her rebellious face. He kissed her slowly and deliberately on the forehead, then stroked the side of her face with his finger. She refused to shrink away from his menacing touch. Instead, she pictured him broken and bleeding as she ran over him with his limousine, his smug face smashed into the pavement.

Dropping his hand to her waist, Leo whirled her around and propelled her forward until they caught up to her mother and Sarah. Their table occupied the very center of the dining room, the most coveted spot in the restaurant.

"This is more like it!" Leo looked around, nodding and smiling at the other diners, flaunting his power.

"Only the best for Leo Goss!" he boomed loudly. "Keeps the rest of you in your place...taking care of me...'cause when Leo's happy, everybody's happy!"

Sam kept her mouth shut. Her cheeks burned from the fawning looks and comments directed their way. People knew and feared Leo...especially the ones already caught in his web of intimidation and deceit.

Leo played the doting father to Sarah, laughing indulgently at her enthusiasm. He sat between Melissa and her youngest daughter. Many times during the meal, he reached out and stroked Sarah's hair, running his fingers through the long, blonde curls playfully. Leo looked at Sam, enjoying her obvious discomfort.

"When you come to live with me, Sarah, you can use an entire wing on the second floor for your art studio. I look forward to seeing your art displayed at the Community Center this Sunday evening. I'm sure you'll win first place. Everyone connected to me is a winner. Isn't that right, Melissa?" Leo spoke louder. He enjoyed being the center of attention.

Sam imagined taking her steak knife and cutting off his fingers one by one. Meticulously sawing through the thick flesh and bone while he screamed in pain. She eyeballed him, wondering how long it would take him to bleed to death.

Melissa drank glass after glass of wine, smiling and nodding at her fiance when it seemed appropriate, but appearing otherwise subdued. Leo, on the other hand, had the time of his life--his ego on display for everyone to see.

After the main course, Leo leaned over to Melissa and kissed her. Finally she pushed him away, breathless and flushed.

"Leo, what's gotten into you?" said Melissa warily.

"You have, my dear. You and your beautiful daughters. I love being together like this. I thought about waiting until after we were married," he glanced at Sam briefly, "but I'm moving up the timetable."

"What timetable?" asked Melissa.

"Waiting until Samantha left for Switzerland to move you and the girls in with me. Why wait? I'd much rather be together under one roof as soon as possible. I've already arranged to move everything on Sunday. It's done. I've taken care of all the details," Leo beamed. His chest puffed out proudly. He beckoned to the waiter.

"Bring out the cake! And another bottle of champagne! This is big news! Aren't you pleased?" Leo put his arm around Melissa. She didn't look thrilled.

Sarah gazed at Leo and her mother. A worried look crossed her face. Then the cake arrived, glowing with hundreds of candles. She clapped her hands, the tension forgotten in the flurry of standing, blowing out the candles, and everyone wishing the happy couple congratulations.

Leo put his arms around Melissa and Sarah, pulling them close. Sam didn't trust herself to say a word. She burned with anger.

"I am going to burst into red-hot flames right in front of everybody. Talk about morphing at light speed--my entire world is on the brink of extinction!" Sam thought furiously.

"Mom, what time is the limo taking me and Sarah to Magda's house?" It took every shred of Sam's control to ask the question without screaming.

"Nine o'clock, dear. Are you alright, Samantha? You look feverish. Are you coming down with something?" Melissa touched Sam's forehead with her cool fingers.

"I'm fine, Mom. I think my dress is too tight."

"Can't eat in couture, dear. Let me check the time. Oh, goodness. It's already nine. I'll walk you two out to the limo while Leo chats."

Leo shook his head. "I'll do it, Melissa. This is a special night. I want you to relax and enjoy yourself. I'll take them out and be right back."

Melissa looked torn. She didn't want to make a fuss. She gave Sam a hug and whispered in her ear, "Don't leave Sarah alone, Sam. Stay right by her side. I'm depending on you."

"Yeah, you *and* Dad."

"What do you mean?"

"You wouldn't understand."

Sam shrugged out of her mother's grasp. Leo put his arm around Melissa. "You'll see them tomorrow. They'll be fine. Trust me." He kissed her lips and slapped her rump familiarly. Melissa looked pained.

"Let's go, girls." He held his arm out to Sarah, who took it. She looked back at Sam with an innocent smile.

"C'mon, Sam," Sarah said.

Sam hurried through the restaurant behind them, trying to keep up with Leo's long stride. Suddenly a waiter dropped a tray with a crash. Startled, she turned her head in that direction. When she looked forward again, they were gone!

Leo and Sarah had vanished!

Chapter Fifty-Two

"Sarah, where are you?!" Sam cried in alarm.

The bar opened up to her right, crowded with suits and women in heels. She looked out over the sea of people, but no Sarah. On her left, waiters carried trays of food into another dining room.

"What if he took her to another exit? What if he has another limo waiting?" Sam thought desperately.

Seven long frantic minutes passed as she combed the restaurant looking for her sister's blonde head. She bumped into Adrian.

"Excuse me, miss? Aren't you with Mr. Goss?" Adrian righted the distressed girl.

"Yes! Yes, I am. He's with my little sister. Did you see them?" Sam tried not to overreact, but a note of hysteria crept into her voice.

"Yes, yes," Adrian soothed. "Your sister took an unfortunate tumble and twisted her ankle. Mr. Goss moves rather quickly. She tripped trying to keep up. I left them in the waiting area by the ladies lounge." Adrian delivered Sam to them briskly, then flew off to handle another situation.

Sarah sat on Leo's lap, her head against his suit jacket. Tears streaked her face, her shoe lay in pieces on her lap. Leo had both arms around her, holding her close, his hands caressing her arms and back as he dropped kisses on her tangled curls.

Sam hurried toward them, ready to yank Sarah away. She stopped in her tracks when Leo looked at her, shook his head in mock severity, and remarked, "the airport's not too far from here."

Sarah put her head up and said, "who's going to the airport, Sam?"

"Nobody, baby. Not tonight, anyway. We have a date with Magda."

"Smart girl. You learn fast. I like that. Hold on to your shoe, Sarah, honey." Leo scooped Sarah up into his arms and held her firmly against his chest. "I'll carry you to the limo. Gotta stay off that ankle."

Leo settled Sarah into her seat. He took a long time buckling her seat belt and getting her foot in a comfortable position, running his hands over her leg to make sure nothing was broken. Sarah liked the extra attention and said so.

"Thank you for taking care of me. It's very nice of you," said Sarah shyly.

Leo threw his head back and laughed. He leaned in and kissed her on both cheeks.

"You keep thinking that way, darlin', and we'll get along just fine."

He stepped out of the limo. Sam waited on the sidewalk to get in. She looked like a cat whose fur had been brushed the wrong way. He grabbed her hands and pushed her back against the limo.

"Leo Goss always gets what he wants. Always. No one gets in my way." Sam struggled to free her hands. "That pretty little thing in there who thinks I'm her hero? She's mine. Like your very hot mother. I got it made. You, I'm not so thrilled with, kid. Be careful how you play this or you might end up dead like dear old daddy."

Sam gasped. He let go of her and she fell back against the car.

"Get in," Leo commanded.

In a louder voice, he said, "take 'em home, Vinnie."

Sam watched the figure of Leo Goss grow smaller and

smaller as the limousine headed toward the George Washington Bridge. Sarah, worn out by the excitement, fell sound asleep. Sam's teeth chattered as she tried to calm down after Leo's threats. Her mind raced.

"That egotistical, disgusting thug would love to pay one of his goons to make me disappear in some cement Manolo Blahniks. Only the best for the pervert pig! He thinks he's so damn clever, threatening to send me away, even kill me if I don't play nice! Check and mate. Well, maybe I don't feel like playing nice, jerk!" thought Sam wrathfully.

She reached down into the cabinet next to the wet bar, pulled out two of Leo's fancy, monogrammed handkerchiefs, and stuck them in her backpack. She sent her father a quick message.

It's bad, Daddy. Leo's after Sarah. He keeps touching her, Daddy. He said I'd end up dead like you if I got in the way. I have to stop him. He's the one who had you killed, Daddy! He practically admitted it!

anime's father
works for Leo

What???!!

he gave
anime
video of mom
also set up
mugging

Oh my God, I knew Anime had something to do with it!

leo is
behind it all

*you have to
get rid of him*

Sam stared at the phone. She trusted him. He had brought her this far and kept her safe. She hesitated for a fraction of a second, took a deep breath, and tapped out:

He's got really bad allergies and asthma. It's pretty serious.

*use it, honey
save sarah and mom
don't get caught
he's lethal*

Got it. I have a plan that might work.

*good
stay strong*

I will, Daddy. As long as I have you, I can do anything. But don't leave me again. I need you. I don't know who I am without you. You're the only one keeping me sane. I don't feel alone anymore. I love you so much.

*i'm here now
love you, too*

Sam put her phone away and glanced at her sleeping sister. She wouldn't mind seeing the two pristine, white handkerchiefs in her backpack wrapped around Leo's neck like a hangman's noose.

Sam closed her eyes and silently declared, "I'm about to get in your way, Leo. My dad and I aren't so thrilled with you, either."

Chapter Fifty-Three

Magda hung up the girls' cocktail dresses as soon as Sam and Sarah arrived at her house. She made them change into their pajamas. Sarah didn't want to scrub off the makeup or comb out her fairy princess curls.

"But I'm beautiful, Mag! Mr. Leo said so! He said I am the prettiest girl he had ever seen!" Sarah exclaimed.

Sarah sat on Mag's sofa with a large, blue ice pack on top of her foot. She gestured excitedly as she described in detail the entire spa experience and the evening at Mancini's.

"We're moving into his house on Sunday before my art show. You're coming to my show at the Community Center right, Magda?" asked Sarah.

"Oh, it's your show now, is it? Of course I am. I've only been hearing about it for days. Goodness, what a chatterbox you are tonight. I'll bet you talked everyone's ear off! How did you hurt your ankle, sweetie?" Magda sat down next to Sarah, taking care not to jostle her leg.

"I held on to Mr. Leo's arm as we walked to the front door-- then he made a sudden turn. I guess he wanted to speak to somebody. I don't know. I tried to keep up...I practically ran! But my heel broke off my shoe and I fell. Adrian saw and picked me up. Mr. Leo looked kind of mad, though. I thought he got mad because I broke my shoe so I started crying. Adrian brought us to that room with all the couches where Sam found us." Sarah yawned.

Magda and Sam exchanged a long look. Sam felt ill. She

resolved to put an end to Leo Goss one way or another.

"There's lots of people who are helpers in this world, Sarah. I'm so grateful Adrian rescued you. I think your ankle will be fine by morning. You just need to rest it. Who's up for some buttered popcorn and a movie?" Magda picked up Tigger and nestled him on top of Sarah's lap. She asked Sam to come and help her in the kitchen.

Magda took out the oil, poured some into a big pot on top of the stove, and lit the burner. She tossed in two or three kernels of popcorn, put the lid on, and waited for them to pop.

"I don't like that man at all, Samantha. What is this about you moving into his house on Sunday?" said Magda.

Not paying attention, she grabbed Fred's ashes when the oil was ready and almost tossed the lot into the pot before realizing her error. Magda put them down with a shaking hand.

"Damn it, Fred. I nearly boiled you in oil that time," she exploded.

Magda reached for the correct canister containing the popcorn kernels and poured them in. In a few moments, they heard the steady pop-pop-popping against the lid.

"It'll be okay, Mag. I don't think my dad will let anything happen to Sarah. And we still have a day to think of something. It'll work out. One way or another," Sam answered automatically.

Sam felt light-headed as though someone had replaced all her hot, angry blood with a fizzy liquid. It energized her, making her hyper-alert and aware. One part of her brain watched herself talk to Magda, saying all the right things to reassure her. The other part of her brain whirred busily: calculating, rejecting, and re-vamping the exact steps to take to neutralize Leo.

"Who are you and what have you done with my Sam?" Magda pulled the overflowing pot of freshly popped hot popcorn off the burner. She unwrapped a stick of butter and put it in a quart-size saucepan to melt.

"Oh, Magda. I'm tired of fighting everything and everybody, you know? Let's just stuff ourselves with popcorn and watch something on Netflix. I don't want to talk about stuff I don't have any control over right now, y'know?" Sam poured the popcorn into a giant bowl. Magda poured on the melted butter and added salt.

"Okay. I'll leave it for now. But I am definitely having a talk with your mother tomorrow. I would never forgive myself if I didn't let her know my concerns about this new living arrangement. I love you girls. I won't take this lying down." Magda hugged Sam.

Sam carried the big bowl into the family room.

"Okay, Sarah. Let's eat, drink, and be merry."

"Because tomorrow I may be in jail…," Sam added silently.

Chapter Fifty-Four

Both girls slept late. Sarah's ankle still hurt the following morning. Magda decided to take her into the quick clinic for an x-ray. The clinic operated from nine in the morning to seven in the evening on Saturdays. The kitchen clock already said eleven. Outside, the weather turned cold and windy. Raindrops spattered the driveway. Sam shoveled in the eggs, bacon, and homemade cinnamon rolls Magda set out on the kitchen table. Sarah finished before Sam and turned on the television in the family room.

Magda drank her umpteenth cup of coffee, a thoughtful expression on her face. She sensed someone, probably Fred, in the room with her. An eerie feeling prickled between her shoulder blades, but every time she turned around...nothing, nada. She glimpsed a shadowy something out of the corner of her eye, but it disappeared every time she focused on it.

"Come on, Fred," Magda thought. "If you've got something on your mind, figure out a way to say it. Leave off the theatrics. Just some plain old words will do."

Shaking her head to clear away the fog, Magda went over to the counter to make a fresh pot of coffee. She rinsed out the carafe and replaced it in the machine. She went to dump out the coffee grounds, but missed the trash can. Coffee grounds went all over the floor.

"Damn it to hell and back again...what an unholy mess!"

She hated spilling coffee grounds. They spread out like an oil slick in the Gulf.

"Need any help?" Sam called over her shoulder on her way to get dressed.

"No, honey. I've got it. The most important thing is containment," Magda grumbled. She dampened a few paper towels, then got on her hands and knees in order to push them into a manageable heap before attempting to pick them up.

"Oh sweet, Lord Jesus," she thought, "the grounds are moving." She didn't take her eyes off them as they gathered together in a pile, pushed into place by an unseen hand.

Magda hissed softly, "if this is your idea of a joke, Fred, just kill me now. This is not good for my blood pressure."

One letter at a time appeared, painstakingly drawn in the wet grains. The white tile gleamed through the dark grounds, making them easy to read.

S...... A...... M...... D...... A...... N...... Then, nothing.

"SAMDAN? What is SAMDAN?" Magda felt frustrated and more than a little spooked. Still nothing. Then she realized Fred didn't have any space left to write.

"What is this? Wheel of Fortune, Fred? I don't know what you're trying to spell!" Impatiently, she took her hand and wiped over the grounds like a messy Etch-A-Sketch. "There! Finish!" She looked down at the grounds and waited.

Three more letters emerged. At least a minute or two passed between each attempt. Each letter got shakier and harder to read. G....... E...... R. Magda could barely make out the R.

"GER? SAMDANGER? SAM... DANGER? Sam is in danger? I know the situation with Leo Goss is bad, but danger? Physical danger? From who? Goss?" Magda rocked back on her heels. She sat flat on the floor in shock.

"Mag? Who are you talking to?" Sarah called from the family room.

"Fred, honey. Just talking out loud..."

"Okay, tell him I said hi." Sarah turned the volume back up, engrossed in the show she was watching on The Disney Channel.

"Good Lord, Fred," Magda moaned softly. "Your first message in the coffee grounds couldn't have been 'Hi, Honey, having a great time...wish you were here?!'"

Her vintage black cat Halloween mug began to rock back and forth, moving closer and closer to the edge of the sink.

"Sorry! This must be really hard. Don't break my mug!" She waited, worry curling like a little worm in her stomach.

"Please, Fred. You're scaring me. Who is trying to hurt Sam?" Magda stared at the grounds, willing something, anything to appear.

Finally, one final letter began to take shape. The tension in the kitchen grew thick. Magda held her breath.

"It looks like a B?"

"G?"

"D?"

"Maybe an R?"

"Oh, Fred. I'm so sorry. I can't read it." Magda dropped her head into her hands.

"Magda?" Sam yelled from upstairs. "Can we leave soon? Gray wants to meet me at the Mall. It's close to the clinic. I could walk over."

"Sure, honey." Magda pushed the grounds into a pile, obliterating the letters. She picked them up with the damp paper towel and threw them into the garbage. She felt the sensation of eyes staring at her between her shoulder blades again.

"This isn't over, Fred. Let me go and take care of the girls. Rest up. We'll try again later. I'll keep an eye on them both, I promise." Magda hauled herself to a standing position, wincing at the stiffness in her knees. "Never would have thought of coffee grounds. Whatever works, I guess."

****

The three of them piled into Magda's car. The rain came down harder. Booms of thunder preceded flashes of lightning that lit up the sky in the distance. They drove down the street. The intense rain made driving treacherous and visibility limited.

Magda concentrated hard on her driving. The windshield fogged up after she turned on the heater. She never could remember which combination of buttons operated the front defroster. She glanced down and fiddled with a couple.

"Sam," Magda began. "Would you help…"

Magda glanced back up. To her horror, she drove right through the four-way stop sign. A light blue Mercedes loomed directly in front of her. Magda stomped hard on the brakes. Her car hydroplaned, skidding out of control.

"Hold on!" she yelled.

Magda gripped the steering wheel and braced for the crash!

Chapter Fifty-Five

The driver in the Mercedes saw Magda's Lexus SUV lose control. He made a hard right-hand turn to avoid a collision and pulled to a stop on the side of the road. He watched Magda fight to control her car. An empty church parking lot came into view up ahead on the right. The Lexus veered into it and spun around before coming to a halt.

The man jumped out of his car and ran over to check on them. Magda opened her window, apologizing profusely. Shaken and flustered, she didn't recognize him at first.

"Are you alright?" he asked.

"I think so. I am so, so sorry." She peered at him through the rain. "Oh, my goodness! Peter! That was you? My defroster doesn't work very well. That's no excuse for going through the stop sign, but I took my eyes off the road trying to push the right button."

"It's okay, Magda. No harm done. I'm a pretty defensive driver. I saw you miss that stop sign so I moved out of your way. Didn't Fred ever tell you never hit the brakes hard in the rain? Hydroplaning is no fun. Lucky the traffic's pretty light in this weather. I see you've got some very precious cargo on board. Hi, girls! You okay?" Peter looked inside the car at Sam and Sarah with a worried smile.

Both girls nodded at their dad's friend, their eyes wide after this unexpected turn of events. Sarah looked back down at her iPad. Even the threat of a car wreck wasn't enough to tear her away from her newest fashion design app.

"What are the odds of almost literally running into Peter after Fred's warning?" thought Magda. "I don't believe in coincidences. Peter's a good man. He'll help us." She made a split-second decision and spoke quickly before she could change her mind.

"Peter, you must know that Melissa is going to marry Leo Goss. I'm just sick about it. Isn't there anything we can do? He's moving them into his house tomorrow." Magda knew Forbes had put a lot of faith in this man. If anyone could figure out a plan to stop Leo Goss, Peter could.

"What?" Peter looked stunned. "I knew they were engaged, but he can't just disrupt the kids' lives on a whim. I'll talk to Melissa. Leo's pretty devious. He may be forcing her hand, somehow. He's the last person I'd want for an enemy, but this is too much."

"There's more, Peter. Leo's sending Samantha away to school abroad in two weeks. Just sending her away like that. No discussion...nothing. Why isn't Melissa stopping him, Peter? I don't understand this at all," said Magda. "You're Forbes' executor. Can't you put some legal monkey wrench into Leo's plans?"

"I'll take care of it, Magda. No one is going to send Sam away. And they are not moving into Leo's house tomorrow. That's just crazy. The girls have gone through enough. Thanks for telling me all this. I'm on it. Don't worry." He patted Magda's hand and dashed back to his car through the rain.

Sam leaned back against the passenger seat. She watched the cars drive past, lost in her own thoughts, as Magda pulled back out onto the main road.

"You might be a nice man, Peter," Sam reflected, "but you are no match for Leo Goss. You can't stop him before tomorrow. But I can. I know Leo's weakness and I intend to use it."

Her phone went off like a fire alarm--a jarring ring tone she used for anyone she didn't know. Sam looked at the number.

"Probably some random sales call," she thought. She answered it.

"Hello?"

Chapter Fifty-Six

The cloudburst ended. The wind whipped the trees into a frenzy, hurling wet leaves against the dark sky. A moody electricity crackled in the air--perfect weather for the last week in October.

The clinic hummed with allergies, the first cases of flu, and assorted sports injuries. Magda hustled them into the office. Sarah hung on Magda's arm, hopping on one foot, until they reached the nearest available seat. Magda sat her down and went to fill in the paperwork.

"Sarah, tell Magda I went to the Mall. I'll call her later, okay?" Sarah nodded. Sam slipped out the door.

Sam still didn't know how Anime knew her number. She sounded off the wall on the phone, crying and being a jerk at the same time. She kept yelling about her dad getting fired because of Sam. She wanted to meet up at the parking garage behind the Mall.

"As if," Sam muttered. "I'm not stupid. Anime outside of school is still the same person who wants to beat the crap out of me inside of school. Ooooh...let's go meet in an empty parking lot. I don't think so."

Sam took off down the street. The strong winds pushed her along. She practically ran, dodging puddles deep enough to drench her sneakers. She saw the entrance to the Mall up ahead. A group of people waited at the crosswalk for the walk signal. Sam stood and waited with them, anxious to see Gray.

"I just need a couple hours of normal before I have to deal with Leo," she thought. Sam pushed the evening's plans to the back of her tired brain. "All I want is a cinnamon dolce latte and a pumpkin scone at Starbucks. And Gray. I really want to see Gray." The light changed. The WALK sign flashed.

"You decide to show up, loser?" Anime materialized loud and large in Sam's peripheral vision.

"Um...no. Go away, Anime." Sam hadn't noticed her in the crowd on the corner. At least Anime couldn't do anything here. Too many witnesses.

"I said, you decide to show up, *loser*?" Anime crossed the road next to Sam and hit her hard on the back the second time she said "loser." People streamed across the road. Sam didn't think twice. She stuck her foot out. Anime went down like a sack of potatoes right when she reached the opposite curb.

Sam broke into a light jog, trying to lose Anime in the crowd. She took a quick right between Kohl's and Victoria's Secret, darting into a pedestrian passageway between the stores.

"I can take the back way to the coffee shop," Sam decided. "What the hell is Anime's deal? What a head case--she probably got rejected from her home planet for eating her own offspring!"

"Nice move, freak. You're gonna pay for that after you tell me why Goss wants to fire my father," Anime grunted behind her. She seized Sam's arm and threw her against the side of the brick building as hard as she could.

A strip of trees grew down the center of the landscaped, outdoor walkway. The wind blew stronger. Debris and sticks swirled through the narrow corridor. Thunder clapped in the distance. Lightening flashed.

Sam's temper rose from zero to a hundred. She put both of her hands on Anime's shoulders and pushed, hard. "What are you talking about? How would I know, you dirty, low-life?

You gave that disgusting video of my mother to your creep geek at the theater! I could care less about what happens to you or your ex-con father!"

"You liar!" Anime turned red in the face. "You knew it was me all along. And because my dad works for Goss, you figured he gave me the flash drive!" She pushed back, harder, and punched Sam in the stomach for good measure.

"Oof." Sam's back hit the brick wall again with a thud. She winced.

"That's gonna leave a bruise," she thought.

Sam straightened up with difficulty. She looked at both ends of the walkway, trying to estimate the distance.

"I could make a run for it. Maybe. If I could breathe," she muttered.

"C'mon, liar! Don't play dumb!" Anime yelled.

"Really? You admit you did it?" Sam cried. She moved cautiously away from the brick wall, putting distance between her and Anime.

"How could I make your dad lose his pathetic job with Leo Goss? How many different drugs do you take, Anime?" Sam shouted. "I have no power over Leo Goss! Who told you I was the reason? They're wrong! Maybe he's just a crappy employee? I don't really care! Get away from me! Crawl back in your supersize bag of Cheetos and leave me alone! I have enough to deal with right now!"

She reached down and picked up a good-sized stick with one hand, keeping an eye on Anime.

"I am not going down without a fight!" she vowed. If Anime came at her again, Sam was going to let her have it.

"I don't believe you! You think you're better than everybody 'cause Goss is marrying your tramp mother! I bet you think you're too good for Gray now. You think Goss is gonna let you date a landscaper's kid?" Anime yelled.

She threw a rock at Sam's head. Sam ducked. Anime ran at Sam, trying to grab the stick away.

"Have your fat cells eaten away what's left of your brain? What's wrong with you! Go away!" Sam screamed. She jabbed at Anime with the stick. "I wish my dad hadn't died! He'd never let you get away with any of this! Don't touch me!"

Anime went nuts. She grabbed the end of the stick and pulled on it as hard as she could. Sam couldn't hold on any longer. She let go of the stick. Anime flew through the air and landed on her butt. She struggled to her feet and came after Sam again, brandishing the thick branch over her head.

The sound of the two yelling girls attracted a crowd. People gathered at both ends of the passage, drawn by the commotion. The rain drizzled steadily.

"Drop it, Anime!" Sam kept moving out of Anime's reach, throwing her hands up to protect herself.

"No! I'm gonna bash your stupid head in!"

"Not if I can help it!" Sam ran behind one of the trees, slipping on the wet roots.

"You are so dead!" Anime shrieked. She cut behind a bush and landed a stinging blow, catching Sam on the back of her leg.

"Owww! Give me that! I mean it!" roared Sam.

She reached out and wrenched the make-shift weapon out of Anime's grasp with a burst of superhuman strength. She held it high in her hand like an avenging warrior and stalked toward Anime.

"I am tired of being pushed around, tired of being threatened, and tired of being afraid, Anime!" snarled Sam.

Anime backed away, scared by the hard, resolute look on Sam's face. She tripped and fell, landing in a puddle. Sam stopped. She stood very still, breathing heavily. Rain streamed down her face. The wind doubled in strength. Powerful gusts caused the trees to bend and sway. A huge crack of thunder sounded. Sam glared down at Anime.

"I don't know why Leo wants to fire your father, Anime! Everything is not my fault! But what *you* did to my family was wrong and horrible! And you know what? You're gonna pay! Right now, you're gonna pay! 'Cause karma is a bitch and you owe her big time!" Sam howled, her words heard clearly above the roaring wind.

She drew the heavy stick back, prepared to beat Anime senseless. Deep inside her mind, Sam heard her father's voice, *"No! Don't, Sam! Don't do it! No!"*

Sam took another step forward. Anime cowered on the ground, her body pressed up against a tree, unable to move back any farther.

Thunder boomed. Lightning shot across the sky. Rain poured down. A harsh, creaking sound grew louder and louder.

"Anime, look out! Anime! ANIME!"

Chapter Fifty-Seven

A large limb snapped off the tree above Anime. It crashed to the ground, its branches covering the motionless girl. Sam froze in horror. Gray pushed through the crowd.

"Move, Sam! SAM! Move!" Gray shouted. "Now!"

Gray and a man from the crowd of bystanders picked up the end of the heavy tree limb and dragged it to one side. Gray ran back to check on Anime. She started crying.

"Ow-ow! It hurts! I think my arm's broken!" Anime cried, her face wet with tears. A large scrape on her face dripped blood.

Luckily, the main portion of the limb completely missed hitting her. Gray helped her up and gently walked her over to a stone bench underneath an awning on the main street. Anime sat down: dirty, bloody, and soaked from head to toe. She cradled her arm against her chest.

"Sam's a maniac, Gray! She tried to kill me!" Anime babbled, rocking back and forth.

Gray ran back to Sam who just stood there in the rain, dazed.

"What the hell, Sam?" Gray accused.

"What are you talking about? I didn't make a tree fall on her!" said Sam, dumbfounded by the censure in his eyes.

"Why did you push her down? Why were you screaming at her? From what I saw you were about to hit her with a stick! What's wrong with you?" Gray faced away from Anime, but Sam could see Anime smiling meanly at the two of them.

"What do you mean what's wrong with *me*?! There's nothing wrong with me! She fell down on her own, Gray! I didn't push her! Anime tried to hit *me* with the stick! She started the whole thing!"

Sam couldn't stop shaking. She felt like bursting into tears herself, but Anime already owned the drama queen crown.

"Give me a break. Do you really expect me to believe that? It's always somebody else's fault, Sam. Everyone's always out to get you. Anime's a bully, but she wouldn't go after you with a stick. I didn't see her standing over you, Sam. You weren't the one on the ground. C'mon," Gray argued.

"You weren't there, Gray! You didn't see it! Anime deserved everything she got!" Sam teetered on the edge of hysteria.

"Sam. You can't mean…" he stopped. "You know what? I think you do mean it. And I think we need to call it a day, okay? I'm going to take Anime over to the walk-in clinic in my truck. She needs to have her arm checked out and those cuts cleaned up."

"Gray! Please, you have to believe me…Anime started it!" Sam fumed. Behind Gray's back, Anime waved at Sam with her supposedly hurt arm and grinned. "She's not even that hurt! Look for yourself!"

But as soon as Gray turned, Anime cradled her arm again and pretended to sniff back tears.

"Aggghhh!" Sam groaned. She kicked the ground in frustration. Her back throbbed.

"Wow, Sam. Just, wow. You can't blame Anime for this. Look…I don't really want to go out tonight. I'll see you around," he said.

Gray walked over to Anime. He offered her his jacket. Sam watched him drape it around her shoulders. Anime took a few steps and faltered. Sam's heart broke as Gray put his arm around Anime to steady her, then kept it there as they walked slowly up the street to his truck.

Sam stood all alone: wet, confused, and angry. She forced back her tears until Gray and Anime drove away, together.

Chapter Fifty-Eight

Sam called a taxi.

"I don't want to take the stupid bus. I don't want to call Magda and have to explain what just freaking happened. I just want to go home and take a hot shower. I'm freezing!" thought Sam bitterly.

She texted Magda.

I'll be be home by four.

Magda sent a quick text back.

Okay, honey. Thanks for letting me know. Sarah's ankle is fine. Just a sprain. We're going to a matinee at the Cineplex. Be home after that.

"Whatever," thought Sam.

The taxi brought her home quickly. She didn't mind paying the thirty dollars. She even gave the driver a ten-dollar tip. Anything to be home, away from all those staring eyes.

"Jerks. If you'd seen Anime in action, you wouldn't feel sorry for her. Next time I hope Dad drops a house on her," said Sam to herself, wiping tears off her cheeks with unsteady fingers.

Her back ached. Blotchy dark purple and blue bruises bloomed where Anime had chucked her against the wall. The back of her leg also sported several different shades of blue. The oh-so-satisfied look on Anime's face when she and Gray drove by earlier still made her stomach do flip-flops of rage. Anime had flipped her the bird with her "good" hand as they passed. Of course she did it when Gray wasn't looking.

"Okay. Concentrate. Just because Anime is a boil on the butt of life doesn't mean you don't have work to do. Get a grip. You have a family to save." Sam geared up for battle, riding high on a wave of anger. She needed every bit of hostility to keep focused on ridding the world of Leo Goss.

She took the two white, monogrammed handkerchiefs out of her backpack.

"What should I use? Perfume is too much. He'd notice it right away. Flowers or pollen would make a stain or leave a mark. I need something highly allergic, but invisible. Something he won't notice right away," Sam muttered.

She racked her brain. Finally, Sam took out her phone and googled Allergies and Asthma.

"Perfumes, chemicals, pollen, animal dander…," she read. It didn't take long for the neurotransmitters in her brain to connect the dots.

"That's it! Tigger is loaded with animal dander. Plus, he's always rolling in the grass and flowers so he'll be loaded with pollen, too." Sam danced a little jig at her own cleverness.

She looked at the time. Two o'clock. Magda and Sarah wouldn't be back at Mag's house for another couple hours. She threw on jeans, a t-shirt, and a white hoodie. She wanted to see how much, if at all, the dander showed up on white material. She ran downstairs and got a gallon-sized Ziploc bag. She put both handkerchiefs inside, stuffed them in the front kangaroo pocket of her sweatshirt, and took off down the street to Magda's house.

Sam reached the back kitchen door, hoping Tigger had decided to stay in out of the rain. She fumbled in her jean's pocket for her key and let herself in.

"Tigger? Tigger?" She took off her muddy sneakers and left them on the mat in the mudroom.

She found him on the sofa in the family room, curled into the cushions. She breathed a sigh of relief. Sam inched toward him, her hand outstretched.

"Hi, sweet Tigger boo! How's my favorite ki....Ouch! Tigger!" Sam yelped. His paw shot out and scratched the top of her hand. He leaped to the floor and hopped up on Magda's recliner.

"What the...Tigger! Come on, what's your problem? That hurt! Come here, you mangy...I just want to hold you." Sam stopped moving. She eyed the cat. He had never scratched her before. She tried again.

"C'mere, baby. Let me rub your belly." Sam sat down and patted the cushion next to her. "I don't have time for this. What is the deal with you?"

Tigger looked at her. His eyes dilated, the green-gold irises swallowed up by his black pupils. He arched his back and hissed, baring his teeth. Sam stood up and walked over, intent on picking him up and putting him on her lap. If only she could pet him, surely he would calm down.

But as soon as she reached out with both hands and attempted to pick him up, he reared back and struck out again with his paw. Once, then twice. The second time he drew blood, slicing down the side of her finger with his razor-sharp claw.

"Damn it, Tigger!" Sam sucked the blood off. "I need you!"

The room grew cold. The tip of her nose felt chilly. She wondered if Magda had left the kitchen windows open.

"Jeez, Mag! It's nippy in here. Stay where you are, Tigger!" She went into the hall to check the thermostat.

"That's odd. It's at seventy-four degrees. And it's warm right here." She went back into the family room. "Now it's freezing again. What gives?"

She looked at Tigger. He puffed up, meowing and hissing.

Sam cleared her throat and asked, "Dad? Is that you?"

She caught a faint whiff of Hugo Boss, but she also smelled smoke. Like a candle burning. She spoke again.

"Is Fred with you?"

The lights flickered on and off.

"I'll take that as a yes. Can you two please stop scaring Tigger? I need to hold him so I can get all his allergy dander stuff on these handkerchiefs of Leo's. That's my plan, Dad. You two aren't helping! So, go! I'll message you later, okay?"

Tigger jumped straight up in the air, yowled, and ran under the couch. Sam felt a presence behind her. She whirled around. It left.

"Stop it, Daddy! I told you I could do this! Stop interfering!" Sam exclaimed. This didn't make any sense.

"I get why you made the tree limb fall! I get it! I lost it earlier! You didn't want me to hurt Anime in front of a bunch of people and get in trouble. Okay. Thank you. But my plan to get Leo is a good one. I can protect Sarah! Come on, Daddy! You have to let me do this! She can't move into his house!" Sam got onto her hands and knees. She peeked under the sofa. Tigger glared at her.

Sam stood up. She ran into the kitchen and got a pair of Magda's thick gardening gloves. She shoved them on her hands. Kneeling back down in front of the sofa, she stuck her arm in as far as she could and got ahold of Tigger's scruff. He yowled and spit at her.

"Take it easy, Tig," she grunted. "I'm not gonna hurt you."

She dragged him out and plopped him on the couch. Holding him down with one hand, she pulled the handkerchiefs free from her hoodie pocket with the other. Magazines and newspapers zoomed through the air. Invisible hands pulled books off the shelves and threw them on the floor.

"You're gonna make Magda think someone broke into her house!" Sam yelled, ducking as a book landed on the sofa. "Watch it! You almost hit the cat!"

It only took a minute or two to rub the handkerchiefs up and down on Tigger. When they were thoroughly covered in cat dander, she put them safely back in her sweatshirt in their

Ziploc baggy and released Tigger. He streaked out of the room and dashed up the stairs to the second floor.

"I hope he forgives me someday," she said. The room got very quiet--still cold, but quiet. Sam replaced the books on the shelves and picked up the magazines and newspapers. She took off the gloves.

"Don't do it. Don't do it. Don't do it. Don't do it. Don't do it. DON'T DO IT. DON'T DO IT. DON'T DO IT." Sam heard voices clamoring the same phrase over and over in her head, getting louder with each repetition. She clapped her hands over her ears to muffle the sound, but it didn't help.

"I have to do this! You told me you trusted me! You said you were proud of me! I can do this! I can't stop now! Stop saying this!" Sam protested. "What is your problem?!"

She marched to the kitchen, threw the gloves back in the gardening basket, and jammed her feet into her shoes. But when she tried to turn the door handle to leave, it wouldn't budge.

"No! No... no... no... no... no... No... NO!"

She pulled and pushed, trying with all her might to move it. When that failed, she beat on the door with both fists in desperation. She started yelling.

"LET ME GO! THIS WAS YOUR IDEA! WHAT ELSE AM I SUPPOSED TO DO!? WHY ARE YOU TRYING TO STOP ME?!"

"Samantha? Are you alright?" called Magda from the other side of the locked door.

She and Sarah had returned early.

Chapter Fifty-Nine

Magda rushed into the kitchen, grocery bags hanging from her arms. Her purse stuck out underneath one arm. She dropped the whole mess on the kitchen table and hurried over to Sam.

"Honey! What's going on? I heard you yelling from the driveway--what on earth?" Magda examined Sam's red, excited face.

Sam thought fast. As much as she'd like to get Fred and Dad in trouble with Magda for throwing ghostly temper tantrums, she doubted Magda would understand. As open-minded as Magda could be about talking to spirits, Sam didn't know how to explain they had just locked her in the house.

"Sorry, Mag. I came in the kitchen door because my shoes were wet and muddy from the rain. I thought I left my favorite t-shirt here, but I guess it's at home. Gray dropped me off. He had to leave to go help his dad pick up something in his truck." Sam paused, hoping Magda bought her story. "When I went to leave, the door got stuck. So I kicked it. Really hard. I think I broke my toe. It hurts pretty bad--that's why you heard all that yelling and stuff."

Magda shook her head and made a face. "Ouch! I did that once. Kicked the kitchen trash can in a fit of temper getting mad at Fred over something silly. Broke my big toe. Hurt like fire! I cried and hopped around swearing like a sailor! Do you want to ice it? First Sarah, now you."

She chuckled as she put the groceries away. Tigger, hearing

the rustle of bags, came running down the stairs and into the kitchen. He took one look at Sam and skidded to a stop. He turned and took off again.

"That's strange. He didn't look very happy with you. Must have been all the yelling," said Magda.

"Maybe." Sam tried the back door handle. The door opened right away without a problem.

"Don't you have plans with Gray tonight, Samantha? Light Tag or something?"

"Laser Tag. And no, he canceled. Something came up." A shadow passed over Sam's face, but Magda, busy making a pot of coffee, missed it.

"That's too bad. I like him, Sam. I hope to see more of him."

"Yeah. You and me both," thought Sam to herself. "Fat chance of that happening any time soon."

She just shrugged her shoulders and looked at Magda.

"I'm gonna go home, Mag. Is Sarah staying here tonight?" asked Sam, already halfway out the door.

"Yes. I called your mother to talk about this whole moving thing, but got sent straight to voicemail. Then an hour later, she texted and asked if Sarah could spend the night, and that, yes, you are moving tomorrow as planned." Magda pursed her lips. "Time to pray for a miracle, honey."

Sam looked at Magda. She put one hand into her front pocket and touched the bag of handkerchiefs.

"Maybe. Depends what you consider a miracle."

Chapter Sixty

Sam sped back to her house. She climbed the stairs to her room and locked the door. At four-thirty, her mother texted.

Leo and I will be back from the city at six for cocktails. I want you there to discuss tomorrow's move.

The whole ghostly episode at Magda's bothered Sam.

"I know he didn't have time to message me before I brained Anime, but why didn't he send me a message at Magda's? Why did he have to throw books at me and jam the door?" Sam asked herself. "How stupid and dramatic can you be?!" She pulled her phone out and sent her dad a message.

Don't ever do that again!

samantha?

Don't Samantha me...You scared me by pulling that ghost crap and filling my head with your creepy "don't do it" over and over. What gives? You said to protect Sarah--my plan will work!

okay
sorry
scared for you

I'm scared, too, Daddy. But I won't get caught. I'll burn any evidence in the fireplace. No one will even know. Just don't make it harder for me!

so brave
do it
tonight

Watch over me, okay? Keep me safe?

yes
always

Sam tossed her phone on the bed. As soon as it hit the comforter, a text came in from Michael.
How come I am the last to know?
What?
Mall fight.
Sorry.
I'm calling. Answer.
Sam rolled her eyes. The phone rang. Beyonce's *Put a Ring on It* played. She laughed. Sam had forgotten he'd changed his ring tone on her phone again.

"Hey."

"Queen! What the hell? I am your back-up. No throwing shade without me in the vicinity. Have you gone completely Poco Loco?"

"Surprise attack, Michael. No warning. She's the insane one."

"Word on media is you tried to club her to death, dropped a tree on her, broke her arm, and put a curse on her. I didn't know you could do that. Sweet."

"Whatever. She's a big fat liar and Gray believes her. He thinks I'm Public Enemy Number One. He canceled Laser Tag because he thinks I have anger issues."

"Honey, I believe you and only you. Anime hates you with a passion that is unrivaled except by my passion for Beyonce. Gray will come around. He's one of those suckers for crying females, even that jelly belly faker. You want to come over? I have more news. Been going through old yearbooks from your mom's high school and some old records from your grandfather's bank."

"Can't you tell me over the phone?"

"Nope. I want you to look at what I found. See if you draw the same conclusions I do. I don't want to start accusing people for no reason. This is dicey."

"Um...I can't tonight. Mom and Leo have to go over stuff with me. Probably about the impending nuptials. Gag. He might even have a minister downstairs. Who knows? My life is outta control."

"You got me, Queen. I'll never give up on you."

"Thanks. You may regret saying that."

"Never. Call me tomorrow. I really want to show you this stuff."

"Okay. Bye."

"Bye." Michael hung up.

Sam sat on her bed. Her mind whirred and cleared. The familiar anticipatory buzz zinged through her veins. She cracked her knuckles.

"One miracle coming up," said Sam.

****

Across town, the man stared at the latest conversation with Samantha. An unexpected anomaly. What did she mean? The brat usually ate out of the palm of his hand. So insufferably needy. Don't ever do what again? Hmm...oh well, it didn't matter. After tonight, her initiation would be complete. She would be his to instruct, his to direct. Her first kill. Like taking candy from a baby...

He lit a cigarette and inhaled deeply. In a few hours Leo would be out of the picture, his usefulness at an end. Samantha would play her part perfectly tonight in order to protect her little sister. Good. He smiled, thinking about it. She was putty in his hands--doing his dirty work. All for her precious daddy. Forbes must be rolling in his grave watching his daughter get played like an emotional violin.

And Melissa...beautiful, bewitching Melissa. Brought to her knees. Once upon a time she had looked down her elegant nose at him. So superior, so secure in her fairytale life. Such a pleasure to bring it all crashing down around her. He controlled it all...her money, her children...even her freedom.

Soon she would be back in his arms where she belonged. He had waited long enough.

Chapter Sixty-One

Sam showed up in the library promptly at six o'clock. Melissa and Leo were already present, drinks on the table in front of them. Normally, Sam loved hanging out in the library. Immense bookshelves covered the walls on either side of the huge fireplace. Brown leather wing chairs with large footstools and a long, comfortable, overstuffed couch loaded with plush cushions sat on antique carpets. The big floor to ceiling windows looked out over the side gardens, planted with the rosebushes her father had loved so much.

Tonight, the drapes were drawn cozily against the cold, dark night. A large fire burned merrily on the hearth. Sam remembered spending hours in here with her family, playing games, drinking cocoa, and eating popcorn in front of the fire while her mom read stories out loud to them. Her stomach clenched at the sight of Leo sitting in her father's chair.

Sam perched on the sofa opposite them. She had changed sweatshirts, throwing the white one in the hamper in case it had dander on it. The handkerchiefs rested against her belly in the front pocket of the new one. Sweat trickled down her back.

Leo's suit jacket lay draped on the opposite end of the couch. She could see the corner of one handkerchief sticking out from an interior pocket. The other peeked out, barely visible, over the top of his front right hand pocket.

She waited for Leo and her mother to speak first. Anxiety

made her mouth dry. Her mother seemed subdued. If anything, she seemed smaller. More beaten down.

"I guess life with Leo isn't all fun and games," Sam thought unpleasantly.

A can of Dr. Pepper and a glass of ice sat in front of her on the table. Sam opened the pop-top, poured some in the glass, and drank it down.

"The movers are coming at ten o'clock tomorrow morning. I put this house up for sale," Leo stated abruptly, watching Sam's face.

"What?! You can't sell our house! You're not even married to my mother yet...you don't have any right to do that!" Sam couldn't believe the arrogance of this man. She didn't care how many bodies he had buried, he wasn't going to sell her father's house.

"Melissa, tell your daughter not to speak to me in that tone of voice," said Leo. He took her mother's hand in his. "Explain to her exactly what we agreed upon."

"Mom?" Sam's eyes implored her mother to deny Leo's words.

"Samantha, please don't speak to Leo in that tone of voice," her mother repeated in a soft monotone. "We had an offer on the house today. An anonymous offer. For full market value. This person wants to close on Monday. We said...," she stopped.

"We said..," Leo prompted.

"We said yes," Melissa whispered, her eyes downcast.

Leo sat back with a satisfied smile. Sam seethed. She wanted to pick up her glass and hurl it at his head. Leo's phone rang.

"Yes," he barked. "One minute. If you ladies would excuse me, I'll take this out in the hall." He stood and strode out of the room, talking and gesturing.

"Mom, what were you...Mom?" Sam tried to talk to Melissa, but her mother stood up and walked out of the library without saying a word.

"Alright. It's now or never," Sam decided. "And after that choice bit of news, never is no longer an option. Take this, you rat bastard."

She pulled the two handkerchiefs out of her hoodie pocket. She plucked both unsoiled ones out of his jacket and shoved them deep in her jeans pocket. Next, she swapped out the two covered in cat dander. She could still hear Leo talking away on the phone in the hall.

On the spur of the moment she took the one from his outer pocket and rubbed it all over the cushion he had been sitting against. She replaced it quickly and returned to her seat seconds before he walked back into the room.

"Where's your mother?" Leo seemed annoyed Melissa wasn't where he had left her. He picked up his glass and went over to freshen his drink.

Sam didn't know. Frankly, she didn't care.

"Sit down, already!" she thought. She picked at a thread on her jeans, trying to act nonchalant.

"Hey! Answer me! We have reservations. I don't want to hang around here all night." Leo sat in his chair and smirked at Sam. "Excited about moving, kid? Your mother's a piece of work. Started to get a little mouthy about selling this house. I told her, like I told you last night, it's all about making Leo happy. As long as I'm happy, we'll get along just fine. She calmed down as soon as I gave her a couple of these." He reached into his pants pocket and drew out a prescription bottle. "Worked like a charm. Want one, kid? You look a little tense." He laughed and stuck it back in his pocket.

Without warning, he sneezed. Sam didn't pay attention. Her mind reeled at what he had just said.

"You DRUGGED my mother? So she would agree to sell something you have no right to sell? You dirty, rotten, no-good con," Sam spat at him.

"Yeah, I did. Piece of cake. Easy, sweetheart, or I'll grind a couple up and force 'em down your throat with pleasure. Why can't you be easy like your sexy little sister? I don't like your tone." He looked at her in disgust. Then sneezed again. He rubbed his eyes with one hand, while giving Sam a menacing look. And sneezed again.

"Get your mother. Now. I need Benadryl, fast! Damn! I'm allergic to something in here." He sneezed two more times. "Go! Why aren't you moving, you stupid brat?" His voice sounded weak. He loosened his tie and undid the top two buttons of his dress shirt.

Leo's eyes began to water, small red splotches appeared on his face. She stood up. Never taking her eyes off him, she began to inch toward the library door.

"Gimme my jacket," Leo wheezed. He cleared his throat and coughed.

Without hesitation, Sam threw his coat at him. Leo grabbed his inhaler and his handkerchief out of the interior pocket. Taking two quick puffs in succession, he mopped at his eyes with the cat hair covered cloth.

"What the hell? Oh, my God, I can't...breathe," he said, gasping for air. His eyes bugged out in alarm.

Sam watched, too scared to move. She could hear her mother's heels, clicking toward them through the foyer. Leo took two more puffs, then dropped the inhaler on the rug. He clawed at his throat. His eyes rolled back in his head. Noiselessly, he pitched forward into the coffee table. His head struck the corner. His glass shattered under the weight of his body. Blood spattered everywhere.

Melissa entered the library.

"Mom!" Sam cried. "Call 911!"

Chapter Sixty-Two

Melissa paled at the sight of Leo lying unconscious on the floor in a pool of blood. She didn't make a move toward her phone.

"Mom! Mother!"

Swearing, Sam pulled out her own phone and dialed 911. When the operator asked her to put the call on speaker phone and check if Leo was still breathing, Sam almost died right there on the spot. Using her foot, she managed to roll him onto his back. He was breathing, barely. His lips had a bluish tinge. A gash on his head bled heavily. Plus, some broken pieces of glass stuck out of his face and neck at odd angles.

"Yes," said Sam to the operator. "I think so."

"Stay on the line until the paramedics get there. It should only be a few minutes." The 911 operator spoke calmly.

"Okay."

Sam observed Leo bleeding all over the rug. The glass shards glittered dangerously. She remembered something from first aid training about not pulling objects out of puncture wounds. She knew she'd puke if she tried, anyway.

"Mom! Snap out of it! Go get some towels!" In a fog, Melissa left.

Sam hoped her mother had heard. She felt a split second of panic. The handkerchiefs! Moving quickly, she switched out the clean ones with the contaminated ones.

"That's done," Sam thought. "Oh, wait...no! The pillow!" She shoved it into a far corner of the room, tucked out of sight.

Melissa came back with some small white guest towels from the downstairs powder room. Sam gave her an exasperated look.

"Really, Mom? These are gonna be as helpful as a Q-Tip!" Sam snatched them out of her mother's hand and attempted to mop up some of the blood.

In her haste, she knocked one of the pieces of glass out of Leo's neck by accident. The wound began to gush, soaking the towels. Blood sprayed all over her jeans, her sweatshirt, even her hair. Sam held the towel in place as best she could, frightened at the amount of blood.

"Miss? The paramedics are at the door." The 911 operator voice in the room startled her.

"Mom! Open the front door!" Sam ordered. This time Melissa put on a little burst of speed, relieved help had finally arrived.

As horrible as Leo had made her existence, Sam felt sick at being the one responsible for the gory scene in the library. The reality was ten times worse than she ever imagined in her wildest revenge fantasies.

"Don't die, Leo. Just don't die," Sam begged over and over again through gritted teeth.

The paramedics came running in and took control of the situation. Sam watched them work quickly and efficiently to control the bleeding, get him on oxygen, give him a shot of epinephrine, and load him into the ambulance. It seemed no sooner had they arrived, they were back out the door with Leo in tow. Lights flashing, sirens screaming, the ambulance raced to the hospital.

Sam collapsed on the floor of the foyer, exhausted. The adrenaline buzz had left long ago, leaving her as dazed and zoned out as her mother. Melissa, on the other hand, got on her phone as soon as the ambulance pulled away. Sam had no idea who she called.

"Melissa? Melissa?!" A tall figure walked through the open front door. Sam looked up at him, exhausted and spent. He looked like a sane island in an upside-down world.

"Peter?" Melissa appeared on the other side of the foyer. In three large steps, he closed the distance between them and caught her before she fainted.

Sam looked down at her blood-stained hands.

"What have I done?" she thought miserably.

Chapter Sixty-Three

The waiting room by the Intensive Care Unit stood empty except for Melissa, Peter, and Sam. Melissa gripped a cup of black coffee in her hands, taking a sip every now and then. Sam had insisted on riding to the hospital with them. She didn't have time to change.

She surveyed her stained clothing and shuddered.

"I look like someone from The Walking Dead or Vampire High," thought Sam.

She'd scrubbed her hands and face, getting off as much of Leo's blood as possible, but Sam could still see traces under her fingernails. She looked over at Melissa and Peter sitting across from her, talking in hushed tones.

"Who knows how long he'll be in a coma, Melissa? He may be on a respirator for a while until he can breathe on his own again. They don't know how much the carbon dioxide affected his brain. Then, of course, there's the matter of his concussion. We just have to wait." Peter fell silent.

Melissa nodded, her lips a thin line.

"What caused it? Did he have some sort of a reaction to something?" Peter ran his hand through his hair. It had been a long couple of hours.

"No clue. He's obsessive about his asthma. I had no flowers, no perfumes, lotions, nothing. And it happened so quickly. One minute he seemed fine, the next...I found him on the ground, unconscious and bleeding. Madness." Melissa shifted in her seat. She kicked off her shoes and drew her legs up underneath her, trying to get comfortable. "He does make enemies on a daily basis, though. Maybe it was one of them sending a message," she offered tiredly.

"Melissa...that's inhuman. Who could possibly hate Leo this much? To want him to suffer like this? I mean, if he dies, that would be...murder." Peter's face turned livid at the thought. "He's certainly not my favorite person, but no one deserves this. If this happens to be someone's sick vendetta, then they need to be caught and punished." He dropped his face into his hands. He looked up at her and continued, his voice anguished.

"And if that's the case, you've exposed yourself and the girls to real danger by accepting his proposal. Honestly, Melissa, this is serious. You need to be very careful. I think you'd marry the devil himself if he had a large enough bank account. If Leo pulls through, you must think of the girls and how living with someone with his business connections," he looked over at Sam and lowered his voice, "his *criminal* connections will affect them. Forbes hated everything he stood for. He'd be horrified if he knew you were planning to move them into his home. When are you going to put those girls first?"

Melissa said nothing. A look of sadness crossed her delicate features and vanished as quickly as it came. She drew her leather jacket more closely around her shoulders and huddled deeper into the chair. Her gaze focused on the wall somewhere above Sam's head.

"Melissa?" Peter tried again. "Look at me! Do you think that's a possibility? That someone deliberately tried to kill him? Do you think we should get the police involved?"

Sam's heart beat faster and faster. It was going to burst right out of her chest. She swallowed, hard. Her mother remained quiet...*too* quiet. The silence dragged on until Sam thought she would go out of her mind waiting for her mother to respond.

"No. Not yet," Melissa whispered.

Sam sagged against the back of her chair like a limp noodle. Her thoughts ping-ponged around her brain: she was glad Leo wasn't dead, glad she wasn't moving anywhere tomorrow, glad her sister was safe from Leo's roaming hands, and glad her mother had enough self-preservation left to leave it alone and not involve the police...yet. Sam couldn't face that tonight. And she was really, really glad to see Michael appear in the doorway of the ICU waiting room.

Until Sam saw Detective Bateman, his dad, behind him in full uniform.

Chapter Sixty-Four

"Oh, Sam..." Michael took a good look at her. He attempted to give her a hug that didn't get near any dried blood, but it didn't work. He ended up patting her shoulder with outstretched fingertips. "Whoa...I'm sorry about what happened...girl, you need a shower, bad. Mom wanted to come, but Dad said he'd give me a ride. She gets freaky in hospitals after my grandma died last year. Not that Leo's gonna die or anything, I mean. Um...sorry."

"It's okay. Pretty gruesome, I know." Sam looked at Detective Bateman standing quietly behind his son. She was all too aware of the handkerchiefs stuffed in her pocket. She imagined the word GUILTY emblazoned in big letters across her forehead. She managed to get a few words out.

"Hi. Thank you for bringing Michael."

Detective Bateman folded her into his arms and gave her a bear hug. He stepped back and looked at her intently. "Pretty bad business, sweetheart. Are you doing okay? Your mom said you were a real trouper...calling 911, trying to stop the bleeding. You kept a cool head. I'm proud of you, honey."

"Ouch," Sam thought. "That felt worse than when Anime punched me in the gut."

She didn't trust herself to say anything. She just kind of shrugged and mumbled, "I guess." She couldn't bring herself to meet his eyes.

Detective Bateman walked over to Melissa and Peter.

"Melissa." He took both her hands in his. "So sorry to see you under these circumstances." He held his hand out to Peter. "Brandon Bateman, Michael's father." He nodded toward his son.

"Peter Ambroglia. I'm a family friend. Forbes and I worked together at NatureLight."

Peter stood and held out his hand to Detective Bateman, who shook it.

"Yes, I remember. You spoke at the service. Very nice, very heartfelt. Forbes' death hit us all pretty hard." He turned back to Melissa.

"How is Leo doing?" Detective Bateman asked kindly.

Sam noticed one of Peter's eyebrows arch at the familiar use of Leo's first name.

"I wonder if Peter knows Michael's dad is the main detective investigating Leo? Probably not," Sam thought idly. She flicked a piece of dried blood off her knee.

"He's in a coma," said Melissa in a soft monotone.

Detective Bateman studied her for a moment. She rocked back and forth slowly, her eyes fixed on the opposite wall again.

"He had an allergic reaction to something which triggered a very bad asthma attack. He's on a vent," Peter added. "We'll probably stay here a few more hours to see if there's any change." He looked tired. "Thank you for coming to get Samantha. She's been through enough tonight."

"Yes, she has. And you're welcome. Come on, Michael, Sam…" Detective Bateman put his hand gently on Sam's shoulder and guided her toward the bank of elevators.

Peter walked with them. After Detective Bateman pushed the DOWN button, Peter held out his arms to Sam. She hesitated for a moment, then rushed forward, hurtling into his arms and burying her head in his chest. She closed her eyes and pretended, just for a minute, he was her dad. As if none of this had ever happened, and she was safe in his embrace. Then she broke away, embarrassed.

"Thanks for coming when Mom called," she said, looking down at the floor.

"Your dad was one of my dearest friends, Sam. Of course I came." Peter put his hand gently under her chin and raised her head until he could see her eyes. "You can count on me."

The elevator dinged and the doors opened. Peter nodded. He stayed until the doors closed and the elevator began its descent.

"Well. This certainly has been a rough night. Peter's a good man, Sam. Your dad would be pleased he was there for you and your mom tonight." Detective Bateman watched the numbers of the floors go by.

Michael stared straight ahead. He seemed agitated. He hadn't said a word since his initial greeting to Sam.

"What's up, son? Something on your mind?" The elevator stopped. They all got off on the ground floor.

"I heard you talking on the phone, Dad, before we came over here and..." Michael stopped.

"And what?" His dad paused at the front doors of the hospital.

"Sam, I know you've had a bad night and everything, but...Dad, I heard you say Mrs. Harding may be indicted for murder!" Michael burst out. He looked upset, but resolute.

"What?!" Sam couldn't believe her ears. "What did you say?"

"Michael," his father warned.

"No, Dad! I heard you! You said she might be indicted for the murder of Sam's father and her boyfriend in high school, that Tucker guy! Don't you think Sam deserves to know?"

"Good Lord, it's only a possibility, son. Nothing is certain. Please, keep your voice down." Detective Bateman frowned.

"But if you knew it was a possibility, why didn't you question Mrs. Harding about Leo Goss? What if this wasn't an accident? What if she was involved in this, too?" Michael kept his voice down, but stubbornly insisted on following through with his line of questioning.

"Michael, shut up!" Sam hissed. "Are you crazy? You weren't even there! You have no idea what happened tonight! You can't blame my mother for this!" She faced Detective Bateman. "And indicting my mother for my father's murder is nuts...they loved each other! She would never kill him, ever! If you think he was murdered, then somewhere out there is a real murderer! And so help me, God, I will find him!" Sam worked hard to control the trembling in her voice.

"Alright, alright. Michael, Sam, please. I'm sorry you heard what you did, Michael...personally, I don't feel there is a prayer in hell of Melissa being indicted for murder, but there are those in the department pushing for it based on circumstantial evidence. And as far as Leo goes, that man has a lot of enemies. But until there is probable cause to suspect foul play, my hands are tied." He looked hard at the two of them. "Let's go."

Detective Bateman pushed through the revolving door. He walked out to the parking lot. Michael and Sam followed, ignoring each other.

For the first time in the history of their friendship, Sam felt alone.

Chapter Sixty-Five

Mrs. Bateman fussed over Sam, trying to feed her. Sam wasn't the slightest bit hungry. However, she knew Mrs. Bateman wouldn't give her a moment's peace if she didn't at least pretend to eat some of the food piled on her plate. After Sam took a few bites and pushed the rest around for a bit, Mrs. Bateman excused her and Michael from the table. Detective Bateman left for headquarters to check on a few things after speaking with Michael privately in his room.

When Michael came back downstairs, he and Sam went into the study. Michael shut the door. They stared at each other. Michael spoke first.

"I'm sorry. My timing sucked. I shouldn't have said anything about what I overheard. My dad read me the riot act for shooting my mouth off. I guess I freaked out with all the blood on you and your mother just sitting there in zombieville." Michael fell silent again.

"Yeah. Okay. Just, you know, don't accuse my mother of doing anything to Leo. 'Cause...she didn't do anything. She wasn't even in the room."

"Sam, I found something at the library today in some old newspaper articles around the time Tucker died. When your mother turned eighteen, your grandfather gave her a huge sum of money in trust. Two million dollars back in the seventies, Sam. That's like twenty million dollars today."

"So? He made his money in investment banking. Two million dollars wasn't that outrageous compared to his overall worth. He had a bazillion bucks and she was his only child." Sam defended her grandfather.

"*And* a year in Europe before going to college? Several articles rumored both gifts were her reward for staying single and unattached because he wanted to pick her husband--someone worthy of his daughter. All the society columns ate it up."

"What does that have to do with anything?" Sam asked.

"She must have know about it in advance, Sam. What a cool incentive package to make sure she didn't do anything stupid like get pregnant or run off with the wrong person. Tucker said in the yearbook he'd even die for her...maybe she killed him and collected the money. Then your grandfather dies and leaves her everything 'cause she played his game. Then fast forward to your dad. He dies and she collects more money! She dates all these rich guys like Kameron, uses their money, BOOM! Kameron ends up in the hospital. Then Leo, BAM! Even more money...that guy practically prints his own! She could be like a black widow or something!"

"No, Michael! You're wrong! You are so off base! Where's the money from my grandfather now, huh? Gone! Where's my dad's money? Tied up completely! She didn't kill anyone! I know she didn't! She couldn't!" Sam ranted. She looked at the bloodstains on her jeans and became completely unhinged.

"But I could, Michael! I could! I almost succeeded tonight and it scared the hell out of me! You want to know who put Leo Goss in a coma? I did!" said Sam angrily.

"No way! Sam, you couldn't!"

"Yes, I could! And I did! I hate him enough to kill him because he won't stop touching Sarah. He wants me out of the way so he can do what Kameron and all those other boy toys did to *me*," Sam raged. "Well, I wasn't gonna let him! He even threatened to kill me if I got in his way. I knew he had bad asthma. I covered his handkerchiefs with Tigger's fur! I put them in his pocket so he'd use them and not be able to breathe! See?!" She drew in an unsteady breath and pulled out the handkerchiefs to show him.

"Are you insane? If he dies...oh, Sam! That's premeditated murder! What the hell were you thinking? You better pray he lives, girl!" Michael paced back and forth. "We have to tell my dad, Sam. If *I* thought your mom had something to do with Leo ending up in the hospital, then whoever is pushing for an indictment is gonna think your mom did, too! What have you done?"

"Leo had something to do with my dad's death, Michael! My dad refused to touch his money. He terminated the whole *Samantha Project*. Less than a year later, my mom signs the documents, Leo's deal goes through, and they're engaged? I know it looks bad, but I swear Leo is neck deep in my dad's murder. And he's not the only one!"

"What are you talking about?"

"Kameron had the paperwork that stated each of the board members would receive extra added benefits, outlined in individual letters. Maybe someone made my mom part of their extra benefit package. Anime's father works for Goss. They paid Anime to put up the sex video in the movie theater. Leo masterminded the whole thing. He may have hired someone else to pull the trigger, but I think he wanted my Dad's company. When Dad stopped him, he had him killed. He pulled strings to empty her accounts, hold up Dad's estate, and control her completely until he got her to sign. Somehow Leo forced her into this engagement. I hate them all, Michael! Leo most of all!"

"Sam, calm down. You're not making any sense."

"I smashed up the car at NatureLight, Michael! Me! Because that jerk on the board, Don Thompson, hurt my mother! I saw him! He said he'd paid someone for her company and he was gonna get his money's worth. So I smashed his car so his keychain alarm would go off and he'd have to leave her alone. I pushed Kameron's car over the edge at the Recycling Center. I had to! I needed that folder! I pretended I was into him to get his address so I could break into his place. I made him angry by promising I would go to his condo and, uh, you know…" Sam couldn't stop the words from spilling out of her mouth.

"I knew something was different about you," said Michael slowly. "Why, Sam? Why didn't you come to me or my parents? Or Magda? We would have helped you…"

"Don't you get it, Michael? I had to fight back any way I could. Kameron is dangerous. I had to stop him. I didn't mean to hurt him, but having him out of the picture is a relief. And Leo is a brute who stops at nothing. So I stopped him, too! Maybe for good." Sam's voice throbbed with emotion.

"I can't believe you did this stuff, Sam! These are crimes! Even if you're right, you don't have enough proof, Sam. We need to take all the evidence we've gathered--the notes, the memo, everything--and bring it to my dad. He'll know what to do. He'll figure out a way to keep your family safe from Leo."

"No! You can't tell anyone, Michael! I'm not finished yet!"

"What do you mean you're not finished?"

"I need to hunt down everyone who had a part in my dad's death, Michael! They're gonna come after me if I don't get them first!"

"Do you hear yourself? Who's coming after you? How do you know someone's coming after you? This is paranoid delusionville, Queen! You *hurt* people, some seriously! You're no better than they are…I don't even recognize you. Leo could have died. He could still die! That's not justice, Sam, that's murder!"

"You don't know them, Michael. You don't know what they're capable of. I do."

"Really? Is this how you're gonna spend your life? Seeking revenge? Running from shadows? Killing people? Is this what your Dad would have wanted?"

"YES!"

"Oh, man. You've gone off the deep end. I've got to tell Dad. Just because you're out of your mind, doesn't mean I have to play by your crazytown rules. By telling me everything, you've just made me an accessory. Did you even think about that?" Michael snapped.

"Please don't get your dad involved, Michael. Give me one week. As soon as I get proof who the murderer is, we'll both go to your dad. I'll admit everything. Please?" Sam begged.

"One week, Sam. I'll give you one week to come to your senses. But if Leo dies, all bets are off. I'll have to turn you in." Michael stared at her, his face grim. "And don't do anything stupid. Promise me you won't take the law into your own hands."

"Too late. I can't promise that. If one of them comes after me or my family, I'll do what I have to do. It's all I know anymore." Sam bit her lip and tasted blood in her mouth. "It's me or them. Tell your mom I said thanks for dinner. I've gotta cruise."

Michael followed her to the front door. "Are you going back to your house or over to Magda's?"

"Home. I can't show up at Magda's looking like this. Sarah will have nightmares." She clapped her hand to her forehead with a groan. "Damn! I almost forgot! Sarah's art show is tomorrow night at the Community Center. Will you be there?"

"Yeah. I told her I would be. My parents are going, too. They wouldn't miss it. It's a big deal for Sarah. Look, just get some rest, okay? I am so worried about you. And, seriously, take a shower. Maybe burn those clothes..." He mimed giving her an air hug, then watched her go down his front steps before shutting the door.

Outside, Sam took great gulps of the cold night air. She took off jogging, intent on burning more than just her clothes. As she turned into her driveway, her phone buzzed in her pocket. She paused for breath, panting, by the mailbox. She glanced down to see who had texted. Her heart dropped like a stone.

you told

Chapter Sixty-Six

Sam paced back and forth in her bedroom, trying to make her dad understand.

What do you mean, I told?

you told michael

I didn't tell him anything important.

define
important

Nothing about you or how I know stuff. Michael thought Mom tried to kill Leo. I had to tell him it was me. He knows about the memo, the bullets, Tucker...he figured out whoever killed you also murdered this guy named Tucker at Mom's high school. Something to do with the bullets. He even thought Mom had something to do with Kameron's accident. I had to tell him the truth!

no you didn't
he's a liability
get rid of him

What?! Oh, no! Daddy, no!

yes
kill him

OMG! You can't mean that! I can't hurt Michael! I won't hurt him!

not hurt
kill
use gun

You went ghost mental on me about messing with Leo. Now you turn around and want me to murder my best friend? What does he have to do with any of this?

all of you
mortal danger
if he talks
we lose our advantage

Michael's my family, too, Dad! I promise, he won't talk!

He didn't respond. The silence made her frantic.

What if I don't? What if I can't?

if these men
find out
you know
i can't
protect you
they're coming

Sam threw the phone down. Her hands shook

uncontrollably. She couldn't do it. She couldn't. Not Michael. She didn't know what to do. The phone buzzed again. She didn't want to look. She wanted to run as far away as possible. It buzzed again. The insistent noise threatened to push her already screwed up life one more notch into the red zone. She gritted her teeth and looked.

do it for me baby

"Oh, God...," said Sam. "Stopping these creeps from hurting me or my family is one thing, but killing an innocent person like Michael is psycho. This is all my fault. I never should have opened my big mouth and told him anything."

Sam turned off her phone. She couldn't concentrate. Every inch of her brainscape threatened to drown her in emotional quicksand--all the oxygen in the room sucked out by her dad's words, *do it for me baby.*

Images of her father lying in his own blood rose in front of her. She closed her eyes but the vivid pictures remained. She sank to her knees, the pain of her father's death tearing her apart.

"I can't do it. I can't kill Michael. I can't. I have to find another way...I just have to." Sam curled up in a fetal position on the floor and wept inconsolably.

****

The grandfather clock in the foyer struck one. Sam sat up. She wanted to run all the way to Magda's house, throw herself in Mag's lap, and curl up like a child after a terrifying nightmare.

"Yeah, but I'm not a kid and this nightmare isn't anywhere near over," she thought.

Sam crawled over to her closet and dug out the scotch bottle--something to ease her despair. She undid the cap and swallowed. The familiar warmth spread through her chest, dulling her misery slightly. She refused to think about her father's request. She threw that sucker into a compartment in her mind and locked it down tight. She had work to do.

"You still have to destroy the handkerchiefs and the pillow, remember, loser?" Sam took another drink. She looked at herself in the mirrored doors of her closet and cringed.

"I need a shower. I had no idea blood could spray like that, ugh. I could have survived without knowing that...like, ever?"

In the shower, the rinse water turned red, then pink, and disappeared down the drain.

"Like Janet Leigh in Psycho. Gross," said Sam. The alcohol made her tipsy. She threw her jeans in the trash and put on a pair of pink Lanz pajamas.

"Time to do the deed," Sam announced to the empty room.

Downstairs in the library, she stirred up the embers in the fireplace and put on another log. When she had a small blaze burning, she bunched up the two handkerchiefs and laid them on top. The fire roared to life. She tossed in the throw pillow she had retrieved from the corner of the room as well. Soon nothing remained but Leo's initials. Then those vanished, too.

Sam curled in her father's armchair, bottle in hand. She watched the flames die down slowly. She took sips from the bottle every now and then. The fire warmed and comforted her, along with the alcohol. She slipped into a hypnotic trance. She felt sleepy, so sleepy.

Sam....

A gust of wind blew through the room, stirring the last of the embers in the fireplace. A faint whisper sailed in on top of it, circling Sam, asleep in the chair.

Sam....

Sam's head tipped back, her hair fanned out against her pink pajamas. She snored lightly. The bottle fell from her relaxed hand. It rolled to a stop somewhere under the sofa.

SAM...

The words were clearly audible to anyone listening. Forbes

Harding looked at his daughter, tears running down his pale, translucent face, his features etched in grief. Several moments passed, as he watched his eldest child sleep.

Oh, Sam, sweetheart...it's not me...

Chapter Sixty-Seven

Sam woke up in her bed. She didn't remember slipping between the cool sheets. A vague dream shred tickled at the edge of her memory...her dad calling her name over and over again. She seemed to remember him saying something else, too. But anytime she tried to focus on it, it hovered tantalizingly just out of reach.

"Forget it. I need to brush my teeth, big time," she said. Her mouth felt dry and sticky.

She guzzled water from the faucet until it ran down the neck of her pajamas. She stared into the mirror at her own green eyes.

"I wish I had enough guts to pack a bag and get on the next bus out of town. Leave all this insanity behind." She spit toothpaste into the sink.

"Dad couldn't possibly have meant what he said last night. Kill Michael? My Michael?" she thought incredulously. All of a sudden she remembered the awful dream about Michael dying...

"Oh my God, am I the cause of his funeral in the dream?" Sam moaned. "Dad said...oh, damn, what did he say?" She racked her brains. "Be careful. He said to be careful! But I wasn't careful...I talked! What am I supposed to do now?"

She ran into her room and opened her closet. Dropping to her knees, she tunneled through mounds of stuff on her closet floor until she reached the hatbox in the back. She took the lid off.

She looked at the gun. She hoped when it came down to the wire, she could fire the damn thing at her dad's murderer without losing her courage. The longer she stared at it, nestled on top of the scarf on the bottom, the more she knew there was no way on earth she could use it on Michael.

"I'll talk to Magda. She'll know what to do. Mag's a spirit whisperer...maybe she can reason with Dad...come up with another way to keep us all safe...including Michael!"

Sam's energy soared. Eager to go to Magda's, she shoved the hat box into the far reaches of her closet and slammed the door. She stripped off her pajamas, balled them up, and slam-dunked them into the hamper. Five minutes later, Sam ran out the door in her usual uniform of jeans, T-shirt, and sweat jacket.

Outside, she cut across lawns, dodging trash cans and people in their robes picking up the Sunday paper from the grass.

"Excuse me! Sorry! My bad!" Sam hollered as she hightailed it through the neighborhood. She zoomed down the sidewalk and up Magda's driveway. She reached the front door and turned the handle but it wouldn't open. She banged on the wood as loudly as she could yelling, "Mag! Mag! Open up! Hurry!"

"Good Lord, Samantha! It is seven o'clock in the morning! Hush your shouting, for goodness sake!" Magda appeared at the door in her bathrobe, holding a giant cup of coffee. "Get in here before you break some noise ordinance or something. It's okay, Mr. Branchley. It's just Sam. She's a little excited this morning!" Magda smiled, gave a little wave, then hustled Sam inside.

"Sam?" Sarah yawned at the top of the stairs, rubbing her sleepy eyes.

"Go back to bed, sweetie. You can sleep for another hour.

Your art show is tonight. I want you rested." Magda looked up at her.

"Hey, Sarah. Listen to Mag. Everything's okay. I just need to talk to her," said Sam.

"Okay." Sarah yawned again, stretched, and padded back down the hall. Magda and Sam refrained from speaking until they heard the door close and the latch click shut.

"Now, what's this all...oh, Sam. Oh, honey. Sshhh." Magda folded Sam into her arms. Sam shook with silent sobs, tears coursing down her cheeks.

"Mag... M-m-m-mag," she hiccuped. "He wants me to murder Michael. He wants me to shoot him. Dead. He said I had to."

"What? What are you saying? Who does? Who, Sam? Who wants you to do this? Sam? LOOK AT ME! WHO?" Magda demanded, shocked at Sam's words.

"Daddy!" Sam clutched Magda's arms. "Daddy wants me to kill him. I can hear him, Mag. I...um," Sam covered her face with her hands, then jerked them through her hair. "I've made everything worse. If Daddy's k-k-k-killer finds out I'm after him, he'll kill all of us before I can find him."

"Why? What killer? Find out from who?" Sam's incoherent babbling frightened Magda.

"Because Michael will tell his dad and the police what I've been doing. I'll lose my advantage. Daddy said the man who killed him will come after me, Mom, and Sarah if we don't get to him first. Daddy says I'm so close, Mag! I can't screw it up! But I can't hurt Michael! Oh, Mag!" Sam broke down completely.

"Samantha Harding! Listen to me! That is not your father's voice you're hearing. I know your father. He would never, ever ask you to hurt another living soul. He loves you too much to ask you to do something so awful. Sam, dead or alive, Forbes Harding would *never* ask you to murder your best friend in cold blood!" Magda grabbed Sam by the shoulders.

"But he told me so, Mag! He said do it for me, baby! He said I have to do whatever it takes to hunt down his killer," Sam cried.

"Samantha! You're sixteen! This is not your responsibility! We have an entire police force working on this...you can't possibly believe this voice you're hearing is both judge and jury?" Magda tried to reason with her.

"Mag, help me! You know I won't kill Michael! I can't! But I have to convince Dad that Michael won't say anything and I have to make sure Michael doesn't talk and I have to figure out who the murderer is or he'll kill us all!" Sam wailed.

"Sam, honey...please! You're not making sense! The stress you're under is making you talk crazy, sweetie. Look, I know life's a roller coaster these days, especially after last night. I'd snap and think I was hearing things, too." Magda wrung her hands together, distraught at Sam's confessions.

Something really bad was happening. Magda knew with every cell in her body that the spirit of Forbes Harding loved Sam and would never push her to commit murder.

But somebody or something had gotten to Samantha. Magda's insides turned to ice.

Chapter Sixty-Eight

"I am not manifesting, making this up, or hallucinating, Magda!" cried Sam. "Dad told me very clearly he wanted me to kill my best friend! And why! I don't need your psychoanalysis! I need to know why one minute he's locking me in a room to keep me from hurting someone, then telling me the next minute it's okay. I don't get it! And I don't feel any closer to solving the mystery of who killed him in the first place! Which is all I ever wanted to do!"

"Sweetheart, remember when I told you it takes a great deal of energy for a spirit to communicate with the living? Even if your dad could get a message or two across to you, it would be very difficult for him to contact you on a regular basis...." Magda trailed off, thinking about what Fred had spelled out in the coffee grounds.

"Well, what about the picture frames? What about Tigger? What about the lights going on and off?"

"All those things are individual acts that require a great deal of energetic concentration, honey. It's mostly attention-getting...letting you know they're around. Spirits don't usually give you blueprints of how to catch a killer, Sam. Clues, maybe, but not directions. Now look, if there's someone out there, you have to let the authorities know."

"Really, Mag? Let them know that my dad's ghost is warning me to be careful because the guy who murdered him is coming after me and my family? How many people believed you when you started talking to Fred? NOBODY! We all thought you were nutty as a fruitcake!" Sam reminded her.

"Fred wasn't telling me to track down criminals and go around killing people, Sam! Come on, there's a big difference and you know it. Loved ones letting us know they're okay, watching over us, sending messages or warnings, visiting us in our dreams...all of that helps us survive and get through another day on earth without them. But encouraging us to harm one another? That's just wrong and twisted and evil...hold on." Magda grabbed a pack of matches and a candle from the kitchen windowsill.

"Fred? Forbes? Are you here?" Magda lit the candle. "If you are, I need to talk to you, please." She waited.

Sam rolled her eyes. Despite her angst, she still held a grudge from yesterday. "I bet Tigger does, too," she thought.

"Fred! Forbes!" Magda commanded. "I need you. Sam needs you." She raised her hands up, leaned her head back, and closed her eyes.

The kitchen door banged open. A strong breeze blew through the house. It swirled around the two women. The candle flame held steady, flickering strong and bright. Magda and Sam faced each other over the kitchen table, mesmerized by the candle that refused to extinguish. The lights went out. The wind grew in intensity. It began with a low hum, gradually getting louder.

Sam glanced up at Magda in dismay. She tried to speak, but her words died in her throat. Petrified, she found her legs wouldn't obey her silent command to run. Sam's eyes remained riveted on the two forms on either side of Magda.

"It's just Daddy and Fred," she kept reminding herself.

In her yellow bathrobe and happy face slippers, with her unkempt hair slipping out of its scrunchie on top of her head, Magda assumed the aura of a high priestess summoning her dead. On one side of her body, shimmering in the dark, wafted the faint figure of Fred and on the other side, floated the figure of her father, equally translucent.

Both spirits held their hands out to Sam. Fred stayed by Magda, but Sam's father moved directly in front of her. Sam's heart cracked in two. He looked just the same. Forbes' sad, serious eyes met hers.

Tears rolled down her cheeks. He lifted his hand as though to wipe them away, but stopped short of actually touching her. He said something, but she didn't understand him. Sam shook her head, still unable to speak. Forbes drifted nearer, brought his head close to hers, and put his lips next to her ear.

"Peter."

Chapter Sixty-Nine

"Daddy? Daddy!" Sarah stood at the top of the stairs and fainted.

Instantly, the candle flame went out. The lights came back on. The wind died down. The ghostly shapes of Fred and Forbes vanished. Magda stretched her arms and yawned. Sam blinked and realized she could move again. She ran up to Sarah.

"Samantha? Why's the kitchen door open?" Magda yawned again and looked over at the extinguished candle. "Did you see? The candle went out. I told you...that's all they do. They're friendly, loving spirits. Not supernatural detectives."

"Sarah?" Sam squeezed her little sister's hand. "Sarah?"

Sarah opened her eyes and examined her sister's face. "Sam? I think I saw Daddy."

"I'm sure you did, baby. I'm sure you did. Sometimes he visits when we're not quite awake. Looks like you were a little more awake than usual. Did he scare you?" Sam wondered how much Sarah had seen.

"No. I don't know what happened. I saw him kiss your ear. That's all I remember."

"Well, it's your big art show today...he'd probably already been up to give you a kiss and stopped by to give me one before he took off," Sam explained. She wasn't quite sure what she had just witnessed, but obviously both Magda and Sarah were oblivious.

"Why did Dad say Peter's name?" Sam wondered to herself.

Magda walked over to the bottom of the stairs. She looked at the two of them sitting on the landing, talking in low tones. Sam had her arm wrapped around Sarah's shoulder.

"Go get dressed, Sarah. I'll fix some breakfast. We should head over to the Community Center around four this afternoon for set-up. Sam, you need to be there early so you can sit with us. It starts at seven-thirty."

"Seven," Sarah corrected. "I've got so much to do! I'm changing out one of the side panels to make it look extra scary." She scrambled up the stairs to get changed. Sam watched her disappear into the bedroom.

"Magda," Sam started, "If I say the name, Peter, who comes to mind?"

"Peter Ambroglia, of course. As a matter of fact, he called here right before you arrived. He wanted me to tell you Leo hadn't woken up. He's still in a coma, no change. Peter and your mother will be at your house this afternoon to go over some paperwork. Oh, and that your mother would see you tonight at the Art Show." Magda yawned again. "I don't know why I am so blasted tired."

"I know," thought Sam, "but I'm not saying a word."

Magda put her arm around Sam's shoulders. "Honey, I feel terrible about Leo. I would never wish ill on the man. But we did pray for a miracle and it looks like we got one. You're not moving out of your house today! Maybe his illness will slow down the whole marriage process as well, including those ridiculous plans for sending you away to school. I asked Peter to talk to your mother. Hopefully, he'll make her see this is a bad match."

Sam nodded, still confused about why her dad mentioned Peter's name and didn't say anything more about Michael. She tried to remember what her dad had said to her about Peter last summer. She could picture the conversation in her mind…he had said something really important.

"Sam, what you told me earlier is disturbing…that this voice in your head is telling you what to do…especially about, oh Lord, killing people, Sam." Magda poured herself a fresh cup of coffee.

"I get it, Magda. It just seemed so real. It must have been a horrible nightmare… I thought I really heard his voice last night. I'm sorry I frightened you. I had to tell somebody! I mean, this is Michael he's talking about!" Sam felt bad about lying to Magda, but realized Mag couldn't help her.

"This is my problem," thought Sam. "Mine and mine alone. Wait! That's it! That's what Daddy said about Peter!"

Sam, if you ever need help and you can't reach me or Mom, go to Peter. He's the most intelligent, level-headed man I know. I trust him with my life and I would trust him with yours. He'll be there for you. You won't be alone.

"Mag, you're awesome! I feel ten times better. Truly, I do. I have to go. Right now. I'll see you at seven tonight. Promise. Kiss Sarah for me." Sam ducked underneath Magda's arm and snatched a strawberry-frosted doughnut off the counter in the kitchen. She dashed out the front door, down the front steps, and took off running down the sidewalk.

"Sam, wait!"

Magda frowned, wrestling with the urge to chase after her.

"Not so fast, missy," she thought. She pulled out her phone and dialed Peter Ambroglio.

"Yes?" He answered on the first ring.

"Hi, Peter. It's Magda. I just had…"

The line went dead. Magda could only hear static. She tried again, but the call failed. And her text wouldn't go through. No matter how many times she hit Send.

"Fred? What the heck is going on!?"

Chapter Seventy

Peter lived on the other side of Beaconsfield. It took Sam a good fifteen minutes to get to his neighborhood--filled with lavish mansions, sitting on acres of manicured property. Her heart pounded. She kicked up her speed for the remaining few blocks.

"Something's not right," she thought. "It's like Dad has a multiple personality disorder or something. On one hand, he wants the impossible by asking me to kill Michael...as if he's joined forces with the legions of evil. On the other, he teams up with Fred to block my every move. Now he's bringing Peter Ambroglia into it. Well, good. Peter will know what to do. He knew Daddy better than anybody. Dad can only do so much. He must need me to get Peter's help."

By the time Sam reached Peter's front door, she had decided to tell Peter everything. She would confess it all: the Facebook messages, the gun, Don Thompson's car, Kameron, her mom's dead high school boyfriend, the missing money, the memos, Leo...everything.

"I'm dumping it all in your lap, Peter. Who am I kidding? This is way too much...I can't handle it by myself. All I wanted was to have Dad back...to feel safe and secure. Instead, I'm in over my head and drowning fast!" Sam murmured, trying to rub out a stitch in her side.

She knocked on Peter's front door. No answer. Sam remembered her father had given her both the key code and the alarm code to Peter's house last December in case she ever needed it. She pulled out her phone and looked it up on Notepad. She tapped in the four-digit code and opened the door. The alarm code's warning beeps started going off. Quickly, she disarmed the house.

"Where's Peter?" she wondered.

She called out, "Hello?"

She closed the door behind her and stepped into the foyer.

"Mr. Ambroglia? Peter? It's me, Samantha. Hello? Anybody home?"

Nobody. Frustrated, she wandered through the foyer and looked out the dining room window onto the driveway. She realized she'd been in such a hurry she didn't check for his car. Her phone buzzed. She looked and saw her mom had just sent a text.

Back at the hospital with Peter. Leo still in a coma. Staying until after lunch, then heading home. See you tonight.

"Not now!" she burst out. Sam's voice echoed through the empty rooms. "I really need to talk to you, Peter!"

"What is this? Did you have the same interior decorator?" Sam looked around and made her way through the dining room and into the kitchen. Exactly the same layout as her house--same colors, same fabrics. Back in the foyer, she peeked into the library

"Jeez, Dad. I know you two were friends and everything, but didn't this weird you out?" It was an exact replica of the library at their house. "Come on. Use some originality," Sam said in disgust.

Then again, she didn't remember her parents ever coming over here for cocktails or dinner parties. She'd heard them say in passing Peter rarely entertained.

"Maybe he will when he gets married? Who knows?" She glanced up at the painting over the fireplace. Her eyes almost fell out of her head. Shocked, Sam shook her head in dismay. "Or not! What is Daddy's painting doing here?!"

Melissa Harding stared down at her daughter, her naked

body draped provocatively over a deep blue velvet couch. Her father had commissioned the painting by an artist, now famous, in Italy during their month-long honeymoon. One of her father's prized possessions, the painting had hung in a private gallery at NatureLight, along with other pieces of art he had collected over the years.

"How did Peter get this? And why?"

Even though Sam wasn't privy to all the ins and outs of her father's will, she was pretty sure her dad left that to her mother. And she knew her mother would never have given it away. A prickle of uncertainty crawled up the back of Sam's neck.

She saw a group of paintings on the far wall. They were luminous, fantastical landscapes that breathed with a life all their own. Sam walked over and took a closer look. She swore she could hear the waves crashing and the birds singing. She read the artist's name:

Melissa Crafton

"Mom? But these are amazing...why haven't we ever seen them? Why don't we have anything like this at our house? I've never even seen a sketch of yours. I didn't know you could paint like this! This...this is magical." Sam traced her finger over her mother's signature. She turned back to the painting over the fireplace. Something didn't add up.

"This feels like a weird shrine to Mom. Which is seriously sleazy and icky."

A scraping noise at the window interrupted Sam's thoughts. Startled, she looked over but only saw a tree branch moving gently in the breeze, brushing against the window.

Sam left the library. She studied the stairs leading to the second floor. Before she spilled her guts to Peter, she wanted to learn a little bit more about him. Downstairs didn't give her a good vibe at all. A small kernel of doubt lodged in her brain. She figured a little snooping couldn't hurt.

"One quick look around and I'm so out of here," she

promised. "Hopefully the rest of the house is just old people decor and boring. No more surprises, Peter. I really need your help."

The first two rooms contained run-of-the-mill guest bedrooms. Nothing special. Sam breathed a sigh of relief. The hall bathroom was just a bathroom. Nothing stood out. No life-size nudes of her mother waiting to greet her.

"I'm just overreacting," she said to herself, chagrined. "There's probably a reasonable explanation for the portrait and paintings. I'm suspicious of everything these days. Which is only logical, I guess, when there's a killer after you. Lighten' up, girl!"

The master bedroom waited at the end of the hall on the left. She passed another door on the right. Sam assumed it was a bedroom or a home office. Feeling better, she went by it and headed for Peter's bedroom. She peeked in, then pushed open the master bedroom's door all the way.

"Wow. This is huge. Definitely bigger than Mom and Dad's bedroom. Nice fireplace," Sam commented.

She walked over to the massive dresser. Something pink and white caught her eye. She recognized an empty box of Good-N-Plenty. A ball of cement formed in her gut. Sam moved her hand cautiously toward the empty box and picked it up. Inside the top flap were written the words:

I love you, Daddy!

Sam's vision clouded, black spots danced before her eyes. The box slipped from her nerveless fingers and clattered to the hardwood floor.

"Oh no...," she choked.

Sam knew that writing. She had written those words herself before tucking the box into her father's jacket pocket. The morning he went to work. The day he died.

Dazed, she looked at the framed pictures clustered on either side of the dresser and whimpered. Her stomach turned over. Each frame held a different picture of her mother and father: at their wedding, on their honeymoon, at the beach, on a cruise, at a company picnic, and relaxing on the deck of their home. Except, in each photograph, her father's face had been cut or photoshopped out and replaced with Peter's.

She ran to the adjoining bathroom and wrenched open the door. The doughnut she had eaten rose in her throat. Sam made it just in time. She threw up violently, hanging on to both sides of the toilet. After flushing, Sam leaned against the counter weakly, her head drooping over the sink. She turned on the faucet and rinsed the sour taste from her mouth with cold water, wiping her mouth with the back of her hand.

Alarm bells clanged loud and clear in her head. Trembling, she left the bedroom. Leaning against the wall in the hallway, she spied the door to the last unchecked room slightly ajar.

Torn between getting as far away from Peter's house as possible or probing further to get to the bottom of this nightmare, Sam pulled herself together. She pushed the door open with a shaky hand. She took a deep breath, all the way down to her toes, and let it out again.

"You can do this," Sam steeled herself. "You have to do this. Just go inside and look. Nothing in there is going to hurt you. But you have to know if there's anything else." Terrified of what she might find, Sam took a tentative step into the room.

She fumbled around on the wall for the light switch.

"Come on," she muttered. "There has to be one..."

Sam found a switch and flicked it up. A single lamp in the far corner came on. When her eyes grew accustomed to the pale pool of light, she could make out a normal-sized desk and chair, along with a few file cabinets. She squinted at the walls. In the low light all she saw was plain, dark paneling. No pictures or wall hangings of any kind.

Sam walked over to one of the windows on the side of the office and pulled open the drapes. On the wall next to the window she found a small panel with two electronic push pads.

"Maybe these are more lights," she thought. Sam pressed the one on the left. She heard a soft hum. She turned back around.

The paneling on the opposite wall begin to split and slide apart, revealing another wall directly behind. The blood drained from her face. A thick rope of fear coiled and twisted in her chest. Sam stood, rooted to the spot by the monstrosity before her stunned eyes.

"Oh. My. God," she breathed.

Chapter Seventy-One

Pictures of Melissa Harding covered the wall: small ones, big ones, life-size ones. Pictures of their family, of her, of Sarah. Blown-up images of her father from the coroner's office and the medical examiner--showing Forbes' lifeless body covered in blood. The scrapbooking obscenity brought Sam to her knees. She wrapped her arms around herself to keep from shattering into a billion pieces.

Newspaper articles from Tucker's and her father's deaths, the Time magazine article about Melissa becoming the heiress to her father's banking fortune, yearbook photos of Melissa and Tucker, and corporate headshots of her grandfather, all crowded together, impaled on brightly-colored pushpins. The frightening representation of Peter's deranged obsession with Melissa spanned years.

One section had Sam's Facebook letters to her father, along with his responses. These were highlighted in yellow with handwritten notes scribbled next to them. The handwriting matched what she remembered seeing on the valentine in the locked drawer. And on the guest list in her mother's office.

"Oh, sweet Jesus, Peter killed Daddy? But he...look at this...this is sick...this is unreal," Sam stammered. She ran her fingers over the walls, talking to herself. "Sick bastard even did a timeline...when he fell in love with Mom, when he started to work for Grandpa at the bank, when he decided he hated

Tucker...when Tucker would have to die. Oh my God, when he planned to murder him--all the notes he took, how he was gonna do it. The gun he was going to use, here's a note describing how pleased...pleased?...he was to kill Tucker," Sam drew in a sharp breath. "How alive he felt afterwards. How much better he was for Mom than Tucker. He's a complete freaking psychotic headcase. I didn't even know he went to high school with Mom."

Sam looked further down the timeline. "He had a one-night stand with my mother when she came home from Europe?" She saw the note taped next to the picture of them, arm-in-arm at the airport, and read it out loud.

"She's going to be all mine. My promotion came through. I'm a manager at the bank now. Her father thinks highly of me. There's a party at their estate tonight to celebrate her return to the States. I asked to be her escort...she said YES!"

Articles raving about Melissa's success as an artist...her studies in Europe. Sketches and watercolors she had done. Sam looked at the next handwritten note, reading faster and faster, her mind reeling as she tried to take it all in.

"Last night was the pinnacle of my life. I've taken possession of her body and I WILL possess her soul. She is the most exquisite creature on earth. She will be MINE for eternity."

Pictures of her mother and Peter torn in half, then carefully taped back together were carefully placed next to her mother and father's newspaper engagement announcement outlined in black.

"This is disgusting," Sam cried. "You've been stalking my mom for years!"

She viewed pictures of her and her sister as babies...Forbes and Peter playing tennis...Forbes, Melissa, and Peter laughing at parties together. She gasped.

"The picture of our sandcastle at the beach...that's how you knew what my father said!"

The announcement of Peter's promotion to Chief

Operations Officer of Information Technologies at NatureLight, the picture of her father shaking Peter's hand as he accepted the promotion, notes from the *Samantha Project*, memos recommending Forbes bring Leo Goss on board…it was all here. Peter's treachery overwhelmed her.

Sam read the next handwritten note and stifled her anguished cry, her fist shoved against her mouth.

Time's up, Forbes. Time to go. Melissa's father disrespected my advice and my contributions to his company that earned him billions. He left it all to her. Nothing to me. I should have been his son-in-law, not you. I didn't get what was mine. I got nothing. Not even a mention in the will. I advised you to bring in Leo and you said no. I'm done. I'm tired of pretending to be grateful for your crumbs, Forbes. I'm tired of waiting for Melissa. All the power and all the control are going to the one who deserved it all in the first place. Me. The best man is going to take it all. And I mean all. Game.Set.Match.

Up on the wall, she saw a copy of her father's last memo pinned next to the newspaper articles of Forbes' death. Tears poured down Sam's cheeks as she looked at photographs of her family at the funeral and the pallbearers carrying her father's casket.

On the timeline, she saw the date her mother went into New York City last July. Underneath it, Peter had pinned a copy of the bank statement showing her mother's account at zero and a journal entry, ripped out and taped next to it:

Emptied Melissa's accounts today. Sent her a note detailing what she needed to do to keep the lights on…she'll be on her knees begging me to help her in no time…I'll make her crawl to me. I look forward to her suffering. Makes playing the hero much more enjoyable. When she tires of being the town courtesan, I'll be there to save the day. By the time I'm through with her, she'll do whatever I want. Threatening to use the girls is genius.

Little notes from Peter were scribbled on all the posts she had written to her father:

Needy little brat, do you miss your Daddy?

Time to commit a crime for daddy
She's so easy, what a loser
Kameron's getting too close to Melissa
Time to unleash the teen
She surprised me—I underestimated her
Still so needy, why can't your mother be that needy
Want daddy to be proud of you, little girl?
Leo's moving too fast—let the kid do the dirty work
Watch Michael--kid's too smart
So emotional--come to daddy, baby
Bet she'll kill her friend if I push her hard enough

She read a more recent note about the possible indictment:

Melissa isn't caving. She's actually going to follow through and marry him. Time to pin both murders on her, get Leo out of the picture permanently via the brat, get rid of the kid, give the police department fabricated evidence to put Melissa in the middle of both crime scenes, plant the matching ballistic evidence from the gun in Melissa's house, and ride in on the white horse to save the day. Melissa's next and only wedding is going to be with me. Are you ready, love?

Sam's head spun, scared stiff by Peter's brilliant life-long dedication to his lies and manipulation. He had all the evidence he needed to make his master plan work. And everyone in the town trusted him.

"I am so stupid!" she ground out. "Stupid to think I was actually talking to my dad!" Sam wiped away the angry tears that wouldn't stop leaking down her cheeks. "And needy, okay? If you want to call being heartbroken, needy, then okay! You were right about that, but you were also right when you said you underestimated me, Peter. And my real dad? You underestimated him, too." Sam fumed through her tears.

"Now that I know it's you, I will bring you down, you murdering traitor. You trained me well, Peter. Too well. I can pull the trigger and not feel a thing now that I know who you are," Sam yelled, choking back sobs. "You took everything from me, you selfish, sadistic, evil man. My father, my mother, you even dangled Sarah in front of Leo...you enjoyed it! Because you get off on making everybody your victim. I will not be your freaking victim, Peter! You don't hold all the cards anymore." Her throat ached with tears.

Her phone buzzed.

Are you ready?

Chapter Seventy-Two

"I can't message him back. He rocks at this decepticon stuff! He'll probably ping my phone and figure out I'm at his house. I can't let him know! I've gotta get out of here! NOW!" Sam realized quickly.

Paranoid, she powered down her phone and stuck it in her pocket. She hit the other electronic button on the right to shut the panels. After drawing the drapes, she retraced her steps and erased any evidence she had been there as fast as she could. Sam paused, looking at the empty candy box. Peter must have taken it from her father's trash in his office.

Sam shivered, frightened by how easily he had brainwashed her.

"Oh my God," she said. "I destroyed two cars and put two people in the hospital! He told me to jump and all I asked was how high!? And Daddy's been here the whole time, trying to stop me from falling into Peter's trap!"

Sam hurtled down the stairs, wiping her messy, tear-stained face with her sleeve. She ran to open the front door and slip out. Suddenly, she heard a car door slam in the driveway. Her hand froze, inches from the doorknob.

"Say that again? What time tomorrow morning?" She could hear Peter, slowly coming up the front walkway talking on his cell phone. He paused to look in the mailbox. He drew out the pile of mail and leafed through the assorted envelopes. He held a small bag in his hand.

"The alarm!" Sam remembered at the last minute.

Turning to the panel, she tried to remember the numbers she had used earlier. She tapped in a sequence, praying it was the right one. It beeped, letting her know she had ten seconds to hide before it armed the house.

Frantically, Sam dashed into the library and squished her thin body behind the leather sofa, hoping Peter took longer than ten seconds to get inside. The front door opened. The alarm started beeping on cue.

"Thank God!" Sam mouthed.

After Peter disarmed the system, she heard him toss his keys into a crystal dish on a side table in the entry way. The coat closet door opened. Her heart sank.

"NO! Don't stay! Don't take off your coat! Leave! Please, please make him leave!" Sam screamed silently in her head. "If he finds me here, I am dead! Dead!"

She dug her fingers into her leg, willing herself to stay still. She heard his footsteps walk toward the stairs. Sam squeezed her eyes shut and listened, hoping he would go up to the second floor. Instead, his footsteps continued past the stairs and into the library. Sweat broke out under her armpits.

"I'll have it ready by ten o'clock tomorrow morning. No, I have an engagement this evening. Melissa's youngest daughter is in an art show. I promised I would attend. Yes, Melissa's very fragile right now. Leo's prognosis doesn't look good. Indeed. A terrible tragedy. No, it doesn't affect the project; the funds are already transferred." Peter smiled. "I appreciate your concern. We'll talk in the morning."

He ended the call and walked over to the wet bar to pour himself a drink. He settled into one of the armchairs facing the fireplace and looked up at the painting of Melissa. Peter raised his glass in a toast and laughed. Sam watched him from her vantage point, fear drying the saliva in her mouth. Her stomach ached. Just being near him made her want to vomit.

"Tomorrow, my sweet Melissa, you are going to be charged with the murders of Tucker Callahan and Forbes Harding." Peter arched his eyebrow. "I can't wait to see the expression on your face when they set the bail at the impossibly high figure of ten million dollars. How will you ever scrape up that sort of scratch without the help of your good friend, Peter? You're going to look so good in my bed…" He took a long drink, swallowed, and narrowed his eyes. "My old man would be spinning in his grave to see how far I've come. That piece of white trash humiliated me at graduation by getting drunk. Called me an arrogant clown with a puff degree that didn't allow me to get my hands dirty or do an honest day's work. Said I thought I was too good for the likes of him. Well, *Dad*, I did then, and I still do. The only good thing you ever did was die. And you needed help with that, too. You're welcome." He made a low, ugly sound in his throat.

Sam's eyes widened at Peter's words.

"Did he just confess to killing his own father?" she thought, shuddering. Chills washed over her. She tried not to think about the very real possibility of dying that afternoon.

Peter looked down at his phone and tapped out a message. He grunted in frustration.

"Where the hell is that brat? That's the second time she hasn't answered."

Sam almost whimpered out loud in relief, but caught herself just in time. If she hadn't turned her phone off when she did, it would have given her away. Peter kept talking, congratulating himself.

"Having her kill that kid, Michael, is genius. She thinks she won't do it, but she's so messed up, all it'll take is a few more pushes in the right direction. She buzzed pretty high after her first taste of revenge. Didn't take much to get her to land both Kameron and Leo in the hospital. Vengeance sets up a craving, sweetheart. It's like good sex…there's no stopping once you start, you just keep coming back for more. And she gets pretty hot under the collar where baby sister is concerned."

Sam seethed with hatred.

"Hmm...someone needs to kidnap Sarah. Michael's life for Sarah's life? That ought to send Samantha screaming right over the edge and out of our lives for good." Peter contemplated this next move.

"How dare you think you can play with the lives of the people I love, you psycho! I wish I had the power to strike you dead right here and now!" Sam thought furiously. "You are not going to get away with it this time! I'm gonna go straight to the police and tell them...if I can ever escape from here!" Then Sam watched Peter open up the bag he had brought inside from the car.

"Foolish girl..telling me she was going to burn evidence and forgetting to clean up the fireplace." He pulled out a Ziploc baggy filled with ashes and tiny bits of white cloth.

He walked behind the bar and opened a safe on the wall. Peter tapped in the electronic code. The door swung open. Sam swiveled her head, trying to see inside.

"These can join the other bits of evidence left behind. Gloves, hair ties, fingerprints...teenagers just don't clean up after themselves, do they? I have enough in here to put her away for attempted murder of both Leo and Kameron. Michael's death will throw away the key for good. And perhaps, Sarah won't survive the kidnapping..." Peter rubbed his jaw thoughtfully. "Melissa and I could start fresh..."

He shut the safe, closed the cabinet, and put his glass down on the bar. He hit a number on his phone and strode out of the library. Sam could hear Peter's words as he turned and went up the staircase.

"I have another job for you."

Chapter Seventy-Three

"What was I thinking?!" Sam railed at herself for being so irresponsible and leaving behind incriminating evidence.

Peter specialized in being a smooth talker who had the good will and trust of every influential person in town. He helped raise money for numerous causes, women swooned over the highly sought after bachelor, and people asked when he planned to run for public office.

"I'm the only one, except Dad, who knows Peter's a lying, no-good, murdering snake in the grass! And Dad can't do anything about it 'cause he's dead," Sam fumed.

Peter had made sure Sam was deeply entangled in his malicious plans with no way to trace them back to him. He had boxed her in neatly.

"Who's gonna believe anything I have to say if Peter's against me? Especially when my only defense is I thought I was helping my dead father...who was communicating with me via Facebook. Puh-lease. One straightjacket, hold the padded room." Sam couldn't believe how stupid and naive she'd been. She stretched out one leg, then the other.

"Damn! Peter thought of everything," she realized, "except the possibility I might stumble into the real truth about him. If Daddy hadn't used Magda to get a message through to me, I might never have known." Sam shook her head. She had gotten closer to her nightmare's reality than she ever thought imaginable. The memory of Michael's funeral in her dream cut her to the bone.

"Thank you, Daddy," she whispered.

Sam could hear Peter moving back and forth upstairs. She didn't dare make a run for it. She knew he had to go back to her mother's in order to have Melissa sign a bunch of papers. All she had to do was wait him out.

"I hope it isn't too long. I really have to pee." Sam squirmed underneath the sofa. "If only I could turn my phone on and check the time...but, that's definitely not an option."

She wriggled out from behind the sofa, keeping one ear on the sounds upstairs. Sam didn't see a clock of any kind in the library, but she remembered a grandfather clock in the foyer. She decided to risk a peek at the time and get right back to her hiding place.

Sam glided noiselessly out of the library. The clock stood around the corner from the stairs. She could still hear the low, resonant timbre of Peter's voice as he continued his phone conversation upstairs. The few yards of marble tile she had to cross in order to see the clock face seemed like miles.

"Come on!" she urged herself, hating how nervous she felt beyond the safety of the library.

She stole across the floor in her sneakers, holding her breath. She looked up at the ornate clock face and saw it was only two-thirty. Sam felt like she had aged twenty years in the space of a few hours. She turned to head back and bumped her hip into the table by the front door.

The table wobbled back and forth. The crystal dish holding the keys slid to the very edge and started to tip onto the floor. Sam steadied the table quickly. She grabbed the dish with the end of her finger and stopped it from crashing to the floor. Still, the momentum caused the keys to fly up into the air and clatter onto the marble.

Sam didn't stop to think. She picked up the keys, threw them in the dish, and ran back to the library. She jumped behind the sofa just as Peter came thundering down the stairs.

Sam huddled against the wall, praying desperately for something, anything to save her from being discovered. She concentrated on breathing through her nose, not making a sound, intent on calming her racing heartbeat. The seconds dragged on and on. With each passing moment, the tension grew.

Peter walked through the foyer, his eyebrows drawn together in a frown. Nothing seemed out of place, everything was just how he had left it. He cocked his head and listened. He walked over to the library with slow, deliberate footsteps, paused in the doorway, and listened again. Sam held her breath, petrified.

Suddenly the temperature in the room dropped. The tree outside the library window began to move and sway, banging its branches against the glass and making scraping, rattling sounds. The lights in the library flickered on and off, adding to the confusion. The room plunged into darkness. Sam opened her eyes. She saw Peter walk away, shaking his head. She could barely hear him over the racket the tree made, but she thought she heard him mutter something about damn circuit breakers.

Within five minutes Peter had retrieved his cell phone from upstairs, seized his coat from the closet, and pocketed his keys from the dish. His phone rang.

"Hello? I'm on my way, Melissa. Sorry. Will Samantha be driving to the Community Center with us? What? Oh, she'll turn up before tonight. She knows how important the show is to Sarah. I've never seen a more devoted older sister. Hold on." Peter punched in the code on the alarm, but nothing happened. No friendly beep. Nothing. Even the backup battery failed to kick in.

Peter swore loudly. He ran back upstairs. He returned in a few minutes, breathing hard. "Yes, I'm still here. I had to go lock something up, the alarm system is on the fritz. I'll be there in a few…" He closed the front door behind him.

Sam stayed under the sofa, silent and fierce, until she was certain he wasn't coming back. When the coast was clear, she pulled herself out from under the sofa. She bent down and rubbed her legs hard trying to massage the kinks out of her tense muscles.

Thoughts rushed around her brain, crashing and ricocheting off one another like bumper cars at Playworld. Her life had just been handed back to her, albeit inside-out and upside-down. She looked up at the portrait of Melissa over the fireplace, heartsick at the suffering Peter had caused her family.

"He has to be stopped, Dad. I don't know how, but I have to try," Sam vowed. "Thanks for the assist...stick close, okay?" She blew a kiss, hoping it would reach him. A faint whiff of Hugo Boss let her know it had.

She slipped out the front door and went to find Michael.

Chapter Seventy-Four

Six streets and two neighborhoods later, Sam turned on her phone. Waiting for her were four Facebook messages from "Dad," three calls from her mother, and a text from Michael.

She ignored the calls from her mother. She didn't want to have a conversation about where she'd been all day. She sent her mother a quick text.

I'm fine. See you tonight.

The Facebook messages were all the same--just her name, over and over again.

"I can't believe you played me with your ghost crap, Peter. I hate this, but you can't have any idea I know what you're up to," she muttered. "I'll message you later."

Michael sent a straightforward text.

Need to talk.

Sam texted him back immediately.

Me too.

Where?

My house?

Meet you there in 15?

K

Sam hurried. She had so much to tell Michael. Next, she called Magda to check on Sarah. Magda picked up on the first ring.

"Hello?"

"Hey, Mag. It's me."

"Everything okay?"

"Yeah. Mag, is Sarah there?

"Yup. Been here all day putting lots of finishing touches on her project. We got some green and purple battery-operated LED lights to make it look super spooky. She's sitting right here mainlining a batch of cookies. Want to talk to her?"

"Actually, yeah. Put her on, please." Sam waited.

"Hi, Sam! You should see this! It looks so cool...Magda and I spent all afternoon adding the lights," said Sarah happily.

"Sounds awesome--I can't wait to see it! Sarah, I need you to listen to me, okay? I need you to stay close to Magda. I don't want you to go anywhere without her when you leave the house...even to use the bathroom. Don't go with *anybody*. I don't care how nice they seem or if they say Mom or I sent them or if they lost a puppy and want you to help them find it. You have to be really careful. And if somebody tries to grab you, be ready to scream, kick, or do whatever you have to do to get away. Promise?"

"Promise," said Sarah slowly, sounding nervous.

"Good girl. I'll be there tonight. Maybe you, me, and Magda can go out and get ice cream afterward. Lemme talk to Mag."

"Goodness, Sam! What did you say to her? She looks like she's seen a ghost...and not a friendly one!" said Magda.

"Sorry. I heard somebody's been trying to snatch kids in town. I didn't tell her the gory details. I just told her to stick close to you and be aware," said Sam uncomfortably.

"Oh, my! Well, alright. I'll keep a close eye on her. That's all we need. Sam, have you been having any phone trouble today? This is the first time my phone has worked since I saw you this morning!" Magda griped.

"Not that I've noticed. Gotta go, Mag. I'll see you later." Sam hung up.

A few minutes later, she walked up her driveway, wishing

she could stop and enjoy the gorgeous New England autumn afternoon. Red, yellow, and orange leaves drifted down haphazardly, covering the lawn in a patchwork quilt.

Michael waited for her by the front door. She looked at his dear, familiar face and it hit her again how close she had come to being brainwashed by a madman, pretending to be her father, into harming her best friend.

"Stay safe, Sarah," thought Sam, worried about her little sister.

She looked at Michael, eager to confide in him.

Michael held out his phone.

"Your mom and Leo killed your father."

Chapter Seventy-Five

"What? What are you talking about! She did not!" Sam looked at him in disbelief.

"Sam, Peter Ambroglia met with my father earlier today at our house in a closed door meeting. Talk about weird after what I heard yesterday. I listened outside the door. Not proud of myself, but I did. Did you know a glass really works?" Michael boasted, proud of his sleuthing skills. "Anyway, I heard your mother's name and Leo's mentioned...something about new evidence regarding your dad's death. As Peter left, I heard my dad thank him for being transparent and cooperative on behalf of NatureLight."

As soon as Sam heard Peter's name, her legs buckled. She sat down on the marble bench outside her front door. She clasped her hands together to keep them from shaking. Concerned, Michael looked at her but continued talking, his words spilling out unchecked.

"After Peter left, my mom and dad went for a walk. Again, I'm not proud of what I did...my dad would be furious...but I had to see this new evidence. Sam, I saw it with my own eyes-- a folder full of papers reinstating the *Samantha Project*, dated the day after your dad died. Her signature and Leo's are all over them. Don't you see, Sam? They planned this whole thing together! When your father wouldn't agree to funneling Leo's dirty money through the *Samantha Project*, bringing millions of drug-free, human-traffic free money back into NatureLight for the shareholders--*including* your mother and Leo--they killed him." Michael pulled up pictures of the documents on his phone. "Look for yourself."

Sam's mind raced. Magda said Peter planned on going over to her mother's to have her sign some papers. Her mother wouldn't have paid any attention to what Peter asked her to sign, especially today, after being at the hospital most of the night. Because Melissa trusted him, like everyone else in town. Peter had successfully deceived every last one of them, even her father.

"UGH!" Sam exploded in rage.

"My guess is they decided she'd play the grieving widow for a few months, move all her money and combine it with his, then start dating after a short time so it wouldn't seem odd when they got married. Cold. Just...cold. I'm sorry, Sam." Michael sat down next to her.

"It's not true, Michael! Not any of it! My mother had nothing to do with my father's death! Do you hear me? Nothing! Peter is a lying piece of scum...I just came from his house! I saw...I saw..."

Sam stopped. Her throat constricted in fear at Peter's powerful con artist skills, realizing just what she was up against. She reached out to Michael.

"Oh, God! You have to help me, Michael! We have to stop him!"

Michael jumped to his feet. He backed away from her, his hands up in front of his chest.

"Hey! Easy, chica! I know this is really bad news, but you can't go around blaming other people for what your mother did. You and I both know she's been acting strange for months, Sam. Peter's not at fault here. He's been helping. Helping! In a police investigation to find out who murdered his friend!" Michael shouted. "I found out he went to high school with your mother and he testified as a witness in defense of your mom! He worked for your grandfather's bank. He's part of your family's history. He's a good guy!" Michael stared at Sam who refused to respond.

"And what do you mean you were in Peter's house? Breaking and entering again, Sam? Damn, girl! Gonna bust up his car? More petty crime for kicks? You are one scary, out-of-control accident waiting to happen! Maybe lookin' to stick someone else in the hospital? Why don't you take all that anger and put it where it belongs...with your mother! What is wrong with you?" Michael took a deep breath. "Just chill for a minute. I know it's not the answer you wanted, but it is what it is. I don't know what happens next, 'cause I'm not even supposed to know these papers exist. I just wanted you to be prepared 'cause you've been through a lot. I didn't want you to get flattened when you heard. I wanted you to hear it from me."

Sam stared at Michael.

"I can't tell him anything," she realized numbly, "not one thing I discovered in Peter's house. It's safer he thinks I'm one dysfunctional fry short of a Happy Meal, than to expose him to any more danger."

"Well? You wanted to tell me something?" Michael sounded wary.

Sam closed her eyes and shook her head, her lips pressed together.

"Yeah. Okay. I'm gonna delete these pics. Probably a felony to have them on my phone, anyway. You know the scoop and there's no going back. Tonight's Sarah's show. Me and my family are gonna be there. Just hold it together tonight, okay? No major scenes, no accusations...we're not supposed to know *any* of this. We will deal with it when it happens." Michael gazed at her intently, worried she might start having kittens again.

Sam nodded, not trusting herself to speak. She watched him turn and walk down the driveway. This was it. At least she wasn't fighting shadows in the dark anymore. The killer finally had a face.

Her phone buzzed. All her spidey senses went on high alert. She looked at the screen.

samantha?

Yes, Daddy. I'm here.

Chapter Seventy-Six

Sam and Sarah piled out of Magda's car in the crowded Community Center parking lot. Dry leaves scudded to and fro around their feet and a giant, yellow moon hung in the sky...a picture-perfect October night.

Sarah hovered like a mother hen, giving last-minute instructions. Magda opened the back hatch of her Lexus RX 350 to retrieve Sarah's art project. It took both Sam and Sarah, one on either side, to carry it. All three trooped toward the front doors.

"Be careful of the lights, Sam!" Sarah scolded.

"Just concentrate on watching your own end...this side is doing fine. Mag, get the door, please?" Sam reassured Sarah, trying not to trip on the stairs.

Inside, a coordinator told Sarah which section of the auditorium to put her project. Once Sam and Sarah heaved it gently onto its display table, Sarah stood back, hands on hips, and surveyed it critically.

"Why are all the chairs set up? I thought it was just an art show," said Sam. "What are we saving seats for?"

"They added a talent show. Could be fun, could be painful, who knows? But we're here. Might as well enjoy ourselves," Magda answered.

Sarah ran over to say hello to some people she knew. Sam followed behind her, determined not to let her out of her sight. She kept one eye on Sarah while she glanced around at the different tables filled with art. Magda had an armload of jackets which she laid down on a row of seats before settling into a seat herself.

Sam checked her phone: no calls, no texts, no messages. She saw Michael and his parents walk in. He gave her a tentative wave. She waved back and pointed at Magda in the row of seats buried under coats. He nodded and headed that way.

"Sam! Sam!" Sarah zoomed toward her. "Mrs. Silver wants to talk to you!"

Sarah took her hand and dragged her over to the director of the talent show.

"Here's Sam, Mrs. Silver. She'll do it! I know she will!" Sarah exclaimed.

"Oh, Sam! I really need your help, honey." Mrs. Silver pushed her glasses on top of her head. "The middle school is doing highlights from the Wizard of Oz, but the girl who is supposed to sing *Somewhere Over the Rainbow* has a terrible cold. She can speak her few lines, but she can't sing a note. Do you think you could sit sort of offstage and sing it for her? You're the only one I know who could pull it off at such short notice." Mrs. Silver clasped her hands over her clipboard pleadingly.

"Oh, Sam! Daddy loved it when you sang that song. You make it sound so good! It's my friend, Katie, and she's so upset. She wants to wear her Dorothy costume and say her lines. Please?" Sarah begged.

Sam didn't know what to say. The past twenty-four hours had ripped her guts out. She looked over at the door. Peter and her mother had arrived. Her mother looked like a beautiful robot, no expression on her face. Peter had his arm around her. Sam wanted to throw up. She wanted to push his arm away from her mother and scream the truth as loudly as she could. But no one would believe her.

Sam turned toward Mrs. Silver's hopeful face. She looked at Sarah, holding her breath, eager for her big sister to save the day.

"Okay, I guess," she agreed.

"Oh, Sam! Thank you! Here's your sheet music...come over here and talk to the pianist. Don? Sam is going to sing for Katie. Just set the key with her. It'll be great. Sam, I'll come get you in the audience when it's time to go backstage." Mrs. Silver rushed off to solve some other last-minute crisis.

Afterward, Sam wandered around the big room with Sarah, looking at all the different exhibits. She kept Sarah's hand firmly in hers, only half-listening to her sister's comments. She looked across to where Michael and his parents sat with Magda, her mother, and Peter. It seemed so normal, so ordinary.

"What a joke," Sam reflected.

"Sam, stop it! You're squishing my fingers!" Sarah tugged on Sam's hand, trying to make her sister let go.

"Sorry, baby." Sam loosened her grip, but refused to drop Sarah's hand.

She purchased a bottle of water at the concession stand. Sam noticed a man standing by himself just inside the entrance doors. He looked vaguely familiar. He had a sullen, mean look on his face. He wore a green shirt with the sleeves rolled up, dirty blue jeans, and scuffed work boots. His arms were folded over his chest and his piercing eyes searched the crowd.

Instinctively, Sam stepped in front of Sarah, blocking his view of her sister. She relaxed slightly when she caught sight of Anime rush up to the man and bring him over to a table loaded with ceramics. No wonder that hostile expression had looked familiar. Anime was the spitting image of her father.

Sam groaned inwardly when she saw Gray walk in.

"At least he isn't here with Anime," she grumbled. "Not that I care who the judgmental boy hero comes with. That door is closed. Been there, done that, got the brushoff. I just didn't realize the whole world decided to be here tonight or I wouldn't have agreed to sing! Damn!" She ducked behind a wide man as Gray went past.

"Just stick a fork in me now," Sam grimaced. "I am so done with this. Ugh. You gotta mellow out, chick--it isn't about you or a stupid song...just keep Sarah safe."

The lights blinked, signaling everyone to take their seats. As Sam and Sarah went to sit down, Sam bumped into Miss Jenkins and Mr. Davies. They held hands, searching for two seats together.

"Hi, Samantha," said Miss Jenkins. "We saw your sister's artwork. She's very talented. Does she take after your mother or your father?"

"Um...Hi, Miss Jenkins. Hi, Mr. Davies. No clue," said Sam. "Excuse me, we need to go sit down." She pivoted around them, pulling Sarah with her.

The lights dimmed completely as they slid into their seats. Sarah sat tucked in between her and Michael. She tried to concentrate on the woman singing on stage, but it happened to be a really bad rendition of Patsy Cline's *Crazy* so she tuned it out.

"Cats yowling on a fence at midnight would sound better," she said out loud.

"Shh," Magda leaned over and hushed her.

Sam swiveled her head around, taking note of all the exit doors. She ran over the layout of the Community Center in her mind, trying to remember how many other doors led outside in addition to the main one.

"Samantha, stop fidgeting. You are driving me batso. Do you need to use the bathroom?" Magda said in a low voice over Sarah's head.

"No, sorry," Sam apologized. She couldn't help it. Her body vibrated with adrenaline and stress.

The next few acts were okay for local talent. They included a Beatles copy band with their own entourage of screaming girls in the front row, a four-part acapella group singing *Hallelujah*, and a magic act. After all that was over, the curtain opened on the group performing scenes from *The Wizard of Oz*.

Sam turned to Sarah who stared raptly at the stage. She elbowed Sarah gently to get her attention, then motioned for her sister to follow her. Sarah shook her head and pointed at the stage.

"I want to watch it from here, Sam," she said in a whisper.

"No, Sarah," Sam hissed urgently. "Come backstage with me. You can see it fine from there. I promise."

"No." Sarah shook her head stubbornly.

Sam hesitated. Mrs. Silver beckoned wildly. Sam didn't want to cause a scene and make Peter suspicious, but she didn't want to leave Sarah's side. Sam figured Sarah would be so engrossed in the production, she wouldn't move from her seat. Plus, Michael and Magda were there.

"But as soon as the last note of my song is done, I'm coming right back. Pronto," Sam promised herself.

From behind the curtain, Sam could see out into the audience. Sarah laughed at the Munchkins. Anime and her father sat a few rows behind them, a few seats away from Miss Jenkins and Mr. Davies. She didn't know where Gray was sitting, but she didn't want to know, either. Her mother stared off into space while Peter texted someone on his phone.

A few minutes later, Katie got up to say her lines as Dorothy. Sam could hear the congestion in Katie's hoarse voice. Sam kept her eyes glued on Sarah. The opening bars of the song played.

As Sam heard the music, feelings of pain and loss blindsided her.

"You can't break down now, you idiot," she thought and pinched herself in desperation.

Instead she poured all her longing and heartache into the words she'd sung for years. Sarah's mouth hung open, amazed. Sam looked at her mother and saw Melissa crying. Actually crying. For a minute, Sam missed her mother. Peter just looked bored.

When Sam sang the last line, she felt so miserable she closed her eyes. She held the last note, letting it float effortlessly until it faded away. Thunderous applause burst out. Startled, Sam opened her eyes and looked back out into the audience.

Her eyes fell on her sister's empty seat.

"Sarah!" Sam gasped.

Chapter Seventy-Seven

The next act, a salsa band, launched into their first number--a loud song with a driving beat. Sam leapt off the stage. She hit the ground running, tore down the aisle, and pushed through the heavy double doors. She stopped short, not sure which direction to take. She heard a sound to her left.

Turning, she saw Mr. Bloom, Anime's father, pulling Sarah, his hand covering her mouth, toward the side exit doors near the parking lot. Sarah writhed and squirmed, trying desperately to break free. She twisted and kicked her legs wildly, connecting with his left calf. Bloom grunted in pain and slammed Sarah's body into a wall until she stopped struggling. Sam ran toward them.

She had only seconds to reach him before Bloom made it to the doors and disappeared with Sarah into the night. Ahead of her loomed a large glass case with the ceremonial knives and sword that had been gifted to the town from their sister city in Japan.

Without hesitation, she picked up the fire extinguisher in the hall and smashed the case. Sam reached inside, grabbed one of the smaller blades, and ran like hell toward her sister.

Victor Bloom looked behind him when he heard the breaking glass. He saw Sam running toward him, knife in hand. He picked Sarah up, threw her over his shoulder, and pushed the door open. Sam howled in rage. She ran as fast as she could, terrified she might lose sight of him. Bloom looked at her for an instant and sneered, but stopped short when

Sarah's hand snaked out and hooked the middle door jamb, catching him off guard. He wrenched her hand down viciously, but the brief pause gave Sam time to catch up.

"Let her go!" Sam ground out. She clutched his sleeve, trying to tear his hand away from Sarah's mouth.

Bloom kicked Sam hard in the leg with the toe of his work boot, sending her flying. She scrambled back to her feet and launched herself at him, knocking both him and Sarah to the ground. Bloom cried out in pain as Sarah chomped on one of his fingers in front her mouth. He slapped her in the face with his free hand while kneeing Sam in the ribs at the same time. Sam fell, the wind knocked out of her. Bloom stood, breathing heavily, with Sarah collapsed against him, moaning.

"Stupid kid." Bloom kicked Sam in the ribs. "Give it up. You won't win. Whoever he is, he's loaded. I get paid big bucks to do what I'm told. I don't ask questions." He reached down and backhanded her across the face. "I don't know what your family did to piss him off. You might as well have targets on your backs. Good luck crying to the cops. They're on his payroll, too. Nobody'll believe you." He kicked her one more time, harder, and laughed. "Had enough, yet?"

Sarah gazed at Sam with big, frightened eyes imploring her for help. She kicked feebly, straining at Bloom's strong arm pinning her to his side.

Sam went cold with fury. Time slowed down. She tightened her fingers on the knife. Adrenaline shot through her veins, surging through her body.

She sprang forward, hurtling toward Bloom with the knife outstretched. She sliced at his thigh, but missed. She fell to her knees--the knife dropped to the floor. Sam looked up. To her horror, another man ran in from the parking lot. He wore all black with a ski mask to hide his features. Bloom handed Sarah over.

"Go!" Bloom ordered. "I'll take care of this one." The masked man vanished into the night with Sarah.

Bloom stepped away from Sam and ran toward the auditorium doors, yelling at the top of his lungs.

"What's wrong with you, kid?! What do you mean threatening me with a knife like that? You ought to be locked up! Are you nuts? Trying to stab me?!"

People poured out of the auditorium, gasping and pointing fingers. Anime ran to her father who was shouting and carrying on. He gestured at Sam and made wild accusations, one right after the other.

"You shouldn't be allowed out of your house! Came out of the bathroom and there she was, sticking a knife in my face, telling me she was gonna pay me back! For what? Is this what the world's coming to? No-good, lousy teenagers going around and terrorizing hard-working people?!" Victor Bloom pressed one hand to his heart.

"Dad!" Anime glared at Sam lying silent and crumpled on the floor.

Sam's teeth chattered in shock. Moments later, people surrounded her asking all sorts of questions. Sam stared at them. Fog shrouded her brain making it hard to think. It grew thicker with every beat of her heart.

Michael and his parents reached Sam first, followed by Magda, Melissa, and Peter. Miss Jenkins and Mr. Davies hung back, concerned and confused. Michael looked from the shattered display case to the knife on the floor next to Sam and turned to his father. Detective Bateman knelt down and spoke to her.

"Sam? Sam!" he asked urgently. "What happened, honey?"

"Sarah. He took...Sarah. She's gone," Sam whispered, her eyes locked on the detective's.

The fog surrounding her brain drew back for an instant. She looked over at her mother and Peter. Sam saw Peter staring at her, his expression unreadable.

The fog took over. Sam blacked out.

Chapter Seventy-Eight

"Samantha? Samantha? Can you hear me?" The kind, insistent voice wouldn't go away.

Sam opened her eyes.

"Why am I on the floor?" she wondered. Sam drew in a deep breath and pain shot through her body. Then she remembered.

"Sarah!" She struggled to sit up.

"Mr. Bloom had Sarah...I tried to stop him." She took a shallow breath. "He gave her to this guy in a mask...he took her! Oh, God! Oh, Sarah!" Tears rolled down Sam's face as she fought to rise.

"I didn't do anything! I just came out of the bathroom! This guy dressed all in black had a little girl over his shoulder and he disappeared out that door! I would have run after him but she," he said, pointing at Sam, "*she* stuck a knife in my face, accusing me of taking her sister! I had nothing to do with it! She blocked me...I couldn't get around her to go chase the guy! I could have stopped him if she hadn't gotten in the way!" Bloom explained self-righteously.

Anime nodded her head in agreement.

"We have to do something! We have to go after her!" said Magda. "Oh, Lord, I didn't even notice her leave the auditorium." Magda dialed 911, a frantic expression on her face. Melissa turned to Peter, clutching his arm, her eyes dilated with fear.

"Oh, Peter! My baby! We have to find her! Brandon, what do we do?" Melissa looked at Detective Bateman, terrified.

"She's gone," said Sam. "It's all my fault. I couldn't stop him." She coughed and wrapped her arms around herself.

Detective Bateman took the phone from Magda, reported the kidnapping, and called in an AMBER alert for Sarah. He turned to Melissa and Peter. Tears ran down Melissa's face.

"I have a few questions for Mr. Bloom. He may have seen or heard something that might be useful. Sam probably confused him with the actual kidnapper. I'll calm him down. He's not hurt, just badly frightened. Those ornamental blades look pretty fierce. Good thing she didn't actually make contact with that blade. It's pretty damn sharp. It would have sliced him up good. Then he'd definitely be pressing charges. And Sam needs to be taken to the ER. From the look of things, she may have a couple broken ribs." Detective Bateman took Victor Bloom by the arm and walked him over to a quiet corner. Anime followed behind.

"Holy crap, Queen! Look at you, girl! Oh man, look what he did to you! I'd keep you company at the ER, but Dad needs me to take Mom home. She's a mess about Sarah. We all are." Michael paused. "Look, I'll check on you later. Dude must have been huge, judging by the size of the footprint on your shirt." Michael sat on the ground next to Sam, careful not to bump her.

"Yeah, same size as the shoe of the guy over there, but that would be too obvious for this bunch of clueless ostriches," thought Sam. "Head in the sand much?"

"Man, you ran out of there so fast...I thought you had to go to the bathroom bad. What clued you in? You see through walls now? You must have given that guy a run for his money the way he worked you over. Smashing the case and going for the knife was total Rambo, Sam." He winced. "Too bad you missed."

"Not helpful, Michael," said Sam.

"Sorry. Dad'll get Sarah back. He'll put every guy on the force on this case. You did your best. You know, it's a good thing you held him off as long as you did...he couldn't have gotten far." Michael comforted Sam as best he could.

"Melissa? I'll take Sam to the ER if that's okay. You and Peter should be available if there's any news of Sarah." Magda sounded confident and matter-of-fact, but the wobble in her voice gave her away.

Melissa nodded, unable to speak. Her eyes gleamed bright with tears. She held on to Peter's arm like a drowning woman clinging to a life preserver.

Together, Michael and Magda helped Sam to her feet, staying on either side of her so she wouldn't fall. Peter walked Melissa over to her daughter. Melissa pressed a gentle kiss on Sam's forehead.

"I'm so sorry, Mom. I tried so hard." Sam hung her head.

Melissa attempted a smile, but failed miserably as tears flowed down her cheeks again.

"I'm sure we'll find her safe and sound. You did everything you could, Samantha." Peter laid his hand against her cheek. It was all she could do not to recoil at his touch.

Sam kept her head down, reluctant to meet his eyes in case he read the truth in them. Peter pulled Melissa close to him, his arm around her waist. "I agree with Michael. It's amazing. Almost as if you knew something was going to happen."

Sam shrugged her shoulders, fear pricking the back of her neck. Peter's voice sounded rich and comforting as always, but that didn't fool her. She almost foiled his kidnapping plan. He must be wondering what tipped her off.

"Oh, Samantha...you warned me earlier. I shouldn't have relaxed my guard. You told me you had heard of someone attempting to snatch children, but I didn't think anything about it once we were here," Magda wailed, her emotions getting the better of her.

"Really?" Peter's voice was silky smooth, but with an underlying tension that hadn't been there a few minutes ago. "Where did you hear that, Samantha? That's very serious."

"Crap. Shut up, Magda. Do. Not. Say. Another. Word," Sam thought wildly. "Now would be a good time to faint." She pretended to stumble, then gasped in pain. She refused to look at Peter.

Michael and Magda steadied her. Detective Bateman beckoned to Michael. Michael gave her pinky a sympathetic squeeze and went over to his dad.

"Okay, missy. Out to the car with you...we should have left by now." Magda bustled around Sam, getting everyone out of her way. "Peter, I'll give you and Melissa a call as soon as we know if Sam has any broken ribs, poor dear. And please, keep us posted on any news about Sarah."

Sam climbed gingerly into the front seat of Magda's car. She leaned her head back on the seat and gave a sigh of relief to be out of the same building as Peter. She felt Peter's eyes on her as he and her mother made their way to Peter's Mercedes. A wave of anger and raw grief rose in her chest. Sam choked back a sob.

Her ribs throbbed unmercifully, but losing her sister hurt so much worse. The only thing her mom and dad had ever asked her to do was keep Sarah safe. Sam closed her eyes, but she could still see Sarah's face plainly, begging Sam to save her.

She had failed.

Chapter Seventy-Nine

Sam had two bruised ribs along with multiple contusions on her torso and legs. Her eye swelled shut and boasted an ugly purple-blue color. It had taken seven stitches to close the cut on her forehead. Sam looked like the prize fighter who lost the match. The strong narcotic they gave her for the pain made her loopy-sleepy.

Magda didn't say much on the drive home from the emergency room. She would start to speak, then stop. No word yet from Melissa or Peter about Sarah. Sam doubted there would be. She doubted the police would have any luck at all. He would have had Sarah taken to a secure location within minutes of being grabbed. Sam stared out the window.

Back at Magda's house, Sam just wanted to go to bed. Magda helped her up the stairs, gave her a large ice pack, and instructed her to put it on her ribs for twenty minutes before going to sleep. She kissed Sam on the forehead.

"I'll wake you if there's any word, sweetheart." Magda looked old and worn, crushed by the devastating events. She pulled the door closed and left Sam alone.

Sam put her phone on the nightstand. She leaned back against her pillows, wadded up for maximum support, and waited for the inevitable message from Peter. In her painkiller haze, she knew he would try to use Sarah's abduction to coerce her to do what he wanted. He'd use her guilt, thinking Sam would be heartbroken and compliant in his scheming hands.

"Well, that was then, this is now," snarled Sam. "I don't intend on doing anything you say, Peter, but you're not gonna know that...are you? And I'm gonna make damn sure you don't find out. You keep thinking I'm a needy, whacked-out basket case who wants her daddy. And maybe, just maybe, if I act weak and helpless, you'll be cocky enough to let something slip, some clue I can use to find Sarah."

Right on cue, the phone buzzed. Sam bit her lip, hard, in order to shock herself awake.

"Concentrate," she muttered. "You can't afford to screw up again."

samantha

Daddy, Sarah's been kidnapped! Anime's father grabbed her! He took her and gave her to some horrible man! I couldn't see his face! I tried to stop him...oh, God, Daddy, she's gone! I have to get her back! I have to find Sarah!

i know
professionals
you're hurt

I don't care about me...I need to know if she's okay...I'll go crazy unless I know she's okay! Help me, Daddy! Help me find her!

michael

What? What about Sarah?!

eliminate him

I told you I would. I said I'd do it for you, Daddy. I'm working on a plan.

hurry

Anime's dad hurt Sarah! He smashed her into a wall!

kill michael
running out of time

?

knows too much
like father, like son
if he exposes them
you'll never get sarah back
kill michael
find sarah

I'll do it! I know I have to. I'll do whatever you say to get Sarah back! I promised I would always look out for her and I will, no matter what, Dad!

48 hours
or it will be too late

Can you see Sarah, Daddy? Can you try? It hurts so much to move. I can't think straight on these pain meds...I'm scared!

yes
alive
blindfold
tied up
dark
abandoned

Thank you! Thank God, she's still alive. I'm so tired. I can't keep my eyes open. Watch over her, Daddy. Keep her safe. Don't leave her alone.

i won't
i love you
rest

I will. Love you, too, Daddy.

Sam ended the communication and puked into her wastebasket. New levels of pain reverberated through her body. She was fully awake and ready to rumble. Her temper flared at Peter's cruelty--pushing her to get rid of Michael while holding Sarah hostage.

"Homey don't play that game any more, scumtard!" Sam wiped her mouth with the back of her hand and spit one more time into the waste basket.

She studied the message.

"Where in town is it dark and abandoned?" she wondered.

Sam remembered the old Central Station Flea Market two blocks away from the Community Center. People had shopped there for decades. The building was huge. It had housed over one hundred vendors. She and Michael used to spend weekends there just hanging out and treasure hunting. It was definitely their favorite place to blow their whole allowance. Inside were tons of booths filled with antiques, vintage toys and clothing, military supplies, and used books.

It had been sold two months ago. The vendors were given thirty days notice to pack up and clear out, devastating a whole section of the community. She vaguely remembered petitions and media coverage, but in the end it didn't matter. It remained closed for good.

"And right now it's the only place I know that's dark and abandoned! That's it! It has to be! It's the perfect place to stash her! No one would think of looking for her there! Except me," she clarified. "Luckily, Peter thinks I'm out of the way for now, passed out on painkillers."

Sam swung her legs over the side of the bed, tossed the ice pack to the floor, and jammed her feet into her sneakers. She turned off the ringer and stuck her phone in her pocket. Trying not to breathe too deeply, she crept to the door and peeked into the hall.

All the downstairs lights were off. Sam didn't see any tell-tale light shining beneath Magda's door. The pain pill must have been doing its job because Sam could move--creaking like the Tin Man--but inching steadily forward, nonetheless. She stuck the prescription bottle in her pocket next to her phone in case she needed her next dose.

"When, not if, I find Sarah tonight, I'm gonna need to be able to move," Sam planned.

She tip-toed down the carpeted stairs to the first floor. In the mudroom, she grabbed a black hoodie of Magda's and zipped it up, pulling the hood over her head. The hoodie covered her completely, all the way past her knees. Sam also took a small LED flashlight. Tigger gazed at her with unblinking eyes, not making a sound.

"I'll bring her home, Tig," Sam promised. To her surprise, Tigger got up and walked over to her. He rubbed his body against her leg and headbutted her.

"Guess all's forgiven, huh?" she whispered.

Sam unlocked the kitchen door and slipped out onto the back porch. A faint outline of the moon remained visible behind the gathering clouds. The cold night air shocked her system, but she didn't mind. It cleared her head and numbed her body--a welcome change from the pain.

"Sit tight, baby. I'm gonna find you or die trying." Sam didn't bother asking her dad for help. This one was on her, no matter what the cost.

She owed Sarah.

Chapter Eighty

Sam eased through the darkened streets as quickly as her stiff legs would go. It took twenty-five minutes to walk to the abandoned flea market on a good day. The clock in the kitchen had said midnight. She had about five or six hours of protective cover before the sun rose. Sam prayed she would find Sarah at the flea market. If her sister wasn't there, she didn't know where to look next.

Sam kept to the shadows, far away from the bright streetlights on the main road. She didn't want anyone to see her and call the cops. She couldn't take the chance of having her mother notified. She quickened her pace, ignoring her screaming ribs.

"She has to be there. She just has to…," Sam muttered.

After forty of the most excruciating minutes of her life, Sam staggered up against the side of the Community Center. She leaned against it, careful not to jar her ribs, and caught her breath. The flea market loomed large and cumbersome in the distance, a giant rust-colored metal warehouse with a corrugated tin roof and a large set of double doors on each of the four sides.

It looked sinister and foreboding rising up against the night sky. A couple of dark green dumpsters sat out front, filled to the brim with trash, broken appliances, and busted lawn furniture. The parking lot in front looked neglected, overgrown with weeds and grass.

Sam started feeling the negative effects of her walk. In the brief time she had stopped, her muscles cooled down and stiffened up. She glanced at her phone.

"No wonder," she realized.

It had been over six hours since her last dose of pain meds. Sam dug the prescription bottle out of her pocket and shook one of the pills into her hand. She stuck it in her mouth and gamely swallowed it with some spit, grimacing at the taste.

"Just work, damn it. Preferably fast." Sam straightened up, pulling away from the Community Center's brick wall. She covered the remaining two blocks at a snail's pace, limping and hobbling, talking to herself. "Superhero reject. Able to leap tall buildings...not at all. Ouch."

Sam stood across the street from the Central Station Flea Market, blending in with the dark, wide trunk of a tall oak tree. She wondered if she should do a perimeter check of the building to make sure there were no cars or people on guard duty. The moon still hid behind the thick clouds. By now her eyes had grown accustomed to the dark. She could see the main door had been chained and padlocked.

"No way I'm getting in that way," she murmured.

Sam scoped out the parking lot. Staying on the edge of the sidewalk behind the trees, she worked her way up, closer to the line of dumpsters. Getting behind them meant crossing ten feet of open space, but she had to take the chance. She had started forward when a dog barked in the distance. Then a car door slammed. Then another. The sounds came from behind the building.

She froze. A car engine started up. Soon she saw the dim glow of headlights shining, getting brighter as the car pulled around the side of the building toward the front. The car headed toward the tree where Sam stood. She tried desperately to blend in.

"Don't lose it, do not lose it. Be the tree. I am the tree. Be the tree. Be the tree, Sam." As the car came nearer, Sam sidled around the tree, keeping it between her and the car.

Her knees turned to jelly when the car pulled up--right next to the tree. Sam pressed her face into the bark, pulled her hands into the long sleeves, and tried to make herself as small as possible.

The car rolled to a stop. Slam! Slam! Footsteps headed toward the tree. They didn't turn the engine off, so she hoped whatever they had stopped for would be quick. She flattened herself as much as she could, barely breathing.

"Hurry up! I'd like to get home tonight, Vic!"

"Alright, alright! Keep your shirt on...it's not like you got jumped by that headcase. My back still hurts. Plus, the little one bites. I belted her good for the chunk she took outta my finger."

Sam's eyes widened. She recognized that voice.

"That's Bloom, Anime's father! The other one must be the masked dude," she thought. Sam heard a zipper unzipping, then the unmistakeable steady stream of pee splashing down onto the tree roots. Her body relaxed a hair in relief and disgust.

"Gross!" Sam cringed.

"Yeah, she's a little spitfire." Another zipper unzipped. They both stood there peeing. "She'll calm down after a night of being locked up all by herself. Me, I prefer them more docile. I got stuff to put in her food tomorrow morning to make her kind of stupid. Thought I'd have some fun with her to pass the time while I wait to hear what we're gonna do with her." He gave a satisfied grunt and zipped up his pants.

"Over my dead body," thought Sam.

"Whatever, Jasper." Victor Bloom zipped up and cracked his knuckles. "I'm kinda sorry the other one didn't manage to nick me with the knife. I coulda pressed charges and gotten her thrown in juvie. I had my kid get in her face yesterday. Tried to get her to go mental so Anime could press charges. Instead, a freak storm dropped a tree branch and broke it up...go figure! My instructions are to keep the heat on her until she cracks big time...powers that be want her out of the way. I did what I could...kicked the bejeezus out of her...she won't be moving any time soon. Ha!"

Sam trembled with excitement. They *did* put Sarah in the flea market, locked up in some booth all alone! She heard the men walk back to the car. One door opened and closed. The other door opened.

"C'mon, get in your stupid car and drive away, losers." Sam shifted her weight slightly.

"Did you hear that?"

"Nah...just the wind or something. You spook too easy. Get in." Jasper put his foot on the gas and revved it gently.

"I don't know...I think I'd better take a look around, just in case." Sam heard Bloom start to walk back to the tree when a large squirrel skittered down the trunk right in front of him and raced away. "Whoa! Scared the crap out of me...dumbass rodent!"

"Satisfied?! What a wuss...get in!"

The footsteps retreated from the tree. The second car door slammed. Slowly, the car pulled away and headed toward the main street.

Sam gave the tree a final hug and took a step backwards, peeling herself off the trunk. Bits of bark clung to her face, embedded in her cheeks and forehead. She stared hard at the retreating dark blue Nissan, memorizing the license plate number.

Sam wanted to stay far away from the men in that car.

Chapter Eighty-One

As soon as the taillights faded in the distance, Sam took a few steps to get her legs moving again. For the second time, she attempted to cross to the dumpsters. This time she made it. She walked around the brick building, staying close to its walls. Every set of double doors had a padlocked chain.

Disheartened and sore, Sam considered her options.

"There has to be a way inside!" Sam grumbled.

A fat raccoon waddled up the back loading dock stairs, climbed on the railing, and disappeared overhead. When the raccoon didn't come back down, Sam switched on the tiny LED flashlight and looked up. Above the loading dock roof, she saw a raccoon-sized hole in the transom window.

"This would be a good time for any dormant superpowers to activate," Sam thought hopefully. "Not sure how the hell I'm gonna get up there, and when I do, how I'm gonna fit through that hole!"

She walked over to the loading dock. A ladder leaned against the building.

"Okay. Doesn't look like anyone else is volunteering...oh, let me. I'll do it," said Sam to no one in particular. "My meds must've kicked in like Popeye's spinach 'cause I am feeling no pain. Which is a good thing. Because this is a very bad idea."

"Onward, Christian Soldiers," she murmured. She looked around to find a big rock to bash the glass in. She found a sturdy one with a sharp edge and stuck it in the front pocket of her sweat jacket. "And awa-a-a-a-ay we go!"

Sam started up the ladder, swaying slightly. She still hurt, but the big, red PAIN sign in her body seemed to be flashing far off in the distance. Her head drew level with the metal roof. An inquisitive mask eyeballed her, turned tail, and took off.

"Must have been something I said," Sam snickered and her left foot slipped off its rung. She caught herself just in time before sliding all the way back to the ground. That little mishap brought her up short. "Concentrate! You can't rescue Sarah if you break your neck, stupid!"

The next two rungs brought her butt level with the roof. She slid one cheek over gingerly, then the other one, praying the rickety roof would hold her weight. It creaked, but held. She got to her knees. She inspected the window. She took the rock's pointy end and thumped it against the edge of the hole. Big chunks of glass fell inside to the floor below. One piece wouldn't budge. She wiggled it until it came free.

"Hey, Raccoon! Who's your best friend, now, huh? Dude, you can party it up all night. Invite your friends and relations. Whatever." Sam gritted her teeth as she chipped away at another chunk of glass. She examined the hole and decided she could almost squeeze through.

"Almost. I don't need to add getting cut to ribbons to my pain resume," she thought.

Finally, Sam removed the last big piece.

"Okay. Before I drop sight unseen into this big hole of death, let's see the landing strip."

She shined the flashlight and saw an attic. It overflowed with old magazines, newspapers, books, and stuff people had long forgotten about. Directly underneath the broken window sat an old antique desk.

"Headfirst is not a good idea. I really don't want to get up close and personal with a raccoon booty," Sam decided.

She turned herself around and lowered her legs in, one at a

time, dangling them in mid-air until she felt the top of the desk with her toes. Sam dropped down and crouched on all fours on top of the big desk. She heard raccoons chirping and pitter-pattering all over the floor.

"I hope you are friendly, cartoon-y ones, not rabid, death squad ones," she called. Sam knew of a guy who used to feed cat food to some raccoons on a regular basis. When he died at home, all alone and stuck in his doorway, they ate him instead.

"So not helpful, Brain...," thought Sam, trying to lose the mental picture of raccoons dining on someone's face.

"Um...hey! Raccoon people! Chillax. I'm the one who remodeled your entry way? Just have to snag my sister. We'll be out of here before you know it. So, you do your raccoon thing and I'll do my rescue thing. Okay? We good?" Sam eased over to the edge of the desk and shined the tiny light around the room. Over twenty masks and pairs of bright, shiny black eyes stared back at her. The vendor booths were on the first floor. The stairs to the first floor were all the way across the attic. Past all the raccoons.

"Great."

Sam took her first step. Something squished under her shoe.

"Guess you guys don't clean up after yourselves, huh?" said Sam. "Ugh, this place stinks."

She hobbled across the floor in as few steps as possible and made her way down the stairs. Sam looked behind her. The masks and eyes crowded together at the top of the stairs, watching her with more than a little interest.

"That's really uncomfortable," she reprimanded them nervously. "I don't want to hurt your feelings or anything, but I think our relationship needs some space."

She turned the doorknob, ready to power through and barricade the door against her bushy-tailed besties, but it wouldn't budge! Someone had locked it.

"Really?!" Sam cried.

Chapter Eighty-Two

"Crap-freakin'-tastic."

In the dim glow of her flashlight, she saw the raccoons slowly advance, sniffing the air with interest. Sweat rolled down between her shoulder blades.

"I am not your super-sized Happy Meal!" she exclaimed, stamping her foot on the bottom stair, trying to frighten them back.

She trained the flashlight on the door to see how flimsy it was, if at all. No such luck--someone had installed a code-enforced metal fire door.

"I don't have a prayer in hell of kicking through that," Sam realized.

She searched frantically for any weakness. A glint in the flashlight beam at the top of the door frame caught her eye. She reached up and ran the palm of her hand along the metal. Her fingers touched a key-shaped bump underneath a strip of masking tape.

"Jackpot, baby! Now we're talking! Open sesame...oops!" Sam fumbled the key and dropped it on the floor. She picked it up and glanced over her shoulder again at her curious audience.

"No time like the present--let's go, let's go, let's GO!"

Sam jammed the key into the lock and turned the knob. The door swung open. She hurried through and closed it firmly behind her. Panting, she stood in the center of the main floor and shined her flashlight in all directions. On the left, she saw a large, football stadium-sized area divided into individual shops with doors that could be shut and padlocked. On the right, she saw a huge, open area.

She started to call Sarah's name, but stopped.

"Just in case...," she thought.

Sam slid forward warily and turned down the long aisle to her left. Faint, muffled sobs came from the back of the building.

"Yes!" Sam's heart leaped.

Shining the tiny light down the long corridor, she limped toward the sound. She wound her way around empty boxes, heaps of trash, and leftover piles of boards and shelving. Sam knocked over a plastic bookshelf. The sobbing stopped.

"Who's there?" Sarah whimpered. "I'm sorry. I'll st-st-stop crying, please don't hit me again. Please, I promise. I won't make any more noise."

Sam's heart hurt when she heard the fear in Sarah's voice. She vowed she'd make Bloom and Jasper pay for this.

"Hanging upside down in a giant nest of pit vipers would be too good for them," she vowed.

"Sarah, baby, it's me, Sam. I'm going to get you out of here." Sam went to the door of the shop and beamed the light on Sarah.

Sarah lay curled on her side on the floor, her hands and feet bound. A blindfold covered her eyes. Her clothes were torn and disheveled.

"Sam? Oh, Sam! Get me out of here before they come back! Oh, Sam! I heard rats! There's rats in here!" Sarah cried hysterically.

"Easy, Boo. No rats, just raccoons. Lots of them--having a party in the attic. Other than getting smacked around and being scared, are you okay?"

"Yeah. I am. I can smell Daddy. He's here, but he can't do anything. I want to get out of here! Do you think you can get me out of here, Sam?" Sarah begged, in a shaky, high-pitched voice.

"Yeah. I don't *think* I can. I *know* I can. Just let me figure this out." Sam looked at the bike chain and lock securing the door. "Geez. These jerks were really big spenders. This is like from the Dollar Store." Still, she had nothing to cut through any chain, no matter how small and cheap. She examined the lock hinge.

"Hang on. I'm not going anywhere. I just want to look and see if there's anything here I can use."

She rummaged through the pile of junk and wood, shoving it out of her way. At the bottom she found an old tool chest drawer with a couple of screwdrivers and a hammer with half a handle.

"Perfect!" Sam exclaimed.

Using the Phillips head screwdriver, she removed the six screws holding the entire hinge in place. Sticking the screws in her back pocket, Sam laid the whole shebang on the ground and swung open the door. She reached Sarah in two steps and ripped off her blindfold.

"Sam! You did it!" Sarah started to cry.

"No waterworks, kiddo. We still have to get you untied. Plus, we need to get past the raccoon guard, get out of the building, and hide you somewhere safe. Then we can cry!"

"What do you mean, hide me? I wanna see Mom! I wanna go home!" Sarah sat up and squirmed, trying to free her hands.

"Can't do that, not yet anyway. I don't want to scare you too bad, but the guy behind your kidnapping is the same guy who killed Daddy. You, me, and Mom are all pawns in a big, nasty chess game." Sam dug out her pocket knife and cut through the zip ties binding Sarah's hands and feet together. "He figured he could blackmail me into doing bad things for him by taking you: Advantage him. Never once, though, did he think I'd figure out his plan, find you, and take you back: Advantage me."

"Oh, Sam...who is he?" Sarah breathed fearfully.

"Can't tell you, sugar booger, for your own protection and mine. He can't know I'm the one who freed you or I'll never psych him out. Look, you've trusted me all along since Daddy died, right?" Sam put her face close to her sister's.

"Yes," Sarah whispered.

"Didn't I find you when nobody else could?"

"Yes."

"Okay, then. The dude who's behind this is uber powerful. He's ruthless, but if I told you who he was--heck, if I told *anybody* who he was--nobody would believe me. No.One. He's *that* good. I have to beat him at his own sick game," said Sam. "If I make it seem like you disappeared into thin air, then he will start looking over his shoulder and wondering what happened. By hiding you, even from Mom and the authorities, I'll have removed one of his chess pieces. It'll drive him bonkers." Sam pulled Sarah to her feet.

"Okay, baboo. Stretch your hands, stretch your arms, and stretch those legs of yours. Get the blood flowing. We still have a long, couple of hours in front of us." Sam took Sarah's hands in hers and rubbed them briskly. "You good? I'm going to leave all this binding stuff on the floor." She held Sarah's hand and walked her out of the booth. "I'll put the lock back on and make it look like nobody was ever here. You just did a Houdini and vanished. That'll give 'em something to chew on."

Sam bent down to pick up the screwdriver but in doing so, her ribs stabbed with pain. She wrapped her arms around herself and waited for the worst to pass.

"Sam! You're hurt! Oh my gosh, you're really hurt!"

"Mmmhmm. You should have seen the other guy," Sam cracked weakly. "Don't worry, I'll live. Even more important, you're gonna live. Now let's get the hell out of here, huh?" She lifted the padlock, complete with bike lock and chain still intact, back in place.

Sarah held the flashlight while Sam tightened the screws. When she finished, Sam threw the screwdriver back in the rusty drawer. She buried it all back underneath the junk.

"Alright. Here's Plan A. Michael's dad is going to have cops all over our property going through your room, getting stuff for dogs to sniff, etc. Our house is off-limits until they're gone. So, what I'm going to do is bring you back to Magda's house with me. Nobody will think to check there because I'm there," Sam strategized. "In the morning, I'll go down and check the status. When I'm sure our house is cool, we're going to sneak you home and hide you right under their noses in your own room," Sam finished triumphantly.

"What's Plan B?" asked Sarah.

"No clue, chickaboo. I'll deal with that if and when we need a Plan B." Sam realized they needed to leave, now. The painkiller barely masked the pain. Moving in any direction hurt. She leaned on Sarah as they made their way back down the long corridor toward the attic door.

"Sarah, don't let go of my hand. When I open this door, there might be nothing or there might be an army of raccoons pouring down the steps. Don't freak out. Either way, I've got you and we're going to get through this."

Sam really didn't want to go back in the attic. Not only did she dread the raccoons, but she didn't know about getting up and out the window. She knew Sarah could do it, but Sam was afraid it was beyond her own capability. She was losing energy quickly.

"Dad? I've got Sarah. If you, and maybe Fred, are hanging out, do you think you could handle the raccoons? Maybe put some sort of whammo on them so they don't come near me and Sarah so we can get to the desk and get out that window and get out of here and…" Her voice dropped to a whisper. "I don't feel so good."

Sam didn't really expect an answer. When she did catch a comforting whiff of Hugo Boss, she turned her face in its direction, stumbled, and fell on her hands and knees.

"Sam! What's wrong? Sam! Can you hear me?" The

younger girl grabbed the flashlight and shined it in Sam's face. "Oh, no! Please, Sam! Sam?" Sam looked up at her sister and tried to speak, but nothing came out. Her vision clouded, then dimmed.

Sam collapsed.

Chapter Eighty-Three

"*Samantha. Listen to me. Samantha, honey... It's Daddy. Come on, you're stronger than this. You can do this. You can't be found here. Wake up, baby."*

Sam opened her eyes. Forbes stood over her, his chest bloody like in the pictures at Peter's house. She could see people gathered at the gravesite nearby. This time Michael stood with the mourners. Sam looked at her father, puzzled.

"*It's you, Sam...and Sarah. And your mother. When she found out you two were gone, she killed herself. She had nothing left to hold on to. If you don't wake up...if you don't fight, baby, it's over. This is still only a possibility, like the other dream. You can change it. You don't have to let this timeline play out. Don't let Peter take down our whole family."*

Sam lay on the ground, weak and exhausted. A young man walked over and joined her dad--a well-built, high school football player in a Beaconsfield High jersey. Sam recognized him from his yearbook picture. Tucker Callahan, her mom's high school boyfriend.

"*Hey there, Sam. I loved your mother. Peter shot me in cold blood, the same way he killed your father. You will never be out of danger from this man. He will stop at nothing until your mother is his. And she never will be. So he will do everything in his power to destroy her so no one else can have her. You are the only one who knows the truth about him. You can stop him. You have to stop him. Come on, kid. It's the end of the 4th quarter. Time to get some skin in* the game."

Forbes knelt next to his daughter and took her hands in his. His firm, tender look pierced her heart.

"I don't want to go back, Daddy. I don't want to leave you." Sam looked up at her dad, basking in his love.

"I know, sweetheart, but you have to. We can help you, Samantha, but time is running out. Our energy is limited. When you wake up, we can give you exactly one minute. After that, it will be too late."

"No, Daddy! I can't! It's too much. Don't make me go!"

"It's not up to me. I love you so much! You can do this! Do it for Sarah. Do it for your mom. Give her a chance, Sam, to show you how much she loves you. She always has. Come on, my sweet Woodstock, show 'em how tough you really are! Give 'em hell! NOW!"

****

Sam's eyes flew open. She turned her head and saw the electric garage door to their right begin to creak and rise.

"Sarah?"

"Right here, Sam. What's happening? Are you okay?"

"Dad gave us one minute, Sarah. We have to get under that door and get out of here or we're toast. You with me?"

"Y-y-y-esss."

"Good. Give me your hand!"

With all the strength she could muster, Sam rolled up to her knees. Grabbing Sarah's body with both arms, she hauled herself up, ignoring the screaming pain in her side. Together, they raced toward the door. When it had risen about a foot, the girls dove down onto the old hardwood flooring and rolled underneath. They stopped a few feet from the dumpsters.

Sam and Sarah moved close together. A few seconds later, the electric garage door crashed back down.

"Sam?"

"Yeah?"

"Dad did that?"

"Yeah. He had help, but, yeah."

"Did you see him?"

"Yeah."

"Is he okay? I mean, being dead and everything."

Sam made a face in the dark.

"Yeah, short stuff. Dad's okay. And he's doing his best to make sure we stay alive. So...are you ready to move out?"

"Yes. Can you walk to Magda's? You scared me when you passed out for those few seconds."

"Seemed like an eternity to me. Yeah. I'm good. I feel like an alien stuck in a human suit. Making my arms and legs work together is trippy, but other than that, I'm good. Let's boogie."

Sam put her arm around Sarah, relishing the feel of her sister safely by her side. Her own body pulsed with pain again, but they needed to move. They only had a couple of hours before the sun rose. By that time, Sam wanted Sarah hidden away in Magda's house.

The two sisters made their way toward Magda's cautiously, their senses on high alert. Every car in the distance could be one looking for Sarah. Now that Sam had her sister back, she didn't trust anyone.

At least not anyone living.

Chapter Eighty-Four

Sam and Sarah staggered inside the house. Tigger met them at the kitchen door. He marched ahead of them, tail flag high, as they crept upstairs. When Sam and Sarah were safely back in the bedroom, Tigger jumped on the bed and settled in.

Sam hurt all over. She locked the door, then turned on her phone and checked for messages, grateful to see none had come in. She looked at the time.

"Ow! No wonder...," Sam moaned. She'd missed her next scheduled pain medicine. "C'mon, Sarah. Into bed. When you wake up in the morning, do not, under any circumstances, come downstairs or make the slightest peep. Understand?"

Sarah nodded. She stretched out on the bed, fully clothed and half-asleep. Sam covered her with a blanket. Sarah snored gently.

Sam took her next dose of meds, tossing it back with an inch of water from a glass she found on the dresser. She offered a silent prayer of thanks to her dad, gingerly curled her aching body around Sarah, and descended into a dreamless sleep.

****

Sam reached for Sarah's hand as soon as she woke up the next morning. With her other hand, she looked at her phone.

"It's already eleven o'clock?" she thought groggily and yawned. "I guess Peter knows Sarah's not at the flea market by now. My fly escaped your web, creep. And I'm not waving the white flag any time soon. Wonder what you're gonna do about it, hmm?" Sam made no attempt to move from under the covers. She relished the rare moment of peace after yesterday.

Her mind flashed forward to the day ahead. She needed to get Sarah back to their house, without alerting anyone, and hide her. She didn't want to, but she had to get up. Sam eased out from under the covers, swearing as her body protested. At least she didn't have to get dressed. She and Sarah still wore yesterday's clothes.

"Okay, this stinks. It's gonna take me a year to get downstairs," Sam complained. Taking shallow breaths, she tottered toward the door. Tigger raised his head and looked at her, then snuggled back in next to Sarah.

"I feel like I got run over by a truck," Sam groaned softly. "My parts don't fit together like they used to...jeez."

She closed the door and contemplated the carpeted stairs.

"Come on, champeen," she muttered. "You can do this. They take worse hits in WWE. Don't be such a baby."

Sam clutched the railing. She took the stairs one at a time, cursing Victor Bloom and Peter with each step.

"Mag?" she called.

"Oh, Samantha! Honey! You didn't have to come downstairs! I would have brought you breakfast, sweetheart! Oh, my sweet Lord, look at your beautiful face! And your poor ribs. Let me help you. Here, come sit down." Magda rushed over to Samantha at the bottom of the stairs.

"What's the news on Sarah, Mag? Did they find her? Who's out looking? Have they checked our house? Where are Mom and Peter? Did Michael's dad call?" Sam kept up a steady stream of questions, keeping a close eye on Magda's face.

Magda dropped heavily into the chair next to Sam at the kitchen table. Her hands shook as she raised her coffee mug and took a sip. Magda looked at Sam and her eyes filled with tears.

"No word yet. Your mother and Peter were at your house all night with Michael's dad waiting for any leads. The detectives took some of Sarah's things for the police dogs to sniff." Magda's voice trembled. "Let me get you an ice pack for your ribs, Sam. And one for your face. I didn't realize how many stitches you had over your eye. It looks so much worse this morning."

"I don't care about my face, Magda. I just want to find Sarah!" Sam slumped in her seat, masking her relief that the detectives had left her house.

Magda hastened over to the freezer and retrieved two ice packs from its depths, one large and one small. She handed them to Sam. The icy coldness against her injuries made Sam inhale sharply, causing a brief stab of pain. She gave a muffled cry.

"Goodness! You are not going anywhere today. You need to ice, rest, take your medicine, and rest some more," Magda clucked, looking pretty beat up herself. "Peter stopped by early this morning around six-thirty to check on you. He wanted to know how you were doing and if you were having trouble sleeping from the pain. I told him you hadn't moved a muscle all night. Slept like a baby. The pain meds the doctor gave you did the trick. Gave you good, restorative sleep."

Sam's hackles rose. Peter's goons probably discovered Sarah missing early this morning and Peter went to Magda's to check on her! He must have suspected she had something to do with Sarah's disappearance.

"Good thing Magda takes a sleeping pill every night since Fred died," thought Sam. "She'd swear on a Bible we both were sound asleep."

"How long was Peter here? I didn't hear anything," asked Sam.

"Oh, just a few minutes. As soon as he heard you were alright and still sleeping soundly, he left rather quickly. I'd just put coffee on and he didn't even stay to have a cup!" said

Magda.

"Probably needed to get back to Mom." Sam adjusted her ice packs, her heart beating faster.

"I guess. I don't blame him," Magda nodded.

"Probably burning up the town trying to fix this particular loose end and wondering who's on to him," Sam thought triumphantly.

"Are you hungry, dear? I can fix some eggs if you'd like. I made a nice cinnamon coffeecake. You really need to eat something, Samantha. And what about your medicine? It may be time to take your next dose. I'll just run upstairs and get it for you."

"Wait! No! Don't go up there!" Sam cried out. She tried to leap out of her seat, but gasped in pain. She shrank back, holding the ice pack at her side.

"Sam! What are you doing?" Magda stopped and hurried back to Sam.

"Um...sorry! I just wanted to tell you I already took it right before I came downstairs. You don't need to get it," Sam lied. "And I'm really hungry. Could I have those eggs? Please?"

Magda frowned, then gave Sam's shoulder a gentle squeeze, taking care not to jostle her too much. "Okay. Eggs coming right up!"

Magda's phone rang. She answered it right away.

"Hello, Peter. Any news? What? Oh, no. No! They can't!" Magda gripped the back of her chair.

Sam knew it wasn't about Sarah. But she also knew Peter was capable of anything. She sat up, intent on the conversation, her fingers holding the edge of the ice pack tightly.

"Where are you now? Yes, I'll let her know. This is terrible, Peter. And wrong, so very wrong. Please call us when you have news." Magda hung up.

"What is it, Mag? Is it about Sarah? Did they find her? Did something happen to her?" Sam had to say something.

"No, Samantha. It's not Sarah. It's your mother." Magda

took a deep breath. "She's been arrested for the murder of your father, the murder of her high school boyfriend, Tucker Callahan…," she paused. "And for being an accomplice in Sarah's kidnapping…with Leo Goss."

Chapter Eighty-Five

"Oh, no! Magda, that's crazy!" Sam exclaimed.

"Leo's in a coma. He can't testify," she thought quickly. "That bastard is trying to flush me out by pinning Sarah's disappearance on Mom!"

"Peter asked for a special hearing, Sam. He's going to see if your mother can be released on her own recognizance. If not, he's working on getting funds together to post bail." Magda paced back and forth in her kitchen, gesturing with the egg carton. "If they do set bail, it could be impossibly high. How will Peter ever get the money together that quickly?"

Sam knew exactly how he was going to get it.

"By using Mom's own money," Sam mused silently. "Peter must be tripping trying to figure out what happened to his ace-in-the-hole." She adjusted her ice pack, thinking furiously.

"Magda, I need to go home. I'm not hungry anymore. I just need to be in my own house." It dawned on Sam that Peter would be out of the way and occupied for a couple of hours.

"But, honey, you haven't eaten a thing," Magda protested.

"Can't, Mag. I just want to get dressed and go home," said Sam, her voice thick with emotion.

She really needed to leave with Sarah. She stood awkwardly and pushed her chair away from the table.

"Let me help you, Sam," said Magda.

"No. It's okay. I can do it. Just call Michael's dad and see if there's any news on Sarah. Please?" Sam begged.

Magda gave up and nodded. She turned, opened the refrigerator, and replaced the eggs with a sigh. Gathering up the ice packs, she stuck them back in the freezer, and slammed it closed.

Magda heard Sam's footsteps reach the top of the stairs, then listened as the bedroom door closed behind her.

"Fred? You keep my Sarah safe! You hear me?" Magda's voice broke. She didn't try to stop the tears streaming down her cheeks.

For the first time since Fred died, Magda felt afraid.

****

"Sarah! Wake up!" Sam hissed.

Sarah sat up and rubbed her eyes. With all the craprageous 911's going down, it did Sam's heart good to see her little sister, whole and unharmed.

"Hi, Sam!" she whispered. "I'm ready for Plan A. But I have to go to the bathroom..."

"Good. 'Cause it's showtime. Get your dancing shoes on. Here's the deal. Go use the bathroom right now. Magda won't be upstairs for a few minutes. When she does come up to get dressed, we're gonna go down ahead of her and get in the car. You're gonna hide in the very back."

She held the door open and watched Sarah scamper to the bathroom. When she returned in record time, Sam locked the bedroom door again. She checked to make sure she had her meds and phone in her pants pocket. The sisters looked at each other when they heard Magda pad up the stairs.

"Samantha? I'm going to change. We can leave in about ten minutes," Magda said, standing outside their door.

"Sounds good, Mag. It'll take me that long to get out to the car," Sam answered.

"Okay, dear." Magda's footsteps went toward her bedroom. Her door closed.

"Ready?" Sam beckoned to Sarah. The two girls slipped down the stairs. Tigger ran next to them, not letting Sarah out of his sight.

At the back door, Sam pulled the oversized black hoodie from its hook where she had replaced it the night before. Wordlessly, she motioned to Sarah to put it on and cover her head.

"Okay, Daddy and Fred, help me get Sarah to the car without anyone seeing her. Shield us from any nosy eyes," Sam pleaded. She unlocked Magda's car using the remote on the keychain hanging by the door. It was only three steps to the car, but it seemed so far away.

When Sam did open the kitchen door, everyone in the neighborhood suddenly found themselves compelled to look in a different direction, away from Magda's house. The next door neighbor, who sat drinking coffee on her patio next to Magda's driveway, went inside and checked her email. The patrol officers driving by Magda's became interested in the house across the street, running the license plate of the car parked in front.

In a heartbeat, Sam and Sarah left the house and took up their positions inside Magda's car. Tigger meowed, rubbed against someone only he could see, and took off into the yard to hunt mice. Magda came down a few minutes later, locked the house, and settled into the driver's seat.

"Sorry, sweetie. I would have been out sooner, but I put my purse down on top of my coffee cup in the bedroom. What a mess! Took me a few minutes to clean up," Magda apologized. "I don't know what came over me. I'm usually more careful."

"It's cool, Mag. Did Michael's dad have any new information?" Sam scanned the neighborhood through her window, searching for any signs of the car she saw last night.

"I couldn't reach him. It went straight to voicemail. Sarah's kidnapping is all over the news. I'm sure people are burning up the phone lines trying to help. I know we'll be the first to hear if they find her," Magda said in resignation.

The Lexus crawled down the street. Magda tried not to jounce Sam unnecessarily. Sam's phone buzzed. She looked at the message from Peter. She decided to play possum a little while longer and turned off her ringer. Magda pulled into the Harding's driveway and drove up to the front door.

"Magda, would you please go inside and see if everything's okay? I mean, make sure there's no police or anyone there. I just want to change into my pajamas and lounge around the house. I wouldn't feel comfortable if any of them decided to stay." Sam sounded fragile.

"Sure, honey. You stay here. I'll even check upstairs," Magda agreed. She got out of the car and hurried into the house.

"Sarah?" Sam called softly.

"Yes?"

"I need you to get out of the car, sneak around the side of the house, and go in the back door. Don't worry about the alarm. Magda's already inside. Just be really quiet. As soon as you're in, lock the door and deadbolt it as well. I want you to hide in the cabinet under the kitchen window seat until I come get you. The blinds are open. Close them so I know you're inside and safe, then hole up and wait for me. Do not move from there until I personally open the cabinet." Sam squeezed her sister's hand. "Now, go!"

Sarah darted from the car and disappeared.

"One-one thousand, two-one thousand, three-one thousand, four-one thousand, five-one thousand, six-one thousand, seven-one thousand, eight-one thousand, nine-one thousand, ten-one thousand, eleven-one thousand, twelve-one thousand, thirteen-one thousand, fourteen-one thousand..." Finally, Sam broke off counting.

"Come on, Sarah!" Sam worried, wondering what could be taking so long.

Finally, Sam saw the outline of her sister's head behind the blinds in the kitchen. Sarah closed them quickly. Sam let out her breath in a whoosh of relief, not realizing she had been holding it.

"Good girl, Sarah." Sam waited in the car.

"All clear, sweetie!" Magda appeared on the front steps. She went over to help Sam inside.

A dark blue Nissan with tinted windows drove up the driveway. Puzzled, Sam and Magda exchanged glances. The car pulled directly in front of them. Sam took one look at the license plate and froze.

Victor Bloom lowered the passenger side window.

"Hello, ladies."

Chapter Eighty-Six

Bloom unfolded his long, lanky body from the passenger seat and walked toward them.

"Ma'am." He nodded his head in greeting at Magda. "My buddy, Jasper, and I were driving through the neighborhood. We've volunteered our services to help search for the little girl that got kidnapped last night. We saw your car here and wanted to make sure everything was alright. We just feel awful that someone would do such a thing."

An awkward silence fell. Magda struggled to compose herself, not sure what to say to this man who had accused Sam so vehemently last night at the Community Center. Sam refused to say a word, not wanting to make a scene. She knew how violent Bloom could be and she didn't have any way to protect Magda. Hopefully, he'd think Sam was zonked on painkillers.

"Go away, go away, go away, go away," Sam chanted in her head.

"I appreciate your concern. We appreciate everyone who is volunteering their time to help get Sarah back," Magda continued, excitement making her words tumble out faster. "As a matter of fact, I just got off the phone with Detective Bateman. Someone spotted a child, a young girl, with Sarah's description on the outskirts of town by the Arboretum. They're sending people there right now to check out the call. He said it's their best lead yet. The description fit Sarah to a T. It seems she escaped her captives and is running scared. He's not sure how she got that far, but hopes to find her before she gets too deep inside the trails before dark."

Bloom glanced over at Jasper, then back at Magda. He gave Sam one more penetrating look. She closed her eyes, trying to appear as dopey as possible. Her lack of fight and listlessness satisfied him.

"That's great news, ma'am. We're on our way," said Bloom.

"Oh, thank you!" Magda clasped her hands to her chest and smiled.

Bloom jumped into the car which sped off down the driveway. They heard the motor gun into high gear as it raced through the quiet neighborhood. Sam cocked an eyebrow at Magda.

"Really? You forgot to say my hero," she said wryly. "I think I need an insulin shot after that. You know you can go to hell for lying. You didn't talk to Michael's dad."

"I don't care. It would be worth it. Victor Bloom makes my skin crawl. Plus, I picked up really negative energy from that Jasper man behind the wheel. He's bad news. I trust them about as far as I can throw them. Which isn't very far." Magda shook her head.

"You did good, Mag. At least they left."

"I didn't believe him last night. Me thinks he protested too much when it came to a little slip of a girl half his size, lying on the floor with her ribs kicked in. Nice druggy act, by the way. We need to stick together, Sam. Too much is happening all at once. Are you sure I can't stay here with you? What if they come back?" Magda didn't like the idea of leaving Sam here all alone.

"I think if they're telling the truth about helping the cops, they wouldn't have bothered coming up here to sniff around. I bet they had something to do with Sarah's kidnapping. Which is why they took off so fast. Maybe they lost track of her. And they're so stupid they won't even bother checking your story. By the time they figure out she isn't in the Arboretum like you said, the police may have found Sarah." Sam skirted around the truth. She needed Magda to leave.

"Oh. I never would have thought that. What if you're right, Sam? Or what if Sarah escapes somehow? I better get home in case she comes there," Magda replied, her mood a little lighter.

"Good idea, Mag. I'll call you if I need anything. Just knowing you're at your house down the street makes me feel safe. I promise to lock all the doors, keep my phone next to me, and turn on the alarm system. That way if Sarah shows up, I'll be here." Sam dragged her stiff body out of the passenger seat and gratefully accepted Magda's assistance up the stairs.

"Okay, doll." Magda enveloped Sam in a careful hug. "If you hear or see anything out of the ordinary, call. I can be here in a twink. An absolute twink."

"I know. Thanks." Sam returned the hug just as carefully.

"I love you. Sarah will be home soon. I just feel it in my bones," Magda assured Sam.

"I believe you, Mag. And I love you, too." Sam watched Magda get in her car, give a wave, and drive away.

Sam closed the front door and leaned back against it. She took her phone out of her pocket. She had seven Facebook messages from Peter.

"Sorry...," she murmured rudely. "Can't reply right now. Losing control, pyscho-man? I'll get to you in a few...my family comes first."

She hurried to the kitchen to get Sarah. Sam smiled grimly to herself, wishing she could see the look on Peter's face right now. She turned the corner and panicked. The cabinet door under the window seat was open...so was the door to the back yard!

"Sarah? Oh, no! Sarah!" Sam gasped.

Chapter Eighty-Seven

Sam ran to the back door. She stuck her head outside. Frantically, her eyes combed the yard, searching for any trace of Sarah.

"Oh, come on! Peter's goons are long gone...I'm sure of that. I watched them leave. Where are you, Sarah?"

She heard a toilet flush. Sam whirled around and marched painfully to the bathroom next to the kitchen. She rolled her eyes when she heard the water running.

"Glad you remembered to wash your hands! Wish you'd remembered to stay put like I told you!" Sam yelled through the door.

Sarah unlocked the door. She stood in the bathroom doorway, her eyes big and fearful. Sam's heart clenched when she thought about everything Sarah had been through in the past twenty-four hours.

"I'm used to riding the crazy bus," thought Sam. "Poor Sarah, this is her first time on board." She smiled at her little sister.

"Don't look at me like that. I'm not mad at you. I just got scared when I couldn't find you. I can't lose you again, short stuff. My head will explode." Sam held her hand out to Sarah who took it and held on tight.

"I'm sorry, Sam. I wouldn't have moved except I had to pee so bad and I didn't want to pee in the cabinet. And I'm sorry I didn't remember to shut and lock the kitchen door like you said. I tried to signal you and hide as fast as I could." Sarah hung her head, then raised it again. "Can I have a bowl of cereal? I'm kinda hungry."

"Sounds good. I'm hungry, too. Chow down," said Sam. "I'm gonna go alarm the system. Be right back."

Sam set the alarm's perimeter, including all the doors and windows. Back in the kitchen, she grabbed a tray and loaded it up with napkins, milk, spoons, cereal, and bowls.

"Let's go. I want you upstairs in your room with the curtains drawn and the door locked. And here, keep this on you." Sam handed Sarah the cell phone she'd lost in the scuffle last night.

"You found it! Thanks, Sam."

"Yeah, well, what are big sisters for, right? Keeping mushmouses like you in line, huh?" Sam poked her sister who giggled. Sam picked up the tray to carry upstairs. "After you…"

When they had eaten their fill of Cap'n Crunch and Cocoa Krispies, Sam waited in Sarah's room. Sarah took a shower and changed into fresh, clean clothes.

"Thanks for coming after me, Sam. I don't know how you found me, but I'm sure glad you did." Sarah curled up on her bed.

"Anime's father would have had to knock me unconscious to stop me. I think he tried, too." Sam examined her stitches in Sarah's mirror. "Ugh." She sniffed under her armpits. "I smell really bad. Shower time for Stinky Sam. You rest. And do not leave this room! No excuses. One heart attack a day is my quota. Understood?" She dropped a kiss on Sarah's forehead. "Lock the door after I leave."

"Okay." Sarah looked around her room in contentment. "Where's Mom? I want to let her know I'm okay."

"Baby, we talked about that. Mom can't know you're here. The bad guys would just snatch you again. Keeping your whereabouts hidden is our only chance to keep them off balance. Hopefully, they'll make some stupid mistake and reveal their hand."

"But, Sam, it's not fair to Mom. She must be going crazy!"

Sam hesitated. She wondered if she should tell Sarah about their mother's arrest. Magda said they needed to stick together. Maybe she shouldn't keep Sarah completely in the dark.

"The police arrested Mom this morning for Daddy's murder, her high school boyfriend's murder, and conspiracy to commit kidnapping," Sam paused. "Your kidnapping."

"What? That's mental! Mom didn't kill Daddy! She couldn't have hurt anyone! She hates anything violent or cruel. She buys the live lobsters at the grocery store and sets them free in the ocean when we go to Nantucket!" Sarah raged. "She loved Daddy! Nobody who knows Mom would believe that! And you and I know *exactly* who kidnapped me! This is wrong, Sam! How can they do this?"

"Not they, who. One person, Sarah. One evil, powerful person murdered, manipulated evidence, stole money, ruined people's lives...and is still out there, free as a bird. But so help me, God, it won't be for long. All you need to do is stay right here. And trust me. I haven't let you down yet." Sam's hands shook, but her voice remained steady.

Sarah took a deep breath, her face mutinous. Her small hands curled into fists. She relaxed her shoulders and nodded slowly.

"Okay. But I want to help."

"Deal. You will be the first one I ask because I trust you, too. But I need to take a shower and change out of these clothes. Love you. Lock the door. That means *now*, poker chip."

Back in her own room, Sam filled a cup of water from the bathroom sink, sank down into her big, overstuffed armchair, and propped her feet up on the ottoman. Her ribs pulsed a steady, painful drumbeat. She started to take her pain meds, then stopped and stared at the bottle.

"I really can't take the chance of falling asleep with those neanderthals on the loose looking for Sarah," she thought slowly. "Besides, pain reminds me how much I hate them."

Sam looked at her phone. Three more Facebook messages from Peter.

"Sucks to be you…" Sam threw her phone on the bed and went to take her shower.

The phone buzzed two more times like an angry hornet. Then, silence.

Chapter Eighty-Eight

Sam dressed. Every movement was a fiery reminder of Victor Bloom and his work boot. She took the hatbox out of her closet, placed it on her bed, and removed the lid.

"Meet Plan B." Sam drew the gun out of the box and expertly loaded it with the bullets from her father's safe.

She surveyed the large pile of plush Woodstocks on her bed. She smiled at the one Magda had given her--Woodstock held lovingly in Snoopy's arms. Sam picked up the big one from Peter. She laid it face down on the bed. Using the utility knife, she cut a large slit in its back and tucked the gun inside.

"Backstabbing Woodstock...how appropriate."

Satisfied with the weapon's concealment, she picked up her phone and read her messages.

samantha
need to talk

"I'll bet you do." Sam narrowed her eyes and kept reading.

samantha
worried
danger

"Yup. That one's been overused." Sam kept scrolling.

samantha
help me
find sarah

"Did already. Took her right out from under your nose, freak."

samantha
important
killer coming

"Same old, same old. Except you're the killer, dude. And I have your gun." It dawned on Sam that all the stuff in the office safe had been Peter's, not her father's. She shook her head, again, at how easily she had believed him.

samantha
talk to me
you have to
help Sarah

"Okay. Those were from earlier. You're fishing, trying to see if I know anything." She looked at the next three. "Ooh...getting pissed off, aren't we, Peter?"

samantha
michael
plan
running out of time

samantha
take care of michael
save sarah

samantha
sarah
crying
hurt

"Damn." She rolled off her bed, swore again as pain knifed through her, and walked across the hall to Sarah's room. She called Sarah on her phone and knocked on her door at the same time. Sarah answered her phone, then let Sam in.

"What?" Sarah asked. A Disney movie played on the television in the background.

"Just wanted a handful of Cap'n Crunch," Sam lied. She took the box in her shaking fingers.

"Keep watching. Thanks!" She stood outside the door and waited while Sarah locked it again.

"God! Peter's so good, he makes me doubt my own sanity! I know she's safe, but he still spooks me...ugh!" Sam shivered, wondering if even Plan B could stop this man.

Back in her own room, Sam picked up her phone.

Dad?

are you okay
so worried

"I'll bet," thought Sam.

Just really groggy. I keep falling asleep with these meds. Oh, Daddy, I can't do anything to find Sarah. It hurts too much to even move. And Mom's been arrested for your murder! What's going on? Everything's so messed up!

try samantha
get rid of michael
now

sarah's life in danger
don't wait

"Seriously? Still trying to scare me into killing my best friend by using my sister as bait? You don't even have her! And Michael's probably the only one smart enough to figure out your game pretty soon. Wow! Do you think I can be controlled so easily?" Sam realized that's exactly what Peter did think. No wonder Michael thought she was a loose cannon with serious anger issues. He had every right to be suspicious and question her every move.

Yes, Daddy. How? I can't think straight.

serious
sarah is the next to die
kill him

I can barely walk, Daddy. I need some time.

try
time is running out

What about Mom? You know she didn't kill anybody...what can I do?

nothing
powerful men
will stop at nothing
to destroy our family

I'm so scared. And I'm so tired.

do your best
for us

love you
stay strong
hurry

"He's right. I can't do anything. Unless I can somehow *prove* Peter is behind all this, my family and I are screwed." Sam threw the phone down on her bed.

"Why does he keep harping on Michael? Oh no, what if he thinks Michael is the one who's on to him and took Sarah? He knows Michael's brilliant. If he's desperate enough, he'll go after Michael by himself." Sam's stomach churned.

She picked up her phone and punched in Michael's number, determined to make him listen to her. The call went directly to voicemail.

"Damn it, Michael! I know I'm a jerk, but this is serious! I need to talk to you, please! You're in danger--as much as Sarah is! You have to believe me! Please call me back!"

Sam's insides contracted. She couldn't help her mother, she couldn't warn Michael, and she couldn't leave Sarah. And her ribs hurt like fire any time she moved. The awful truth of how helpless she was at that moment threatened to drown her in a sea of panic.

"Stay calm," Sam warned herself, breathing slowly in through her nose and out through her mouth the way the school nurse had taught her. "You're no good to any of them if you're comatose. Think. What can you do right now?"

Just then she heard a car crunch into the driveway and brake to a stop. Sam struggled to the window as fast as she could. She saw Peter behind the wheel of his light blue Mercedes.

Every thought flew out of her head except one...she had to get Sarah out of there! Now!

Chapter Eighty-Nine

Sam raced across the hall and pounded on Sarah's door.
"Open up! It's an emergency!"
"What is it?" Sarah's frightened face appeared.
"Bad guys...here...in the driveway," Sam panted. "We have to get you out of here, fast!" Sam took Sarah by the hand and dragged her over to her window. "You're leaving this way. I'll lower you down to the back deck railing...stay low and stay hidden--don't go *near* the front of the house. Head for Magda's. Keep off the road...cut through bushes, yards, behind garages...whatever. Don't let *anybody* see you!"

Sam opened the window. Sarah hopped on one foot, trying to put her shoes on as fast as she could.

"No time, sweetie. Forget the shoes. You've gotta go!" Sam grabbed the shoes, wrapped them in Sarah's hoodie, and tossed them into a bush below where they landed in a noiseless heap. "Put 'em on later!"

Sarah climbed over the window sill. Holding onto Sam's hands, she angled her body and slid, facing Sam, down the side of the house. Sam held onto her in a death grip as she lowered her down, bracing her body against the bedroom wall.

"Let go!" Sarah hissed. "You're gonna fall out!" She wiggled one hand out of Sam's grasp and clung to the indentations in the brick. "I can do this!"

Sam closed her eyes and let go, praying Sarah would be

alright. Waves of pain washed over Sam as she collapsed against the open window. When Sam opened her eyes, she saw Sarah scampering, unharmed, with her hoodie and shoes, into the woods behind their house.

"Protect her, Dad! Please get her to Magda's!" It scared Sam to think about Sarah all alone out there without her.

Sam went back to her room and peeked out the window. Peter stood in the driveway, leaning against the passenger side of the car, talking on his phone. He hadn't moved.

Sam pulled on her hoodie. She made sure her phone was on, turned the ringer to silent, and shoved it in the front pocket. Next, she went over to the bed and took the gun out of the slit in Woodstock's back. She took the safety off and replaced it in the stuffed animal. Finally, she put the Swiss Army knife in her back pocket.

Sam stepped back over to the window. Cautiously, she raised it a few inches. Peter, still engrossed in his conversation, didn't notice.

"Listen up, you mental defective. You work for me now, not Leo. I don't care how, why, or when it happened. All I know is that it did. You find that spoiled little brat and bring her to me. I'm at her house, 445 Hawkins. If you want to live to see tomorrow, I suggest you find her...quickly. If not, don't bother looking over your shoulder. You'll already be dead," Peter warned. He ended the call and opened the door to the back seat.

Sam panicked. Peter hadn't bothered to hide the fact he called the shots and these men answered to him. She had rescued Sarah. But by backing him into a corner, he had morphed into an even bigger threat. Sam didn't know if he was losing it or he figured he had nothing left to lose. Either way, Peter seemed more dangerous than ever.

Chapter Ninety

"Come on, Melissa. Let's go inside." Peter offered his hand to the woman inside the car.

Sam hid behind the curtain, listening. She watched as her mother's long legs, ending in navy blue Jimmy Choos, appeared, then the rest of her in a tailored, navy blue dress. Melissa reached out and gripped Peter's arm, swaying, a silver flask in one hand.

"I'm going to jail, aren't I, Peter? For killing the two men I loved more than life itself...and for risking my baby girl's life in the hands of some vile kidnappers? My sweet Sarah? How? How is this even possible?"

She turned to Peter and stumbled into his arms, weeping. He gathered her close to his chest. He looked over her head at the house and the grounds, a smirk lifting the corner of his lips. Keeping one arm wrapped around her, Peter guided her toward the front door.

Sam grabbed up Woodstock and raced as quickly as she could down the stairs to the library. She placed Woodstock on the far end of the sofa, nestled among the throw pillows. She had no clue what to do next, so she hid behind the door in the library and waited.

The front door opened. Peter and Melissa walked in. Melissa stood in the foyer, weeping and clutching at Peter. He calmly closed the door behind them. Once inside, Peter removed the flask from Melissa's hand and placed it on the marble table to his right. He took her by her shoulders, tracing his index finger down the side of her face.

"Melissa…," Peter whispered, staring at her.

She drew back, wariness flickering in her dull eyes.

"Nothing's going to happen to you. I won't let it. That's why I put up the bail. Me, Peter. All ten million dollars. I rescued you. And you should be very, very grateful. So grateful you'll do whatever I say. Because I can make all the charges go away and I can find Sarah. Just say the word." His mouth curved in a confident, arrogant smile.

Peter ran his hands down her arms. He grasped her hands in his, raised them to his lips, and kissed them. "I love you. I've loved you since the moment I saw you trying to open your locker on the first day of high school. I recognized your helplessness, your inability to survive on your own. You were so easy, so trusting…so beautiful. I knew, no matter what it took or how long, you would finally, irrevocably, belong to me. All of you…"

Melissa's eyes widened. She looked up at the amused expression on his face and wrenched her hands away.

"What? What are you saying? No, Peter! Never! I'll never be yours! Ever! You're insane!" The awful truth of his words dawned on her. She beat his chest with her fists. "Where is Sarah? How do you know how to find her? What did you do with her!!"

Peter backhanded Melissa across her face. He gazed at her, a superior expression on his handsome face. She put a shaking hand up to her reddened cheek, her eyes blazing. He shook his head and pushed her up against the wall.

"Temper, temper, Melissa, my love." He kissed her neck. "I own you. I control *everything*. I can bankrupt you, put you in jail, make your daughter disappear for good…or, you can come to your senses and play nice." He began to slowly unbutton her dress with one hand, pinning her arms above her head with the other. He murmured in her ear, "you're going to enjoy the life I've planned for us...I've waited a long time." He covered her mouth with his own, kissing her again and again.

Melissa succumbed to his kisses, letting her body relax against his, then broke free, desperately lunging toward the front door. Peter laughed and looked at her with contempt. He walked over, twisted her arm behind her back, and slapped her across the face several times, her head ricocheting violently.

"Now, where were we?" he sneered. He threw her down on the marble floor of the foyer. Her head hit the ground with a terrible thud. Her legs twitched, then were still.

Sam, forgetting all about the gun, launched herself at Peter in horror, screaming her mother's name.

"Oh, my God! You killed her!" Sam tore at Peter's clothes, scratching and kicking, all her pent-up hatred for the man unleashed in her fury.

"Enough!" Peter roared. He pushed her with such force she tripped, hit her head on the marble table, and fell.

The last thing Sam remembered before losing consciousness was her mother's still body next to hers.

Chapter Ninety-One

Sam opened her eyes. She sat next to her mother, propped against her shoulder, on the sofa in the library. Melissa looked at Sam and gently murmured her name. Both had their hands bound behind their backs with zip ties. Sam felt something wet drip off her forehead onto her nose. She looked down and saw little red drops pooling on the leg of her blue jeans.

"Nice. My stitches must have opened," she murmured groggily. Sam leaned against her mom, trying to remember what happened.

"Oh, no!" Sam exclaimed. She sat bolt upright and winced at the pounding in her head.

"Why did I go all kamikaze when I have the stupid gun stashed in Woodstock...Woodstock!" Sam thought, afraid Peter had discovered it.

She cast her eyes casually down to her right. Looking in any direction made her seasick, but she was relieved to see his bright yellow beak still poking out from the tasseled throw pillows. She had no idea how she was gonna access Plan B, but at least it remained an option.

"Samantha?" Melissa asked weakly. "What is it?"

Peter walked into the library before Sam could answer. He had a beer bottle in one hand and carried a sandwich on a plate in the other. He put the food on the coffee table and sat down across from them. His left cheek boasted three red, ugly scratches.

"I wondered when the two of you would come around." He reached across the table and cracked Sam across the face so hard she saw her second set of stars that day. Peter pointed to the scratches on his face. "Not a good move, sweetheart."

Melissa drew in her breath sharply. "Peter, stop! What's wrong with you?!?"

"Save it, Melissa," said Peter, taking a bite of his sandwich. "Nobody cares. I'll do what I want with you and your daughters. No one's coming through that door to save you. Your reputation is trashed--so's your daughter's. And, Sarah? That remains to be seen. I'm your own personal Obi-Wan. I'm your only hope."

"I'm okay, Mom. Peter's right. Nobody's coming. He's got it all wrapped up." Sam leaned her body closer to her mother's, angling her hip closer to her hands.

One more fraction of an inch and she'd be able to use two fingers to shimmy the Swiss Army knife out of her back pocket with its little pair of very sharp scissors. Her fingers closed on the tip of the knife. Sam grasped it and eased it slowly out of her pocket. She counted the indentations on the knife with her fingers and pulled open the second one to free the scissors.

Looking pitiful, which wasn't hard with blood dripping down her face, Sam maneuvered the scissors between her wrists and poised them on the edge of the zip tie. Snip! Her hands were free! Sam didn't dare move a muscle. She glanced idly in Peter's direction, but he wasn't paying attention to her. He stared down at his phone with an irritated expression.

"What is taking so long?" he complained.

Just then, the front door crashed open! Victor Bloom and Jasper came in carrying a squirming, hooded bundle between them, its legs bicycling like crazy trying to get free. The men walked over and stood in the library doorway. Bloom yanked off the hood, revealing an angry, tear-stained face with a gag over her mouth.

"Sarah!" Melissa gasped.

"Drop her!" Peter ordered.

Bloom dumped her on the rug. Peter gestured to Jasper.

"Get a chair," he demanded.

Jasper returned from the dining room with a chair, yanked Sarah to her feet, and pushed her onto the seat. Peter swiftly zip tied the girl's hands and ankles to the chair.

"Luck," Peter allowed, unimpressed with Sarah's return. "You shouldn't have lost her in the first place. Get outside, both of you. I don't want to be disturbed." Peter waited until the front door closed before turning his attention to Sarah.

"I missed you, sweetheart," he mused, taking hold of her hair. He pulled Sarah's head back until her frightened eyes met his. "I worried. I don't like worrying. I don't like anyone disrupting my plans." Peter took both his hands, placed them around her slender throat, and squeezed. "It won't happen again, will it?" When Sarah didn't respond, he flexed his fingers and applied more pressure. This time she shook her head back and forth vehemently, petrified, unable to speak with the gag in her mouth.

"You're a monster, Peter!" Melissa cried, fighting frantically to free her hands.

"Thank you," he tossed over his shoulder. He kept his hands on Sarah's neck, watching the fear grow in her eyes. Pleased, he rewarded her by relaxing his grip.

Another disturbance at the front door interrupted Peter's concentration. He sighed. Bloom and Jasper walked back in, this time dragging Michael between them, his ripped clothing covered in mud.

Sam's heart sank.

Chapter Ninety-Two

"We found this kid in the driveway. He wouldn't leave. Said he needed to see her," Bloom jerked his head in Sam's direction. "Said he wasn't leaving. Mentioned your name, too. Figured you might want to know that."

Michael stared at Peter, locking eyes with him defiantly. "I finally put two and two together. You're not the only one who can hack a computer. Those documents Mrs. Harding signed were created in the past week, not last spring. You forged Leo's signature. And you almost had me going, believing you like everybody else except for one little detail. Mrs. Harding would never agree to having either of her daughters kidnapped. She'd die first. I know what you are. And I know what you did. You have everyone in this town believing you're a saint. But you're a liar...a liar and a murderer who will say or do anything to get what you want."

Peter laughed. He motioned for the two men to bring Michael closer. "So easy. You've just saved me the trouble of finding you. Bloom, hold him. Jasper, fix his attitude. I'd prefer him more...cooperative. Don't close your eyes, Samantha, or I'll have them repeat the process. You need to see exactly what snooping in my business has cost your friend."

Sam forced herself to watch as Jasper beat Michael mercilessly. His fists battered Michael with blow after blow until the boy collapsed on the floor, panting and bleeding—one eye swollen shut.

"Enough." Peter glanced down at the glaring, unrepentant teen. "Bloom, get another chair and tie him up. Then both of you get back outside."

Bloom didn't waste any time. He got the chair and jerked Michael into it roughly. A few minutes later, he had zip tied the boy's hands behind his back and attached each foot to a chair leg. Michael's head lolled to one side. Blood dripped from his nose.

"Looks like the gang's all here, Samantha." Peter studied Michael. "I knew that boy was trouble from the beginning. Too bad you didn't kill him like you said you would.

"As if, you loser!" Sam flared in anger.

"Oh, really? Not even for your precious daddy? You would have done anything I said, especially if it came down to a choice between Sarah and him. But I've made other arrangements." Peter kicked Michael in the leg. "Pay attention, boy."

Michael didn't say a word. He just raised his head slightly and looked at Sam, then back at Peter.

"What are you talking about?" Melissa demanded.

"Your stupid twit daughter thought I was Forbes, sending her private messages on Facebook. I had her trash Don's car as well as put Kameron and Leo in the hospital. Her next task involved executing Einstein over here. She's so easy...I have enough on her to put her away for a long time. She's not very talented at cleaning up evidence and I'm very good at cataloging it. Who would believe an angry, truant teen who almost got expelled for attacking her fellow student, Anime Bloom, twice, and went after Victor Bloom with a knife just last night? The Blooms are very loyal to me. They were paid well for their services...with your money."

Melissa looked at Sam, horrified. "Samantha, is this true?"

"Yes! He's behind everything, Mom! Peter killed Daddy just like he killed Tucker! He conned me into doing horrible things.

He created the *Samantha Project* to bring Leo on board! He stole all your money, Mom...he's some kind of tech genius. He's responsible for that video of you and Leo, he kidnapped Sarah, he even killed his own father! And he pretended to be Daddy the whole time. He said he needed my help: to save you, to save Sarah, and to find his murderer!" Sam's words spilled out of her mouth, tears clogging her throat.

"Well, well, little girl. I certainly did underestimate you." Peter frowned, then shrugged as he walked over to Sarah and stroked her hair lightly.

Melissa bent her head and pressed her forehead against Sam's. Sam looked at her mother, terrified she would see anger and accusation in Melissa's eyes. Instead, her mother's eyes filled with tears.

"Oh, sweetheart," Melissa whispered. "I didn't know. I am so sorry. It wasn't your job to save our family. It was mine."

Chapter Ninety-Three

Melissa turned and stared at Peter. Her gaze hardened. "Murdering two decent, loving men wasn't enough? You had to prey on my daughters and turn Sam into a criminal so you could keep your hands clean? This is your sick, twisted idea of love?"

Peter smiled. "That's what I find so appealing about you, Melissa. You act tough, but underneath it all, you were as easy to manipulate as your daughter. Samantha was motivated by an unquenchable love for her father. You were motivated by fear. It's so much fun to watch. Like this."

He bent over and expertly knuckle-punched Michael in the chest as hard as he could. Michael groaned in pain. Next, Peter drove his fist into him with an uppercut, knocking the wind out of him, then struck the boy in the kidneys for good measure. Peter tilted Sarah's chin up and slapped her viciously across the face. He nodded in satisfaction as Sarah made a small, muffled sound through her gag while tears rolled down her reddened cheeks.

"Stop it, Peter! For the love of God, stop hurting them!" Melissa cried out in anguish.

When Peter turned his attention to Michael and Sarah, Sam used the opportunity to slip her hand into her front pocket. In one smooth motion, she reached for her phone, dialed 911, dropped it silently under the coffee table with the line open, then quickly placed her hand behind her back again.

Peter watched Michael and Sarah with interest, a pleased half-smile on his face. There was little, if any, fight left in the two. Their bodies sagged in the chairs, the zip ties the only thing keeping them upright. He prodded each of them with his shoe, but there was no response.

"Good. Fighting back gets you nowhere...and I'd prefer my next shipment not have any permanently damaged goods. Your bruises won't show in a day or two and should heal nicely. My clients prefer their purchases to be extremely marketable. More profit that way. It's a win-win for us both." Peter tilted Sarah's chin and turned her head from side to side, examining her face.

"Peter? What clients? And why would they be concerned with these kids?" Melissa demanded, unable to control the tremble in her voice.

"Oh. These three are about to disappear, permanently. Remember the document you signed in the boardroom on Thursday, placing your fiance, Leo, on the Board of Directors? That enabled NatureLight to launder the money he earns in all sorts of nefarious ways, including human trafficking. It's become a big part of the company's bottom line."

He grabbed hold of Michael's chin. Michael tried to jerk his head away and spit in Peter's face, but that just earned him another solid gut punch.

"So, really, the choice is up to you, Melissa. A) You agree to take all I have to offer you--my love and a life together. This buys you an out-of-jail free card and these three healthy, young people will be sold into a less seedy situation in another country and are kept alive, or B) you refuse me, go to jail, and these three meet an unfortunate end when they can no longer earn their keep. Also, in another country. Somewhere in Asia, I believe." Peter checked his phone. "Either way, it'll be talked about for years...the day three Beaconsfield youths vanished into thin air...no clues...just another unsolved mystery. Fingers will be pointed at you, most likely. With my protection and connections, you might weather it. But without me, you'll just end up another inmate on suicide watch."

Sam could see the edge of her phone, barely visible under the antique table. She prayed Peter wouldn't find it. If she didn't answer the responder's questions, someone would ping the cell phone and send help.

If it wasn't too late.

Chapter Ninety-Four

"Peter, no! I'll do anything...go anywhere with you! Please, oh God, please don't do this!" Melissa pleaded.

"Too late. I take it your choice is A? Keep the little darlings alive? Excellent choice. This calls for a drink. Care to join me? Oh, sorry. I forgot. You're all tied up. I'll have one for you." Peter brushed off her concerns and walked over to the bar. He poured himself a neat scotch and tossed it back, then poured another.

Quick as lightening, Sam snipped the zip tie joining her mother's hands together. Melissa's eyes widened and met Sam's. Sam shook her head slightly and indicated her own hands still behind her back. Her mother gave a tiny nod and leaned against the pillows, hiding the fact her hands were free.

Sam drew the gun out of Woodstock's plush body. She sprang to her feet and held the gun on Peter. He turned.

"Well, aren't you handy." Peter's eyes narrowed and his smile faded. "The gun. I wondered if you had the nerve to use it without someone coaching you from the sidelines. You do realize you're holding the same weapon I used to murder your father? How does that feel?"

Michael raised his head and glared at Peter. "And the same one you used to kill Tucker, too! Why did you give that to her?" He stopped, aghast, as he realized why.

"That's right," said Peter. "You were next. Too smart for

your own good, Boy Wonder. No matter, I'll make more money this way. They love it when I send a male."

Sam's legs trembled, but her hands on the gun were steady. She didn't say a word as Peter taunted her. She just concentrated on keeping the gun trained on her target.

"Do you really think you're going to be able to shoot? You've never shot a gun in your life...what did you do, google it?" Peter swirled the amber liquid in his glass with one hand and calmly took another swallow. He rolled his eyes and placed a call on his cell phone.

"Stop!" Sam snapped. "Hang up and throw your phone over here. Now." She looked wildly from her mother to Michael and Sarah.

Taking a deep breath, she squared her shoulders and focused her gaze at the man who had taken her father from her. Her arms, holding up the gun, began to shake from fatigue and fright. Her right index finger began to draw back on the trigger.

"Sam..." Michael coughed and spat blood. "Don't ruin your life, Queen. He's not worth it."

Sarah's eyes implored her to do something, anything. Sam could feel her own heart pounding furiously in her chest. The energy in the room intensified. Everything seemed a little brighter, more high-def. She smelled the familiar Hugo Boss surround her. She heard her father's voice in her ear, as though he was standing right next to her.

"Give Mom the gun, Sam. It's time. Trust her. She loves you more than life itself. You don't have to be the parent anymore. She's got this."

"Samantha," Melissa breathed. "Give me the gun, sweetheart. Please."

"But, Daddy...," Sam choked out.

"Would want me to take care of you. It's not your job to save our family. It's mine. You never should have been put in this position. But I can do something about that now. Give me the gun, Samantha," Melissa insisted gently, keeping one eye on Peter. She rose from the couch and held out her hand.

"I love you, Sam. I am so sorry for everything you've been through, what this deranged lunatic has put our family through. I don't blame you for wanting to hurt him. He has hurt you so badly. But, please...please don't do something that will ruin your entire life. Don't give him that satisfaction. He's taken enough. Don't let him turn you into a killer like him."

"Mom? Oh God, Mom?!" Sam swayed uncertainly, unable to move, her finger still poised on the trigger.

Melissa saw Peter edge forward, taking advantage of Sam's hesitation. She lunged and closed her own hand over her daughter's.

BANG! The gun went off.

"Mom!" Sam screamed.

Chapter Ninety-Five

Peter clutched his arm. Blood leaked through his suit jacket. Furious, he looked down where the bullet had creased his upper arm and lodged in the wall behind him. Melissa held the gun on him, shielding Sam behind her body.

"Where do you think you're going with this, Melissa?" Peter snapped angrily. "You're out on bail for two murders that were committed with that gun. As far as anyone is concerned, the murder weapon has been in this house the whole time. If you kill me, you'll go to jail for all three murders. I've already cooperated with the police by providing evidence that puts you at both crime scenes. And if you don't kill me, no sane person will believe your word against mine. I'll concoct some story that has you responsible for everything, and when you're off in jail, these three will disappear as planned."

"I don't know, Peter. I think jail will be worth it. You'll be dead. My daughters and Michael will be alive and unharmed." Melissa kept the gun pointed at Peter. "No regrets on my end. What did you call it? Oh, yes...win-win."

"All of this is your own fault, Melissa," Peter pressed. "You're weak. You couldn't make a decision on your own when you were with Forbes and you fell apart when he was dead. I made you into the most desirable woman in Beaconsfield again. You never once protested. You wanted this as much as I did. I gave you back your life. You owe me. You're my soulmate, Melissa, in every possible way. You're not some suburban housewife...these children are collateral damage. A broken leg you suffered in order to win the war." He made an impatient gesture with his injured arm and winced.

"My children are not collateral damage...they are my *life*, what's left of it! Why, Peter? Why did you kill them? Tucker had his whole life ahead of him, Forbes was a good man and a wonderful father..." Melissa's voice shook.

"You deserved better than a football oaf like Tucker. Forbes was vanilla...no vision. You were a jewel in need of a better setting." Peter looked smug. "And my father...he laughed at me. Said I'd never make anything of myself. I smothered him with his own ratty pillow. My family thought he'd died in his sleep. I idolized your father. I followed him around like a lost puppy. That man could sell ice to the Eskimos. He chewed up tin cans and spit out gold..." He laughed. "Give me the gun, Melissa. You obviously have no idea how to use one of those properly."

Melissa shuddered. How could someone who looked so good and played the part of a model, upright person with such conviction be so obscenely evil? She felt Sam hiding behind her, looked at Sarah watching her with panicky eyes, and saw Michael's shoulders sagging hopelessly. Peter walked toward her.

She fired. No regrets.

Chapter Ninety-Six

Detective Bateman looked at the three kids. They sat close together on the couch, Sam in the middle, all huddled in blankets. He couldn't believe how close he had come to losing his own son, as well as Sam and her sister, Sarah.

The paramedics carted Peter off in an ambulance. Melissa's shot hit him in the shoulder. At the last second, she decided not to kill him outright with a good, clean finish. She wanted him to live and pay for every single crime he had committed.

Bloom and Jasper were booked and fingerprinted for their involvement in the kidnapping and their ties to Leo Goss. Detective Bateman figured they'd be wetting their pants and spilling their guts about Leo Goss' whole crime operation at the station right about now. He frowned thinking about Peter Ambroglia.

"If it weren't for Peter's arrogance and obsession with Melissa," he realized, "I bet Peter's own ties to Leo would have gone undiscovered."

Detective Bateman's cell phone rang.

"I see," he said. "Yes. I'll let her know. Thank you."

He turned and gazed down at Melissa, sitting on the floor in front of her daughters. She had one arm curled protectively around each set of her children's legs, her eyes closed in exhaustion. Her hair was a mess and she had bruises blossoming on her face, but he thought she looked more at peace now than she had in the past months.

"That was the hospital, Melissa. Leo came out of his coma. He's off the ventilator and his doctors expect him to make a full recovery."

Melissa nodded without opening her eyes.

"I'll send someone up there to get a statement. Meanwhile, I'll make sure he's under twenty-four hour police guard. We've been trying to get the goods on him for a long time. What we heard from Peter via Sam's 911 call will help us close the book on him. Leo's extremely slippery, but now we have it recorded," said Detective Bateman. He turned to Samantha.

"Samantha, during your statement you said you discovered evidence in Peter's house detailing every crime he had committed against your family, including the computer hijacking of your mother's bank accounts, plus information regarding Tucker Callahan's murder."

"It's all in a room upstairs on the second floor. It's probably locked. He locked it before he left his house yesterday afternoon. Everything's in there: from the time he met my mother in high school until now." Sam rested her head on top of Sarah's.

"You're very brave, Sam. Rescuing Sarah despite your injuries...standing up to the man who killed your father and blackmailed your mother. Not many girls your age would've had the courage or the presence of mind to do what you did." He smiled at her before taking another call.

"Thanks," said Sam. Her grip tightened on Michael's fingers. He squeezed her hand in response.

"I'm sorry," she mumbled.

"What?" He could barely hear her.

"I'm sorry, Michael. I should have told you what was going on with Kameron and Leo and the stupid Facebook messages. I was afraid Sarah and I would be taken away from Mom if anybody knew. I thought I could figure it out by myself and keep us together at the same time. I wouldn't have done anything to you...I couldn't. You're my best friend." She hung her head.

"Hey, Queen...this is me, remember? You're one of the strongest people I know. Yeah, you lost it when your dad died...who wouldn't? But the Sam who believed her dad was on the other end of a Facebook message was the same Sam who knew something was really wrong with your mom. And the same Sam who beat Peter at his own game. Smooth move with the knife...and the gun in the fat yellow bird."

"Woodstock, you moron," Sam interrupted.

"Whatever. You blew it up, girl. But next time, don't go all ninja and do it yourself. Take advantage of this superior brain and the amazingness that is at your disposal and use it." He gestured toward himself grandly. Sam cracked up.

"Okay, you're on. Except I don't want there to be a next time, y'know?" Sam looked down at her mother and slumped against the cushions. "I thought it was some kind of a miracle...somehow Dad had figured out how to reach me. I'm sorry about putting Kameron in the hospital. But if he had gotten hold of me, he would've done worse. And Leo scared the hell out of me. He threatened to kill me. Plus, he was sending me away so I couldn't protect Sarah. I didn't want him to die, but I don't know what else to do," said Sam.

"Don't blame yourself, Samantha," said Melissa, turning to look up at her. "Peter manipulated you. He used your weakness and vulnerability to control you. He used Leo's desire for power. He used your love for your father. And he used my fear that something would happen to you girls. Good thing he underestimated you. I'm so proud of you. Your father would be, too. You're a force to be reckoned with."

Sam smiled, relieved and grateful to have her mom back. Her stomach bubbled with a shy happiness as she let her mother's compliments wash over her. It felt different. It felt good. For the first time since her dad died, Sam felt strong and back on solid ground.

"Mom, I wanted the messages to be from Daddy so badly. I didn't know who I was without him."

"Oh, Samantha...sweetheart," said Melissa. "You are so much like your father...quick-witted, intelligent, loyal, and resourceful. But all those qualities of his, and some of my own," she teased, "mixed together and created someone who is uniquely you. Someone we couldn't live without."

She rose up off the rug and bundled Sam into her arms. Michael scooted over to make room. Melissa wiggled in between Sam and Sarah on the sofa, hugging them both close. Detective Bateman cleared his throat to get their attention.

"Samantha, you will be facing some charges," said Detective Bateman. "These include vandalizing the car at NatureLight, totaling the car at the recycling center, and aggravated assault of Leo Goss using allergens. However, based on the extraordinary circumstances surrounding all these incidents, I have a feeling the charges will be dropped." He walked over to the sofa and gave his son a bear hug. "I'll come pick you up in a couple of hours, Michael. If I know your mother, she'll be cooking every single one of your favorite foods. I doubt she'll let you out of her sight for days."

The quiet, exhausted atmosphere in the library was suddenly interrupted by a car screeching up the driveway, beeping its horn wildly.

Chapter Ninety-Seven

"Hallelujah!" Magda burst into the house. She blew by the surprised detectives who were heading out the door.

She rushed over to the sofa and gathered them all up into her arms. She patted their faces, reassuring herself they were alright, and gave them all huge hugs.

"Mag! I can't breathe!" squeaked Sarah, coming up for air.

"Ribs!" Sam laughed and protested at the same time.

"It does my heart good to see the four of you alive and safe on that sofa. And you, Melissa, oh my word! What you have been through...dear Lord, never, ever in my wildest dreams did I imagine Peter Ambroglia to be capable of such treachery." Magda stepped back and stared at them, tears running down her cheeks.

"And when did you ever learn to shoot a gun, Melissa? You never said a word about guns the entire time I've known you."

"My father never trusted Peter," said Melissa dryly. "He always thought there was something off about him, but he could never put his finger on it. Peter idolized my father, but the feeling wasn't mutual. Father trained me to become an expert marksman as soon as Tucker died. Peter tried to weasel into my father's affections for years, making himself indispensable at the bank creating computer systems and financial programs. My father told me learning to defend myself would come in handy one day. He made me promise to always keep my skills up, which I did privately. Peter didn't know. I never advertised the fact. Forbes knew, but at my father's insistence we never spoke about it to anyone outside the two of us." Melissa dropped a kiss on Sam's head. Sam tilted her head and met her mother's pain-filled eyes.

"I'm sorry I shut you out, sweetheart. You must have felt so alone...so abandoned. I failed...us." Melissa gestured to include herself and her daughters. "I lost your trust. I've never been so afraid. I received so many threats. I blindly followed his instructions...what he told me to do in order to keep you safe. So wrong. It didn't keep you safe. I should have confided in Magda or trusted Michael's parents. I should have told them about the threats and that my money had vanished. If only I had reached out to someone, this whole nightmare would have ended sooner. I blame myself," she confessed.

"You did the best you could, Melissa." Magda took both of Melissa's hands in her own. "Who's to say if you had come forward sooner that anyone would have suspected Peter? Or connected him to Leo? Peter could have covered up his tracks and surfaced later on down the line, hurting God knows how many others? Sometimes events have to play out until the perp gets cocky and makes a mistake. Thank God, Sam figured it out," said Magda.

Melissa nodded.

"Perp, Mag?" Sam raised an eyebrow.

"*Murder, She Wrote*, missy. Angela Lansbury uses the term all the time," Magda explained.

"I know. I watch it with you, remember? I'm just pulling your chain," Sam smiled. "I did have help, Mag. Dad was there all the time. I just didn't realize how much until the end."

"I'm so glad, sweetie." Magda gave Sam another hug.

Detective Bateman stood in the foyer talking on his phone. When he finished the call, he walked back into the library.

"Before I go, Melissa, I want to let you know we will have some forensic accountants working on Peter's financials along with your bank accounts. We're going to get this straightened out and get your money back to the rightful owner...you. Also, I'll notify the life insurance company and the lawyers of the estate that Peter Ambroglia is under arrest. He's no longer the executor of Forbes' estate and you've been cleared of all charges."

"Thank you," she said simply.

"Sam, we sent some detectives over to Peter's house. It was just as you said. The evidence we uncovered there is enough to put him away for a very, very long time. He is one sick individual. Once all this comes out, I don't believe he'll have anyone vouching for him in Beaconsfield." He shook his head.

Sam nodded and leaned into her mother, grateful it was all over. She watched as Michael's dad said his goodbyes and shut the front door behind him. Magda talked to Michael who gave her a play-by-play of what happened. Sarah slept against her mother. Sam shut her eyes and listened contentedly to the sounds of familiar voices and Sarah's soft snoring.

Someone knocked at the front door. Sam opened her eyes. It pushed open. Gray stood in the doorway, his hands in his pockets, unsure of his welcome. He gazed at her steadily, a question in his eyes. He gave her a tentative smile.

Sam elbowed Michael discreetly. She widened her eyes, giving him a "what now?" look.

"Don't be looking at me, Queen. It's a small town. News travels fast. Now that Bloom's in custody, Gray probably figured you were telling the truth about Anime. Or maybe he's here to ask for your hand in marriage. Because you look so good working the bruised, fragile look with that attractive drool coming out of the corner of your mouth. Oof!" He grunted as her elbow dug in harder.

Sam turned her head and wiped at her mouth furiously.

"Kidding! Go for it...you know you want to..." Michael made a kissing sound with his mouth.

"Remind me again why I put up with you?" Sam murmured in disgust.

Sam looked at Gray waiting in the doorway. And smiled.

Chapter Ninety-Eight

Later that night, Sam waited while Sarah arranged the Ten Chosen. After she finished, Sarah plopped down among them. The bouncing, fresh-faced pre-teen, smelling sweetly of shampoo and lavender bubble bath, bore no resemblance to the frightened child zip tied to a dining room chair earlier that day.

"C'mon, chicken nugget. Prayers." Sam sat on the end of the bed, careful not to make any sudden moves due to her aching ribs.

"Okay." Sarah closed her eyes, folded her hands, and said her prayers out loud while Sam listened. Melissa was downstairs talking on the phone with Magda. For the first time in months, they had eaten pizza in the family room and watched a movie together on Netflix. And Sam hadn't even minded that Sarah sang along to every song during *Frozen*. It was actually kind of nice, considering.

"Sam, do you think Daddy will come around any more? I mean, now that he knows we're safe and everything?" Sarah looked at her with a serious expression on her sleepy face.

"I do. I think he's only ever a thought away, baby. You'll feel him...you might even hear him. And if we ever *really* need him the way we did last night, he'll move heaven and earth to try and help us. I know he will. Not for something stupid like a test, but for the really important stuff. He's still our Dad." Sam leaned down and kissed her on the forehead. "Night, junebug."

"Night, Sam. I love you."

"Yeah? I love you more."

Sam turned off Sarah's light and headed across the hall. When she entered her room, she could smell Hugo Boss floating on the cool breeze coming in through the open window.

"Hey, Daddy," she whispered. "Thanks for everything."

She stood still in the moonlight playing across the room. As she relaxed, Sam felt a wave of warmth and happiness wash over her as though someone had given her the most amazing hug. She turned and saw her father behind her, sort of. He was there, but he wasn't. She could vaguely make out his features in the dim glow. His lips didn't move, but she heard his voice in her mind.

"I'm here, Sam. In spirit. Always. I love you."

He gradually faded away until Sam couldn't feel his presence anymore.

"I know. We'll be okay, Daddy. I love you, too."

Chapter Ninety-Nine

Three weeks later, Sam, Michael, and Gray sat at a table during lunch. They only had a few more days until their Christmas break. Gray draped his arm comfortably around Sam's shoulders while Michael scarfed the rest of Sam's french fries.

"Three more torture tests until Colorado," Sam complained. "Is D still a passing grade?"

"Sam, you're never gonna get into college with that attitude. There's a really good antidote to failing. It's called studying. That's where you open the books and actually read them." Michael frowned in mock chagrin.

Miss Jenkins stopped by their lunch table. She sported a small diamond on her left hand. She and Mr. Davies had gotten engaged over Thanksgiving.

"Hi, Samantha. Don't forget we have a session after school today at three o'clock. I think that will be our last one until January. Your mother told me she was taking all of you skiing over winter break." She glanced around the table before hurrying off. "Have a wonderful time!"

"You seem to be getting along better with Ms. Shrinky-dink." Michael bit the ends off two Twizzlers and drank his orange juice through them.

"Yeah. She's been really helpful now that I'm actually telling her stuff. She said we're only as sick as our secrets. True dat." Sam helped herself to some of Michael's candy.

"It was nice of your mom to invite us skiing," said Gray in his deep voice.

He and Sam had been inseparable ever since he had shown up at her house after "the incident." Sam still busted his chops about falling for Anime's wounded bird routine, but all was forgiven now. He had apologized so nicely. She never could resist his soulful green eyes and that "awe shucks, ma'am" sweetness. Couple that with his WWE John Cena physique and she was a goner.

"Yeah. Mom's amazing. Peter's in jail. With the help of her lawyers, she got Leo kicked off the Board of Directors, got her money transferred back into her name, and put a stop to the *Samantha Project* for good. She fired Kameron. He's being charged with sexual assault of a minor in the fourth degree. And she cleaned house of anyone involved in Peter's scheme. She wants NatureLight to reflect Daddy's ideals again. Two weeks of relaxing and playing on the ski slopes in Vail is mandatory after all the crap that went down." Sam stood up at the sound of the bell. "Time for trig. Yay."

"I'm gonna be king of the slopes," bragged Michael, throwing out his orange juice container.

"And I'm gonna be Queen Snowbunny and drink hot cocoa with whipped cream. I'll just watch, thanks," giggled Sam, holding hands with Gray.

The three of them left for class. Sam's cell phone sat, forgotten, on the table, nestled underneath the empty Twizzler wrapper. It buzzed three times, then fell silent.

Enjoy Colorado. I know I will.

****

Victor tossed the prepaid cell phone through the bars. The guard caught it, dropped it on the cement floor, and ground it to bits under his boot.

Victor nodded. "Tell the boss it's go time."

The End

There's always something new around the corner...

Stay in touch with the author via:

Email: annetalmage@gmail.com

Website: http://annetalmage.wix.com/annetalmagecooksey

Instagram: https://instagram.com/annetalmagecooksey

Facebook: www.facebook.com/annetalmagecooksey

Twitter: https://twitter.com/talmageanne

If you liked *Spirit Dad*, please post a review at Amazon and let your friends know about the book.

Made in the USA
Columbia, SC
20 November 2017